CITIZENS UNITED

By

Hollis Joslin

If, as the Supreme Court said in the Citizens United case, the political speech of corporations is no less protected by the 1st amendment than that of individual natural persons, then the 1st amendment implies a right for corporations to speak from elected office. That is the basis upon which Vizion Inc. justified the corporation's direct candidacy for the presidency of the United States. But the New Republic of Texas is having none of it.

Dedication

This book is dedicated to the people who are the spirit of the land of the free- Texas and what remains of the United States of America; to those throughout the world yearning to be free; to those who fought and died for freedom; to those who fight to preserve it today; and to those who strive to make the world a better place, forever cognizant that individual liberty is the essential ingredient for sustainable health, wealth, and happiness – the increasingly illusive American Dream.

Acknowledgments

I owe a ginormous debt of gratitude to Richard Peltz-Steele, who humored me and encouraged me as a Umass Dartmouth law student as my would-be policy paper on 1st amendment implications of campaign finance regulation went rogue, morphing into *Citizen United, the Novel*. As a *real* Journalist, lawyer, law professor, constitutional scholar, and mentor of many (among other things), Professor Peltz-Steele was and is an invaluable resource, and I am grateful to call him a friend. Likewise, I acknowledge my friend, Attorney James Freeley III, an incredible man and an amazing business organizations professor who primed the pumps of my imagination by sharing his experiences in the rough and tumble world of corporate America. And thank you to Constitutional law professor, Dwight Duncan, whose knowledge, insight, and unassailable values were instrumental in my motivation and creative process here. And to Dr. John Quinn, Professors Wendy Davis, Patrick Francomano, Dylan Malagrino, Justine Dunlap, William Manganiello, and Spencer Clough, Judge Rudko and Judge Larkin, as well as Dean Robert Ward, Dean Philip Cleary, and Dean Michael Hillinger; To Dr. Deborah Kaye and Dr. David Graizbord of the University of Arizona; To Tiffany West who was a huge help in getting the formatting right here. I also thank my son, Hollis NT and his wife Jennifer, my awesome proof-readers, as well as my girls, Jessica Nicole and Courtney Brooke, both of whom are an infinite source of inspiration; Giuseppe Lo Fiego for the terrific job he did creating promotional materials for this book – Grazi, Amico!; my sweetheart, Dr Cheryl Wathier who stood faithfully by me through this challenging project; To Garth Brooks and his amazing assistant, Carol Gabbert- thank you for the song *The River*, and for the hospitality you showed Cheryl before the Phoenix show; to my parents Robert and Dyanne; the late Ken Lamkin and Gene Church, two great writers the world sorely misses; and, finally, thank you to my many friends, colleagues, fellow libertarians and others who encouraged me and inspired me along the way with a shared belief in arts and entertainment as an effective medium for fanning the flames of liberty. May God Bless you all.

Chapter 1

While the nation was distracted with the conflict with Texas, Vizion Inc.'s CEO, Ricky Santana went quietly about the business of having the corporation added to the 2028 presidential election ballots in the remaining U.S. states. Dueling democrat candidates Helen and Max Baxter along with the sitting republican president promptly responded with a lawsuit seeking to enjoin the company's candidacy; and the federal district court just as promptly dismissed the suit for lack of standing. Helen and company subsequently appealed and lost on the same basis. What, if anything, the Supreme Court would have to say on the matter if it went to the next level was anybody's guess.

Mr. Miller, attorney for the complaining parties, expected the high Court would reverse the decision and force the court below to hear the merits of the case. Joshua Horowitz, attorney for the defendant, thought otherwise. Gabriella Meir, television talk show host for Global and Beyond News – GABN in common parlance – was conducting a nationally televised studio interview with Mr. Miller about the case this evening and Max and Helen Baxter agreed to a truce long enough to watch it together.

Max carried a tray of caviar and wafers over and plunked into one of a matching pair of high-tech luxury recliners that performed various functions, including heated back and foot massages. Now sixty-four years old and suffering from the aches and pains often associated with that age, he had a great deal of appreciation for those features. He gazed out at the massive icicles clinging to the crumbling New York City skyline beyond the glass penthouse wall while the massager hummed away at its work. Then he glanced back at Helen in the other recliner.

Despite Max's preference for younger women, he still found Helen attractive. Although not nearly as attractive as she should be after all the money her cosmetic surgeon had drained from his bank account. Not that it mattered now. He scooped a lump of caviar onto a wafer and shoved it into his mouth, and said as he chewed, "I've missed this chair."

"Not half as much as I'm going to miss the Big Apple," Helen droned. "Why couldn't they have chosen someplace like Boston for the new capitol? We were happy there, once, back when you worked for the police officers' union. Before you…well."

"Boston is a ghost town now, or have you forgotten," Max growled.

"Oh, you know what I mean, Max darling, someplace a little less primitive than Dodge City, Kansas, for Heaven's sake. Surely Dodge City wasn't the only other town in America that could be abbreviated D.C....Oh well, I suppose it might be tolerable if I could come back here to New York from time to time but almost everyone else is gone. Not that I wouldn't enjoy some solitude, but what would I do for power? The generator for this apartment is far too noisy. Can you believe President Farnsworth caved to the enviro-nuts and ordered the last coal-fired plant closed? Rather extreme, wouldn't you agree? Closing the last one? How much greenhouse gas could just one possibly emit?"

"Yes, yes." Max sighed. "Completely unreasonable not to keep a plant operating for the sole purpose of powering one very spoiled lady's penthouse – a spoiled lady who's profited handsomely from the climate change business. Do you suppose this chair might be shipped to father's Dodge City mansion rather than left here?"

"Surely you aren't suggesting there's anything unseemly about my investing in carbon credits," Helen said. "Can you imagine a more effective way to save the planet from the peasants than pushing the price of its destruction beyond their reach?" She commanded the seventy-inch flat-screen on the wall across from them, "GABN," and it tuned to Gabriella's program where the television camera had just zoomed in for a close-up of the host as though drawn to her exotic emerald eyes and the chestnut curls framing her slender face.

"Oh, Max darling, doesn't our little project look just lovely. They did such a fine job with the eyes. If only they were real. Well, Levi tells me that since Ricky Santana brought in that African-American doctor woman, Dawn Wise or whatever her name is, he may finally be getting somewhere with the artificial sight project. After all these years." Helen sighed. "Too bad about that unfortunate ban on transplantation testing."

The camera zoomed in closer on Gabriella, and Helen gasped. "Dear God, she's wearing that pitiful little trinket of a necklace. Do you suppose she knows? Someone should have told her."

"Did you hear what I said?" Max garbled through another mouthful of wafers and caviar.

Helen's gaze never left the television. "What's that, Max darling?"

2

"I said I miss this chair and I'd like to have it shipped to Dodge City."

"Is that all you miss?" Helen said, still fixated on the image of Gabriella on the screen. "A pity you left me no alternative but to divorce you."

Yeah, sure, I'm the bad one, Max thought. Never mind Helen having gotten herself knocked up by another man early in their marriage. His eyes swept around the room, taking mental inventory of various items the divorce had cost him.

Helen reached over and patted Max's hand before he could complete the growing list in his mind. "Let's be quiet now, Max darling, Gabriella's getting ready to speak."

"Counselor," Gabriella began, "thank you for coming on the show tonight despite being a bit under the weather."

The camera zoomed out for a wide shot, contrasting seventy-one year old red-faced pot-bellied Attorney Miller and considerably more delicate and refined fifty-two year old Gabriella seated in chrome-framed contemporary chairs a few feet across from one another. The studio lights added a soft sheen to Gabriella's Lebanese complexion.

Miller covered his mouth with a fist and nodded while battling through a wheezy cough. Then he took a sip from a glass of water and said, "You're welcome."

"Now," Gabriella continued, "my understanding is that the district court dismissed the case without hearing your argument because your clients lacked standing to sue and the circuit court affirmed that decision. But before we get into your thoughts on that and what your next move will be could you explain to the viewers who the parties to the case are, and their respective arguments."

Bombastic Miller half-chuckled through another cough. "Vizion Inc. is the defendant, my clients' opponent. And Vizion's counsel, your special friend Joshua Horowitz cites *Citizens United v. Federal Election Commission* as support for the proposition that *corporations are people too*, or something to that effect." He slapped himself on the chest and let loose a bellowing laugh, and after calming himself, went on to say, "Well now, that might make an interesting topic for some misguided grad student to write a postmodern thesis on, but show me where it says that in the presidential qualifications clause of the Constitution."

3

After a short pause, Miller muttered, "Corporations running for office. Makes as much sense as a washing machine practicing law. With all due respect to washing machines, not a one of which would ever come up with such a ridiculous legal theory."

Gabriella maintained her professional composure despite Miller's swipe at her very close friend Joshua's intellect. She knew Josh could be gullible for the right amount of money or recognition and this would seem further evidence of that if not for the fact that Levi Baxter was the mastermind behind Vizion Inc.'s candidacy. "So that's your argument then, that corporate entities don't meet the qualifications to run for president?"

"In a nutshell, yes." Miller smiled smugly, pulled a pocket constitution out of his suit jacket, slipped a pair of reading glasses on, and flipped to the page he was looking for. "Says right here in article two section one that, 'No person except a natural born citizen,' etcetera, 'shall be eligible to the Office of President; neither shall any person be eligible to that office who shall not have attained to the age of thirty-five years, and been fourteen years a resident within the United States.' So there you have it."

"And you've mentioned a second theory that isn't included in the complaint?"

Miller pulled his reading glasses off. "That's correct. In my view, the defendant's candidacy or any other non-human candidacy would violate the guarantee of a republican form of government as provided for in article four section four of the Constitution. You want me to recite that for you too?" He smirked and put his reading glasses back on.

"That won't be necessary." Gabriella sighed. "You've said Vizion Inc. is the original defendant in the case. Now remind us who your clients, the original plaintiffs, are."

"Young lady, you know very well who my clients are."

Gabriella sighed again. "For the benefit of the viewers, please."

Miller's eyes glazed over momentarily. "Yes, oh yes of course. I filed the lawsuit on behalf of Helen Baxter, the democrat party's frontrunner, her ex-husband and primary challenger Max Baxter, and President John Farnsworth, the incumbent republican seeking a second term. Our objective was to get this monkey business out of the way before the general election because there's no good to come from complicating things with a rogue independent corporation running

4

against real and respectable people from the real and respectable parties, to wit – my clients, the democrats and the republican."

"Anything else, briefly, before we go to break?"

Miller began to cough and wheeze again and finally managed to say, "Yes. I'd like another glass of water, please."

The set dissolved into a silent commercial produced for Leviathan Corp:

A towering image of Levi Baxter appeared onscreen. Except for his enormous size, he could have easily passed for a beloved great grandfather, a family patriarch – his neatly combed white hair and razor thin mustache, the perfectly pressed denim overalls he wore, his arms folded proudly across his chest, and his even smile and captivating sky blue eyes exuding the confidence and wisdom unique to men of his years.

Levi stood at the center of the screen on a hilltop amidst a sea of lush-green plains with a silhouette of distant Dodge City, Kansas as a backdrop. Unmanned farming machinery comparatively the size of children's toys reeled busily across the land. Similarly sized drones soared gracefully overhead, their appearance more like doves than all-seeing eyes in the sky. A platoon of human-like saluting harmonizers stood shoulder to shoulder at Levi's giant feet. Then the following words appeared in bold black letters:

WORLDWIDE HARMONY
BROUGHT TO YOU BY LEVIATHAN

The next advertisement featured Helen Baxter knee high in a mound of imitation snow, bound up in a thick winter coat, hugging herself tightly while pretending to shiver as though she were just short of death by hypothermia. "A vote for Helen is a vote for an increase in carbon credit redistribution from greedy corporations to individuals," she promised through feigned chattering teeth. "Vote for Helen on election day, your life just might depend on it. I am Helen Baxter and I approve this message."

Max sat his now empty tray down less than gracefully on the table between the recliners and got up and stood over Helen with both hands on his hips and glared. "So your plan is to scare the people into voting for you?"

"Never mind what my plan is Max darling." Helen made a shooing motion. "Would you please sit down and be quiet. I'd like to watch the rest of the interview and I can't do it with you standing there carrying on like that. Perhaps if you lost a few pounds it might be easier to see past you."

Max cringed and shoved his hands in his pockets and retreated to the glass wall. Tilting his head just so, he glimpsed a Global Trade Partnership – GTP – flagged patrol boat crisscrossing the harbor. One of Leviathan's subsidiaries somewhere undoubtedly manufactured those pesky vessels. He mused. With all the technological advances and a new multinational agreement signed seemingly daily, the world was shrinking at an ever-increasing rate. And the smaller the world got, the larger his father Levi and Leviathan Corp seemed to become – and the tinier Max felt. But Max would be larger than all of it when he became president. He needed this, damn it; unlike Helen, for whom becoming president would merely provide a larger playground for her social engineering hobby.

"Max darling, come and sit," said Helen. "You're missing the program."

On the television, Miller babbled on, "...my clients will suffer irreparable harm if this nonsense is allowed to move forward and so will the American people. Our system of government, the American dream, democracy as we know it, the whole shebang will be out the window," Miller snapped his fingers, "just like that. Big greedy corporations will rule the world!" Veins bulged from his forehead. He jabbed a finger viciously up into the air as though accusing God himself, until he succumbed to another prolonged fit of wheezing and coughing, and finally collapsed, toppling from his chair onto the floor, clutching his chest.

Chapter 2

At the conclusion of Gabriella's program, Dawn powered off the IPad she and Ricky had viewed it on from the breakroom at Vizion Inc.'s Dodge City headquarters. Her lime green medical scrubs slid to the side, exposing the smooth ebony flesh of her shoulder. "What an unfortunate way to end an interview," she said. "I hope that man is alright."

Ricky nodded. "Had to be stressful for Gabby, that happening on her set." He couldn't help noticing the absence of bra straps and the near cantaloupe-sized breasts beneath Dawn's scrubs which apparently had no need of artificial support. A lifetime of bachelorhood was clearly taking its toll on his manners.

He shifted his gaze downward and reached for his lower leg to scratch an imaginary itch. Both of his legs were prosthetic, and had been since his real ones were severed below the knees in a plowing accident on his family's farm when he was a young boy.

His cheeks warmed with embarrassment as he glanced back up at Dawn, this time into her hazel eyes – pretty eyes that distracted from the brilliant mind behind them. As one of only a handful of ophthalmologists also certified in neurosurgery, the thirty-six year old doctor would be indispensable to Vizion's effort to cure the blind with artificial eyes if the Federal Medical Ethics Department – FEMED – ever lifted the ban on animal testing, and then allowed human trials.

Of course, even if Ricky were to get the opportunity to prove the artificial eyes could work, practical application would be limited unless he figured out a way that transplant recipients could be detached from the bulky computing equipment he anticipated would be necessary to replicate the neural code for sight electronically. "Doc," Ricky said, "Can you imagine any circumstance under which you would defy that testing ban?"

"No." Dawn sighed. "As frustrating as it can be at times, I play by the rules."

"Would that be the case if you had a loved one who was blind?" Ricky pressed.

Dawn considered this angle on the question. She knew the matter was deeply personal to Ricky. But that didn't change the fact that what he wanted her to do was illegal. "No, Ricky, I would not. I'm not throwing away my future to perform illegal tests of a procedure that we have virtually no evidence will even work."

Ricky shook his head. "Have a little faith. If I'd taken that attitude on my theory that our magnification process would be capable of detecting insects on the ground from low-Earth orbit, the harmonizer sight system that put Vizion on the map wouldn't even exist."

"Might be better if it didn't," Dawn said, well aware of Ricky's own reservations about the harmonizer program. "Regardless, those

7

tests were not against the law. And anyway, it was Levi's money, not faith that made that happen."

Ricky couldn't argue with that. Faith or not, if it hadn't been for the financial backing of Levi Baxter of global giant, Leviathan Corp., Vizion Inc. would probably be buried in the graveyard of unfunded worthy objectives instead of enjoying phenomenal success as the sole supplier of the Department of Homeland Security's robotic officers' camera eyes. Even so, it troubled him that all he had to show for thirty-five years of effort on Vizion's original mission of developing artificial sight was a handful of partial sight restoring retinal implants in animal test subjects. Exactly how much sight had been restored in those animals was unknowable given the communication barrier between them and humans, but his observation that his old St. Bernard, Bernice no longer routinely stumbled into things as she had prior to the procedure greatly encouraged him.

Ricky's cell phone rang. "Hello," he answered... "Hi, Gabby.... Yes, I saw it. Is Miller alright? ...How are you doing? ...I'll be right over."

Chapter 3

Ricky slipped and slid his way past the ambulance and up the icy steps to GABN studios as quickly as he could on his prosthetics, then scrambled down the hallway to Gabriella's office where he found her slumped over in her chair with an elbow on her desk, and a hand pressed against her forehead. He glanced at the antiquated Nikon camera serving as a bookend on the bookshelf behind her. It had been the top of the line in photographic equipment back in the early 90s when Gabriella, then a freshman Harvard photojournalism student, hauled it with her everywhere she went. "I got here as quick as I could," Ricky said.

"Thank you for coming." Gabriella sniveled. She wanted to reach up and touch his hand but her pride would not allow it. "I didn't know who else to call." She blew her nose. "And by the way, it's quick-*ly*, not quick. Your grammar is as atrocious as ever."

Ricky caressed her shoulders. "Gabby, it wasn't your fault."

She brushed his hands away. "No kidding. Everyone knows Miller's heart was a ticking time bomb. I'm just the lucky contestant whose set it decided to explode on this time. So yes, it obviously was not my fault. What is wrong with you?"

Ricky lowered his gaze to the toes of his shoes. Of all the comforting words he could have offered, the best he could come up with was, *It wasn't your fault*? "I'm sorry. I guess I just ain't much good at these situations."

"Ain't? Listen, Ricky, your language skills need serious help. And the only situation here is that I've misplaced my electronic navigator and I need an escort on the train. Like I told you on the phone."

"Yeah, right." Ricky felt stupider than ever now.

Gabriella shook her head. "I'm sorry if this is an inconvenience for you. I called Josh first, but Mr. big-shot's with the president and he couldn't break away."

"With the president, huh?"

"Yes. As you know, Josh has been President Farnsworth's lapdog slash unofficial on-call *advisor*" – she twirled a finger above her head – "since he interned for him during law school back when his majesty was *Congressman* Farnsworth."

"What's Josh advising him on?"

Gabriella spun around in her chair to face Ricky. "If you're worried he's revealing Vizion's secret legal strategy, don't be, because there's obviously nothing secret about it. Not that Josh would violate your confidence if it weren't common knowledge, seeing as you're his employer and you all have been friends like forever. Besides, there are rules against such things."

Ricky laughed. "I reckon that's right. So what's he over there for?"

"Did you just say *reckon*?" It was Gabriella's turn to laugh, and man, it was good to hear her laugh.

"I reckon I did say reckon." Ricky intentionally stretched the words out in an extended drawl. "You reckon there's any reason this ol' cowhand from Texas ought not be able to say reckon?"

Gabriella laughed even harder, until her stomach hurt, and when she finally settled, she said, "You've done such a mighty fine job of hiding that there accent that I forgot you was from Texas, partner." She flicked at the brim of an imaginary cowboy hat on her head.

"Hey, there wasn't any sense jeopardizing Vizion's contract with Leviathan Corp over an accent. You know every link in the contractor chain has to be approved by the Department of Homeland Security. And about the only thing a Texas accent is likely to get a body from

DHS nowadays is a quick trip to a harmonization camp. You know what I mean?"

"I know exactly what you mean. As a matter of fact, you didn't hear it from me, but the president asked Josh over to discuss the Texas situation."

Ricky's eyes narrowed. "What's happening with Texas? The prez looking to kiss and make up?"

"To the contrary, there's talk of war. Although they can't technically call it war. Apparently the Texans are demanding a return to some early 1800s borders encompassing half of New Mexico, part of Colorado –"

Ricky took over from there, "And parts of Oklahoma, Kansas, and even a piece of Wyoming. I'm well acquainted with the history of the Republic of Texas, both the old republic and the new one. And just so you know, if the Bureau of Land Management – or BLM, as they call it – hadn't tried to steal that ranchland along the Red River none of this would be happening."

Gabriella shook her head defiantly. "We only have one world and there is global consensus that the environment and natural resources must be protected at all costs. If those barbarians hiding beneath their cowboy hats had been properly managing that land, there would have been no need for the BLM to do what they did." She flipped an unruly curl of hair off her forehead.

"Give me a break," Ricky said. "The conflict had nothing to do with the environment. And as for natural resources, well, cattle are a natural resource, and those *barbarians*, as you call them, were doing a right fine job of managing them." He felt the temperature rising in his face. "By the way, some of those barbarians happen to be friends and family of mine."

Gabriella clutched his hand. "I'm sorry, I didn't know. Honestly, I'd forgotten you had any connection at all to Texas. But regardless of that, scientists have determined that cow poop is a source of greenhouse gasses and we really don't need cows. And anyway, according to Josh, the president seems to think the Texans – with the exception of your friends and family, I'm sure – are a stubborn lot and impulsive, and no offense, but not any too bright either, and he's hoping Josh might persuade them to think before they act this time. This is all strictly between you and I of course."

Ricky nodded. "Of course…So, how are Max and Helen holding up after that spanking in the court of appeals?"

"Helen will be fine," Gabriella said. "She's a strong woman. But I am worried about Max. He hasn't been feeling well lately. He's returning from New York the day after tomorrow and I was thinking if the weather clears up maybe you could fly me out to the Baxter mansion in your corporate helicopter so I can check in on him."

"That's a mighty big *If.* I don't remember it being this snowy and cold in March even during the Deep Freeze. Global warming, go figure."

Gabriella drew in an exasperated breath. "It's *climate change,* Ricky. The experts revised the terminology long ago to more accurately describe the threat, and you well know it. Now, stop, you're beginning to sound like one of those kooky deniers."

Or they changed the terminology to more accurately *disguise* the threat, Ricky thought as he peered out the window at the snow fluttering down. He remained unpersuaded that a problem that had not definitively resulted in the loss of a single life justified the unproven solution that destroyed the economy and brought about the deaths of more than half the population of the northern states through skyrocketing energy prices that made it impossible for people of modest means to heat their homes in the winter.

For the survivors – with the exception of the elites who could afford unlimited carbon credits – the devastating winter of 2025 would always be remembered as the manmade Deep Freeze. It seemed surreal that it happened only three years ago. Ricky helped Gabriella up from the chair. "Come on, we better get going so you don't miss your train."

"So, are we on for the flight to Max's Wednesday?" Gabriella said as they walked toward the exit.

"Weather permitting."

"Great. You want to go grab a bite to eat?"

"Gabby, I'd love to, but I've got to get back to the office."

"Seriously? It's almost nine o'clock." Gabriella pursed her lips. "Oh never mind. Josh invited me for dinner after he finishes up with the president. I guess I'll take him up on it. As a matter of fact, he also asked me again to marry him. I might just take him up on that too this time."

Chapter 4

The Dodge City presidential office was rectangular, not oval, but it would have to do until contractors completed construction of the new mansion. If recent trends in in internal Whitehouse polls continued their downward slide, Farnsworth would no longer be president by then. Time would to tell whether offloading Texas and its thirty-eight anti-establishment electoral college votes would change that.

Farnsworth paced one way across the office, and Josh the other, passing one another back and forth as they talked. "Congratulations on finalizing the global carbon emissions agreement," Josh said, looking up at the six-foot tall president towering above his modest five-foot eight inches.

"Thanks," Farnsworth grumbled. "Shifting the responsibility off me and onto the Global Trade Partnership for freezing what's left of our snot-nosed middle class out of their suburban paradises was a great idea. It's just too bad we weren't able to conclude the agreement soon enough to blame the GTP for the Deep Freeze." He folded his arms across his chest and donned a more serious expression. "Listen, Josh, I'm not going to pretend I'm happy about you representing Vizion against Helen and Max and I in the lawsuit."

"Mr. President, my representation of Vizion should not be construed as an endorsement of its candidacy. It's simply a matter of my obligation to zealously advocate on behalf of my client's wishes."

Farnsworth rolled his eyes. "Spare me the legal ethics spiel. I'm well aware of Levi Baxter's interest in Vizion and the history you two have. Not that any of that matters right now. I sent for you to discuss the Texas situation, not the election. DHS reports covert Texas Ranger activity as far north as southern Colorado approaching the Arkansas River. It seems the Texans may have been serious about returning to their historic borders. Any thoughts on a strategy to persuade them to back off?"

Josh tilted his head back and scratched beneath his chin as he made another pass across the plush golden carpet. "Well, sir, you certainly can't threaten to eject them from the union since you've already ejected them."

Farnsworth sighed deeply. "In retrospect, that may not have been the wisest decision. It has put us in a bit of a box, given the abolition of national militaries and the prohibition against unilateral international kinetic action. But in light of the GTP directive on proportional use of force in domestic matters, I'm hard pressed to imagine what else I could have done."

He snatched a document off his desk and handed it to Josh. "That's the GTP opinion paper I requested regarding the Red River land dispute early on in the conflict. As you can see there, those SOBs seem to think the use of force to defend territorial integrity from domestic insurrection is unavailable unless the defending government's forces are inferior to the insurgents. By that logic, a government is only permitted to defend its territory if it can't defend it. That's why I said to hell with it and booted Texas out."

Josh looked at Farnsworth skeptically. "You're suggesting the BLM was defending United States territory in that action?"

"If ejecting trespassers from federal land doesn't constitute defending federal territory, I don't know what does," said Farnsworth.

As far as Josh was concerned, the whole affair had been idiotic. Attorneys for the feds had transformed the rulings in a pair of 1980s legal disputes between private landowners into fairy dust and sprinkled them over the 1819 treaty between the U.S. and Spain, effectively reducing competing land claims between the feds and the Texas ranchers into a debate over whether accretion or avulsion created the southern bank of the Red River.

The 1819 treaty established everything north of the middle of the river as belonging to Oklahoma. Logically, everything south of the middle of the river would have belonged to Texas. But, because Texas was a Spanish territory then and the U.S. had had no intention of ceding any part of a major waterway to a foreign power, the terms established everything below the *south bank* as belonging to Texas instead. Consequently, a strip of land between the south bank and the middle of the river belonged to the federal government. No one gave that a moment's thought until more than a century later natural forces had shifted the river northward causing that strip of federal land to merge with the south bank adjoining private ranchland.

Whether the U.S. government's claim to that land was valid or not, its interest in controlling the river certainly was not when Farnsworth sent the BLM agents in, because Texas had long since been a part of the United States at that time. As far as Josh could tell, the only remaining interest in that land was Farnsworth's interest in making

13

Texas an example for any other state pondering a challenge to federal power. Josh understood that. What remained a mystery to him was why Farnsworth had chosen to antagonize the Texas ranchers to arms by attempting an in-their-face land grab rather than just boiling them away in a pot of regulation.

"With all due respect, Mr. President," said Josh, "in the Red River land dispute, we weren't dealing with a federal building, a national forest, or even so much as a federally owned statue. And no one disputed ownership of the river itself. All that was at issue was a river *bank*. Now, don't get me wrong, I don't have any sympathy for a bunch of trash-talking, flag-waving rednecks with shotguns threatening revolution, but in my view, you never should have sent the BLM agents in in the first place."

Farnsworth banged his fist on the desk. "What, I should have cowered to Governor Grant?"

"It's *President* Grant," Josh interjected. "Texas is its own country now. Remember?"

"Whatever," Farnsworth said. "The point is Grant would have cleaned my clock in the upcoming election if I'd caved in on the Red River problem. It wasn't about private property rights, it was about Grant's ambition to take my job. Her big talk about seceding and all." Farnsworth began to laugh. "Well I showed her, now didn't I? No way she could have seen it coming. But the question right now is, What are we going to do to prevent these Ranger encroachments from escalating into a bigger problem? My information is Texas has even brought land survey crews into southwestern Kansas."

"Hmm." Josh thought for a moment. "Have you considered offering them money?"

"I will not pay blackmailers," Farnsworth said. "You do that once and they keep coming back for more. Besides, we're seventy trillion dollars in the hole, not counting unfunded liabilities. Where are we supposed to find payoff money?"

Josh peered over the frame of his round-lensed glasses. "With all due respect, sir, this country has a long history of payoffs to private parties and state actors alike – foreign aid, loan guarantees, social programs, subsidies, tax credits, strategic regulation. And the carbon emissions agreement. That agreement is probably the biggest payoff in human history to those appropriately situated. As for the money, you know very well that we haven't had any real money since FDR confiscated privately held gold, long before President Nixon actually admitted we were broke and took the dollar off the gold standard and put it on the atomic bomb standard back in the 1970s. So, my advice is to do what has always been done, have the Federal Reserve digitize some more dollars and make the drop."

Farnsworth drummed his fingers on the desk. "Hmm. The way you describe it makes it sound more like bribery funded by counterfeiting than blackmail."

Josh chuckled. "Tomato, tomahto, potato, potahto."

"I see your point," said Farnsworth, "but the deal would have to be approved by the GTP central bank. And you can be sure I can't politically afford whatever they'd want in return. So where does that leave us?"

Josh and Farnsworth both stopped pacing and stood eye to eye, so close that Farnsworth's slightly protruding belly pressed up against Josh's near skeletal frame. The bulging pupils inches from Josh's face told him that Farnsworth had reached his own conclusion, and then Farnsworth said it, "We send in some harmonizers to apprehend the rangers and make examples of them."

"That could work." Josh held up a finger. "Of course, it'd be best to get the GTP board's consent. Capturing the Rangers could be construed as an international operation. If you go it alone you might be charged with obstructing commerce."

What Farnsworth would have liked to do was to send a message to the Texas president's mansion strapped to the belly of a precision guided missile, the GTP be damned. But he couldn't risk Texas' most probable response – a retaliatory strike on Dodge City. He gazed out the window at the progress on what was to be a magnificent new presidential palace and imagined Texas bombs raining down on it before it was even completed. "Maybe we shouldn't have moved the capitol from old D.C. We may well have been better off taking our chances with the GTP patrols along the east coast rather than these lunatic Texans here. At least GTP board members are reasonably rational actors, give or take Caliph Rafsanjani."

"Not to get off topic," Josh said, "but the Caliph and his Persian Caliphate would not exist if we'd supported the Iranian people's popular uprising in 2009 instead of backing Ayatollah what's-his-face and standing idly by while his thugs with machineguns mowed peaceful protesters down in the streets."

15

Farnsworth scowled. "That was before my time. Now, let's stick to Texas."

Josh nodded. "Yes sir, Mr. President. There might be one other less controversial option."

"No!" Farnsworth shouted and banged his fist on the desk again. "I'm telling you now before you even say it, I will not have the GTP's so-called free trade enforcers anywhere on U.S. soil, if that's what you're going to suggest. They're even more worthless than U.N. peacekeepers were and considerably more violent and destabilizing. Foreign spies with guns is what they are."

"I suspect GTP forces will ultimately be unavoidable," said Josh, "unless you bring Texas back in."

Farnsworth raised an eyebrow. "You think Grant'd be interested in a reunion? Better question, if we were to strike a bargain to bring Texas back in, do you think the Texas people might be persuaded to vote for me or do you think they're stuck on libertarian crazy?"

Josh threw his hands in the air. "Hard to say. Grant wouldn't be a contender this late in the game. She couldn't get on the ballots if she wanted to. And I seriously doubt many Texans would support a democrat. They might go for Vizion though."

"Assuming Vizion is allowed to run, which I seriously doubt." Farnsworth clapped his hands together. "Fine, I'll look into it... So, speaking of the Vizion case, you do know that Miller filed for a writ of cert from the Supreme Court? I'm sure someone at his firm will follow up if he doesn't recover from whatever that was that happened to him during the interview."

"No, I didn't know that. But I'm not surprised."

"Listen, Josh, for the sake of argument let's assume the Supreme Court agrees with the lower court's conclusion that in our capacity as candidates, Helen and Max and I don't have standing. Do you suppose the appropriate party bringing suit on behalf of the United States government to have Vizion Inc. removed from the presidential ballots would have standing?"

"Under what theory?"

"The same theory – that corporate candidacy violates the election rules set forth in the Constitution. In my hypothetical, the federal government would be the injured party."

Josh nodded. "In that context, yes, I believe it would."

"And as counsel for the defense, how exactly would you respond?"

"My position would remain the same as it has been: If, as the Supreme Court said in *Citizens United,* the political speech of a corporation is no less protected by the first amendment than that of individual natural persons, then corporations have as much right as anyone else to speak from public office."

Farnsworth put his hands together in the shape of a steeple beneath his chin. "Seems a tad attenuated to me; although I suppose in the post-reality world we live in today it could be persuasive. But that still doesn't answer the question of substantive qualifications. You know, natural born citizen, residency, age, and all of that business."

Josh smiled. "I don't have time to go into all that right now. I promised Gabriella I'd join her for dinner. But I discuss the topic at length in the series she and I put together on the *Citizens United* case and what the ruling means for freedom of speech and associated candidacies. The first of the four prerecorded segments airs at eight PM tomorrow evening on GABN. I hope you can find time in your busy schedule to tune in."

Chapter 5

Dinner with Gabriella went well, exceptionally well as far as Josh was concerned. After chit-chat at a quaint little jazz club until the early morning hours she had finally said yes. He laid down to sleep thinking about how she had caressed that huge diamond after he slipped the ring on her finger. But she hadn't shown the excitement he had hoped for.

The telephone rang and Vizion Inc. appeared on the caller ID.

Josh glanced at his watch. 4:00 AM. Ricky must be working another all-nighter. "Hello."

"Hey, it's Ricky."

Josh propped himself up on a pillow. "The sun isn't even up yet, Ricky. What do you want?"

"A ride to my meeting, if you wouldn't mind," Ricky said, his tone annoyingly insistent for this time of the morning. "The activation code for my car expired again and I can't reach anyone at IT to reset it at this hour. I'd take the helicopter but that wouldn't exactly be discreet."

"Alright." Josh hung up, and after a thirty-minute ride in his self-navigating limo, he arrived at Vizion. From the outside, the steel framed sheet-metal structure looked like a typical, if unusually large, warehouse – although the surrounding electrified fence topped with razor-wire and marked every few feet with signs warning of severe consequences for trespassing gave the place an ominous feel.

The limo pulled up to the entrance gate and honked twice, alerting the harmonizer in the guardhouse. Josh marveled at how nearly human the harmonizer – one of Leviathan Corp's latest models – appeared compared to the first model he'd secured a patent for for Levi Baxter. It pulled a lever, raising the crossbar and the limo drove Josh in and across the paved lot to the office.

The small placard bearing the name Vizion Inc. on the solid metal office door provided no clue as to the nature of the business conducted here, and even less of a clue that in a few months this company might actually be the president of the United States.

Josh stopped briefly, listening to the muffled hum of conveyor belts and the rhythmic thump thump thump of the automated fabricator stamping out lenses from the manufacturing side of the facility. It may as well have been a money printing machine, one that he would soon control, one way or another. He swiped his security card through the electronic box beside the door and stood still for a retina scan. The lock disengaged.

Inside, Josh almost gagged from the pungent cocktail of animal odor, ammonia, and antiseptic emanating from the research area. He cupped a hand over his nose and made his way down the hall, guided by a slanted ray of light beaming out from a powerful reading lamp in Ricky's office.

Ricky sat alone at his desk staring into a microscope, manipulating something with a pair of tweezers. Josh rapped his knuckles lightly on the door. "Hey, boss," he said, his shoulder resting against the door jam.

Ricky looked up from the microscope, the weariness of too many consecutive all-nighters apparent in his face. He laid the tweezers down next to the microscope. "Pull up a chair."

A grimace from Ricky this early in the morning irritated Josh. "You're not going to start in on me about those goats again, are you?"

Ricky's eyes narrowed. "I told you that last shipment needs to go back."

Josh sighed. "And I told you I don't do shipping and receiving. I'm general counsel, that's the legal department, in case you've forgotten."

18

"Damn you and your little jokes," Ricky fired back. "I've been very clear that we do not practice animal cruelty here, and there is absolutely nothing wrong with the eyesight of any of those goats. If traumatizing animals with a complex surgical procedure with no prospect of any benefit to them isn't the very definition of animal cruelty, then I don't know what is. Besides, thanks to that stupid testing ban, we couldn't experiment on them even if it weren't a slap in the face to decency. So what are we supposed to do with them, start a petting zoo?"

Josh scrubbed his tired eyes with the balls of his hands. "Listen, Ricky, those goats were on their way to the slaughterhouse, so what difference does it make?"

Ricky raised an eyebrow. "They were? I thought they came from Helen's outfit that rescues blind animals."

Josh wished he could unsay what he'd just said. After all, he was the one who signed the deal on Vizion's behalf to purchase sight deficient animals at a pretty penny from Helen's phony animal rescue. It took an altruistic idiot like Ricky not to realize they were domesticated animals that she deliberately had blinded. Except for this batch, not a one of which had any obvious visual impairment at all. What a royal screw up. "I don't know why I said that. There was obviously some kind of a mix-up in shipping or something."

Ricky glared. "A mix-up, huh?"

Dawn interrupted the back and forth, shuffling in with a tiny male chimp fast asleep in her arms. She yawned. Her hair could have passed for a bird's nest and her tired puffy eyes resembled a raccoon's.

"Good morning, Doc," Ricky said. "What brings you in so early?"

"I couldn't sleep for worrying about this little rascal." She gave Ricky a little peck on the cheek and nodded an acknowledgement to Josh.

"What's going on with him?" said Ricky.

"He's still got a fever. Which is hardly surprising since I can't get him to swallow the antibiotics."

Ricky reached up and as he stroked the baby chimp's head, Dawn noted his rippling bicep and overall rock hard physique. Six-foot four-inches of solid muscle – less the titanium below the knees – with a hard bronze chiseled face and salt and pepper military style crewcut. A somewhat battered version of the fabled Latin lover.

Josh tapped the toe of his oxford loafer impatiently against the tile. "I thought you had a meeting to be at this morning, Ricky."

Chapter 6

Very little irritated Ricky more than untimeliness and yet here he was almost ten minutes late. But at least he had made it. He hadn't missed one of these 5:00 AM meetings for more years than he could remember.

Before he got out of the limo a report came over the radio.

"In international news," the broadcaster said, "speaking from the Persian Caliphate's capitol in Istanbul this morning, his holiness, Caliph Rafsanjani once again accused Israel of providing weaponry, fighters, and financing to the Kurdish individualist rebels – flagrant acts of commerce interference. The Caliph called on his fellow GTP board members to strike down UN resolution 181, the 1947 resolution that created the State of Israel.

"When pressed by reporters as to why he believed the GTP had the authority to overrule a UN resolution and dissolve a nation, the Caliph – relying on opinions from global law experts who have long argued that GTP decisions supersede UN resolutions and that the Jewish state is a legal fiction – remarked: 'What the global community giveth, the global community can taketh away.' Anticipating the logical follow-up about what such a precedent might mean for the future of the Caliphate, his holiness added: 'The Persian Caliphate's legitimacy comes from Allah, whose authority supersedes *all* manmade law."

Josh laughed. "I was there at the GTP vote to recognize the Caliphate and I don't recall seeing Allah anywhere in the chamber."

"Even those of us who weren't there remember the controversy when Rafsanjani insisted on language granting Allah authority over the territory," Ricky said. "I recollect it made front page news all over the world when the GTP board agreed to it."

Josh nodded. "The GTP's mission is to keep the wheels of commerce turning. It does whatever it takes to accomplish that."

"If you say so," Ricky said as he got out. "Thanks for the ride." He shut the limo door, slipped on a pair of mirrored aviator sunglasses, tugged a blonde wig onto his head, and hustled up the snow-covered steps.

The stench of cigarette smoke, stale coffee, and mildewy indoor-outdoor carpet filled Ricky's nostrils as soon as he stepped inside the cramped little meeting room on Wyatt Earp Boulevard. He walked up to the front of the three short rows of folding metal chairs and took a seat. "Good morning," he said to Chick, who was busy dusting a yellow particleboard bookshelf behind the podium.

Chick turned and smiled, and his lone gold tooth gleamed in contrast to the Sub-Saharan pigmentation of his face. "Good morning to you, *John*," he said with a wink. Ricky, AKA John, took his anonymity considerably more seriously than the others that came here. "Sorry about the mess with the animal cages back at the shop," Chick went on. "I had to fill in for the chair of the afternoon meeting here yesterday. I'll get on over to Vizion and get that cleaned up soon as we're done."

Ricky nodded. "Josh call you about that?"

"Uh-huh."

"Well, don't let him get to you. I'm the boss and if I didn't have confidence in you, I wouldn't have made you Vizion's sanitation director."

"I appreciate that," Chick said, and pointed to a flimsy tin service cart near the entrance that was as yellow as the bookshelf except for the rust that had begun to bubble to the surface of it here and there. "Coffee and doughnuts are where they always are. The fresh brew's in the pot on the right. And double-check that the door's closed tight, please. We're almost at our carbon credit limit for the month and we still got twelve days left to make it through." The iron radiator heater beneath the street-front paned window gurgled and sputtered like a worn out diesel engine.

"You got it." Ricky gave the doorknob a sturdy shove, then started to peel out of his overcoat and scarf but decided against it after noticing his breath looked like exhaust from the mouth of a fire-breathing dragon. He grabbed a doughnut and took a bite. "You get these from the Smithsonian?" He tossed the rest of it in the wastebasket and swished a sip of coffee around in his mouth. "Those ought to be against the law."

Chick grinned. "They are." He went back to dusting the bookshelf and started whistling a tune.

"Oh, Chick, you didn't?"

21

Chick turned back to Ricky with an expression of feigned indignation. "Hey, that time I done in Bridgewater was for grand theft auto, remember. How you get doughnut thief out of that?"

"Always bragging about your resume'." Ricky chuckled. "So what's up with the doughnuts then if you didn't steal them?"

"They're day-old, which makes consumption of them illegal under the Uniform Code of outdated doughnuts or some such." Chick snickered. "And that makes that bite you took a violation of law on account of you consumed it. But I ain't done nothing wrong because the code prohibits consuming outdated doughnuts, it don't say nothing about serving them."

"What are you, a lawyer now?"

Chick shook his head. "Nah, I'm pretty sure they won't let me in the lawyer club on account of I exceeded my immoral turpitude limit. But I did spend my fair share of time in the prison law library while I was locked up. Studied con-law mostly."

Ricky grinned. "I'll just bet you did."

"Con as in con-stitutional law, not con-vict law, if that's what you was thinking," Chick said. "Not that they ain't the same thing. Matter of fact, if the politicians was doing it right, all law'd be constitutional law. You want to know why that is?"

"I'll take your word for it," Ricky said. "So how's the ice cream business?"

"Been slow with this nasty weather and all. Too cold out to go pedaling that cart around town. If you hadn't hooked me up with that janitor job at Vizion, I'd be dead broke."

Ricky hung his head. "I'm sorry I couldn't bring you on as a programmer. I know you're more than qualified in software development. But –"

"I know," Chick interjected. "Government contractors are prohibited from hiring felons for jobs around sensitive stuff. I should've known all I'd get out of them computer classes I took in prison was a fancy piece of paper." He glanced at the cheap round plastic clock on the wall behind him. "It looks like it's gonna be just me and you."

"I guess I can lose this mop then." Ricky pulled the wig off.

Chick laughed. "Alright, let's get started. Welcome to Alcoholics Anonymous. I'm Chick and I'm an alcoholic."

"Hi, Chick," Ricky said, per AA tradition.

Chick nodded a greeting to him as if Ricky was a newcomer, and then read the AA preamble which ended with the admonition that those who are incapable of being honest with themselves and grasping a manner of living that demands rigorous honesty with everyone else too are unlikely to recover.

Ricky pondered whether he was one of those incapable of honesty or whether he was simply unwilling. The campaign Vizion Inc. was about to embark on would be a deliberate act of dishonesty against the voters. At least to an extent it would be. After all, his only interest in the presidency was money and power – the money to fund increases in his artificial sight research and the power to rule the regulatory agencies that were the chief impediments to innovations in medical technology; most notable among the offenders since 1906, he had read somewhere, the FDA.

And Ricky couldn't deny that he'd been dishonest with Gabriella. He'd done what he'd done, despite his having no recollection of it. And what about being honest with himself? Was his memory loss about the car accident the result of some sort of trauma, or was it just a trick his dishonest mind had played on itself?

His attention returned to Chick who proceeded to recite the twelve steps to recovery: "We admitted we were powerless over alcohol and that our lives had become unmanageable. We came to believe that a Power greater than ourselves could restore us to sanity....We made a searching and fearless moral inventory of ourselves...."

A chill ran the full length of Ricky's spine. He was far too busy to take inventory of all the mistakes he'd made in life, although not a day went by that he wasn't haunted by that terrible one he'd made during his and Gabriella's freshman year at Harvard.

"We made a list of all the persons we had harmed, and became willing to make amends to them all," Chick went on. Ricky fought back tears. *I'm so sorry, Gabby.* "We made direct amends to such people wherever possible, except when to do so would injure them or others....And finally, having had a spiritual awakening as the result of these steps, we tried to carry this message to others, and to practice these principles in all our affairs."

Ricky sucked in a deep breath, relieved as Chick rambled off the last of the twelve steps.

"Anything you want to share?" Chick asked after that, and when Ricky said, "no" like he always did, Chick asked him, per AA meeting convention, how long he'd been sober, even though Chick already knew the answer – assuming Ricky hadn't gone on a covert bender sometime.

"Since the accident." Ricky ground his teeth.

"And that was thirty-five years ago today." Chick closed his eyes for a second, recalling. "I remember it well. You know, there's something I've always wondered about that night."

"What's that?" Ricky said.

"You. You were passed out cold when they threw you in that jail cell with me. I don't see how you could have even gotten to a car in your condition, much less drove one."

Ricky ran that night's events through his head as he had a thousand times. He and Josh and Gabriella had been at the Green Dragon Tavern in Boston. Max – Max Baxter, a regular there that neither Gabriella or Ricky knew at the time – sat at the end of the bar. Ricky ordered a drink, went to the men's room, came back and took a sip. It all went black after that; until he woke up in a jail cell the next morning with Chick stretched out on the bunk above his. The jailer released Ricky later that day without explanation. "I wish I knew the answer to that myself." Ricky sighed. "Had a blackout I guess."

Chick reached with both hands into a rusty coffee can and scooped out a heap of one-year sobriety chips and pressed them into Ricky's hands. "Happy birthday, brother man, and congratulations. You earned the mother-load."

Ricky held his cupped hands over the can and let the chips dribble through his fingers like as many years of his life. After the last of them clinked back into the can, he joined hands with Chick and together they prayed, "God grant me the serenity to accept the things I cannot change, the courage to change the things I can, and the wisdom to know the difference. Amen."

"No matter how many times I pray that prayer, it never works," Ricky said. "Could be I just ain't religious enough."

Chick nodded. "I used to call my mama whenever I was feeling that way. Fine Christian woman, she was."

"Used to?"

"Yessir, before the Deep Freeze killed her. Your folks still living?"

Ricky rubbed his forehead. "Got no reason to think otherwise."

Chick shook his head. "You tell me all them stories about that fine life back at you all's home on the range in Texas. And you ain't even bothered keeping up with your folks? You don't even know if they're still living? Ain't no wonder God ain't answering your prayers. Then again it might be because you ain't never been straight with Gabriella. Ain't right you letting her carry the guilt like that."

Ricky could not argue with what Chick said. When the right time came, he would make it right with Gabriella. He'd tell her everything. And he'd also make a point of going to visit his parents. Assuming they weren't dead. The thought of them having passed without him seeing them in over thirty years made him shiver even though the room had finally warmed up some.

Chapter 7

Ricky arrived back at his office at Vizion a few minutes after 7:00 AM, and as soon as he got to his desk, the telephone rang. "Hello, Ricky Santana here."

"Good morning, Ricky darling. It's Helen Baxter. I hope it isn't too early."

"Not at all, ma'am. But if you're calling about the case, my attorney says I ain't supposed to talk to you about that." Ricky settled into his chair with the phone cradled to his ear.

"Well we certainly wouldn't want to do anything to upset Joshua, now would we." Helen chuckled. "The reason I'm calling, darling, is to inquire whether you've given any more thought to my offer to purchase your work on the artificial eye. Not the one used in machines for spying and all of that unsavory business, the one for humans. My offer was quite generous, and with the ban on artificial eye transplantation testing I can't imagine your technology has any value to Vizion now."

"If it doesn't have value, why are you willing to pay so much for it?" Ricky wondered aloud.

So I can put it on ice because my company's value depends on preventing a cure for the blind, you rank amateur, Helen wished she could say. And should the day come that that's no longer possible, I intend for my company to be the one that profits from the cure. "What I said is it doesn't have value to *Vizion* now. My company, however, has a well-established track record of advocating for the visually impaired, as well as the financial resources to hold out for an end to

25

the testing ban. Surely you must see that I'm in a much better position to see this through."

"Ma'am, I am truly touched by your concern for the blind. But I'm afraid I have to decline."

Helen sighed. "Very well. Call me when you come to your senses. But remember, I may not be able to maintain the same level of generosity if you keep me waiting long."

"Yes, ma'am."

Ricky spent the rest of the morning and into the evening holed up in his office scouring online journals for more information on a fiber optic prostheses concept for the visual pathway that might work without the aid of external computing equipment. Apparently every other effort underway to develop a technology to replicate the neural code required for sight had been suspended after the ban on animal testing went into effect. He wondered if maybe he should take Helen's offer. But every time he thought about it, he saw images of his years of research collecting dust in a file cabinet in a dank basement somewhere. Helen's purported concern for the blind just didn't ring true.

"That's enough for today," he mumbled to himself, and prepared for the mindless job of feeding the research animals. He took off his watch, pulled on a lab coat and buttoned it up to the collar, then slipped a pair of rubber gloves and goggles on to protect against the flying feces that Brutus – a blind adult male Chimpanzee with an attitude – routinely hurled at him. Ricky didn't much blame the chimp. He imagined if he were in Brutus's situation he'd do far worse.

He reached into a drawer for a pair of silicone plugs to prevent his eardrums from bursting from the raucous whoops and chatter – another unpleasantry of hungry primates.

"Here you go," he said when he arrived at the first cage. He poured a cup of monkey chow into the chimp's food bin and refilled her water. Then he moved on to the next cage, and then to the next. Each animal's cage had a nameplate affixed to it. He'd read somewhere that people tend to treat animals that have names more humanely.

The place quieted down after all the primates ate. Ricky pulled his earplugs out. "Dawn?" he called out, "what time it is?"

Dawn glanced at the digital clock in the exam room where she was doing her best yet again to persuade the baby chimp to swallow an oral antibiotic. "It's a couple of minutes to eight. Why? You got a hot

26

date?" she hollered back to Ricky. "Come on baby," she said to the chimp as she attempted to shove the pill down his throat, "I know it tastes bad but just swallow it and it will make you all better."

Ricky raised his goggles so that they clung to the top of his head, and then went to the washroom. He tossed the rubber gloves in the wastebasket next to the sink and scrubbed his hands before shuffling down the hall to the exam room where Dawn was. "That thing picks up television, doesn't it?" he said to her, pointing to the flat-screen on the wall there.

"Um-huh. Ouch." Dawn jerked her hand out of the baby chimp's mouth. "Little urchin bit me." She shoved the tiny primate into Ricky's arms and grabbed the remote control off the counter and powered on the flat-screen. "What channel?"

"GABN, please," said Ricky. "The first segment of Josh making the case for corporate candidacy on Gabriella's program airs tonight."

"No kidding?" Dawn selected the channel, then filled a syringe with a liquid antibiotic and jammed the needle into the baby chimp's shoulder. "Sorry, little one but you gave me no alternative." She took the chimp from Ricky and returned him to the cage with his mother.

Ricky hopped up on the side of the exam table, and Dawn came back in and sat beside him. Both of them watched as the television camera zoomed in on Gabriella.

"I am honored to have a very special quest on the program today," Gabriella said, "my longtime friend and now fiancé, Attorney Joshua Horowitz."

Ricky's jaw dropped. "Did she just say Josh was her fiancé?"

"Sure did," said Dawn. "Isn't that exciting? I wonder why Josh hasn't shared the big news with us."

Because apparently he's a backstabbing weasel, Ricky thought.

Onscreen, Gabriella gave a brief bio on Josh: "Josh completed his undergraduate degree in robotics engineering at Harvard." She smiled for the camera and injected, "That's where he and I met. He earned his Juris Doctorate at Harvard Law and during his summers as a law student, he interned for then freshman Congressman Farnsworth whom as you all know is now president of the United States. Today, Josh regularly counsels the president on a variety issues." She batted her eyelashes. "After graduation, Josh officially began his law career as a clerk for the patent court. Later he joined the legal department at Levi

Baxter's Leviathan Corp, a company renowned worldwide for its public health and safety technologies, among other things.

"After a number of years at Leviathan Corp, Josh accepted his current position as general counsel and right-hand man to Mr. Ricky Santana, founder and CEO of Vizion Inc., a company, which, like Leviathan Corp, is committed to the greater good of humanity. It goes without saying that as lead counsel for Vizion Inc. in the first and only case to date challenging corporate candidacy, Josh is the foremost expert on our topic today. Please welcome attorney Joshua Horowitz."

Gabriella rose from her seat.

The camera zoomed out for a wide-shot revealing a backdrop of faux cherry-wood shelves stuffed with dated law books and a small stand with a brass statue atop it of the blind-folded lady in a toga holding the scales of justice – props that had been brought in for the purpose of imbuing the set with a law office aura. The contrast with the contemporary chairs and quarter-moon glass-top news desk, however, resulted in an unfortunate eclectic quality instead.

Josh walked onto the set, straightening his tie as he did.

Gabriella met him at center stage, her slender hand extended. In her platform shoes, she stood a good three inches above him.

Ricky rolled his eyes. What a miss-match. Gabriella with her striking features in contrast to Josh's slight build and ordinary face may as well have had a neon sign hanging around her neck that said, "I'm obviously blind."

After a handshake and a quick mini-hug, Gabriella and Josh took their seats at the news desk that doubled as a discussion table.

"Josh," Gabriella began, "Let's begin with a brief overview of the *Citizens United* case and what relevance it has to the associated candidacy at the center of all the recent controversy."

"Brief?" he said, grinning. "I'll do my best."

Gabriella rubbed a fingertip around the face of her brail wristwatch, and a little wrinkle appeared above the bridge of her nose. "We only have half an hour."

Josh glanced over the rim of his glasses at Gabriella and nodded. "Alright, but first I want to explain a little about why we've prevailed in our case so far:

"In order for a court to hear a case, the party bringing suit must have standing. For our purposes, that means the plaintiff must be able to show he or she was or imminently will be actually injured in some

28

way by whatever the issue is. Now, a candidate showing actual injury will result from other candidates running against him or her in an election is difficult regardless of the opposing candidates' qualifications or lack thereof. I mean, think about this, what is the worst injury a candidate can suffer in this context? Losing the election, right? And what is the objective of each and every candidate? You got it, to inflict exactly that injury on opposing candidates.

"So, when a case is brought by one candidate against another, the relief sought is most always for the court to take some action that will at least increase the probability that the defendant candidate will suffer that injury instead of the plaintiff candidate. That's why I think the appeals court ruled correctly in upholding the lower court's conclusion that the injury asserted by Max, Helen, and President Farnsworth in their capacity as candidates was not an injury at all, but rather a potential election outcome. And frankly, I'd be surprised if the Supreme Court even hears this case. Shall we move on to the significance of the *Citizens United* decision to corporate candidacy now?"

"Please," Gabriella said. "I was beginning to think you were waiting for a drumroll."

Josh laughed at that. "Alright. The central question in the *Citizens United* case was the extent to which the government can restrict speech through regulation of expenditures on electioneering communications without violating the Freedom of speech and of the press clause of the first amendment. That clause says, *Congress shall make no law...abridging freedom of speech, or of the press*. We'll take a closer look later at what exactly that means, but first I think it's important for the viewers to understand a little about who Citizens United is and specifically what the lawsuit bearing its name was about.

"So, Citizens United is a political advocacy corporation that produced a documentary entitled *Hillary* that it wanted to make available on cable television through video-on-demand within thirty days of the 2008 presidential primary elections. Because the film unquestionably advocated for the defeat of Hillary Clinton – Hillary was competing with Barrack Obama for the democrat party nomination for president at the time – running the film on cable that close to the primary would have violated campaign finance regulations; specifically, section 441b of the Bipartisan Campaign Reform Act, otherwise known as the BCRA.

"Among other things, the BCRA prohibited corporations from using their general treasury funds to make independent expenditures for speech that was an electioneering communication within thirty days of an election or primary. An electioneering communication is any speech that expressly advocates the election or defeat of a candidate. Anyway, the short and sweet of it is that Citizens United felt like the law was unconstitutional, so it sued, asking the court to prohibit the government from enforcing the law against the organization."

"Thank you for that explanation," Gabriella said to Josh. She turned and smiled into the camera. "More to come following these brief messages from our sponsors."

After three back-to-back attack ads in which congressional candidates hurled various insults at each other, followed by a variation on Leviathan's usual elaborate PR spots, Gabriella reappeared onscreen. "For those of you just joining us this evening, we have Attorney Joshua Horowitz with us sharing his views on the prospects for associated candidacies and explaining the legal basis for his views." She turned to Josh. "Before the break, you mentioned that Citizens United believed that the BCRA's provision on electioneering communications was unconstitutional."

Josh nodded. "That's correct, and the Supreme Court agreed with them."

Gabriella massaged her forehead, fatigue clearly setting in. "Okay, listen, what the viewers need to know is, what any of this has to do with corporations running for president."

"Bear with me," Josh said, "we're getting there, but to understand the significance of the *Citizens United* decision you need to have some basic knowledge of the history of campaign finance regulations leading up to it. You see, the roots of the whole problem go back to the mid- 1800s when the federal government began ramping up pervasive regulation of corporate activities and the courts began upholding those regulations. Corporations responded, as one would expect in this new regulatory environment, by becoming much more politically engaged as necessary to protect their interests. That political engagement manifested itself in several ways, including, but certainly not limited to, advertising for and against candidates.

"In 1907, reacting to the supposed threat to the integrity of the electoral and political system posed by this corporate spending,

Congress passed the first campaign finance law – the Tillman Act, which banned corporations from giving direct contributions to federal candidates. Four decades after that, Congress passed the Taft-Hartley Act, which prohibited corporations from making independent expenditures in support of or in opposition to federal candidates."

Gabriella raised a hand. "Wait, wait. You're telling me the government started passing all sorts of legislation that seriously impacted various industries and when corporations raised concern, the government responded by passing laws prohibiting them from speaking out on behalf of themselves and their own interests? Prohibiting corporate support for political leaders who might actually listen to them?"

Josh nodded. "That is what I'm saying. The government criminalized all but a very minimal amount of direct corporate political speech. But the leaders of those corporations didn't just throw their hands in the air, lay off all the employees, shutter the doors, and wave the white flag of surrender. What they did was create the predecessors of today's super PACs, and then funded those PACs from their corporate treasuries to speak on their behalf. Ironically, under the new regulatory scheme, big corporate money in politics did not decline. It skyrocketed."

Gabriella smiled into the camera. "I'm afraid our time is up for this evening, so we'll have to leave it there. But be sure and join us next week when Josh will pick up right where he left off. As always, thank you for tuning to GABN."

Chapter 8

Wednesday morning, Max Baxter clawed his way through the tangled silk sheets to the edge of the California king and lit a scented candle on the bedside table. The vanilla aroma helped to soften the smell of aging hardwood exuding from the walls at the Dodge City Baxter Mansion. He laid there for a quiet moment, missing New York again already, but glad to be back in Kansas, just the same. Seeing the once grandest city in the world in such decay reminded him of his own decline and the freight train of mortality speeding his way. Unless he managed to seize the presidency, he would meet his end without ever having amounted to anything but just plain old Max – the pathetic ex

31

union boss whose signature labor strike on Leviathan Corp was crushed beneath the heavy foot of his father, the great Levi Baxter.

He switched a lamp on and the light pierced his swollen eyes like icepicks through a pair of marble-sized jellyfish. His face contorted and he released a moan just short of a scream as a jolt that felt like two hundred and twenty volts shot through his brain. He pressed firmly against both temples and kneaded until the pain subsided enough that he could sit up. The migraines – which occurred with increasing frequency lately – were becoming unbearable.

Max slung his legs over the side of the high-rise bed and slowly lowered his five-foot-six-inch's of chubbiness until his feet contacted the icy slab of a marble floor. "Brrr." He stepped into a pair of slippers and reached for the velvet robe hanging from one of the granite bedposts.

He held the robe out for a moment, admiring his golden monogrammed initials on it. Then he tugged it on and attempted to tie the strap around him. It must have shrunken in the wash, he told himself, but he knew that it had not. That robe had fit perfectly when Helen gave it to him as a birthday gift. He could not recall what year that was, only that it was before he moved back into Levi's Dodge City mansion after Helen divorced him; sometime after Gabriella came into their lives. Poor Gabriella. Life had dealt her such a terribly nasty blow. But she was okay.

He sucked in his gut, holding his breath as he did, and gave the strap another pointless tug. Some changes were in order – a diet perhaps, maybe a health club membership, a personal trainer. Losing a few pounds might improve his now virtually nonexistent ability to attract beautiful young women. The sound of the shower running, the squeaking of the old iron pipes as the water coursed through them, and the steam seeping from beneath the bathroom door, reminded him of how badly it had been going lately. Any moment now the twenty year-old Newman U Sophomore would come prancing out of the bathroom with her hair bound up in a towel like a turban and another towel wrapped tightly around her body, strategically revealing her considerable cleavage.

She would raise her eyebrows wantingly or wink and lick her lips sensually or something of that nature, and after imagining his unspoken answer in the affirmative to her inviting eyes, the towel would drop to the floor and she would throw her arms around him and her fingernails would gently scrub the back of his neck while his face was buried in bosoms. Etcetera.

After countless experiences with college-aged girls it had all become so very predictable. Not that Max didn't appreciate predictability. In this case, however, the stunningly beautiful young woman he had gone to bed with would vanish when that towel hit the floor just as suddenly as she had appeared in his imagination when the lights went off last night, leaving a pathetically average reminder of his decline in her place. That was a prediction he was not looking forward to. The thought of it worsened his headache.

He fished a handful of aspirin from his robe pocket and choked them down, ignoring the bottle of more potent pain relievers on the dresser next to several other medications – all of them unopened, except for the Rohypnol and Viagra. He flipped a wall switch, igniting the oversized natural gas fireplace and scrubbed his hands together in front of the flames. "Ah the pleasures of an enormous carbon credit account."

Max mused, considering the peaceful countryside beyond the double layer of blackout shades and heavy draperies covering the bedroom windows. The chimneys of vacant dwellings dotting the surrounding landscape had all gone cold. He smiled. Such a pity that millions perished in the Deep Freeze. But most of the deceased had been poor and ignorant and generally too stupid to use birth control – a heretofore perpetually self-replicating drag on society. The latter provided Max some measure of solace despite the collateral reduction in his former union's membership.

Yes, all in all, comprehensive carbon emissions regulation – sealed permanently in international law now by the recent global agreement – had accomplished so much more than merely staving off a potential climate catastrophe. He closed his eyes, basking in the relative absence of humanity around him. He had need of only one person. No person in particular, just a prettier version of the young woman in the shower – one he could promptly dispose of when he was finished with her.

Riiiiiiiiiiiiiiiiing.

Max winced at the rattly ringer of the antiquated rotary telephone, echoed by at least six others just like it dispersed throughout the mansion. Another jolt shot through his head. He glanced at the clock. 11:30 AM. Anyone that knew him also knew that he rarely got up before noon these days. Who in the world was calling?

Riiiiiiing...squeeaak.

Dear God!

The noise from the old plumbing pipes intensified. And the crescendo – the slapping, flapping whir of a low-flying helicopter so close it sounded as though it were landing in the living room. Then, pounding at the front door. A conspiracy of noises to make his head explode.

Riiiiiiing.

Max yanked the receiver from the hook. "Who is it!"

"Max darling, did you wake up on the wrong side of the bed?" Helen answered back.

He ran his fingers through the precious few strands of white hair remaining on top of his scalp and made a conscious effort to control his breathing. He'd read about the importance of controlled breathing in some women's yoga magazine. "Sorry. Rough night."

"Still having trouble sleeping? Why don't you try taking those pills your doctor prescribed for your insomnia? Rohypnol, wasn't it?"

"My doctor told you about that? That's a violation of Hippo regulations."

Helen chuckled. "Max darling, it's HIPPA, not hipp-o, and by the way, everything is a violation of something these days. But never mind that, I'm worried about you. I can hear the wheels of paranoia churning in your mind. Have you forgotten we were married for over twenty years? Your doctor was prescribing you that medication even back then.

"Was I supposed to overlook the stockpile in the medicine cabinet? Close my eyes before reaching in and just hope somehow I might recognize whatever I was looking for by the feel of it? I suppose we could have had everything labeled in brail or –" Helen stopped herself. Her company had retained the most prestigious lobbying firm on Wyatt Earp Boulevard to lead the charge to require federally mandated brail labeling on pharmaceutical products – labels which her company printed at a healthy premium. She should have chosen her words more thoughtfully.

Max sat silently for a moment, considering the implications of it all. One small error had permanently altered the course of his life. That error was perhaps a very close runner-up to his leading that failed strike against Leviathan Corp. back in the 90s.

"I'm sorry, I got lost in a thought," Helen finally said.

34

Max heard the shower shut off and another round of pounding at the front door. He sucked in a deep breath and then let it out. "Me too," he said. The pounding on the door grew louder. "Listen, Helen, I've got to go. Someone's at the door?"

"Another of your young floozies?"

Max grunted. "Don't start, Helen." He hung up the phone and shrugged into a larger robe he'd purchased for himself recently and went and tugged the massive front door open.

Gabriella stood on the stoop, shivering. "It's about time," she said through chattering teeth. Ricky stood silently behind her, bombarded by chunks of blowing snow.

Max shoved his hands anxiously in and out of his robe pockets as the bitter wind stung at his bare legs. "I'm in the middle of something right now," he said. "Can you all come back later?" He glanced at the security harmonizers stationed at either side of the door. "I hope you two useless wastes of innovation aren't expecting a year-end bonus," he grumbled. One of them appeared to stare mockingly at him through a pair of camera eyes manufactured by Vizion.

"How do you do?" Gabriella said – her teeth still chattering – to the slightly plump young woman who appeared behind Max.

Max glanced over his shoulder at the woman with hair tied up in a towel and another towel around her body, just as he had predicted. But he had not anticipated a crowd here to witness it.

Gabriella pushed past Max and extended her hand. "Gabriella Meir," she said as she and the young woman shook hands. "Max is a dear friend, like a father to me, sort of. And you are?"

The woman shrieked when her towel dropped to the floor in the course of the handshake.

Gabriella moved quickly along to the den.

Ricky's jaw dropped.

Max planted a hand over his eyes and shook his head.

The woman snatched the towel up from the floor.

"Well," said Max through a prolonged sigh as she clutched the dangling towel to her bulging breasts, "I guess the cat's out of the bag, so to speak." He snorted. "It might be best if you got dressed, young lady."

She scampered off to the bedroom.

Ricky still stood outside the door, his flight jacket and cowboy hat now almost solid white from the heavy snowfall.

"Well, you may as well come in," Max said.

Ricky followed Max into the den where Gabriella had already switched on the gas fireplace beneath a massive portrait of Levi Baxter seated on a medieval throne much like the one in his office at Leviathan Corp.

"How did you know the girl was there?" Max said to Gabriella as he settled into an oversized leather chair by the fire.

Ricky sat down on the matching leather sofa.

Gabriella smirked at Max. "A woman can always smell the presence of another woman."

Max tapped a finger against his pasty chin. "Hmm." That might explain why Helen never got over her endless suspicions back when they were a married couple despite his having covered his tracks meticulously, except for that one time – certainly more meticulously than she, who had tried to pass her pregnancy off as a thyroid malfunction that caused her to swell up like a humanoid melon. He clasped his hands together. "So to what do I owe this surprise?"

"Just wanted to see how you were doing," Gabriella said.

Max glanced at Ricky. "And I suppose you're here to gloat."

"Excuse me," Gabriella said, and left for the kitchen to get a glass of water.

"What do I have to gloat about?" Ricky said.

Max lit a cigar and leaned back in his chair. "The Supreme Court refused to hear the case. Just as Josh predicted. They announced it earlier this morning."

"Really? I hadn't heard."

Max glared at him. "So, now that the court case is over, where do we go from here? What I mean is, do the gloves come off now or shall we handle this like gentlemen?"

Ricky got up and paced the den, stopping at an antique handgun display case. He opened the glass lid and carefully lifted out an early 1800s vintage flintlock single-shot pistol. He wagged it in the air. "What did you have in mind, a gentlemen's duel?"

Max waved the backside of his hand at Ricky and said through a cloud of smoke as he puffed his cigar, "Put that thing back. Levi would have an aneurism if anything happened to it. As to your question, what I had in mind was you withdrawing Vizion from the race. It's the least you could do in exchange for my continuing to keep your little secret safe and sound."

Ricky extended his arm, aiming the pistol directly at Max's forehead, then cocked the hammer back and aligned his eye with the sight. "And what secret might that be?"

Josh stepped into the den, and Ricky lowered the pistol.

"What are you doing here?" Josh said.

Ricky frowned. "Funny, I was going to ask you the same thing. By the way, thanks for giving me a heads up on your engagement to Gabriella."

"Visibility on the road back from some business in Kansas City last night was almost nonexistent," Josh said, ignoring Ricky's comment about the engagement. "Max was good enough to let me ride out the rest of the blizzard in a guestroom here."

Gabriella came back in with her water in hand. "Did I miss anything important?" .

Max smirked. "Why, yes, Gabriella, as a matter of fact you did. Ricky was admiring Levi's firearm collection and out of nowhere he mentions that he's considering withdrawing Vizion from the race. Something about a campaign distracting him from his research."

Ricky put the pistol back in the display case and returned to the sofa.

"It's a shame," Max went on, "I was really looking forward to a vigorous debate in the marketplace of ideas. They say that sort of thing is healthy for the democratic process."

"Wow," Gabriella said. "Are you really thinking about withdrawing, Ricky?"

"No," Ricky growled.

Max glared at him again.

The room went quiet after that, then Ricky said, "The storm is whipping up again and conditions are expected to continue to deteriorate so we better get going."

"I presume from all the racket earlier that you all came by chopper." Max relit his cigar. "Are you sure it's safe to fly in this weather?"

"You forgetting my pilot here has been flying since he was a young boy?" Gabriella said. "He can handle a little weather."

"I suppose you are in capable hands," Max said, and rose from his chair. His gaze shifted to Josh. "And it would be helpful if you could drive the young lady to the transit center so she can get back to the dorms over at Newman U or wherever it is she's going."

Josh nodded. "Sure."

Chapter 9

The wind picked up dramatically after the Vizion corporate helicopter lifted off from the Baxter estate, forcing Ricky to fight fiercely with the controls throughout the flight. But he managed well enough to deliver Gabriella and then himself safely to their destinations – notwithstanding a near miss when a forty-five knot gust almost blew the chopper into his virtually invisible white cinderblock cottage as he hovered to land on the snow-covered patch of dirt behind it.

After tying the chopper down, he gathered an armful of firewood from the shed and made his way up the creaky porch steps. He stomped the snow off his boots and contemplated the barely legible name on the rusted placard adjacent the door – The Swansons. "Thank you for your hospitality, Mr. and Mrs. Swanson," he said to the image of the elderly couple his mind had conjured up.

The federal government owned that cottage now and leased it to him and he liked to think that the Swansons – whom he had learned called this place home for the better part of fifty years – had left voluntarily and not frozen to death. He imagined them in a nice assisted living facility in sunny Florida where others kept them comfortable in their advanced ages. But then, Florida would be unbearably hot and humid in summer without air conditioning, so that would not be a happy ending either. What was wrong with those aristocratic idiots who thought declaring war on heat and air conditioning was a service to mankind?

He stepped into the modest one-bedroom dwelling, hugging the firewood to his chest, and laughed at the thought of himself, a man well on his way to becoming a multi-millionaire, living in a place like this – even if it did come with a slightly higher carbon credit limit than most. But he was a simple man from humble beginnings and cared little for fancy digs. Although a lifetime ago he had fantasized briefly about the palace he'd build for Gabriella after they married.

His Saint Bernard, Bernice greeted him with a drooling baritone bellow. He smiled affectionately at the old dog. The goggles that housed the video cam and microcomputer portion of her mechanical retinal correction system made her look like an enlarged version of the Snoopy Red Baron dog, less the scarf.

At eleven years old, Bernice had already exceeded the average life expectancy of her breed. She was near deaf and so arthritic that she strained to stand for more than several minutes these days and she had been almost completely blind before the retinal implants. Ricky loaded the wood into the fireplace and after lighting it, gave her a few strokes between her floppy ears. "How ya doing, Bern."

Bernice looked up at Ricky though her goggles and groaned.

After filling her food bowl, Ricky brewed a pot of coffee and sat down with a cup in a badly worn armchair upholstered in the same orange plaid burlap as the equally badly worn couch and draperies. He hadn't chosen the furniture or the drapes or the boxy 1980s vintage TV he never watched or much of anything else here. With the exception of some of old framed photographs on the fireplace mantle, most everything here had been left behind by the Swansons.

He held the cup to his nose, enjoying the earthy aroma of the coffee.

Bernice chomped away until her bowl was empty, then stumbled across the deteriorating hardwood and plopped down on the braided rug in front of the fireplace. The worn off finish gave the floors a rustic appearance reminiscent of those at the Santana ranch in Texas where Ricky grew up. He could almost hear the hollow clickety-clack clank of his father, Ricardo's boots and spurs...Papa.

It seemed surreal that more than thirty years had passed since he last saw his father and his mother, Isabella. But shame prevented him from going home after what he'd done to Gabriella. He'd been raised better. As a boy, Isabella had doted on him like a mother of an only child often does, and Ricardo had taken the time to teach him everything he could, despite being bat-shit crazy. How could the son of such loving parents had done such a horrible thing? He winced as a memory of Ricardo trying to reattach his severed legs after the tractor accident when he was six years old unexpectedly invaded his mind. He felt the pain of the plow slicing through his flesh.

The pain subsided and Ricky peered out the window into the distance at the setting sun seeping through the dull gray haze that remained in the aftermath of the blizzard. As the crackling fire warmed the room, the frost on the windows melted into tiny water droplets creeping down to powdery accumulations of snow in the bottom corners of the rotting wooden panes forming a sort of white mud.

Ricky's gaze shifted to the 5x7 simple-framed photos on the mantle.

To the left was a portrait of Ricardo in uniform after returning from Viet Nam. Next to it, a photo of him with Ricky as a young boy standing next to the old Pitts Special biplane they used for crop dusting. By nine years old, Ricky had learned to fly the antique bird, prosthetic lower legs and all. A couple of years later, Ricardo introduced him to the 1954 Hiller UH 12B helicopter they monitored the herds with.

Things had changed a lot since then. No way Ricky could have imagined he'd one day be the CEO of a major company or that that company might become president of the United States. His gaze returned to the fireplace mantle – to another framed photograph, this one of him with Josh and Gabriella when they were all freshmen together at Harvard. Ricky had saved for months to purchase the simple silver necklace Gabriella wore in that picture. But for that God forsaken car accident, they would all be as happy today as they appeared in the photograph. Except Josh. Josh might not be so happy, and Josh sure as hell wouldn't be Gabriella's fiancé...fiancé. She wouldn't really go through with it, would she?

He took a sip of coffee, then his cell phone rang. "Ricky Santana," he answered.

"Hey, it's Josh. You anywhere near a television?"

Ricky glanced at the set across the room. "Yeah, but I don't have any idea if it works. Why?"

"It's Max. He's giving a campaign speech under a ruse of a press conference."

"Really? It's only been, what, a couple of hours, since we left there? He sure moves quick...uh...ly." Ricky went over and pushed what appeared beneath the caked on dust to be the power button to the TV. Surprisingly, the set came on.

A tease from the upcoming 5:00 news on channel three: "Remands to harmonization for landscaping without a license surged to over one million so far this year; Dodge City is declared a gun-free zone; DHS begins implementing plan to replace human police officers with harmonizers; and Congress debates President Farnsworth's proposal to strengthen unity by abolishing the outdated concept of state sovereignty. Those stories and more, coming up at five."

"What channel?" Ricky asked.

"I've got it on eight here," said Josh.

Ricky tuned the set to channel eight, and there stood Max, behind a podium in the mansion's expansive living room feeding the crowd of reporters a line about how under a Max Baxter presidency, workers would no longer be exploited by evil greedy corporations.

"Modern society is characterized by class conflict," Max declared, "with the upper end of the so-called middle class – doctors, engineers, small-time entrepreneurs, those sorts of crooks – conspiring to satisfy their appetites for more and more luxuries by robbing the hardworking men and women of basic essentials. How much is enough? I say they have more than enough already and its time we take it back!"

The reporters whistled and applauded, urging Max on.

"You should have left that college chick there," Ricky said to Josh. "That would have been a juicy morsel for the press to chew on."

Josh faked a laughed.

Max went on, playing to the cameras. "You, the American workers, are steadfast, patient, and generous. And too much of all of that. You've given your oppressors centuries to prove their precious capitalist system can work for you. But it hasn't worked for you. You have worked for it. It's been your master and you have been its slave. I say, NO MORE. It's time for a new revolution – a revolution led by the working class to eliminate classes altogether and make all men equal as our founding fathers intended when they wrote those precious words in the declaration, 'all men are created equal.' And the first step to that revolution is electing Max Baxter to the presidency of the United States."

The reporters roared their approval.

"Wow, are you hearing this?" Ricky said.

Josh said, "Unbelievable, isn't it? If Max can keep that level of intensity up, Vizion Inc. might be in for a battle at the ballot box."

Ricky nodded, his phone pressed tightly to his ear. "I'll say. But I'm dumbfounded why people keep buying that same old line of bull. Some filthy rich dude gets up on his high horse and rails against the upwardly-mobile of the middle class for making too much money, then once elected they get even richer skimming off them. And at the

41

end of the filthy rich dude's term, the cycle begins again. Doesn't make a lick of sense."

"That was a mouthful for a man who's never been into politics," said Josh.

"Hey, I'm apolitical, not unconscious." Ricky laughed. He pulled back the curtains and peeked outside, curious why no reporters had come by to get his response to the Supreme Court's decision, and he saw that maybe one had. Gabriella weaved her way up the walkway with her electronic navigator in hand.

Chapter 10

Ricky awoke early the next morning with Gabriella nestled next to him, her cheek resting comfortably against his bare chest as she slept, her soft breath warming his skin. He tilted his head and nuzzled her hair, then laid back against the pillow and fell fast asleep again until a couple of hours later when the smell of coffee and something cooking filled his nostrils.

He sat up and stretched his arms. It had been decades since he'd slept so well.

The indentation in the mattress where Gabriella had lain made him smile. Whether it was a new smile or the reappearance of one that had hidden dormant since the accident he couldn't say. But it felt like he'd been smiling forever. He attached his lower legs, threw on a t-shirt, and shuffled out to the kitchen.

Gabriella stood at the stove, dressed in the navy blue casual business outfit she'd shown up in yesterday. Despite the wrinkles from sleeping in it, she looked as beautiful as ever.

"My goodness, what's all this about?" Ricky said.

She giggled and kept stirring the zucchini and carrots. "I underestimated the difficulty of cooking in an unfamiliar kitchen, but making you breakfast to thank you for looking after me last night seemed like the least I could do."

"Looking after you? All I did was carry you from the couch to the bed. You must have been totally exhausted to fall asleep on that worn out old thing."

Gabriella kneaded her lower back with both hands. "Your bed wasn't much better." She laughed. "And it would have been nice if you'd helped me out of my clothes before tucking me in."

Ricky blushed. She had no idea how badly he would have liked to undress her last night. He watched the morning sunlight from the kitchen window dancing in her glass eyes. If only they were her natural eyes, soaking up all the beauty in the world and reflecting it back on him the way they once did. "I'm sorry you didn't sleep well," he said.

"I slept fine," said Gabriella.

"So, you and Josh are engaged?" The words tumbled awkwardly out of Ricky's mouth.

Gabriella filled a coffee cup and handed it to him, then poured herself one and sat down at the table, considering Ricky's comment or question or whatever it was. Why should he be surprised about her finally agreeing to marry Josh? Ricky had had more than thirty years to make good on his own proposal back in college. He'd given her that necklace until he could afford a diamond ring. She would have happily settled for a ring out of gumball machine. And she had waited…and waited.

She thought back to the first lonely hours and days immediately following the car accident. How she'd woken up in the hospital surrounded by a cloud of impenetrable darkness, and the doctor had told her she'd never see anything again. Days and weeks went by and Ricky never came to her bedside. A world that couldn't get any darker somehow did.

Three years – that's how long it was before Gabriella even heard Ricky's voice again. He claimed he'd been at the University of Missouri in Kansas City where he transferred after being dismissed from Harvard for poor grades. The first part was true. He had transferred. But the last part was a lie and she knew it. His grades had been exemplary. Regardless, he could have called. And when he did finally come back, he could have been man enough to tell her where things stood instead of treating her as if they'd never been anything more than friends.

"Are you okay, Gabby?"

She thought a minute longer. Was it selfish of her to judge Ricky this way? She supposed it was. After all, despite his rise to success, he was still a simple man and the prospect of caring for a blind woman the rest of his life probably scared him half to death as it would any sane person.

And even if Ricky had been willing to sign onto a life as a caretaker, she couldn't imagine he would have been capable of actually doing it. Not that wasting decades of his life chasing a pipedream of artificial sight wasn't something, but she needed help with her reality, not his fantasy. Someone to just be there for her; to drive her places; to take out the trash or help unload a dishwasher once in a while – practical things. Didn't he know that? Or was he just too... too...dense? Well, whatever the case, he just should have told her he wasn't up to dealing with a blind person, instead of running off like that. She would have understood. Wouldn't she have?

It hit her suddenly. He wasn't dense. Okay, maybe he was dense. But there was more to it than that. He was angry. Angry with her for having put him and Josh in danger by driving drunk. And he had every right to be angry about that. She was angry with herself about it. "I'm fine, Ricky," she finally said. "I just have a lot on my mind."

"Anything you want to talk about?"

Gabriella's thoughts shifted to more recent events, one in particular lurking beneath the surface of what she knew was an unhealthy layer of self-pity mixed with self-condemnation. "You know that Newman U student from yesterday?" she said. "When I went back to Max's bedroom to let her know Josh was ready to drive her to the transit center, she was sitting on the bed crying and I tried to comfort her but she was hysterical. Like out of her mind hysterical."

"I imagine finding one's self buck-naked in front of a mess of strangers might do that to a gal." Ricky chuckled.

Gabriella scowled. "It's not a laughing matter. That girl told me that she had no recollection whatsoever of going to the mansion or anything else that went on afterwards until she woke up in bed with Max. It's like she had a complete blackout. One minute she's at a bar partying with friends, the next she's in the sack with some old man she's never met before in her life."

Ricky could relate to the blackout part. That had happened to him the night of the accident that left Gabriella blind. But the waking up in bed with an old coot part, not so much. "There's something to be said for beer goggles," he said.

"This is not about drinking," Gabriella shot back.

"If it's not about drinking, then what? ... Oh, you're not thinking that it was –"

Gabriella tugged at her hair. "Date rape drug? Yes, that's exactly what I'm thinking. Remember when that slew of women were drugged and raped in Boston back when we were at Harvard? Recently a similar pattern has been documented here in Dodge City."

"And are half the victims claiming they were abducted by aliens and experimented on like they did in Boston?"

Gabriella clenched her teeth. "They were drugged, Ricky. Just like my big sister was."

"I didn't know your sister was –"

"I think *raped* is the word you're searching for," Gabriella said, "but murdered would be more accurate. It happened before I met you. I was in high school then. She slit her wrists after. I found her in the bathtub." A dribble of wet mascara rolled down Gabriella's cheek, reminding her that tear ducts are not actually part of the eyes.

Ricky draped an arm around her. "I'm sorry."

Gabriella dabbed at the mascara with a napkin. "Forensic evidence recovered from the girls who were willing to give samples suggests the rapist in Boston may have had an accomplice, an accomplice who according to the DNA markers happened to have been a close relative of the rapist. And those DNA profiles are the same as the perps here in Dodge City. Unfortunately there's no match for either in the national database."

"Which means the perps were born prior to the Infant DNA Collection Act and neither has been arrested for anything in recent years," Ricky said. The hair on the back of his neck stood on end as he thought about it. Max was born decades before passage of the DNA collection law and as far as Ricky knew, Max had never been arrested for anything. "So there are connections between the Boston incidents and the ones here in Dodge City, and you think one of those connections is Max?"

Gabriella balled a hand up into a fist and shook it in the air. "Dear God, no. Max is definitely a horn-dog, no question, but he wouldn't do something like that. His ego wouldn't allow it. I'm thinking the rapist spiked the girl's drink and maybe Max stumbled upon her unwittingly while out carousing and maybe he thought she was woozy from one too many whatever cocktails and he took advantage of the situation. He's certainly not above taking advantage of situations. But he's no rapist. Besides, he doesn't have any living relatives except for Levi. Does he?"

Ricky considered the flaws in Gabriella's rationale. Taking advantage of someone who was semi-conscious whether from ingesting a date rape drug or too much booze *was* what it *was* regardless of what the pervert taking advantage knew or didn't know about the cause of his victim's condition. She did have a point about Levi being Max's only living relative though. It was highly improbable a man nearly a century old was a serial rapist. But with Viagra...no. Ricky thought a minute longer before suggesting, "Maybe she should go to the police."

Gabriella took a sip of coffee. "That was my first thought, but you know as well as I do that Max would be questioned as part of any official investigation and the tabloids would have a field day with it. That would be the end of his candidacy. Not that I'm picking sides in your slugfest for the Whitehouse."

Ricky rubbed his forehead. "So you're putting politics above –"

"I'm not putting politics above anything," Gabriella snapped. "You know very well that I'm necessarily both personally and professionally neutral about the election. But every candidate deserves a fair chance. Anyway, it isn't as though I prevented that girl from going to the police. I just didn't encourage her to."

"So, what do you suggest then?" Ricky said.

"I was thinking maybe I could look into it myself. Do some real investigative work. Important work. Just memorizing lines I'm given by my producer and regurgitating them for the camera is not what I had in mind when I chose a career in journalism. As you know, what I really wanted to be was a photojournalist. But that's neither here nor there." Gabriella took another sip of coffee. "Anyway, it's probably just wishful thinking that I could ever be more than a mindless mouthpiece under the circumstances."

They sat silently for a couple of minutes and then Gabriella said, "There's something else," she twirled a lock of hair around her finger. "The perfume that girl wore, I smelled it all over Josh when he came into the den at Max's yesterday."

"Gabby, you know as well as I do that Josh's work requires him to interact with a lot of people every day," said Ricky. "Some of which happen to be females that, surprise, surprise, wear perfume."

46

"Yeah, uh-huh, meetings with bimbos that all happen to wear the *same* perfume. What's he moonlighting as general counsel for a brothel now?"

Ricky couldn't help but laugh at that. "Look, I've known Josh a long time, and…" He paused. Why was he defending Josh? Could be Josh did have a threesome with Max and the college girl, or whatever it was swirling around in Gabriella's mind. Now, that was a disturbing image.

Gabriella gave Ricky a nudge on the shoulder. "Are you going to complete that thought?"

He nodded. "I don't know what to say, Gabby. Maybe Josh did do something inappropriate, but I doubt it. He glanced over at the calendar hanging next to the refrigerator. "We best get going. I've got a meeting at Leviathan Corp at noon."

Chapter 11

"Woo." Ricky bent over, hands on his knees, breathing heavily after running the nearly half mile from the Santa Fe Depot Transit Center to Leviathan headquarters. He glanced at his watch. Fifteen minutes to spare.

After catching his breath, he straightened his back and gazed up at the building – a thirty floor iron and glass monument to Levi towering above the surrounding conventional and mostly old-west style wooden and brick structures. A repeating sign across the top of the building streamed generic information – date, time, and, temperature, followed by *Leviathan Corp* flashing in bold red-lighted letters on a black background, and then back to date, time, and temperature again.

Ricky stepped through the automated glass doors, and a harmonizer stopped him and demanded identification and to know the purpose of his visit. He tossed his Vizion badge at it and growled. "I'm here to see Levi Baxter. He's expecting me." Most harmonizers, this one included, displayed an arrogance that severely irritated Ricky. "Without Vizion's camera eyes, a tin tub like you wouldn't even know I was here," he grumbled beneath his breath as it scrutinized the ID badge.

"You are cleared to enter, Mr. Santana," said the harmonizer.

47

Ricky stepped into the tube-shaped elevator and strapped himself in and it rocketed up.

Several floors up Ricky found Levi waiting outside the elevator in a black custom tailored business suit complete with yellow power tie – his usual attire whenever he wasn't posing as a commoner for one of Leviathan's PR spots.

The two men shook hands. "It's good to see you, Ricky," said Levi.

"Likewise," Ricky said. His Texas drawl – which had reconstituted itself in full force after relocating to Dodge City where similar accents prevailed – contrasted sharply with Levi's annoyingly proper British sounding English.

Levi swept his arm toward his office's soaring double doors. "Shall we?"

The custom furnishings, posh carpet, fine art, and various antiquities beyond those doors reeked of obscene wealth. Levi sat in the throne behind his desk, one that had belonged to some middle-eastern despot deposed by Leviathan mercenaries on behalf of the GTP before the organization formed its own military wing. He slid a marble chess set aside, then folded his hands in front of him. "Please have a seat." Levi pointed to a chair opposite the desk that although also resembling a throne was merely an unusually ornate chair. "So what did you think of Max's press conference?"

"Press conference?" Ricky squirmed in the uncomfortable chair. Pretentious furniture was highly overrated. "More like a pep rally. Ol' Max is quite the performer. That nut apparently didn't fall too far from the tree. You sure you'd rather not support him instead of Vizion in the election?"

Levi smiled. "Once I've made a decision, I stay the course. Which is precisely why I asked you here. We need to go over a few particulars of that course. You'll be pleased to know I've already formed a super PAC and its balance currently exceeds a half billion dollars. Naturally, I will have my marketing experts put those resources to good use saturating cable television, radio, internet, and perhaps some newspapers with a message consistent with Vizion's. Or perhaps not the papers." Levi debated it with himself. "We've got a bit of homework to do yet to determine whether making the papers available free has increased readership. Frankly, I don't anticipate that it has. Reading comprehension isn't exactly pervasive among the imbeciles that make up our fine citizenry these days."

"A half a billion dollars! Good Lord." Ricky could not begin to fathom what Levi's anticipated return on such a mind-boggling investment in Vizion's campaign must be. This was really happening. Nothing could stop Ricky now – his blood suddenly ran cold – except Max's threat to reveal his secret. But what secret? Did Max know about Ricky's role in the accident? If Max did know about that, leverage couldn't hurt, and a sample of Max's DNA could be just the leverage Ricky needed. But how to get that sample? Ricky put it out of his mind for the time being. "Okay then," he said, "so if your people are doing all that, what should I do?"

Levi grinned. "Campaign finance law forbids coordination so I can't tell you what to do, otherwise I would encourage you to get out on the stump and greet the people face to face. Kiss some babies. Press some flesh, as they say. And most of all, talk about harmony, how Vizion will bring us all together again.

"Your opponents' messages will undoubtedly be some variation of the same old *Us versus Them* rhetoric – Rich versus Poor, Every color versus Every other color, that sort of nonsense. A tried and true strategy, to be sure, but I sense the people have grown weary enough of it that it can be soundly defeated by a live and in person message of global harmony – a declaration of war on otherness. And Vizion Inc. is just the warrior to lead the charge."

Levi handed Ricky a book entitled *Engineering Global Harmony*. This will help you get up to speed on the battle plan, as it were, for the war on otherness before your campaign tour bus arrives this afternoon. I'll expect you to be on that bus and making your way round the country spreading Vizion's message in" – he glanced at his watched – "well, let's say by 8:00 AM tomorrow. And you might be comforted to know that Gabriella will be riding along for media coverage. Take good care of her. She's been a bit out of sorts lately."

The thought of spending a few weeks on the road with Gabriella was comforting to Ricky, or maybe exhilarating was a better word for it. "I assume Gabriella has agreed to this?" he said.

"*Agreed* is hardly the word for it, she was ecstatic," said Levi. "Can you imagine the boost Gabriella's play by play coverage of the first corporate presidential campaign will give GABN's ratings and her own professional prestige? Not that both are not already in extraordinarily high standing." He stood. "Now, are you ready for that grand behind the scenes tour I promised you of the harmonizer project?"

Chapter 12

The subterranean facility beneath the Leviathan building housed a brigade of harmonizer pilots paired in cubicles from which they remotely operated the machines. Each cubicle contained a wrap-around video monitor, an instrument panel, and two sets of identical controls and communications headsets. The GPS surface navigation systems built into the harmonizer control stations were more or less variations of a manned aircraft's glass cockpit.

Levi and Ricky made their way down the center aisle and Ricky glanced over at the monitor in station three where the pilots laughed and jerked wildly at the controls as their assigned harmonizer battered a man onscreen.

Ricky grabbed one of them by the shirt collar.

"I'll handle this," Levi said, urging Ricky to release him. "Gentlemen, that's quite enough."

Both pilots leapt to their feet and saluted. "Yes, sir!"

"As you were," Levi said.

Ricky said, "Jerks," and he and Levi continued down the aisle to an unmanned cubicle. "Captain seat's yours," Levi said.

Ricky sat down and examined the equipment. "As a pilot," he said, "I appreciate redundancy. It's comforting to know if the need arises there's someone else in the cockpit with his own set of controls to keep the shiny side up. But, in this context, two pilots per machine strikes me as overkill, an unnecessary and undoubtedly costly inefficiency. Why not just have a few backup pilots on duty to step in in cases of emergency instead of having two at every station?"

Levi sighed. "You're quite right, of course. It is overkill, but it isn't our call. Government regulations, you know. This one alone costs Leviathan close to a billion a year in unnecessary duplicative hardware. Not to mention the increased payroll. On the other hand, the regulations also reduce competition by increasing the price to play. What's more, like a great many other government contracts, the harmonizer contract is cost-plus. Which means the government is obliged to compensate Leviathan for the cost, plus an agreed upon percentage of profit on top of that cost. In this case, twenty percent. So that extra billion in government mandated inefficiency has the net effect of increasing our bottom line by two hundred million dollars. Quite a nice silver lining."

Ricky, like most people, had a general awareness of the government mandated inefficiencies Levi spoke of. But he'd never given more than a passing thought to the cost-plus contracts that resulted in twenty thousand dollar toilet seats and their equivalents culminating in hundreds of billions in unnecessary expenses billed to taxpayers.

Levi powered up the monitor. It displayed real-time video recorded by the camera eyes Ricky designed and manufactured at Vizion.

Ricky watched the screen with interest as elderly men and women shuffled into the senior center for Sunday afternoon bingo. A much smaller monitor positioned like an automobile's rearview mirror above the main monitor displayed video from a fixed camera across the street that kept an eye on the harmonizer itself. "This is cool stuff," he said as he fiddled with the controls. "So why isn't there a team operating this one?"

"The harmonizer on site has been decommissioned due to nonpayment," Levi said. "Seems our friends at city council don't value our esteemed seniors enough to provide them security."

"Really. Maybe you should have decommissioned the council's harmonizers instead."

"Oh, I'd like to, but Leviathan Corp is merely a provider. The politicians make the decisions. And by the way, among those decisions is the phasing out of seniors, so the issue will be moot soon enough."

"Phasing out?"

"Yes. You know, euthanasia. The Department of Health and Human Services determined that healthcare costs for the elderly far exceed whatever value their playing bingo adds to society so it's drafted a rule mandating euthanasia at the age of sixty-five rather than continuing down the road of denying them treatment and allowing them to suffer. It's the humane thing to do."

Ricky shivered at the revelation. For years, government officials had denied that a euthanasia program would be implemented as a cost-control measure, yet here it was, the ugly truth come to pass. "Not everyone over sixty-five just sits around playing bingo," he said. "You, for example."

51

Levi patted Ricky on the back. "Yes, well, thank you for your concern, but I'm grandfathered in, no pun intended. Those of us who have attained to the age of sixty-five before the rule goes into effect will be exempt. Of course there will also be waivers for those who can prove our contribution to society substantially outweighs the cost of our existence."

"How very George Bernard Shaw of the DHHS," Ricky said. "Ain't there some way President Farnsworth could stop them?"

"Of course," Levi said, "but why would he? It's for the greater good. And speaking of the president, he telephoned this morning. He's contemplating an increase in DHS harmonizers. It seems he suspects Texas may have been serious about reorienting its borders and he'd like to be better prepared to respond with force if necessary. We're ready to ramp up production on our part here at Leviathan. Will there be any problem with Vizion increasing production of the camera eyes?"

Ricky continued to fiddle with the harmonizer controls. "It depends on how many you need," he said. He hadn't planned on his technology being used against Texas. "Say, could we try this thing out?"

"By all means, let's give it a go." Levi powered up the rest of the system in the cubicle and demonstrated how the various controls work. He gripped a joystick to his left. "This operates the harmonizer's arms. The joystick next to it controls the legs," he explained. "The one beside it is for head movement. The harmonizer's eyes are your cameras, of course, at least they are on these 2.0 models. They enable you to see what's taking place where the harmonizer is stationed. As you know, they have advanced zoom capability which provides a number of advantages.

"The throttle allows you to control the leg speed," Levi went on. "It's one of the more difficult features to learn. You can walk the machine relatively easily, but running it is quite another matter. The microphone and earphones on your headset are used to communicate through the harmonizer with persons on scene. All you have to do is tune to the harmonizer's local frequency. An alternate frequency to communicate with Central Control as you would ATC from an aircraft. A secondary mic and intercom system is used to communicate with other pilots when necessary."

Levi ran a fingertip lightly across a row of bright red buttons. "And these little gems are what we call the hot-buttons. They fire the harmonizer's various weapons." He pointed to a switch labeled *Deharmonization* to the right of the row of hot buttons. "And this jewel is the mother of all control switches, for use under extraordinary circumstances. I retain an independent master switch for this feature in case a pilot were to become too squeamish to make use of it."

Ricky twisted the joystick that operated the harmonizer's head movement, and an elderly woman scurrying up the sidewalk came into view. She pointed a feeble finger at the harmonizer, the look on her face expressing both relief and vindication. "Well, I'll be," she said in a downhome west Kansas accent. "Looks like the city council decided we deserve a little protection after all. Funny how the local bigshots have a sudden change of heart about looking after us old folks when the U-nited States Government sets up shop in town."

A man rushed up behind the old woman and ripped her purse away.

Ricky grabbed the control for the harmonizer's legs and worked frantically to turn the machine toward the fleeing mugger. Then he eased the throttle forward and glanced up at the small monitor and saw the harmonizer off to a stumbling start. At least it was headed in the right direction. But the mugger was getting away. Ricky shoved the power in full throttle and the harmonizer sped ahead swiftly but clumsily.

Levi pulled back on a joystick on his side, raising both of the harmonizer's arms simultaneously. A finger on his other hand rested on a hot-button. "Stop at once or lethal force shall be deployed against you," he commanded into his headphone mic.

The harmonizer closed in on the mugger but it collided with the old woman. She and the harmonizer both crashed to the ground. The mugger stopped briefly and looked back at the tangled mess of human and machine, then he disappeared around a corner.

Levi noted the coordinates flashing in longitude and latitude on the monitor, and a squiggly red line that traced the fleeing mugger's route. He grabbed the standalone mic and called for backup units.

A few minutes later, two more harmonizers appeared in full view, each of them gripping an arm of the mugger as they dragged him back to the scene to await an offender transport vehicle.

Levi switched the monitor off.

"Dang, that was intense," Ricky said, wiping the sweat off his brow. He knew that harmonizers didn't operate themselves, but he'd had no idea the skill required of the pilot. Still, skillfulness did not excuse the conduct of the pilots he had mentally dubbed assholes number one and two in cubie three. From this day forward, his interactions would be tense with these entities whose thoughts, movements, eyes, and decisions were not their own but those of others whose actions were at least to a degree dictated by yet others still. Even if he thought he knew who he was really dealing with when encountering one of these machines, he could never be certain.

A bit unwieldy, aren't they?" Levi said.

Ricky nodded. "That's an understatement."

"So we've made some improvements." Levi handed Ricky a dual triggered mock M-4 rifle with a USB cord attached to it. Levi plugged the cord into a slot in the instrument panel.

"What's this for?"

"You'll see," said Levi. "It works in conjunction with these." He held out a pair of what looked much like night vision goggles. "So, the rear trigger on the weapon is a view selector. The front trigger is for firing. Put the goggles on and tell me what you see."

Ricky situated the goggles over his eyes. "Looks like a brick wall."

"Yes." Levi said. "Well, the side of a brick building actually. Now pull the view selector."

Ricky did as instructed and now he saw a cardboard target with a flashing red bullseye on another brick wall.

"What you see there is the opposite side of the building," Levi explained. "Pull the view selector trigger again. You should see the building's roof now, a target there as well. Continuing on, you will see the entire exterior perimeter, the rooftop, and then the interior as well as any persons or other warm-blooded entities within the interior."

"Interesting," said Ricky.

"Think so?" Levi said. "Wait until you see this. Turn to your left."

Ricky turned and saw a harmonizer now, with a rifle identical to the one he held.

"Walk in place."

Ricky did that and as he did, so did the harmonizer.

"This is the new harmonizer, harmonizer 3.0," Levi said. "Now pull the view selector again until it returns to the target on the opposite side of the building."

Ricky clicked to that view, and the target appeared in a small window above the harmonizer.

"Now fire your weapon," Levi said.

A millisecond after Ricky fired, a bullet pierced the bullseye.

Levi peeled the goggles off of Ricky's head and smiled. "Impressive, yes?"

Ricky nodded. "I'll say. How did it do that?"

"What, zoom around from the opposite side of the building and strike the target?"

"Yeah."

"Smart bullets," Levi said. "They work the same as smart bombs. As for the rest, that was Josh's contribution. His training in robotics engineering has turned out to be quite useful. What actually happened just now was that the harmonizer at the testing center you saw through the goggles precisely mimicked every move you made. According to Josh, it wasn't particularly difficult to make this work. He simply modified the motion and gesture tracking technology used in interactive game consoles such as the Wii so that harmonizer pilots' movements are mimicked by remote robotic hardware rather than by graphic images on a screen. So, what do you think?"

"I think it's brilliant," said Ricky. "Beats the heck out of having to manage all those clunky external controls on that manually operated harmonizer. So, are there closed circuit cameras around the building and inside it, is that how the various views are generated?"

Levi shook his head. "No. No. We've moved far beyond that. The external views are collected by satellite cameras and transmitted in real time to a server which distributes the images to the appropriate harmonizer pilot based on the respective harmonizer's specific geographic location. This gives the pilot a birds-eye view of the harmonizer's operating environment, drastically improving situational awareness over the harmonizer 2.0 which is limited to the machine's direct line of sight."

"If the new harmonizer 3.0s are not equipped with Vizion's camera eyes, why did you ask me to ramp up production?" Ricky said.

"Oh they are equipped with them," said Levi. "As backups in case of signal interruptions. Better to see something than nothing at all. And of course the satellite is equipped with Vizion's magnification technology – the all-seeing eye, as it were. Would you like to know how the harmonizer pilots are able to see inside buildings now?"

"I'd love to."

"Good," Levi said. "As you are undoubtedly aware, the federal building code requires interior video images to be submitted for every structure in existence, and the compliance rate is very nearly one hundred percent because the penalty for noncompliance is demolition. So the images are exact maps of interiors which are catalogued under precise GPS coordinates for each structure. Remember when I had you upload that data into the harmonizer sight system? This is why. That data gives the pilots the practical equivalent of being able to see through walls."

Ricky raised an eyebrow. "That part's pretty straightforward, but how are pilots able to see *people* inside?"

"Simple," Levi said. "Infrared heat signatures. But rather than be satisfied with the somewhat indistinct impressions produced by conventional infrared technology, we've added overlays from an electronic library of lifelike human images – and other, not so human images – making the experience entirely realistic."

Levi could see that Ricky didn't entirely understand. "You're familiar with the various glass cockpit systems available for aircraft," Levi said. "My favorite is the one that superimposes video images of the Earth's topography, manmade obstructions, runways, etcetera, on a day of perfect weather over the same topography on days of low visibility due to fog or other conditions. As you are well aware, this feature enables a pilot to fly as if he were flying visually, even on zero visibility days. The harmonizer sight system overlays work in much the same way, only with the added ability to superimpose any of a vast number of images.

Ricky nodded. "Got it."

"Excellent," Levi said. "Now let me show you one last thing." He held the goggles out. "Put these on again, and let me know when you're ready."

Ricky slipped them on. "Okay. Ready."

Levi clicked through the view selector to the interior view. "Tell me what you see."

"Looks like a little girl sucking her thumb."

Levi nodded. "Yes. A sweet little girl. How old would you guess? Four? Five?" He handed Ricky the rifle and said, "Kill her."

Ricky yanked the goggles off. "What! Are you crazy?"

Levi's eyes narrowed. "Congratulations. I'd have been disappointed in you if you had reacted any other way. Now put the goggles back on, please." He discretely flipped the deharmonization switch on the instrument panel.

Ricky yelped, and stumbled backwards firing off several rounds at the fanged beast he saw lunging at him through the goggles. A stream of smart bullets pierced the walls of the building and struck the beast between its eyes, exploding its skull.

Ricky fell to the floor, his heart pounding in his chest. "Jesus, what is this thing?" he said as he inspected what was left of the dead creature.

Levi tugged the goggles off of Ricky's head. "It isn't real. It's an overlay."

Ricky felt a lump in his throat restricting his airway. "Oh my God." He choked. "Are you saying I just killed that little girl?"

"No." Levi grinned. "She was an overlay as well. You killed a heated cardboard target."

After a relieved sigh, Ricky said, "So that was all just a simulation?"

Levi nodded. "In a manner of speaking, yes. Demonstrates the enormous psychological power of the overlays, does it not? By dehumanizing and depersonalizing the target, the overlays eliminate any hesitancy a pilot might have in engaging it. In cases of civil unrest or a conflict with Texas where the targets may be perceived as brethren, the feature will be indispensable."

Ricky shuddered.

"If you think about it, the overlays are a natural extension of the harmonizer concept," Levi said. "It's well documented by psychologists that human propensities for violence become exponentially more accessible the further one is removed from direct contact with the object of his or her acts. That's one of the reasons the government has decided to begin replacing all human police and DHS ground forces with harmonizers."

"Really?" Ricky said.

Levi nodded. "Well, now that we've had our play break, let us return to the important business at hand. According to my sources, Farnsworth is considering filing another suit challenging Vizion's candidacy. But this time his plan is to have the Attorney General file on behalf of the federal government. Which is precisely why it is imperative that you get out and start campaigning straight away. Ricky, If you can sell the idea of a corporate presidency to the public, it is quite possible that Vizion will have already won the election before a final judicial determination is made. And a court removing a sitting president by ruling on unsettled law – particularly if that president happens to be popular among the people – would be unprecedented, to say the least." Levi glanced at his watch. "We better head back up, I have a meeting soon."

Chapter 13

Helen strolled into Levi's office shortly after Ricky left, her movements so graceful that she appeared to float. She and Levi hugged, and shared air kisses. Then she flung her scarf cavalierly over the shoulder of a nearby marble sculpture of a Greek goddess with no arms but voluptuous bosoms that she estimated in silicone would cost a good bit more than Max had paid for her implants. "You really must do something about that insufferable harmonizer down in the lobby," she said, "Its disposition is absolutely dreadful."

"Which is precisely why I've stationed it there. Keeps undesirables away." Levi ran the tip of his nose down the back of Helen's neck as he helped her out of her coat, revealing the teal pantsuit beneath it. "You smell lovely. New perfume?"

"Stop, that tickles." Helen pulled away, giggling.

Levi folded her coat over the back of a chair and pressed the intercom button on his desk and ordered tea brought up. "So to what do I owe this pleasure? Miss me after all the years?"

Helen licked her lips provocatively. "We did have quite a night."

"Indeed we did." Levi smiled, recalling the night Helen spoke of. She had only been thirty-one then, and she'd arrived on Levi's doorstep, distraught after discovering a call-girl receipt in Max's wallet when he returned from some union business in Vegas. Infidelity, she had explained, she could live with, but foolishness was unforgiveable. "What kind of idiot keeps a receipt for a hooker in his billfold for his wife to find?" Levi recalled her having said it was the ultimate insult.

Helen lost herself in thoughts of that night as well, recalling how Levi had comforted her and then reassured her of her womanhood with a night of passion that lasted well into the early morning hours. She had never before or since felt so irresistibly desirable. And she had had no less desire for him. Power was an aphrodisiac, and despite his age,

Levi did not disappoint. The man had stamina, far more stamina than that pathetic son of his that she had married. She pulled herself somewhat reluctantly back to the present moment and gazed into his eyes. "You're thinking about it right now too, aren't you?"

Levi nodded. "It's unfortunate you didn't conceive a male that night, an heir to all that's mine." Had she conceived a boy, he would not have had to engage in what – thanks to Max's lack of self-control – was turning out to be a rather problematic alternative method of perpetuating his bloodline. "Do you ever think about it, Helen?"

"Absolutely not," she lied. "Like you, when I make an important decision, I never look back." The truth was Helen thought often of the decision to abort. She supposed her troubling herself with poor Gabriella's maintenance was a response to some subconscious yearning for the child she could have had later if her uterus had not been perforated during the procedure.

But whether or not Helen wished for it, a real mother-child bond simply was not possible with Gabriella, a girl who had been twenty years old already when she came into Helen's life. It might have been different had Gabriella been an infant then. Besides, Gabriella was defective and needy. Helen's relationship to her was merely one of charity. The abortion had been charitable too, in its own way. It would have been unfair for a married woman to bring the child of Levi's into this world. Her husband would have despised it; the public would have shunned it; the child would have hated itself. She'd given it careful thought, maybe too much thought, having waited until well into her third trimester to go through with it. Helen shrugged. Some memories should not be dwelled upon.

"Care to try again?" said Levi.

The words penetrated a part of Helen she wished did not exist. "And risk tainting a beautiful memory?" she said.

Levi brushed her cheek with the backside of his hand. "You do have a gift with words, my dear. I don't believe I've ever been rejected quite so eloquently." It was the age difference, he knew. At some point, age simply cannot be overcome. And that had made the business of creating an heir to his empire all the more urgent. Helen could no longer be of any use for that even if she wanted to. He swallowed a chuckle. That didn't mean it wouldn't be fun to go through the motions. "So, if you haven't come to jump my sexy old bones, then why are you here, my dear?"

"Come now, Levi darling, you know exactly why." Helen fiddled with his collar with one hand and slipped her other hand beneath his tie and rested it gently there.

Levi grasped her hand and pulled her closer, his grip surprisingly powerful for a man in his nineties. She gazed deeply into his eyes, batting her eyelashes like a flirtatious schoolgirl. Now they were getting somewhere – until Levi's white-gloved assistant stepped in and cleared his throat. "Pardon me," the assistant said, and placed a silver tea set on a serving table.

Helen scurried over to the not-throne and sat with her back to the assistant. He filled two cups, then folded his hands behind his back. "Will there be anything else, sir?" he said to Levi.

"That will be all," Levi said, and as his assistant exited, Levi carried the cups over to his desk. He settled into his throne and reached for Helen's hands. "Now, where were we?"

Helen steered the conversation away from Levi's advances and to the reason she'd come. "I believe we were about to discuss all the wonderful things a President Helen could do for Leviathan Corp."

"Or perhaps what wonderful things Leviathan might do for a candidate Helen," Levi countered.

"Damn you, Levi Baxter. You know how hard I've worked for this. I've devoted my entire life to public service through my foundation and the good works my company does. Imagine how much more difficult life would be for the blind if not for my advocacy efforts for mandatory brail labeling on everything from prescription bottles to computer keyboards. Not to mention all the rest. I've paid my dues. I deserve to be president. Which is more than I can say for that despicable son of yours."

There was no need for Levi to remind Helen that her lobbying efforts had also produced a sea of regulation on medical research that had slowed the progress of potential cures for the blind to a crawl while her company made hundreds of millions of dollars providing that brail labeling and other aids for the visually impaired. Neither was there any need to remind her that her foundation provided her with a handsome salary of several million dollars a year and her own personal on-call flying five-star resort in the form of a luxuriously customized 747 – all on the donors' tabs. "Helen, dear, I should think you might be a bit more concerned about Vizion than Max. And by the way, I've long since forgiven Max for that silly attempt at a labor strike on Leviathan if you're suggesting I've a motive to plot against him."

"I'm not suggesting anything of the kind. Max is hardly competition. And don't even get me going on that business about corporations holding electoral office. You can't seriously think Vizion Inc.'s candidacy will survive a hearing in the courts on the merits. And the issue will be heard on the merits. According to my sources, the Attorney General will be filing suit on behalf of the government very soon. When the smoke clears and the ashes of Vizion's candidacy are swept away that leaves me and Farnsworth. Surely you aren't in favor of a second Farnsworth term."

Levi tapped a finger against his chin in mock deliberation over what she'd said. The truth was, of course, that the outcome of the election made very little difference. One way or another he would continue to own the Whitehouse as he had for as long as he could remember. Nevertheless, he would prefer a Vizion Inc. presidency. Short of waiting and hoping for the appointment of more authoritarian justices to the Supreme Court that would overrule the *Citizens United* decision, Levi could think of no more efficient way to resurrect the invalidated provisions of the BCRA than to use the decision itself to install a corporation into the highest office in the land. The public would demand the Court overturn the decision after that and things could get back to business as usual. In the interim, he would see to it that Max and Helen both had a seat on Vizion's board of directors.

In the unlikely event the plan failed, Levi would persuade Helen to join Max on the democratic ticket rather than her continuing to oppose him. She and Max would have to work it out amongst themselves which of them would be at the top of that ticket and if they couldn't come to terms he would indeed settle for a recycled Farnsworth presidency. "Helen, dear, I'd love to help, but whom becomes the next president isn't up to me. The voters will make that decision and you and I both know how fickle voters can be."

"Fickle indeed," Helen said incredulously. "They're only as fickle as those that herd them, namely you and your media interests, and you very well know it." She caressed his fingers. "Come now, Levi darling are you going to make a lady beg?"

"I will mention your thoughts to the herders." Levi winked. "And I suppose this might be of some help as well." He reached into his desk drawer and pulled out a Leviathan Corp check made out for five-million dollars. "I've left the payee line blank so you can fill in the name of your favorite political action committee. We wouldn't want to create any appearance of coordination. Naturally, I've also contributed the maximum allowed under law directly to your campaign as well as to the democrat party." The time-honored tactic of owning every horse in the race was a strategy that had always served Levi well.

Helen snatched the check from his hand and rose from her seat. "I knew I could count on you, Levi darling."

Levi rose as well. "Leaving so soon? You haven't touched your tea."

"Oh I know how terribly rude it must appear for me to just take the money and run, but I've been under a great deal of stress lately and my physician suggested cutting back on caffeine. Perhaps I could make it up to you. Dinner one night, perhaps?" Helen batted her eyelashes again.

Levi smiled affectionately. "That sounds splendid. Oh, and Helen?"

"Yes?"

"Any progress on acquiring Ricky's patent for the artificial eye?"

Helen shook her head. "You know better, but assuming I don't meet any resistance in keeping that testing ban in place, it's only a matter of time. Until then, the status quo is working out just fine. If it drags on past the election...well, if I win it won't make any difference."

After Helen left, the intercom on Levi's desk buzzed. He pressed the button. "Yes?"

"Mr. Baxter, Tom Cole of Cole Brothers Industries is calling," his assistant said.

"Put him through."

Tom Cole came on the line. "How are you, Levi?"

"Very well. And you?"

"Fine, fine. Listen, the reason for my call is that I noticed your warehouse next to Vizion hasn't been in use for some time and I was wondering if you might be interested in selling it."

Levi closed his eyes and thought for a moment. For as long as he could remember, the Cole Brothers had been nipping at his industrial heels and the last thing he wanted to do was help them sharpen their bite. But there wasn't any sense in continuing to pay property taxes on a building he had no use for. He would have sold it already if not for the red tape and astronomical cost of compliance with the recycling regulations for the obsolete machines stored there. "What do you plan to do with it?" he said.

"We were thinking we'd use it as a local distribution center for construction material," said Tom Cole. "Can't keep enough in stock to meet demand with the facilities we currently have here in Dodge City, and our customers don't like waiting for it to come from Wichita."

"I see." Levi quickly ran the pros and cons through his head. By the time the cost of removing those junk robots from the warehouse was added to the end users' price, the Cole Brothers' products might be less than competitive against his own considerable interests in building materials. "I suppose there isn't any harm in a little competition. It would be an as-is transaction and you all would be responsible for the cost of clearing the place out. I'll have my bean counters contact yours to work out a price."

Chapter 14

With images of assholes number one and two in cubie three still fresh in his mind, Ricky confronted the harmonizer at Vizion's entrance gate. "Identify yourself," he demanded.

"I am harmonizer ninety-nine," it said in the emotionless robotic monotone of the voice altering technology used in all harmonizer audio systems.

"How about a name?"

"Harmonizer ninety-nine," it repeated.

Ricky snarled. "So that's the way you're going to play it. Well, how about the jerk-off sitting next to you in Leviathan's dungeon? Or the one who covers during your lunch break, or when you go to take a piss? Are their names all ninety-nine too?"

"I am Harmonizer ninety-nine."

"Okay. Well, answer me this then, is ninety-nine also your station number?"

"Harmonizers are not permitted to disclose station numbers," it said.

Ricky thumped it on its titanium forehead. "How about I come straight over there to your little cubie and see for myself, huh? How'd that be?"

The harmonizer inspected its forehead with a mechanical hand and said, "Unauthorized contact with a harmonizer is a violation of federal law. Please refrain from further contact."

"Screw you." Ricky stormed off to his office and sat at his desk a minute to cool off. Then he dialed Chick's number.

"Hello?"

"Hey, Chick, it's Ricky."

"What's up, brother man?"

"Heading out on a campaign tour tomorrow. Reckon you can look after Bern while I'm gone?"

"Wow, you really going through with this."

"Yes, sir. So what do you say?"

"You know I will. Anything else you need me to handle for you while you're away?"

Ricky smiled. "It'd be right helpful if you could get me a sample of Max Baxter's DNA."

"You mean like ex union boss running for president Max Baxter? You gotta be out of your mind. What do you need with his DNA anyway? You thinking of cloning him?"

Ricky laughed. "Not hardly."

Chick scratched his head. "Let me think on it."

"Thanks, buddy."

After they hung up, Ricky opened the book Levi had given him. It began with the usual explanation of methodology used to define the problems and citations to references from which its conclusions were drawn. Several seemingly self-evident mini-conclusions were included, such as, *A percentage of committed extremists released from detention will return to the mischief.* "This author is clearly a genius." Ricky chuckled.

Beyond the page-filler mini-conclusions, the book focused primarily on the author's main conclusion that diversity of nationality, ethnicity, gender, language, sexual orientation, disability or lack thereof, wealth, age, and so forth creates a sense of relative isolation among groups that causes them to subordinate self-interest to the interests of the group. Because the interest of any given group requires government protection from other groups and equalization of resources, all groups coalesce around a powerful central authority and the resulting harmony is the greater good of the collective whole.

The individualist, a type interchangeable with libertarian or extremist, the author explained further, presents a more difficult challenge because the core characteristic of the individualist is that he or she is not a group at all. For the individualist, self-interest is necessarily the highest priority. To the extent an individualist group exists, its members participate voluntarily, unlike groups with membership based on common intrinsic traits such as skin color or gender.

The individualist group may be comprised of members of any or all of the other discreet groups with broad ranging viewpoints within the context of the overarching view that all views and beliefs may be held and all acts permitted so long as those acts do not infringe upon the rights of another individual. In the individualist's view, the government's role is to protect the life, liberty, and property of the individuals who make up the collective.

No centrally dictated equalization is necessary for the individualists. Resources tend to flow naturally to those who put them to the most productive use; and the maximization of productivity ultimately benefits all. Because such a view and those who espouse it lack uniformity, predictability, or in many instances, predetermined beneficiaries in the abstract, the individualist is incompatible with an orderly modern society and poses the greatest threat to global security. Moreover, individualism is the enemy of equality because membership in individualism, adherence to its precepts, is voluntary whereas membership in the other discrete groups is inherent at birth. Universal reason must triumph over individualized thought and belief.

The solution to the individualist problem, the author suggested, was to identify deviants through a surveillance system pervasive enough to collect generally innocuous personal data on all individuals' public and private day to day activities, movements, transactions, relationships, and so forth, and then to analyze that data for patterns. Those patterns are matched to profile models. So long as an individual's pattern remains consistent with the model global citizen profile, all is well. Otherwise, preemptive action must be taken.

In most cases, the recommended action for a deviant would be a mandatory commitment to a harmonization center and enhanced monitoring after graduation from the program. Ricky shivered. Whether or not it was good for society, this level of intrusion struck him as excessive in the extreme and he wondered to what extent his camera eyes had become an integral part of it.

In conjunction with exhaustive monitoring of all individuals, the author advocated the phasing out of nation states; a goal that could be accomplished by affirming the belief systems of certified model global citizens through endorsement and patronage, thus tethering citizens' identities so soundly to the concept of a global government that they would regard themselves as a diaspora longing for a global homeland and determined to get there. They would become cultural antibodies imbedded in populations, their influence inoculating all but a few against the deeply rooted plague of nationalism. A benevolent global administration made possible by the necessity of free trade enforcement would do the rest, bringing the model global citizens' defiant individual counterparts into the fold through a comprehensive harmonization program.

Ricky looked up and saw Josh standing in the doorway.

"How goes the studying?" Josh said.

"Disturbing," said Ricky. "This book makes it sound as if we've all been transformed from free American citizens to American suspects caged in an electronic concentration camp."

Josh flipped the book over to the front cover. "Oh, Levi's got you reading that one."

"I assume by the response that you're familiar with it, "Ricky said

"Sure am. Questions?"

"Some, yes. This book talks about comprehensive data collection on everyone to create global citizen models. How is all this data collected and by whose authority?"

Josh scrubbed his chin. "The data was being collected primarily from smartphone activity, customer loyalty cards, and bankcard transactions. You'd be surprised what you can learn about a person by monitoring his shopping habits, travel routines, and associations."

"They're able to get all that from cell phones and bankcards?" Ricky said.

Josh nodded. "Uh-huh. And those cards you use for discounts at grocery stores and what not. But data collection has been expanded far beyond that. The whole process is consolidated and almost entirely automated now under the Harmonization Project which incorporates a complex software program that works like a digital octopus with a million all-seeing tentacles reaching into every corner of the electronic world from not just smartphones, shopping cards, and bankcards, but all internet activity, email, government databases, and even the television in your living room. You gotta love smart-TVs. As for the authority you asked about, that was a gift of the 9/11/2001 terrorist attacks which resulted in the Patriot Act and the creation of the Department of Homeland Security. The Patriot Act provides the authority and DHS is the conduit for the funding to Leviathan Corp to run the program and perfect the models."

Ricky laughed. "I doubt that all-seeing freak of electronic nature reaches into my 1980s vintage television."

"It does if you have a cable box, satellite dish, or voice operated remote," Josh said. "Anyway, the bottom line is that DHS doesn't need to go looking for deviants anymore because it's automatically notified when the Harmonization program detects an individual has strayed outside the parameters of the model global citizen."

Ricky raised an eyebrow. "So what exactly constitutes a model global citizen?"

"Have you had a call from DHS lately?" Josh said.

"Nope."

"Then take a peek in the mirror if you want to get a good look at a model global citizen."

Ricky shook his head and laughed. "Me, global? Nah, I'm just a plain jane American citizen all spiced up with a heaping helping of authentic Mexican genetics, and that suits me just fine. So, cable boxes, huh? They putting my cameras in those?"

Josh ignored the question. "Where's Dawn?"

"I don't know," Ricky said, "but if you happen to see her before I do, I'd appreciate it if you'd tell her I need a lift over to the campaign bus tomorrow morning."

Chapter 15

From a half block away, Ricky and Dawn could see the mammoth self-navigating tour bus in front of the Leviathan building – *Vizion Inc. for President in 2028* painted boldly across the side of it. A harmonizer stood guard at the bus's door. Ricky glanced at his watch – Tuesday, 7:40 AM. Enough time left to give that obnoxious waste of titanium a crash course in manners before hitting the road. He ran ahead of Dawn and gripped the harmonizer around its neck. "Who are you? Asshole number one? Asshole number two?" Ricky shook it violently.

Dawn rushed up behind him. "Ricky, stop it! For God's sake, it's just a machine." She tugged at his shoulders. "And it's also a potentially lethal machine."

"A machine operated by real live human assholes," Ricky said, and backhanded it across its titanium face. "Ouch." He rubbed his bruised knuckles.

Chick rolled up the sidewalk in his ice cream cart with Bernice on the seat next to him, her tongue dangling and saliva dripping from the corners of her mouth as usual. He jumped off the cart and dashed over to join Dawn in her effort to pull Ricky off the harmonizer, which kept repeating monotonously, "Vandalism of federal government contractor property shall be construed as vandalism of federal property in violation of federal law. Severe penalties may apply."

"Tell it to someone who gives a rip," Ricky said and then Josh's limo pulled up.

The limo door flew open and Gabriella stepped out.

Ricky gave the harmonizer a powerful shove, knocking it to the sidewalk.

"Gabriella, can't we talk about this?" He heard Josh pleading from inside the limo.

"We are officially on a break," Gabriella told Josh tersely. "And if you can't even give me enough space to do my job, I'm calling it off for good." She slammed the limo door.

Ricky, Chick, and Dawn turned together – all of them breathing heavily still – and watched as Gabriella stepped onto the sidewalk next to the bus, sniffing the air and snarling.

"Ricky, what's gotten into you?" said Dawn. "You're acting like a crazy man."

"What you mean *acting*?" Chick said, and laughed. "They don't make 'em no crazier."

"There's something about those harmonizers I just don't like. Especially that one." Ricky eyed the machine.

"Well, crazy man, you'd better learn to like them," Dawn scoffed, "because they're here to stay, there's more on the way, and their eyes account for almost all of Vizion's annual revenue, from what I understand. Anyway, I've got to get going since I'm minding the store while you're gone." She glanced over at Gabriella again, sensing Ricky's attraction to her and tried to imagine what he could possibly see in such an incessant little witch – besides the very attractive physical aspects of her. Typical man. She gave Ricky a quick kiss on the lips. "Be safe." She headed down the sidewalk back toward the Santa Fe depot Transit Center.

Ricky wiped the pinkish lipstick off his mouth with the backside of his hand and hollered after Dawn, "Thanks for seeing me off."

The bus's electric motor whirred and the folding door thumped open.

"Ready for departure," the harmonizer said. "Please board."

Bernice stumbled off the ice cream cart and limped over to Ricky's side.

Chick grinned big at Ricky and his gold front tooth twinkled with the reflection of the morning sun. "That Dr. Dawn sure got one fine be-hind. You hitting that?"

"No, I ain't *hitting* that."

"Damn shame, that going to waste." Chick climbed back into the ice cream cart and whistled to Bernice, and she stumbled back over and hopped up into the seat beside him.

Ricky waved Chick off. "Thanks for looking after Bern. Let me know what you decide about the DNA thing."

"You got it."

"Ricky?" Gabriella called out.

"I'm here." Ricky reached for her hand and helped her up onto the first step of the bus.

Josh bolted from the limo and ran to her. "Gabriella, please," he said, and grabbed her by the arm, almost knocking Ricky off his feet in the process.

She pulled away and felt her way up into the bus, leaving Josh and Ricky alone on the sidewalk to resolve the question that neither of them had an answer for.

"Ricky," Josh choked. His eyes pleaded.

Ricky turned without saying a word and climbed onboard, followed by the harmonizer. "Where the heck do you think you're going?" he asked it.

It said, "I have been assigned to your security."

"You have got to be kidding me." Ricky left it at that and went and had a look around the bus, noting the satellite television and two plush

69

bench seats across from one another up front, and a bedroom and bathing facility in the rear. Looks like I'll be sleeping on a bench, he thought.

Gabriella sat, brooding.

"Trouble in paradise?" Ricky said. He peered out the window at Josh standing in the middle of the road looking hopelessly pathetic as the bus pulled away from the curb.

"I should have turned him down," Gabriella said. "He's smothering me."

The bus accelerated down the street. "Sorry to hear that, but hey, Kansas City here we come."

Gabriella pulled a bottle of water out of her handbag. "To Kansas City." She toasted and took a sip.

"Gabby?"

She wrinkled her nose. "What, Ricky? It's only water? You're the one who needs meetings."

"You know about that?"

"Everybody knows about that…Well, maybe not everybody but Josh knows and I do too because he told me about it. So, at least two people know."

Ricky wondered what else Josh might have told her.

Gabriella draped an arm across his shoulder and reached over with the other so that the two of them wound up holding hands around the water bottle. "Give it back," she said, giggling and tugging at the bottle.

Ricky tightened his grip on it and pulled it his way.

Gabriella tugged it her way again, and after a few more rounds of the back and forth, she reached into her purse and pulled out another bottle and chugged a mouthful. "Brains beat brawn," she said and laughed so hard that half the sip spewed out all over Ricky.

"Oh now you've done it." He chuckled as he wiped his face. "That cannot go unpunished." He pulled Gabriella across his lap and swatted her buttocks.

She laughed hysterically, slapping back at him, but all she could reach was his rock hard lower legs. "Ouch. I think I broke a nail. Let me go, you brute."

"You promise you'll be a good girl?" Ricky glanced toward the single seat by the door and noticed the harmonizer observing them. He'd forgotten about that creep.

"Okay, okay, I promise." Gabriella giggled and Ricky let her up and whispered in her ear, "What do you say we ditch the peeping Tom?"

"What?"

"The harmonizer," Ricky whispered.

"Oooh. How?"

"Watch."

Ricky shouted to the harmonizer, "Hey dummy, what's wrong with that door?"

It maneuvered over to have a look and as soon as it turned its back, Ricky pressed a button, the door popped open, and he gave the harmonizer a swift kick in the hind end and watched sparks and pieces fly as it tumbled thrashing and bouncing down Interstate 70 behind the bus.

"Woohoo," Ricky hollered over the shrill of the frigid wind rushing in.

"Close it, Ricky, its freezing," Gabriella pleaded through chattering teeth, her hair blowing in the wind and her arms wrapped tightly around herself.

Chapter 16

"Levi, I just lost the feed from harmonizer two-twenty, are you receiving anything from it?" Josh said from his cell phone as his limo bumped along, trailing about ten miles behind the campaign bus. He glanced out the window at a large group of people herded by harmonizers on electric golf carts marked *Harmonization Patrol*.

"Not presently," Levi said, "hold on a moment." He laid the phone down on his desk, picked up a remote control, and leaned back in his throne. He aimed the remote and pressed the power button, and doors recessed into the wall, revealing the large screen there. Nothing but fuzz and static.

He selected the HISTORY key and the earlier scene of Ricky's and Gabriella's frolicking that culminated with Ricky ejecting the harmonizer from the bus played out onscreen. "I must say I hadn't anticipated you'd do that, Ricky," Levi chuckled.

Chapter 17

"Ricky, get over here." Gabriella shivered. "I need your body heat."

He pulled the lever to close the bus door, then slid in beside her and wrapped her in his arms. She burrowed her freezing nose into his open shirt collar. "Woo, you are cold," he said, and rested his chin on top of her head while gently stroking her back.

"Ricky," Gabriella's tone was almost a whisper now, "do you ever think about us? I mean what might have been if –"

"Every day," Ricky said. "Every Single Day since the first time I laid eyes on you in that ridiculous gender studies class they made us take at Harvard."

"It was a silly class," Gabriella agreed. "Like I needed some egghead to tell me it's okay for little girls to play with boy toys or for big girls to have big boy careers…or for little boys to play with dolls"

Ricky grimaced. He hated dolls. Then he laughed and Gabriella laughed with him. She lifted her face to Ricky's. In her mind's eye she saw him gazing back at her, his eyes confessing his love for her and pleading for a second chance. "Why did you go away?" she whimpered. "Why did you leave me all alone? I know it wasn't about your grades."

"I –"

Gabriella interrupted Ricky before he could respond. "I'm sorry. I know why. It's haunted me all these years. Can you ever forgive me for putting you and Josh in danger?"

Ricky hurled a water bottle across the bus. "Gabriella, there's nothing to forgive."

She pulled away, startled by his reaction, and the bus's navigation system said, "One hundred ninety miles to your destination, Liberty Memorial, Kansas City."

"Maybe I ought to rehearse a little," Ricky said, quickly changing the subject.

Gabriella nodded. "Good idea. I'll be your audience."

Ricky lifted his briefcase from beneath the seat and popped it open and sifted through it for the prepared speech Levi had provided him. "Here it is." He unfolded the stapled pages and held them out front of him, shuffling and shifting until he felt his stance was sufficiently profound. "Okay. Four score and uh…how many years ago today was it?" He laughed at his botched beginning of the Gettysburg address.

Gabriella laughed too. "I don't remember how many years ago it was either but we've got to get serious now. The clock's ticking. Oh, hey, why don't we record this so you can use it to polish up after."

Ricky nodded less than enthusiastically and helped Gabriella set up her video camera.

"Okay, so are we ready?" she said.

Ricky sighed. "I'm really not into this right now. How about we listen to the radio or something mindless for a little while?"

"It's your campaign." Gabriella's disappointed tone reminded Ricky of a grade-school teacher whose star pupil had just turned in an incomplete assignment. He switched on the radio.

"Ricky Santana is definitely no politician," a talk show host said.

"That he is not," a cohost agreed, "but I bet he winds up being just another self-interested robot reading off a teleprompter before it's all over."

"I don't know that he's self-interested," the host countered, "but if he starts with the canned speeches from political consultants, people'll think he is. He should just tell it like it is."

"How is it?"

The host chuckled. "It's simple, that's how it is. What Ricky Santana should do first is debunk the myth the mainstream media pushes about corporate candidacy and just explain to the people that there's nothing new about corporations ruling from electoral office. For much of this nation's existence, a cartel of the most powerful companies – de facto corporate electoral office-holders – have ruled, operating under competing wings of the mammoth corporate partnership of the republican and democrat parties. I call it the *republicrat partnership*."

Ricky angled a thumb toward the speakers in the bus's ceiling. "You hear that, Gabby? They're talking about me on the radio."

She held a finger to her lips. "Shh, I'm trying to listen."

The cohost laughed and elaborated, "Yep, and because the republicrat partnership *is* the government, its grip on power remains no matter what. But that could change if the people wake up to the fact that the big two political parties don't actually represent the people, at least not most of the people. George Washington warned about the evils of political parties, how they would be used to divide the citizens into opposing factions. It's the timeless divide and conquer routine, and the first part of how the republicrats did it was by snookering the people into believing that primaries are elections."

"Right, and most people don't realize that the parties are free to rig up their nomination process whatever way they want," the cohost added. "Although that should be obvious after Hillary/Bernie debacle. Shoot the parties don't even have to have primaries. They could just pick whoever they want to run and be done with it. The only reason they go through the primary dog and pony show is to brainwash the voters in advance of the real election into thinking that the partnership's choices are the only real choices – that the real election is a *binary* choice."

"I think that's right," the host agreed. "And once the republican and democrat wings of the republicrat partnership have made their choices, the election is more or less entertainment, intramural gladiator games between the republican and democrat in their dysfunctional political family. It doesn't much matter which of them prevails because they both represent the lords of the partnership. And at the risk of repeating myself, without the approval of those lords, it's virtually impossible for an individual – with the exception of an occasional billionaire here and there – to attain to the office of president or most any other elected federal office. That's where Vizion comes in. A well-funded and wily corporation like Vizion Inc. might be able to change that and it'd be a good bit harder to contain than a single billionaire like Trump."

"So you're saying the republicrat partnership maintains its monopoly on power by handpicking the individual candidates the voters must choose from," the cohost clarified.

"Right, they pick the candidates the voters *think* they must choose from, and then fund them through the treasuries of the corporate membership and through various nonprofits flush with government grants. In other words, as a general rule, the voters don't get to choose their representatives, their senators, or even their president, so long as they vote for a republican or democrat party candidate.

"When you vote for party candidates, you're nearly always limiting your choices to a slate of front-person individual proxies prescreened and preselected by the republicrat partnership to represent the members, a cartel of the elite, not the people generally. The only political party that actually represents the individual is the Libertarian party. And the republicrat partnership has done a dandy job of branding Libertarians as radicals, nutjobs, extremists, potheads, isolationists, pick your political pejorative. None of which is true. But most voters don't know that."

"If the republicrat partnership is only concerned with its own interests, why doesn't it just run its own corporate members directly and cut out the middlemen?" the cohost probed.

The host sighed. "There's a one word answer to that question, and that word is – accountability. By using individual person proxies, the cartel members are not *technically* office holders so they can operate behind the scenes to grant themselves lucrative government contracts, subsidies, and to promote regulations and a rigged tax code that crushes competition with no accountability whatsoever to the American citizens."

"So what should the people do?" the cohost wondered aloud.

"They should do their homework. Know the candidates. And for goodness sake, vote for a libertarian or independent. As long as they vote republicrat, the cartel's game continues uninterrupted, business as usual, and the republicrat monopoly on the government grows ever more impenetrable. I pray that this time the voters seize on the opportunity provided by Vizion's independent candidacy to put an end to the revolving door of republicrat cartel proxies and put a president in office that represents the people. If not, we're probably doomed."

"But couldn't an independent individual accomplish that just as well," the cohost pressed.

"Hey, look, I'm not saying I'd rather see a corporation running than an individual, if that's what you're thinking. The idea of direct corporate electoral office holders is way creepy. But I can't see how an individual can bust through the power bunker constructed by the republicrat partnership, the *government*, to keep itself in and keep the American people out. A corporation with enough resources, on the other hand, maybe could. And if it's got to be a corporation, better one like Vizion Inc. that's run by a man that…well, from what I hear, Ricky Santana is a good man and comes from a good family. Plus he's a Texan. So there's a bonus. And that's where we gotta leave it. Until tomorrow. Thank you to all the loyal listeners out there for tuning in to the Ben Black radio show!"

Gabriella clapped. "Woohoo! Vizion should get all kinds of grassroots support with a message like that spreading around. You ought to put that Ben Black guy on your campaign's payroll."

Ricky's head spun as he realized how little he'd thought about politics and how huge the responsibility of running for office actually was. He certainly hadn't thought of his company as a revolutionary tasked with reclaiming the government for the people. All he wanted with the presidency was to put an end to that ban preventing him from moving the artificial sight project to the next level.

"Ricky, are you alright?" Gabriella rested a hand on his shoulder.

"I don't know. I'm exhausted suddenly. Drained."

Gabriella yawned. "Me too. Why don't we take a nap."

Ricky stretched his arms and yawned also. "Good idea." He followed her to the bus's bedroom where he grabbed a pillow and started back to the front.

Gabriella grasped his hand. "Where are you going?"

"I figured I'd go stretch out on a bench seat," Ricky said.

She laced her fingers through his and pulled him down to the edge of the bed beside her. "You don't have to do that."

"Gabby, I –"

She silenced him with a kiss, then wrapped her arms over his shoulders, lacing her fingers behind his neck, and fell back against a pillow, clinging to him with their lips locked together so that he couldn't help but follow her down.

When they broke for air, Ricky said, "I was thinking about that college girl at Max's and what you said about those other girls and the DNA." He had no idea what caused that subject to pop into his head.

"Later," Gabriella said, breathless, and kissed him again.

Chapter 18

The bus rolled up to the Liberty Memorial in Kansas City around 2:00 in the afternoon. The intercom crackled to life with the navigation system announcing, "You have arrived at your destination."

Ricky's eyes popped open. He lifted his arm to check his watch. "Oh no." He was late for his first speech.

Gabriella stirred, tightening her leg more firmly around Ricky's waist and shifting her head into the safety of the hollow between his muscular pecs. "Mmm," she purred dreamily, then a violent pounding on the bus door startled her out of her sleep.

She and Ricky sprung up together in the bed. "What in the world is going on?" Gabriella said, massaging her forehead.

"Ricky, Gabriella, open the damn door," someone yelled. The pounding continued.

Ricky peeked out the blinds. "It's Josh."

Gabriella pulled the bedsheet up all the way to her nose, hiding the panic in her face.

"Gabby, you've got to get up." Ricky tumbled out of the bed and tucked his shirt in.

"Open this door right now," Josh yelled again and pounded even harder.

Ricky slipped his boots on and scrambled out to the door. "Hey Josh, what are you doing here?" He glanced past Josh and saw a thinning crowd of journalists meandering about the lawn below the tower at the monument, their crews packing up video equipment.

"Don't screw with me, Ricky. You destroyed a million dollar machine and you're supposed to be up at the tower giving your campaign kickoff speech in," he glanced at his watch, "an hour ago, and you look like you just fell out of bed. So, you tell me what's going on. And where's Gabriella?"

She strolled out just as Josh asked the question, her clothes wrinkled and her hair disheveled. She folded her arms across her chest. "What are you stalking me now?"

"I knew it." Josh slammed his fist into the side of the bus.

"Chill out," Ricky said. "She was just napping."

Gabriella growled. "It's none of his business what I... *we* were doing."

Josh glanced at her and then back at Ricky. He handed Ricky a legal-sized envelope. "That's your itinerary. You left it on your desk."

"And you couldn't figure out how to send it electronically?" Gabriella smirked.

Josh stomped off to his limo without a response, and sped away.

Ricky shut the door and Gabriella buried herself in his arms. "What do we do now?" she said softly. She hoped he'd suggest racing to the nearest wedding chapel to get the formalities out of the way so they could finish what they'd started before their nap. But there was still the matter of her engagement to Josh – a matter she suspected weighed more heavily on Ricky's mind than hers. She pulled the engagement ring off her finger discreetly and slipped it into her pocket.

Ricky petted her hair and fiddled with the little silver necklace he had given her. She had worn it every day for thirty-five years. "I guess I do the speech for the reporters that are left and we figure out the rest after that."

Gabriella smiled up at him and whispered, "Okay."

Chapter 19

Gabriella sat in Ricky's lap with her head resting against his chest as they listened to reports of the afternoon's bungled attempt at a speech while the bus bumped along eastbound down interstate 70. According to clearly erroneous reports, Ricky had broken an ankle when he tumbled down the steps at the memorial on his way up to the tower where he was to speak. He pulled a sock down and rapped his knuckles against his near indestructible titanium lower leg and they both laughed.

"Ricky?"

"Yeah?"

"You really aren't into this at all, are you?"

"Nope."

"Well then why do it?" Gabriella tossed her hair out of her face. "I mean, I know Levi wants you to. But he's a grownup, he can handle *no*."

Ricky took her face in his hands and kissed her on the forehead. "It's not all about what Levi wants; except for our shared financial interest, of course. But he seems to think if I win this election, Vizion's stock will soar so high it'll be a fortune fifty company overnight. With my share of all that wealth to spread around Congress, I'm confident I can bring a swift end to every last regulatory impediment to artificial sight research. Of course, we've still got a lot of work to do yet…Anyway, Levi knows how much I care about you and, stock prices aside, I like to think he supports what I'm trying to do for you."

Gabriella stroked the side of Ricky's face. "What did you just say?"

"Listen, I don't want to give you false hope, but we have made a lot of progress on the artificial sight project."

"Not that, you silly man. I'm grateful for what you're trying to do for me and all the other blind people in the world but I'm long past the fantasy that I'll ever see again. I'm talking about the other thing you said."

Ricky cocked his head. "Oh, that. I'm sorry. I shouldn't have –"

Gabriella put a finger against his lips. "Don't be sorry. Say it again."

He hesitated, "Okay, I uh… I care for you."

"Care?"

"Alright." He took a deep breath. "I *love* you. I never stopped loving you. But you and Josh are –"

"Shh." Gabriella quieted him with a finger on his lips again. Something inside her prevented her from telling him that she still loved him too, but it didn't stop her from devouring his mouth. After the kiss, Ricky took her by the hand and led her back to the bedroom where he watched and she listened to *Breakfast at Tiffany's* and some other classic movies, napping in between, until the sun rose the next morning.

Ricky gazed at Gabriella sleeping while the first light of day trickled in through the blinds as though drawn to her. She seemed to attract everything light and bright. The only gray area in her life was him, and maybe Josh. Yet she lived in a world of darkness. It was so unjust. He traced her perfect brows with a fingertip, and then he traced her lips. God, she was beautiful.

A semi-truck crawled past on its way out of the parking lot, it's blasting horn rattling the bus's windows.

Ricky peeled the blinds apart and peeked out at the chrome stack spewing black smoke, and the human driver tugging at the horn. Apparently a few of the old relics were still on the road.

Gabriella sat up and stretched her arms. "Good morning. Where are we? And what's all the noise?"

"According to the sign on top of that building yonder, we're at Sally's Truck-Stop & Diner," Ricky said. "What do you say we go in and see what's on the menu? I'm hungry enough to eat the ass out of a dead skunk."

Gabriella laughed. "Hopefully they have something better than skunk butt on the menu."

They got dressed and Ricky grabbed the envelope Josh had given him and they went inside where they were greeted by the clattering of plates, the scrape of spatulas against iron griddles, and the hum of

79

lively conversation mingling in the air with the aroma of coffee and eggs and bacon and other traditional southern breakfast fare.

"Tators, smothered and scattered," a middle-age bleached-blonde waitress with thick red lipstick hollered to the cook. She wiped her hands on her apron and looked over at Ricky and Gabriella. "What's wrong, y'all can't read?" She pointed to the sign by the door that said, "Seat yourself."

They chose the only empty booth in a row of others along the wall of windows across from a counter lined with red vinyl covered swivel stools bolted to the floor. Gabriella sat first and Ricky slid in next to her.

The waitress gave them each a laminated menu. "Coffee?" she said.

"Yes, thank you," said Ricky. "For both of us, please."

The waitress filled two cups, then plucked a pen off her ear and an order pad out of her apron and glanced out the window and noticed the Vizion slogan on the bus and a platoon of harmonizers marching past it. She chomped on chewing gum as she pointed out at the campaign bus. "Y'all come in that?"

"Yes Ma'am," Ricky said. He looked up from the menu. "I'll have the country fried steak and eggs with biscuits and extra gravy."

The waitress snatched the menus out of their hands and patted herself on the chest, chuckling nervously. "My goodness, I brought y'all old menus. I'm sorry, we don't serve the stuff anymore. Not since the new regulations. No sir, this diner here is as compliant as they come." She scurried off and returned a minute later with different menus. "Here ya go," she said.

Ricky looked the new menu over, impressed by the talent it must have taken to come up with so many different ways of preparing carrots, kale, broccoli, spinach, and some other vegetables he hadn't even heard of. The small print at the bottom of it said:

Global Agricultural, for a Healthier World
A subsidiary of Leviathan Corp

Ricky handed the menu back to the waitress and he surmised from her nametag that she must be the owner of the place. "Sally, I really got my heart set on the country fried steak and eggs. It'll be just between us." He winked.

"And I'll have the same," said Gabriella.

Sally winked back at Ricky. "Say, aren't you the fella that fell down them steps at the Liberty Memorial yesterday? I hear tell you're running for president as a corporation or something crazy like that, which makes me wonder if that wasn't the first time you took a fall." She didn't wait for a response before going on, "Well, mister, I wouldn't know how many tumbles you've taken but you certainly don't look no worse for the wear and anyway you make good sense to me, so, corporation or not, you can count on me to deliver you a whole mess of trucker votes come November. You want some hash browns too? It's on Ms. Sally's tab."

Ricky nodded yes and thanked her.

"That was sweet of her," Gabriella said when Sally left to put their order in to the cook.

"Yeah it was," Ricky agreed, "Maybe I'll make *End the ban on country fried steak* my new cattle call." He pulled up the navigator app on his smartphone. "Looks like we're about sixty-five miles west of St. Louis."

Gabriella sipped her coffee. "Is that our next stop?"

"I'm not sure. Levi told me the bus's route is preprogrammed but he didn't say exactly what the route was after Kansas City. The only control we have is a smartphone app for the bus's activation." Ricky unclasped the envelope that Josh had said contained their itinerary. "Maybe this will be of some help."

He turned back the cover page to a page detailing the Liberty Memorial event from yesterday, then turned to the page after that. "Yep, next stop's St. Louis. Tomorrow at noon." He sifted through the rest of the pages, disappointed at the less than twenty-four hours break between each of the remainder of the scheduled events. He had hoped there would be more time for him and Gabriella to share alone before the inevitable – before she returned to Josh and traded her fiancé title for the title of wife. "Gabriella," he said, and took her by the hand, "I wish we could go someplace where we could have some time together, just me and you, without this campaign stuff and all."

She smiled. "Mmm. Me too. Someplace where I could lay in your arms forever."

Ricky caressed her hand. "I was thinking, you know how the other candidates are doing recorded town-halls and such? I wonder if we could do something like that for this tour. Except make it appear like live events. Is that possible? I mean, the only reason we're doing it this way anyway is so the media will show up and broadcast it, right?"

"You mean like prerecord an entire campaign tour?" Gabriella said. "You are a nut." She tapped a finger against her chin. "Hmm, well, actually, there might be a way. If you can get me some digital images of the locations where you're scheduled to speak off the internet and some video of enthusiastic crowds, we could record you giving your speeches right here on the bus and I can use my media editing software to do a little dubbing, a little copy and paste. Once that's done, we dribble the clips out over the next couple of weeks as after-the-fact footage."

"That sounds terrific."

Gabriella fidgeted, a mischievous glow rose in her cheeks. "Ricky?"

"Yeah?"

"What do you think about throwing away those canned speeches you got from Levi and modeling your message after what that guy on the radio show said?"

Ricky scratched his head. "Well, I don't know. I hadn't really thought about that."

The enthusiasm drained suddenly from Gabriella's face. "Ricky, if the bus's route is preprogrammed we'll still have to go wherever it goes. Maybe we can figure out a way get some alone time after the tour."

"Who says we have to go where the bus goes?" Ricky countered.

Sally brought out their breakfast and topped off their coffees. "Y'all need anything else?"

"As a matter of fact, yes," Ricky said. "Do you happen to know if any manned rigs are heading down Texas way this morning?"

"You mean like going *in* to Texas?" Sally whispered. "Don't you know that's dangerous?" She hesitated for a minute and correctly sensing that Ricky wasn't the least bit worried about that, hollered out, "Anybody headed southwest going near Texas?"

A man two booths down raised his hand, and his unbuttoned flannel shirt spread open just enough to reveal a *TEA Party Patriot* t-shirt underneath it. "I'm going as far as the Lawton, Oklahoma harmonization camp to drop a load of canned goods," he said. "That close enough for you?"

"That'll do," said Ricky.

Gabriella said, "Ricky, what are you doing?"

"Lining us up a ride. I know a place where we can go to get away for a few days."

"What! Where?"

Chapter 20

Noon the next day, Ricky heard keys jangling and then the clang of the heavy iron cell door opening. He suppressed a flashback of his release from that Boston jail the morning after the accident.

"Alright, mister," a guard said, "the deputy chief wants to see you. Come on out of there, face the wall, hands behind your back so I can put the bracelets on you."

Ricky slipped his hands behind his back. "How's Gabriella?" he said.

"Who?" said the guard.

Ricky's face scrunched up as the guard clamped the handcuffs tightly onto his wrists. "Ouch. The woman that was with me when we got detained last night."

"I didn't work the graveyard silly-shift, but I'm sure she's fine," the guard said. He took Ricky by the arm and led him down the hallway to the deputy chief's office where Ricky almost tumbled over with surprise when he saw the Latino man beneath the big cowboy hat behind the desk.

"Juan?" Ricky said.

"Well I'll be, if it ain't the ghost from Texas past," said Juan, his smile extending the full length of his handlebar mustache. "Unshackle him and turn his gal loose," he told the guard.

Ricky rubbed his wrists when the cuffs came off, then opened his arms. "Man, it's good to see you, hermano."

Juan hugged him. "It's good to see you too. What's it been, like twenty years?"

"More like thirty-five," Ricky said. "And it looks like you made good use of the time. So you're the border patrol deputy chief now?"

Juan folded down a corner of his uniform collar and polished his badge with it. "Yes, sir, somebody's got to stop them Oklahoma gringos from crashing our border." He chuckled. "And I'm up for another big promotion when we switch back to the old borders. Did you ever imagine I'd be Chief one day? Well, I guess that ain't such a big deal compared to maybe being president of the U-nited States."

"*When* you switch back?" said Ricky. "I thought going back to the old borders was an *if* proposition."

"According to rumors from on high, it's definitely *when*," said Juan. "Negotiations are well underway with officials from the affected states. I expect in exchange for a little gold and a lot of good will they'll do the neighborly thing and cede the territory back to us peacefully. So, speaking of the big dogs, what's this I hear you're running for president as a corporation? I know crazy runs in the Santana family but I never figured you to be that crazy."

Ricky laughed. This made the third time or more in twenty-four hours he'd been accused of being a lunatic and he was beginning to wonder if it might be true. "Does sound a little off the wall, doesn't it?"

The guard escorted Gabriella in and she felt her way across the office. "Ricky? They took my phone, and my navigator app is on it."

Ricky reached for her hand. "Right here babe." He silently lipped in answer to the question glaring from Juan's face, "Blind."

Juan nodded, and told the guard to go get their personal effects. "So is this lovely lady your wife? What brings y'all to Texas?"

Gabriella's and Ricky's faces both turned shades of crimson.

"Gabriella here's an old friend. I brought her out to meet the family," Ricky said.

Juan grinned. "So you swam across the Red River with your gal. Why didn't you fly in? You forget we got a seventy-five-hundred foot runway at the ranch?"

"Flying would've been a good bit less hectic," Ricky said, "but with the campaign and the tension between the States and Texas and all, it seemed like we ought to keep a little lower profile."

The guard came back in with their belongings.

Ricky checked his phone. Two missed calls. One from Josh. One from Levi. Damn, he'd forgotten to activate the bus and Levi had probably called to find out why they weren't following the itinerary. Josh had other reasons for calling, no doubt. Ricky activated the bus with the remote smartphone app and sent it on its way out of Sally's parking lot while Juan grabbed the keys to his patrol truck off a hook on the office wall.

"Where are we?" Gabriella said.

"Wichita Falls, Texas, more or less," Juan informed her as they headed out to the parking lot. The temperature outside was a crisp fifty-two degrees and not a cloud in the sky. What a difference being a few hundred miles south of Dodge City made.

Ricky smiled as the sunshine soothed his face.

Juan opened the passenger door of his truck for Ricky and Gabriella, then slid in behind the steering wheel and started the engine. "Ricardo won't be back until tomorrow," he said.

"Where's he at?" said Ricky as they drove away toward the ranch.

"Houston. My brother, Francisco took him to see a specialist about his Alzheimer's."

"Alzheimer's? I thought he had bipolar or PTSD or something like that from Viet Nam."

"Well, he does. But a couple of years ago they found out he also has Alzheimer's. The thing is, his age disqualified him for treatment under the U.S. healthcare system even if he paid out of pocket, so it's gotten a lot worse. Bipolar, PTSD, and Alzheimer's is a nasty combination. Especially untreated."

Ricky shook his head. "I'm glad he's getting treatment now at least. So, why'd your brother take him? Seems like Mama would've wanted to do that."

"Oh, she did want to." Juan flipped on his turn signal. "But she fell and broke a hip a short while back. Doc Langford said it's best she don't travel until she's had more time to heal."

The reality of how long it had been since Ricky had last seen his parents suddenly sunk in. His parents had grown old now.

Juan turned onto a gravel road that dead-ended at the Santana property.

Ricky smiled and rolled down his window to get a better look at the Santana Ranch sign hanging from the crossbar over the entrance gate.

Clanging of the iron bell at the main house, cows mooing, and a couple of hoots and hollers from a woman and her two boys mixed with the sound of crunching gravel beneath the patrol truck's tires. "That's Francisco's wife and kids," Juan said, apparently they're excited to finally see the legendary Ricky Santana in person."

Ricky scanned the scene and he smiled when he saw the old Pitts-Special biplane tied down next to the barn. Cackling chickens pecked around. A half-constructed windmill and a stack of PVC pipe lay in the dirt beside the old water well. Rooftop solar panels were in process of either being installed or removed. He couldn't tell which. The little wooden frame guesthouse was one of the few things that hadn't changed much in the thirty plus years he'd been away. "What's happened here?"

Juan said, "Regulation, what else? US and GTP mostly." He pulled his hat off, brushed his hair to the side, then put the hat back on. "First they confiscated the dairy cows. Said selling raw milk was a violation of GTP international health rules. Then they burned the cornfields. Said non-GMO crops were forbidden because they didn't meet the land use efficiency standards promulgated by…I think that was the USDA. Made us disconnect from the well because the water wasn't fluoridated as required by some other department. Demolished the barn because we built it from lumber cut here on the ranch and I guess our lumber hadn't been approved by whatever department approves construction material. The EPA had a hand in that also. They said cutting timber diminishes natural carbon filters or some such. Made no mention of the fact that we planted two trees for every one we cut. And so on. Then the BLM came in and tried to confiscate the land. You know how that turned out."

Ricky shook his head. "Vizion's had its share of trouble with regulation too. All but shut down our primary objective for being in business in the first place."

"Sorry to hear that." Juan pursed his lips, then returned to telling Ricky about the ranch. "So, the place was really booming before all that regulatory crap and the BLM raids and all. At one time we were up to more than three hundred workers. People come from miles away for a job here. We had over five-thousand head of cattle. It's just me, your folks, and Francisco and his boys now. We're back up to about twenty head. Been a slow recovery, but we're making a comeback. The extra income from President Grant's Texas Miracle is helping a lot. I'll fill you in on that later. Thank God the nightmare's finally over…At least I hope it's over. But I guess we won't know for sure until we see what the outcome of the war's going to be."

"War," said Ricky. "Do you really think it's going to come to that?"

Juan said, "Maybe not. I reckon it might depend on how the election turns out, if things don't get out of hand before then. You know what I mean?"

Ricky nodded. "I reckon I do." He gestured with his chin at the solar panels. "What's going on with those? Y'all taking them down?"

Juan sighed. "Nope. Already done that. We're putting them back up now."

"I don't understand."

"Regulations, like I told you. Regulators from the GTP Climate Commission ordered us to take them all down or pay a thousand-dollar a day fine on account of we made them ourselves and we weren't on the approved list of manufacturers," Juan explained. "Same thing with the windmill. That all happened around the time the BLM made its move, and then, as you know, Texas got ejected from the States." He took a deep breath. "Which means we ain't under GTP jurisdiction no more."

"No?"

"No," said Juan. "Texas never signed any agreement with the GTP. We're not a member."

Ricky nodded, digesting Texas' unique position of being the only nation state in the world that was not only not a GTP member, but wasn't even recognized by the organization. Harder still to digest was the fact that GTP regulations had ever been binding on anyone anywhere in America, much less binding on family ranchers in Texas. When had all this happened? Had he been so sheltered in the cocoon of his single-minded work at Vizion that he had missed the fundamental transformation of the whole dang world?

Francisco's wife and boys whistled and chanted, "Ricky. Ricky. Ricky."

"What's happening?" Gabriella said anxiously, her ears alert and her busy nostrils taking in the mixture of steam rising from a cast iron pot boiling with corn on the cob over an open fire, smoke from the barbeque pit, and the powerful scent of cedar trees.

Ricky patted her on the knee. "It appears we've got a fan club, darlin.'"

The welcome party of three quieted to a whisper when Isabella – now in her late seventies – limped out onto the front porch of the main house and leaned on her cane. "Hijo," she cried out with an accent that had barely changed since she and Ricardo waded across the Rio Grande from Mexico together more than a half century earlier. A tear rolled down her weathered cheek.

Juan stayed with Gabriella while Ricky ran to Isabella and took her frail body in his arms. "Mama."

Gabriella and Ricky spent the next couple of hours at the picnic tables gorging themselves on barbeque and getting to know Francisco's wife and sons. Afterwards, they went to the guesthouse and worked until the early morning hours producing the campaign video clips.

Ricky fiddled with an old pair of binoculars that he'd used to peer down on the herds from the helicopter when he was a boy. Seeing a rabbit on the ground like it was right in front of his face through those lenses is what first got him interested in optical engineering.

"Thank goodness for Five-G mobile internet," Gabriella said as she pecked away at her laptop's brail keyboard. She produced more impressive work than most people with perfect vision.

"You're amazing," said Ricky, and pulled the shades down to block the early morning sunlight. He drew in a deep breath, comforted by the familiar scent of the knotty pine walls, an aroma that took him back to simpler times.

A calico kitten hopped up into Gabriella's lap and meowed.

She stroked the tiny fur-ball's back. "Well hello, kitty. Where did you come from?"

Ricky draped his arms around her from behind and nibbled at her ear.

"Stop," she giggled. "I've got a couple more lines to go on this press release." She typed for another minute or so and then pressed SEND. "There, it's done. I can't wait to hear it when it comes out this afternoon. Is there a television here?"

Ricky glanced around the room on the odd chance something here had changed, but it hadn't. "I'm afraid not."

"What about a radio?"

"I don't see one of those either. But I'm sure there's one in the main house. Always has been." Ricky nibbled at her ear again. "You ready to get some shuteye?"

Gabriella nodded, and they fell asleep in each other's arms until a knock on the door at noon woke them. Ricky stretched his arms and went and answered it. "Hey, Juan."

"Hey, Ricky. Isabella told me to come get y'all for dinner. Oh, and Ricardo's back."

Ricky rubbed a hand over his belly, still swollen from yesterday's barbeque feast. "I forgot how serious y'all take eating around here. I reckon it wouldn't take long to get used to it again though. You joining us?"

"Wish I could, but I've got to go into town for a briefing about the border changes."

Ricky nodded, troubled by the conflict that was sure to erupt if Texas went through with the plan to expand its territory. He shuffled back to the bedroom and woke Gabriella.

"Mmm." Her eyelashes fluttered as she smiled up at him. She laced her fingers through his and tugged at him. "Why don't you lay back down here and let's snuggle a while longer."

"There ain't nothing I'd rather do right now, believe me." Ricky leaned down and tasted her lips. "But Mama takes mealtime real serious."

"Oh, alright," Gabriella said, and he tugged her up from the bed.

They walked hand in hand to the main house and Gabriella's nostrils pulsed with anticipation when they gathered at the dinner table with Isabella and Ricardo. "It smells wonderful, Mrs. Santana," she said.

It pleased Ricky that Ricardo seemed as lucid as most any man of his age, although Ricardo's subdued reaction to Ricky's presence after thirty-five years away seemed odd. Maybe Juan had exaggerated the deterioration of his mental health. Ricky hugged his father warmly. "Papa, this is my good friend Gabriella."

Gabriella winced. Good friend?

"Are you going to marry her?" Ricardo said bluntly, his Mexican accent every bit as pronounced as Isabella's. "There will be no fornicating here."

Gabriella blushed. She appreciated the question but not the suggestion.

Isabella squeezed Ricardo's hand. "Let us bless the food, Papa."

They all joined hands and Ricardo said a short prayer, half in English, half in Spanish, and then Isabella passed a basket of hot rolls to Ricky.

"Thanks, Mama."

"De nada, you are welcome, hijo."

"So," Ricardo sliced off a chunk of steak, "I hear you are in the thick of it now."

Ricky said, "That's one way to put it."

Gabriella said, "Isn't it exciting, Mr. Santana? Your son's company could be president soon."

Ricardo took a bite and grunted, his eyes fixed on the meal still. "Is that why you are here, Ricky? Are you scouting for the enemy?"

"Ricardo, please stop it," Isabella pleaded.

"Fine." Ricardo tossed his napkin on the table and got up and turned on the AM radio on the dining room sideboard just in time to catch the tail end of Ricky's fabricated live St. Louis speech. "...vote Vizion Inc. for president in 2028 and together we the people will take our country back."

Ricardo glared into Ricky's eyes and said, "You are an imposter, no?"

"Ricardo, please come back to me." Isabella began to weep.

The old man growled at Ricky, then put his straw hat on and went outside. The screen door clapped shut behind him.

Ricky moved to the seat next to Isabella and wrapped an arm around her. "It's going to be alright, Mama."

"It will not be alright." Her weeping grew more intense. "I am losing him. Every day, a little more of him is gone." She took the napkin from her lap and dried her eyes, then passed a bowl of fried okra to Gabriella.

After lunch, Gabriella helped Isabella with the dishes and Ricky went outside and found Ricardo swaying on the porch-swing puffing away on his pipe and admiring the Palo Pinto mare and the stocky mustang saddled up and tied to the hitching post there. "You okay, Papa?"

"I am okay. How have you been?" Ricardo said, seemingly himself again. His gaze drifted off into the distance.

"Doing fine," said Ricky.

Ricardo abruptly turned angry again. "You have some explanation why you left us for thirty-five years wondering what happened to you?"

"Did it ever occur to you that your being too paranoid to get a telephone or internet service might make it a little difficult for anyone outside the ranch to communicate with you?" Ricky shot back.

"You never have heard of writing?" Ricardo took another puff of his pipe. "I guess we are not worth the price of a postage stamp."

Gabriella stepped out on the porch, her nostrils busy again. "Is that horses I smell?"

"Horses and cherry tobacco," Ricky said.

Gabriella smiled. "I thought so. Reminds me of Boston. Remember when you took me on that tour of the city in a horse drawn carriage? The day you asked me…" She fondled the silver strand around her neck. "Those Clydesdales were just gorgeous. Is there a carriage here?"

Ricardo looked at Gabriella like she might be crazy and he and Ricky both managed a laugh. The closest thing on the ranch to a chariot was an old hay wagon.

Chapter 21

Ricky briefly entertained attempting to pass off the hay wagon as a chariot, but decided instead to take Gabriella on a tour of the ranch on horseback. He reckoned Ricardo intended that when he saddled the two horses up.

Silhouettes of cattle grazed in the distance among aging cedar trees in odd twisted poses like elderly ballerinas with the glowing orange ball of the sun melting slowly into the horizon beyond as Ricky and Gabriella rode north toward the riverbank that had sparked all the controversy with the U.S. Ricky glanced at Gabriella on the mustang, a subtle expression of contentment on her upturned face as she absorbed the sunset and drew in a deep breath of fresh air.

"Mmm. I love the smell of springtime?" she said.

Ricky gazed out at the field of mostly dormant prairie grass peppered with freshly blooming wildflowers – yellow and pink buttercups, rust orange Indian paintbrushes, and bluebonnets – bluebonnets everywhere. "I wish you could see the flowers."

"Me too," Gabriella said. "If they're half as pretty as they smell they must be the most beautiful flowers in the whole world. I wish you had brought me here before. When we were young, I mean. When I could see."

They got off the horses at the river and Ricky plucked a bluebonnet and gave it to Gabriella as they walked down to the water. She held it to her nose and breathed in the fragrance. "Mm." She slipped out of her shoes and Ricky kicked his boots off and they walked hand in hand barefooted along the riverbank.

Gabriella dipped a toe in the water. "Woo. That's cold."

Ricky pulled her close and kissed her. "I love you, Gabby."

He should tell her the truth now. There would never be a better time. But he didn't want to spoil the moment, didn't want what they had to end, as surely it would.

Gabriella said, "I love you too," then they climbed up on their horses and started back.

"Whoa." Ricky saw something he hadn't noticed on the way out, something behind an ancient oak tree just a stone's throw from the riverbank. He halted the Palo Pinto.

Gabriella pulled back on her horse's reins as well. "Why are we stopping?"

"There's a big ol' tree just ahead and I thought I saw something there – a person maybe, kneeling or hiding behind it. You stay here and I'll go have a look."

Gabriella clutched Ricky's arm. "I'm going with you."

"Feeling courageous are you?"

"To the contrary, I'd rather not be left here alone."

"Alright then," Ricky said and they rode up together and dismounted.

Gabriella looped an arm through his and held on firmly as they crept around the tree.

Ricky lurched back.

Gabriella gripped his arm tighter. "What is it?"

"A headstone." Ricky's voice was barely a whisper. His legs went wobbly as he resumed his approach.

"Really?" Gabriella ran her hand across the surface of it, her fingertips reading the inscription etched into the granite:

Ricardo Santana Junior, Beloved Son
July 18, 1971 – April 1, 1975

"Oh my God, it's...you. Except –" Gabriella covered her mouth.

"Except I'm not dead and I wasn't born..." Ricky reached for the trunk of the tree to steady himself.

Dust rising from the adjacent meadow and the pounding of hooves interrupted the haunting moment as Juan charged up on horseback. "Come quickly," Juan said. "It's started." He pulled back on the reins and his horse reared up on hind legs as he twisted it around back toward the main house. He slapped the horse on the hindquarter. "Gitty up."

"Wait," Ricky hollered after him. "What's started?"

"What's happening?" Gabriella said.

"I don't know but we better go find out." Ricky helped her up into her saddle and they raced back.

Juan waved them inside the main house where Ricardo and Isabella stood at the radio, listening intently. The broadcaster was in mid-sentence. "… tension further exacerbated by reports of a new trade deal between Texas and Israel in defiance of the GTP embargo against the noncompliant nation. "I repeat," the broadcaster began again, "President Farnsworth has announced the deployment of a brigade of DHS harmonizers along the Red River in response to reports of an accord signed in a secret meeting this morning by the governors of New Mexico, Oklahoma, Colorado, Kansas, and Wyoming, recognizing the historic borders of Texas. While the purpose of the deployment is said to be purely defensive to prevent further incursions into U.S. territory, residents of the Red River sector and surrounding areas are advised to exercise extreme vigilance. Stay tuned for further updates."

Ricardo turned to Ricky. "Do you still want to be president of the United States?"

Before Ricky could respond, the broadcaster announced another breaking news story: "The Dodge City Times reports it has acquired documents from an anonymous source purporting to show that Ricky Santana – whose company, Vizion Inc. is vying to become the first corporate president of the United States – was the driver in the head-on collision some three and a half decades ago that resulted in the blinding of GABN's famed talk show host, Gabriella Meir."

"Noooooooo," Gabriella shrieked. She felt her way into a bedroom and slammed the door behind her and locked it.

Ricky knocked gently on the door. "Gabby, please."

She dialed Josh's number on her cell phone. "It's Gabriella," she cried when he answered, "I'm in Texas. Can you come and get me?"

Chapter 22

Ricky woke up the next morning to the sound of a Texas state trooper rapping his nightstick against the side of the Pitts-Special's open cockpit. When he reached atop the instrument panel to pull himself up, a half-empty bottle of bourbon tumbled off the edge of his seat and rolled between the rudder pedals. He cupped a hand above his eyes to block the glare from the trooper's mirrored sunglasses. "Good morning, ossiffer. What seems to be the problem?"

"Well now that's exactly what I was gonna ask you, seeing as how you're the one camped out in an airplane in a liquor store parking lot," the trooper said.

Ricky twisted his head and looked around. "I dang sure am, ain't I. I reckon I must've run out of gas."

"Is that so?" The trooper titled his Smokey-the-Bear hat back and lowered his sunglasses. "Say, ain't you that fella that's running for president of the United States as a corporation or some such? I hear you had some trouble catch up to you."

"Where am I?" Ricky slurred.

The trooper raised an eyebrow. "Just outside Amarillo. Don't you know?"

Ricky nodded. "Oh. Is there any place nearby I could lay my head down for a spell?"

"There's a mo-tel up the road a piece if you don't mind a dive. I could give you a lift, but what you gonna do about your airplane? It is yours, ain't it?"

Ricky didn't answer.

The trooper shook his head. "Is this airplane stolen?"

This time, Ricky answered. "Borrowed."

The trooper peered skeptically over the rim of his sunglasses. "Borrowed, is it? From who?"

"My pop, Ricardo Santana."

"Well, I'll be darned. You're Ricardo Santana's boy?"

"You know him?"

"Why, sure. Everybody in Texas and half of Mexico knows Ricardo Santana. He's a good man. A little ornery, a lot crazy, but a good man. Come on down and let's get you to the mo-tel."

Ricky grabbed the bottle from between the rudder pedals and climbed out of the plane.

The trooper gave him a friendly slap on the back. "So how is ol' Ricardo these days?"

Chapter 23

A pungent waft of eggplant and curry followed Ricky as he stumbled out of the motel lobby with a key and a newspaper. He turned and looked at the dilapidated sign out front when he got to his room – Color TV and Free Local Calls. He slipped the key into the lock and twisted the knob. A couple of cockroaches ran for cover when the door creaked opened. Ricky glanced at the boxy nineteen-inch TV of roughly the same vintage as the one at his cottage in Dodge City, and was relieved to see it didn't have a cable box to record him peeling down to his boxers.

"Brrr." He switched on the electric heater, then powered the TV on and tuned it to a 1970s rerun of *Family Feud* to drown out the heater's annoying hum. "Survey says!" Richard Dawson shouted on the TV. Ricky stacked the pillows against the headboard and plunked back against them and took a gulp of bourbon. "Ahh." He burrowed under the blankets, too tired to remove his prosthetics, and reached for the newspaper:

GTP BOARD TO CONSIDER FUTURE OF ISRAEL
HEARING DATE YET TO BE DETERMINED

"Hmm." Ricky flipped the newspaper over to the headline above the fold:

VIZION INC. STOCK PLUMMETS AMIDST NEWLY DISCOVERED EVIDENCE CEO RESPONSIBLE FOR RENOWNED TALK SHOW HOST'S BLINDING

"No. This can't be happening," he gasped. He grabbed his cell phone off the nightstand. The screen flashed, warning that only twenty percent power remained. He dialed Gabriella's number. It went straight to voicemail. He took another sip of bourbon and rolled over and passed out until a few hours later Gabriella's voice jolted him back to consciousness.

"Gabriella?" he breathed. Sweat dripped down the side of Ricky's face. He threw the blankets off as his bloodshot eyes scanned the room. His heart sunk when his gaze finally settled on the image of her on the television. He watched intently.

"When we left off in the last segment," Gabriella said to Josh on the television screen, "you were explaining that corporate participation in the political process increased exponentially in the mid-1800s in response to pervasive regulations affecting corporate interests. The federal government then countered by passing campaign finance regulation that forbade corporations from making direct contributions to candidates for federal office or from making independent expenditures in support of or in opposition to a federal candidate."

"That's correct," Josh said, "first the Tillman Act in 1907 and then the 1940s Taft-Hartley Act. And corporations fought back by creating the predecessors of today's PACs. Almost twenty-five years later, in 1971, Congress passed the Federal Election Campaign Act, or FECA, which maintained the corporate restrictions contained in the Tillman Act and the Taft-Hartley Act and codified the ability of corporations to use PACs to make independent expenditures.

"However, as amended, FECA also placed significant limits on those independent expenditures. But it threw corporations a bone by allowing them to make some limited contributions to candidates. Congress justified all this campaign finance regulation as necessary to further two compelling government interests. The first, to prevent quid pro quo corruption or the appearance thereof – in other words, to prevent bribing candidates for favors once they assume the office. The second was to protect minority corporate shareholders whose views might differ from those expressed by the majority or management or whatever."

Josh continued, "The limitations imposed by FECA were soon challenged in the case of *Buckley v. Valeo*. A diverse coalition of plaintiffs – including conservative party Senator James L. Buckley, former democrat party presidential candidate Eugene McCarty, the ACLU, the American Conservative Union, the Peace & Freedom Party, the Libertarian Party, and numerous others – argued that the legislation violated the first and fifth amendment rights to freedom of expression and due process, respectively. As an aside, you can see from the wide range of the various plaintiffs' political viewpoints, there was nothing remotely partisan about this challenge.

"For our purposes, the most important finding in that case was that independent expenditures in this context are, in fact, political speech, which is protected by the first amendment. Paraphrasing the Court's rationale, it takes more than a loud mouth and an opinion to get a meaningful message out in a nation of several million people dispersed across a vast continent. It takes expenditures. Summing up, money talks – literally. Hence, limitations on expenditures are without question limits on protected speech and thus those limitations violate the Constitution.

"Now, although the *Buckley* Court addressed limitations on expenditures by individuals, any lawyer that wasn't unconscious at the time could clearly see that the ruling might inadvertently, if not intentionally, validate corporate rights to make independent expenditures directly from their treasuries also. Predictably, in a preemptive response to this potentiality, Congress passed yet another new and improved piece of campaign finance legislation. That legislation, BCRA, was the law at issue in the *Citizens United* case."

Josh cleared his throat. "Before I delve into the *Citizens United* ruling itself, I'd like to explore the first amendment a bit more and sort of walk through the evolution of case law leading up to the decision. Again, the relevant portion of the text of the first amendment states as follows: 'Congress shall make no law…abridging the freedom of speech, or of the press.' Many constitutional scholars and historians agree that the most probable reason the founders drafted freedom of speech and the press in the same clause rather than as two separate clauses was because they viewed speech and the press as one and the same.

"The word 'press' describes literally a machine, the printing press, the primary medium used for production and dissemination of speech at the time the framers drafted the Constitution. Today this would include television, internet, and even smartphones. The idea is that if you or I got up on a soapbox on the corner of Wyatt Earp Boulevard and Central and shouted out our views about this or that proposed legislation or this or that candidate or some other matter of public concern, none but those people directly within earshot would hear us. What impact would that have on the governance of our country? Probably none whatsoever.

"On the other hand, if we printed our views and distributed them throughout the nation or had them broadcasted electronically, either of which would cost us money, our views might very well have some impact. Hence, what legislation passes, who will represent us, and other public policy matters would have a better chance of being determined by We the People in the marketplace of freely disseminated competing ideas instead of in the proverbial smoke-filled back room.

"Now, one last point on the freedom of speech and press clause to put this all into context, and we'll move along: The first amendment protects speech from government infringement, but it does not necessarily protect speakers. What I mean by that is that speakers are only protected to the extent required to protect the speech itself. This is what the Court meant when it said in the *Citizens United* case that corporate political speech is no less protected than that of individual natural persons. The Court was not equating a corporate charter with an individual natural person as has been commonly suggested. Rather, it was equating the respective political speech.

"Moreover, the Court's conclusion in *Citizens United* was not new nor was the rationale it based that conclusion on new. Both were actually reaffirmations, albeit in a slightly different context, of what it had said – before a brief detour – in its opinion in a 1978 case, *First National Bank of Boston v. Bellotti.*

"In the *Bellotti* case, the Court addressed the constitutionality of a Massachusetts state law that banned corporate independent expenditures to influence opinion on ballot initiatives as opposed to independent expenditures related to federal elections. But despite the differences in the regulations in question, for all practical purposes, the issue in *Bellotti* was identical to the one in *Citizens United* – although there was arguably at least some wiggle room for debate as evidenced by the detour I mentioned. And we will get to that detour in short order.

"So, in *Bellotti*, the U.S. Supreme Court rejected the State of Massachusetts's asserted interests in preventing diminution of the citizens' confidence in government and protecting dissenting stockholders whose views may differ from those expressed by corporate management. Recall, though worded slightly differently, these were the same interests asserted by the federal government to justify its campaign financing regulations up to the BCRA, which, again, was the regulation at issue in *Citizens United.*

"Returning to *Bellotti* though, the Court in that case overruled the state court's decision that, because the aggrieved party was a corporation whose first amendment rights are incident only to its property interests, where the outcome of the ballot initiative would not have any material effect on the corporation, the ban did not violate the corporation's first amendment rights.

"According to the U.S. Supreme Court, the Massachusetts state court erred when it framed the question as whether a corporation's rights are coextensive with those of natural persons. The correct question, it said, was whether the restriction abridges the expression the first amendment was meant to protect. The Court explained that, quote, 'the constitution often protects interests broader than those of the party seeking their vindication.' The broader interest the Court was referring to was the interest of a democratic society in *access* to the speech itself over and above the interest of the speaker regardless of a speaker's corporate identity or otherwise.

"In support of its holding in the *Bellotti* case, the Supreme Court expressed the view that the most important speech the first amendment is meant to protect is speech intimately related to the process of governing. It then enunciated a number of the purposes of political speech that make it essential to a democratic form of government. Among those purposes it said were discussion of matters of public concern, debate, dissemination of ideas, decision-making, and enabling members of society to cope with the exigencies of their period.

"Presumably, that shortlist of purposes, which, incidentally the *Citizens United* Court reiterated in 2010, was not intended to be exhaustive. And I contend that even if it was, its inclusion of 'decision-making' and other functions performed by elected representatives implies that prohibiting corporations from holding electoral office violates a fundamental purpose of freedom of speech by restricting the relative power of corporate political speech in those processes. Hence, by the Court's own rationale the first amendment freedom of speech clause implies a right for corporate entities to hold electoral office – provided those entities can win elections, of course."

The camera shifted to Gabriella. She smiled. "We pause now for these brief messages from our sponsors."

Ricky muted the television during the commercial break and he thought about leaving it muted for the remainder of the program. The topic was no longer relevant to him. Plus, hearing Josh's annoying voice reminded him that despite the past few blissful days with Gabriella, the wall between him and her, between them and happiness, had been re-erected and fortified. This time probably for good.

His mind wandered to the headstone at the ranch. It was too bazaar to make any sense. Had he imagined it? No. That would mean Gabriella had imagined it too. They couldn't have both imagined it. But Gabriella obviously did not see it. Maybe in his haste he misread the inscription and her fingertips had fallen victim to the power of suggestion. He picked up his cell phone. Only eight percent power remaining now. He dialed Gabriella's number again. It rang this time, several times, before finally going to voicemail again. "Damn it."

Josh and Gabriella appeared onscreen again and Ricky decided not to keep the television muted after all. He needed to hear Gabriella's voice again and if that required him to hear Josh's annoying voice too, he'd suffer through it.

"For those viewers just joining us," Gabriella said, "before the break, Attorney Horowitz explained that, in his view, even before the *Citizens United* case, the Supreme Court had interpreted the freedom of speech clause in such a way that it implied a right for corporate entities to run as candidates for electoral office. Do I have that right?"

Josh nodded. "Yes. That is my view."

"But you also mentioned that the Court later took a detour from that position," Gabriella said.

"Indeed it did," said Josh, "and it's a real head-scratcher. In all the legal research I've done, the only explanation I can come up with is that it must have resulted from changes in the ideological balance of the Court. In theory, Supreme Court justices are apolitical on the job. But in the real world, I suppose one can only judge according to what one sees, and what one sees depends on the lenses one is looking through.

"For the past many years, U.S. judicial lenses seem to have come predominantly in only two shades. One shade adheres as closely as possible to the text or original intent of the document, assuming the founders agreed on and specifically intended the Constitution as drafted. The other view is that the Constitution is a living document that was deliberately drafted ambiguously by founders who couldn't agree on much of anything and intended to leave it to jurists to interpret in accordance with the needs of the people of the times.

"Both sides have interesting arguments. On the one hand, proponents of the living document theory argue that originalists suffer from levels of arrogance and ignorance so toxic that it's warped they're minds such that they believe they're clairvoyant and can see

100

into the minds of dead men whom they must also believe used their own supernatural powers to see into the future.

"Originalists, on the other hand, cite their ability to read as the primary means by which they glean original intent. They point to the Constitution's amendment provision as the method by which the Constitution can be...amended, rather than circumvented by creative interpretation, to address events which might have been unforeseeable to the founders. The amendment provision, the originalists argue, is evidence that the founders foresaw their inability to foresee all and did not leave the potential consequences of that to chance.

"I'm not going to question the sincerity nor the commitment to justice of jurists who espouse either point of view but it seems clear enough that a stint with those of the former persuasion in the majority at the Supreme Court explains the detour.

"One of the more interesting cases heard during this interim ideological shift was *FEC v. Massachusetts Citizens for Life ("MCFL"),* a 1986 case in which the Court carved out that exception I mentioned to the federal government's general prohibition on a corporation's use of general treasury funds on independent expenditures. The exception articulated by the Court applied to a small class of ideological non-profit corporations. In that case, a non-profit corporation, MCFL, used general treasury funds to distribute a newsletter that endorsed certain federal candidates. The Court found that MCFL's expenditure violated the federal prohibition, but that the restriction could not be constitutionally applied to that particular organization.

"Note that if the Court had ruled consistently with what it said in *Bellotti,* it would have struck down the provision altogether rather than carving out an exception for certain non-profits. But I digress. The *MCFL* Court adopted a three-pronged test to determine when a corporation fits within the Court's exception to the general prohibition on a corporation's use of general treasury funds for independent expenditures: First, was the corporation formed for the express purpose of promoting political ideas, and not engaged in business activities? Second, does the corporation have shareholders, and do those affiliated with the organization have any economic reason to remain affiliated if they disagree with its political activity? And last, does the corporation accept funding from for-profit corporations such that it could act as a conduit for for-profit corporate electoral spending?

"Here again, one would have to have been comatose not to recognize that this test was just another way of asking whether the entity's independent expenditures might lead to quid pro quo corruption or result in a corporate message that conflicted with the views of a minority of stockholders. Both of which the Court had previously found insufficient to justify a prohibition on independent expenditures.

"Four years later, in *Austin v. Michigan Chamber of Commerce*, the Court modified its analysis of prohibitions on independent political expenditures, creating what in legalese is commonly termed the anti-distortion rationale. Some argue this new rationale was an attempted distraction from the contradiction in its rulings. Others believe the Court genuinely viewed this new rationale as a compelling enough government interest to override the first amendment in this context.

"So, getting to the facts of the case, in *Austin v. Michigan Chamber of Commerce*, the Court upheld a Michigan state statute modeled after the federal prohibition on a corporation's use of general treasury funds on independent expenditures. It concluded that the Chamber of Commerce did not fall within the exception elucidated in *MCFL* because it was formed for a variety of purposes, including but not limited to promoting political ideas; because it had members who would be reluctant to leave the corporation even if they disagreed with the corporation's electoral speech since they economically benefitted from being a member of the Chamber; and because more than seventy-five percent of the Chamber's members were business corporations who could use the Chamber to circumvent the restriction on a corporation's use of general treasury funds for independent expenditures. Therefore, unlike in *MCFL*, the corporation's speech in *Austin* could not be traced to its members, and the corporation had members who might object to the speech but would feel compelled to remain affiliated with the corporation. Thus the restriction was upheld.

"The justification for upholding the restriction included yet again the previously rejected theory of protection of dissenting shareholders. And it also included the new anti-distortion justification – to prevent 'the corrosive and distorting effects of immense aggregations of wealth that are accumulated with the help of the corporate form and that have little or no correlation to the public's support for the corporation's political ideas.' This is the view that got most of the media attention, which is probably why very few of our citizens have a clue what was really at stake in the *Bellotti* case, much less in *Citizens United*.

"The Court's next major decision in this arena came in 2003 in *FEC v. McConnell* when the Court reviewed the constitutionality of the BCRA for the first time. Without going into needless detail, the *McConnell* Court upheld the BCRA's prohibition on corporations' use of general treasury funds for electioneering communications, once again supporting its decision with the anti-distortion rationale and the previously rejected protection of dissenting shareholders concern. In so ruling, the Court relied on its resurrection of its previously rejected conclusion that political speech may be banned based on the speaker's corporate identity.

"That's the same conclusion it reached in the *Austin v. Michigan Chamber of Commerce* case that we just discussed. Which, as we also discussed, directly contradicts what it said in the *Bellotti* case. And that brings us back to the *Citizens United* case and how a corporate entity could satisfy the substantive qualifications for electoral office, such as age, residency, and citizenship – assuming any of that even matters."

An earsplitting series of beeps accompanied by a multi-colored programming-end test card disrupted Josh and Gabriella's discussion. A newscaster appeared onscreen – "We interrupt this program to bring you breaking news. The Whitehouse has just confirmed that the U.S. Attorney General will file a lawsuit against the State of Kansas on behalf of the federal government tomorrow morning seeking an injunction against Vizion Inc.'s candidacy. According to our sources, the lawsuit will allege that the state's admittance of an associated candidate to its presidential ballots violated the supremacy clause of the U.S. Constitution because Kansas, in essence, substituted its own alternative substantive qualifications for those constitutionally prescribed for the presidency.

"Commenting on the decision, President Farnsworth explained that the Attorney General will name the State of Kansas as defendant in order to avoid months of litigation in the lower courts. 'By naming the State,' the president said, 'we establish original jurisdiction in the Supreme Court so that this corporate political circus act can be brought to a swift and final conclusion and legitimate candidates can proceed to present their visions for the nation to the people without the distraction of unqualified challengers.' "

Ricky guzzled down some more bourbon. "Circus, huh? I'd invite you to join my campaign, Mister President. Every circus needs a clown. But it's over. All over. Everything is over." He slipped into a near hypnotic state as he watched the lawsuit story replayed for the next several hours like it was on an endless loop.

Then his cell phone rang. He snatched it up. "Hello? Gabriella?"

"Levi actually," the chilling voice on the other end said. "Sorry to disappoint you. I trust you've seen the news reports. Can you believe the Attorney General thought to seek original jurisdiction in the Supreme Court? I may have underestimated him."

Ricky hesitated before saying, "Have you heard from Gabriella?"

"She's...," Levi began to answer, then Ricky's cell phone went dead. He chugged down the last of the bourbon and hurled the empty bottle against the wall. "Damn! Damn damn damn." He tried to call Levi back using the landline in the room, but it would not connect. He dialed Gabriella's number next and after getting the same result, he called the front desk.

"May I help you?" The manager seemed to say – though comprehending him over the phone with that Indian accent was difficult.

"Yeah, this is Ricky in room three. I can't get an outside line from the phone in here."

"What number are you trying to reach? I will try to connect you."

He gave the manager Gabriella's number.

"I am sorry but that is long distance number. You will need to bring a deposit to call long distance."

"Fine." Ricky slammed the phone down. He shrugged his pants on and searched around the room. "Where's my wallet? Dang it, I must have left it in the airplane." He reached into his pocket and pulled out his cash clip and found a single twenty-dollar bill. He took it to the front desk. "Will this do?"

The manager shook his head. "We do not accept that worthless paper here."

Ricky wadded up the bill and fired it over the counter and it bounced off the cowboy hat the manager wore. Apparently this Indian embraced the Texas culture – a stark contrast to so many of the U.S. immigrants who bought into the crooked politicians' lie that American culture was one of pervasive racism and bigotry that should be condemned rather than celebrated. Certainly not assimilated into.

"Sorry," Ricky said. "Can't say I blame you." He staggered out to the street and stuck a thumb out and waited about a half hour before a car finally stopped. A DPS cruiser.

The trooper lowered his window and lit Ricky up with his flashlight. "You got some ID on you?"

"Nope," Ricky said, "I ran off and left my wallet in the airplane. That's why I'm standing here alongside the road with my thumb in the air like a jackass."

"The what?" The trooper began to laugh. "Oh, you must be that crazy sumbitch Trooper Tom told me about. Hop in. I'll give a lift."

When the cruiser pulled into the liquor store parking lot Ricky saw Juan sitting in his pickup truck in front of the Pitts Special and Ricardo up on a wing dumping fuel in from a five-gallon gas can. Ricky thanked the trooper for the ride and got out and climbed up on the opposite wing and reached in and grabbed his wallet off the cockpit floor. "How'd you find the plane?" he said.

"Transponders leave tracks," Ricardo grumbled and kept pouring, "you know that."

Ricky nodded. "So, you going to tell me about that headstone?"

After no response from Ricardo, Ricky hopped down and went into the liquor store to buy another jug and when he staggered back out with it Ricardo had the airplane running.

Juan jumped out of the truck and waved his arms, pleading with Ricardo to shut the engine down.

"Get in," Ricardo hollered to Ricky over the noisy propeller and then they all saw the landing lights of a helicopter hovering down. Apparently Ricardo and Juan weren't the only ones who followed transponder tracks.

Chapter 24

Ricky leaned against the plush leather backseat of the Leviathan Corp chopper and gazed out the window. From less than three thousand feet AGL he could clearly see a stream of eastbound headlights below plowing through the snow-covered terrain along the U.S. side of the border just east of the Oklahoma panhandle. He took a swig of bourbon.

"Perhaps you'd like a glass," Levi said, and reached into the onboard service cabinet.

"No thanks. Is that what I think it is down there?" Ricky turned the bottle up again.

"It's a DHS harmonizer transport convoy, if that's what you mean. I'm afraid the Texans may have overplayed their hand this time round."

"That shows how little you know about Texans," Ricky said.

Levi grinned. "I'm rather banking on it."

Josh wiped a hand across his face. "So an invasion then?"

"I wouldn't think so at this stage," Levi said. "Just posturing. I'd say it's designed more to send a message than anything else."

They were quiet for a few minutes.

"I guess Vizion's campaign is over," Ricky said.

"Well," Levi rested a hand on Ricky's shoulder, "it certainly seemed so when news of your youthful indiscretion first broke. But that was before Farnsworth saved the day with his announcement. I can't tell you how delighted I was to see reports of his new lawsuit gobble up the allegations of your involvement in that unfortunate accident. Not that I wouldn't rather he hadn't filed a new suit. Nevertheless, with the scandal of your having abandoned your campaign tour and now this business about the accident, Farnsworth's timing could not have been better."

Ricky ran a hand through his hair. "Aren't you going to ask me if it's true?"

"It's none of my concern," Levi said, and peered into Ricky's eyes. "Now listen to me. Vizion will survive this provided you pull yourself together. And I insist that you do just that. I've entirely too much invested in the campaign to call it off at this point. So, speaking of campaign business, I've scheduled a press conference for you tomorrow to respond to Farnsworth's new lawsuit. It will be an excellent opportunity for you to reintroduce Vizion to the voters and an equally good opportunity to mount a counteroffensive against Farnsworth and his silly legal tactics. But stick to the script this time, no more of that anti-republicrat revolutionary nonsense."

Ricky stared off into the night sky. "I think Gabriella's back in the U.S. already."

"Yes," said Levi.

Ricky said, "Have you seen her?"

"No. But I'm told she's in New York helping Helen pack the last of her things there. Max is there too, as I understand." Levi handed Ricky a folder. "Your prepared statement and talking points for tomorrow's press conference."

Chapter 25

Gabriella took a quick shower after an hour on the treadmill at the fitness center in Helen's New York penthouse. Then she stood in front of the mirror, imagining she could see herself – naked, exposed, vulnerable. That's what she had been since the accident, thanks to Ricky.

Having had time to think through that recent revelation, she was reasonably certain that she could forgive Ricky for it. After all, it was an accident. And as for him having left her, well, it wasn't as if he left her for another woman. Being near her must have reminded him of his guilt and that's why he left. But he had come back. Although not all the way back; not as a lover, not as the husband he had promised he would be.

A tear rolled down Gabriella's cheek. Part of her already had forgiven Ricky for the accident and for not standing by her through what had turned out to be an almost unbearably difficult life. But he had allowed her to go all those years believing she had been the driver, believing that but for some divine intervention she could have harmed him or Josh as badly as she had been harmed, or even killed them. To withhold the truth from her even as she lay in his arms basking in his I-love-yous at the Santana ranch was a betrayal of the worst kind, a direct contradiction of what it means to love someone. That, she could never forgive. Still, like all the rest, she would have to learn to live with it. She toweled off and slipped a bathrobe on, then went to the living room and stood at the glass penthouse wall, trying to picture the magnificence of the scene beyond it.

Max joined her there. He'd come to New York for his chair. "It's a lovely view even without the city lights at night, isn't it?" he said as he peered out at the glowing fleet of Leviathan Corp cargo ships steaming across New York harbor toward the Hudson.

"For God's sake, Max," said Helen. "How cruel can you be."

"Oh, yes, I forgot. My memory has been just terrible since the migraines started."

Helen glared. "Memory problems? Is that the best you can do?"

Gabriella began to sob.

Max wrapped his arms around her. "I'm sorry. It was terribly clumsy of me."

She sniveled. "It's not what you said. I don't mind hearing about beautiful views. It's Ricky. I just can't believe he could let me go on all those years believing I did this to myself."

Max patted her back. "There, there. I know how disturbing that report must have been for you, but you don't know for certain it's true. It is the political season, after all. What if it turns out the supposed evidence against Ricky is just a bit of fiction invented by some unscrupulous presidential candidate to diminish Vizion's odds in the election?"

Helen interrupted, "Max darling, I hope you're not suggesting that I'm involved in this in some way, considering I'm the only legitimate candidate with any chance of winning. It seems to me that you have more motive than anyone for such a prank."

"Actually, Farnsworth is who I was thinking," Max said coolly. "Although your defensiveness is hardly indicative of innocence."

"What would you know about innocence?" Helen said.

Max's eyes narrowed. "As much as you know about burglary, undoubtedly. Perhaps I'll give Gabriella an exclusive on your using that chair to lure me out here so you could have that felon friend of Ricky's break into the mansion. I can see the headlines now – desperate candidate conspires to steal campaign secrets from the frontrunner. Rather reminiscent of Watergate, or perhaps the Russian hacking into the DNC server in 2016 or the intelligence community hacking into Trump's campaign." He wagged a finger at her. "Tsk tsk."

"Would you two please stop it," Gabriella snapped.

Helen gasped. "How dare you speak to us in that tone, you belligerent little peasant."

Gabriella pulled away from Max and hugged Helen halfheartedly. "I'm sorry."

"As well you should be after all we've done for you," Helen said. "If not for my foundation sponsoring your education and the special equipment you've needed to have a successful career and a relatively independent life you'd be dead or institutionalized. And of course Max has been as generous with you as could be expected from such a miser."

"I'm grateful for all you've done for me, both of you. Really I am," Gabriella said meekly. "Since the day of the accident you've been like parents to me."

"And you've been like a daughter to us," Helen said. "Hasn't she, Max?"

Gabriella's thoughts drifted back to the morning she woke up in the hospital with someone at her bedside caressing her hand, the sound of Helen's and Max's voices, and the commotion of the television crew Helen had brought to broadcast her charitable pronouncements. Gabriella had been too distraught to object to Helen's using her as prop. "Ricky," she had cried out and reached for the hand that held hers. But Josh, not Ricky, answered back, squeezing her hand tighter.

"Hasn't she been like a daughter to us, Max darling," Helen said again.

"Yes, yes, of course," said Max.

Gabriella fished a tissue out of her robe pocket and blew her nose. "I'm going to bed."

Max yawned. "Me too. Care to join me, Helen?" He winked.

"Don't flatter yourself," said Helen.

Max said, "Your loss," and shuffled down the hallway to a guestroom where he swallowed a handful of aspirins and fell asleep imagining the media devouring Ricky at Vizion's press conference tomorrow.

Chapter 26

A caravan of media vehicles had already lined up at Vizion's entrance gate when Ricky landed the corporate chopper in the parking lot. He shut the engine down, then with shaky hands, took his first sip of bourbon for the day. "Ahhh." He shoved the pint back into the inside pocket of his sports coat and glanced over at Bernice sprawled out in the copilot seat. "I gotta go entertain the crowd for a minute and figure out what happened to Chick. Then we're going over to see Levi," he said to the old dog. "I won't be long."

A campaign aide hurried over and took Bernice by the leash and led her to Josh's limo.

Ricky scrubbed the stubble on his chin, then grabbed the talking points and hopped out of the chopper.

Josh rushed out, glancing obsessively at his watch. "Glad you could make it," he said. "You had me worried."

Ricky ignored the comment. "You don't happen to know where Chick is, do you? He was supposed to look after Bernice while I was away but when I got home she was there alone."

"Hard to find reliable help these days," Josh said and Ricky concluded from his fidgety body language that he knew more than he was letting on about Chick's whereabouts.

Ricky grabbed him by the collar. "Where is he?"

"Who cares? He's a felon." Josh gripped Ricky's wrists, attempting to pry his hands off his collar.

Ricky gave him a yank. "I said, where is he?"

Josh said, "He was sent to the Lawton harmonization camp for evaluation. Max's harmonizers caught him trying to burglarize the Baxter mansion."

Ricky released Josh's collar. "Damn."

"Do you know something about the burglary?" said Josh.

"No."

Josh sensed that was a lie but any further discussion about the matter would have to wait. The harmonizer at Vizion's entrance gate had raised the crossbar and reporters were flooding in. "Come on, Ricky, we need to get up there."

Ricky gazed up at the enormous American flag draped across the building behind the hastily constructed platform. Then his eye shifted to the red, white, and blue banner suspended from the front of it:

Vizion Inc. for President
An Organization of Real People with Real Vision

"Can you believe they got all this set up so quick," Josh said as they hustled up the steps.

"It's quick-ly," Ricky corrected him.

"Whatever."

They gave a few straggling reporters a minute to work their way in and situate equipment, then Josh stepped up to the podium. "Ladies and gentleman, it's my honor to introduce Mr. Ricky Santana, founder and CEO of the next president of the United States, Vizion Inc."

Ricky took Josh's place at the microphone and nodded appreciation for the dribble of applause. "Thank y'all for coming. I know y'all came here today to hear my response to the new lawsuit filed by the Attorney General and I don't want to disappoint you, so here it is." He wagged his middle finger in the air.

The crowd broke out in a combination of hushed gasps and cautious laughter.

Josh covered his face with his hands. *This press conference is being broadcast all over the world and Ricky is flipping off the Attorney General of the United States.*

After giving the crowd a moment to settle, Ricky opened the folder and began to read the talking points, his monotone voice noticeably devoid of conviction: "For years, American corporations have been treated as second-class citizens, their reputations relentlessly impugned. You've all heard the labels. Evil, Greedy, the One-percenters, etcetera. My friends, those labels may aptly apply to some corporations, just as they may accurately describe some individuals." He strayed from the script, "including some journalists." He paused for a round of boos before returning to the prepared lines, "But because one man or one corporation is corrupt, doesn't mean they all are.

"Notwithstanding a few rotten apples, corporations are the backbone of the economy. They're healthcare providers, shelter and infrastructure builders, food growers, transportation manufacturers, information collectors and conveyors, sources of retirement income. And they are the eyes, ears, and teeth of national security. Without them, we would live in anarchy. Vicious otherness. Everyone forced to fend for one's self. With that in mind, I'd like to make three points and then I'll take some questions.

"First, with respect to the profit motive: There is nothing inherently evil about profit. In fact, we passed the thirteenth amendment abolishing slavery because the opposite is true. A person rightfully expects compensation for his or her labor and he or she negotiates the best price for it. To do otherwise while your family goes hungry, that, my friends, is evil. Similarly, if a corporation earns no profit, the livelihoods of its employees, stockholders, pensioners, and others who depend on that corporation's financial success suffer. And that, my friends is likewise evil.

"Which brings me to my second point: Corporations are comprised of individuals. They are not mysterious inanimate or unhuman

111

heartless entities with unlimited resources. They're people who joined themselves, their efforts, and their resources together for a common purpose. Together, those people are the corporation – a singular entity, a potentially immortal superhuman of sorts, with a super-purpose that no individual could accomplish on his own. And there is nothing inherently evil in joining for a common purpose to push progress beyond conventional individual human limitations. If that were so, how do you explain charities, hospitals, or churches? Or governments, for that matter? And that brings me to my third point.

"Unlike nonprofits and charities, for-profit corporations don't rely on donations. And unlike governments, they don't acquire resources from others through coercion. Nor can corporations crank up the funny-money printing press or reach into the taxpayers' pockets every time their grand utopian schemes fail, like governments do. No. A private-sector corporation must live within its means. As a result, those who operate corporations become skillful managers of resources. They are experts at innovation, adept at rapidly adapting to changing conditions, masters at getting the maximum from the minimum. That, my friends is the kind of leadership this nation so desperately needs. And what better time than now to usher in Vizion Inc., a president run by a team of real professionals with real skills and real vision."

Ricky paused to allow a dribble of skeptical applause that quickly trailed off. "Thank you. Now, as most of you know, Vizion Inc. is unique among corporations in its indispensable role in making the world a safer place through the national security surveillance technologies it produces. But Vizion Inc. also has a much more personal and, dare I say, charitable, mission." An overdue hint of sincerity crackled in his voice. "While that mission has received little media attention, it is no less central to our work today than it was the day I filed Vizion's original charter some thirty-five years ago. That mission – to develop a cure for the blind." He felt tears welling up in his eyes. "And when Vizion is president I will see to it that every regulation standing between Vizion and that goal is struck down. I will not rest until all of mankind sees with twenty-twenty vision."

Ricky cleared his throat, and then continued with a steadier voice. "And I give you my solemn promise that Vizion Inc. will be no less relentless in pursuing a new vision for the nation as together we overcome these difficult times and restore this country to prosperity and, most importantly, to unity." He backed away from the podium and Josh took his place there.

"Mr. Santana has a busy afternoon ahead and so do I," Josh said, "so we'll only have time for a few questions."

Various reporters shouted out a flurry of inquiries that Josh ignored, instead pointing to the first reporter to raise a hand, and sending an aide with a microphone to her.

"Hi, I'm Jill Davis with channel eight news. Could you explain why you think corporate entities should be able to run against people in the presidential election?"

"Sure," Josh said and gave her the abbreviated answer, "because corporations are people too. The Supreme Court has been clear about that for more than two centuries." Josh pointed to the next raised hand and his aide moved with the microphone to that journalist.

"Suzanne Snyder from Pacifist Weekly. My question is for Mr. Santana. There's speculation that the tension between the United States and Texas could erupt into kinetic action. What would you do to resolve the conflict if Vizion becomes president?"

I'd start with abolishing the BLM, Ricky thought, as he moved toward the podium.

Josh held him back. "Mr. Santana can't comment on that at this time for national security reasons. Next." The aide passed the microphone to another reporter.

"John Baker with channel eight," the reporter said, "I'd like to follow up on my colleague Jill's question. As for the Court defining corporations as people, my understanding is that they also referred to corporate personhood as a legal fiction, is that not correct?"

Josh nodded. "John, yes, that is correct, and that's one view. The Court has also recognized corporations as natural persons. In deciding cases, they've used the aggregate persons theory and the natural entity theory in addition to the artificial person theory you mention. I explore corporate personhood in detail in the next segment of my four-part series with Gabriella Meir on GABN. I encourage you to tune in. Next." He pointed to another raised hand.

"Hi, Jane Lake with One World dot com. I know your fiancé well. She's very talented and I look forward to the remaining segments of the series. So how about a tease? What's the punch line in your theory that the *Citizens United* decision created a right for corporate entities to hold electoral office?"

113

"Thank you for the question, but's that's a mischaracterization of my theory," Josh said. "So here's a question for you: Who told you that was my theory?"

"It came from the Associated Press," said Jill.

Josh leaned into the podium. "Who submitted it to the AP and who at the AP approved it?"

"I don't know."

"So, as long as a story comes from the AP it's credible?" Josh resisted the temptation to rip into the reporter, bearing in mind how often he had relied on just such journalistic incompetence to further clients' agendas. "My theory is that the first amendment provided corporations the same protections as individuals from its inception. The same first amendment that prohibits abridging people's freedom of speech and press also protects freedom of association. And a corporation is undeniably an association of people. The *Citizens United* decision simply reaffirmed freedom of association and freedom of speech and clarified for any idiot who thought otherwise, namely the authors of the BCRA campaign finance regulation, that exercising the first amendment right to assemble does not suspend the first amendment right to speak. The Court also made clear that it's the speech itself, not necessarily the speaker, that the first amendment protects. Apparently you missed the segment where I explained all this. But not to worry, all four segments will be available for on-demand streaming soon."

"Isn't Vizion's candidacy really just another clever corporate scheme to enrich its shareholders by manipulating the stock price at the expense of the American public?" Another reporter yelled.

Ricky pulled tongue-tied Josh away from the podium and took his place there. "No, at least not at the public's expense," Ricky began, and the crowd went suddenly silent. "When Vizion is president its first act in office will be to issue each and every citizen of the United States a share of stock in the company." He smiled at the stir that caused among the reporters who responded with a bombardment of questions about the implications of such an issuance.

"Way to go pal," Josh whispered. "We're going to play hell walking that one back." He jerked the microphone off the podium and said hastily, "Thank you all for coming." He tossed the mic and waved with one hand while nudging Ricky down the platform steps with his other.

Josh and Ricky piled into the limo.

"What was that about?" Josh said as the limo sped away.

Ricky stroked Bernice's head. "Voters are entitled to their fair share of the value they contribute to Vizion and I aim to give it to them."

Josh shook his head. "You've lost your mind."

Nothing more was said for the next few minutes as the limo rolled along toward Leviathan Corp.

Josh broke the silence. "I can't believe not a single reporter asked about the accident. What a break."

Ricky nodded with apparent disinterest and Josh let another minute of silence pass between them before saying, "I hope you don't think I had anything to do with those documents about the accident coming out."

"Did you?" Ricky glared at him, then pulled the pint out of his pocket and took a gulp.

"A better question is, Did you sleep with my fiancé during that disaster you made of your campaign tour?" Josh countered.

"Yes, I certainly did," Ricky said and let that soak in a minute before elaborating, "and sleep means sleep. Nothing else happened. Not that it's any of your business." The limo pulled up beside the Vizion campaign tour bus parked out front of Leviathan Corp. Ricky forced a smile. "Well, what do you know, the bus is back."

Chapter 27

Levi put his phone on speaker and leaned back in his throne. "Yes, you heard me correctly," he said. "Put in buy orders for every available share of Vizion stock."

"But Vizion stock is virtually worthless now that the news came out about Ricky Santana's involvement in that accident," the broker on the other end of the speaker argued. "It's barely more than penny stock at this point."

"Indeed, and I can't resist a bargain," Levi said. "Now go to it. And get me a couple of thousand more carbon credits while you're at it."

"Very well. How would you like the stock registered?"

Examine my portfolio, and register a few shares to every domestic corporation I have controlling interest in. That will require a bit of math on your part but I trust you can handle it."

"Consider it done," said the broker.

Levi hung up and smiled. Vizion's stock price would rebound miraculously as soon as Ricky's press conference comments about issuing shares to the public percolated a few hours. Vizion's poll numbers would improve dramatically as well, causing the stock price to rise even higher, which would, in turn, cause the poll numbers to rise more... He appreciated immensely the ease with which a single soundbite could set the self-perpetuating phenomenon of poll numbers and stock prices in motion. The truth or falsity of such a comment be damned.

Line two rang. "Levi Baxter," he answered.

"Levi, it's Josh. Ricky's on his way up."

"Thank you," said Levi, "and while I have you on the phone, Ricky's promise to bring the public in on Vizion, I'll expect you to rewind that. Do whatever you deem necessary to ensure that no such nonsense is ever uttered again."

"I'll handle it."

"I know you will."

Ricky stepped into Levi's office with Bernice at his side just as Levi ended the call. "You wanted to see me?"

"Yes. Please sit." Levi motioned to the not-throne. "There's a matter we failed to discuss during our flight back from Texas. But first I'd like to congratulate you on your quick thinking in response to that reporter's attempt to play gotcha. It was quite impressive. Just make sure you don't repeat that business about issuing stock to the public at the fundraiser Friday. I suspect it wouldn't go over well with the donors. Now, about that little matter I mentioned, I must insist you discontinue association with that felon." Levi sniffed. "When's the last time that dog was bathed?"

"I don't recall," Ricky said.

"Pardon me a moment." Levi stepped out of the office.

He reappeared a few minutes later with a man in a white lab coat.

The man reached for Bernice's leash and said, "May I?"

Ricky grasped his forearm firmly and shot him a threatening glare.

"Relax," Levi said and pried Ricky's hand off the man's arm. "This is Dr. Shultz. He has an excellent animal hygienist among his staff. Your K-9 companion will be much easier on the olfactory senses when they're finished."

Ricky reluctantly let Dr. Shultz take the dog despite an uneasy feeling in his gut about it.

"Now, about your felon friend," Levi said.

"If you mean Chick, he's reformed. And since you brought it up, Josh tells me he's being held in one of your harmonization camps. I'd be mighty grateful to you if you'd turn him loose."

"I'm afraid I can't do that, Ricky. They aren't my camps. At least, technically they aren't. Besides, your obviously not-so-reformed felon friend was detained as required for exceeding the bounds of the GTP's model global citizen. Burglary interferes with legitimate commerce, you see, as stolen items can be traded on the black market. By the way, any idea what he was after when he burglarized the mansion?"

Ricky hesitated, trying to think of a plausible explanation besides the truth. "I...I don't know...Well, actually I do know. I believe I left something when I was over there last, so I asked Chick to go check with Max. And of course since Max is in New York –"

"What, Ricky? What did you leave there?"

"It doesn't matter," Ricky snapped, "and I'd appreciate it if you'd stop referring to Chick as my felon friend. He's been squeaky clean since he got out of prison more than two decades ago and he shouldn't be punished for mishandling a favor I asked him to do."

Levi sighed. "It's not punishment, it's harmonization. And it's only a short term commitment unless he misbehaves in there."

Ricky patted his sports coat pocket, struck by an urge to pull the pint out and chug it down to the last drop. "So we're having a fundraiser this Friday?"

"Yes. Seven-thirty. Black tie for the gentlemen, evening gowns for the ladies. And speaking of ladies, it would be poor form for you to show up unaccompanied." Levi handed Ricky a binder containing photographs and brief bios of several elegant women. "Our guests will be viewing the third segment of Josh and Gabriella's series on *Citizens United* while they dine. Naturally, Josh and Gabriella will be attending in person as well."

Ricky slid the binder across the desk back to Levi. "Thanks, but I'll find my own date."

"Very well," Levi said. "Someone tasteful with no obvious flaws, physical or otherwise, please."

Ricky ignored the comment. "And you say Gabriella will be there?"

"Of course. Assuming she's feeling up to it."

"So, is Chick allowed visitors?" Ricky said.

Levi drew in an exasperated breath. "Visitors are not typically permitted at harmonization but I'll see what I can arrange." He picked up the phone and dialed Dr. Shultz's extension. "Have you finished up with Mr. Santana's animal? ...Splendid. He will meet you in the lobby." Levi turned back to Ricky. "By the way, I'd prefer you were clean shaven and sober for the fundraiser if it isn't too much of a bother."

Chapter 28

Ricky secured Bernice in his cottage, then hiked to the Irish tavern down the block where he spent the evening sucking down bourbon and thinking about what he'd said at the news conference, how Levi had warned him not to say it again, and wondering if that Ben Black fellow on the radio would issue stock to the public if he were in Ricky's shoes.

"Are you sure you wouldn't like something to eat?" a waiter in a kilt that looked entirely inappropriate for the frigid weather asked Ricky for the third time around 9:00 PM.

"No, thanks." Ricky handed him a credit card. "I've got to get going. And, ah, add enough to the gratuity line to buy yourself a pair of pants."

"Bern?" Ricky called out when he got back home. It wasn't like her not to greet him at the door. He called out again as he moved on to his bedroom. "Bern?" He glanced down at his bed and imagined Gabriella lying there waiting for him. "Baby, I'm home," he whispered as he picked up the pillow where she'd lain her head a few nights ago. He held it to his nose. It still smelled like her perfume.

He heard Bernice groan. "Bern, where are you?" He pulled the blanket back and found her curled up beneath the bed, panting heavily. "Hey, Bern. What ya doing under there?" The old dog groaned again and didn't move. Ricky got down and all fours and pulled her out. He grunted as he hoisted all hundred and twenty pounds of her limp body up into his arms. Something was seriously wrong. He rushed outside with her, forgetting he didn't have a car or the helicopter there. "Dang it." He laid her on the porch and quickly punched Vizion's number into his cell phone.

"Vizion Inc.," Dawn answered.

"Thank God you're there."

"Ricky? What's wrong?"

"It's Bern. She's in a bad way."

"Where are you?"

"I'm at the cottage."

"I'll be right there," Dawn said, and twenty minutes later, she rushed up the porch steps. "I got here as quick as I could."

"Quick-ly," Ricky said.

"What?" Dawn dropped to her knees beside the dog.

"Oh nothing." Ricky stroked Bernice between the ears while Dawn probed her with a stethoscope.

"Her heart rate is elevated and I definitely don't like the way she's breathing," Dawn said. "Let's get her in to the office so I can run some tests."

Ricky carried Bernice straight up to the radiology table upstairs when they got to Vizion.

Dawn lowered the imaging device, then went behind the protective screen and snapped the first shot of the old dog's lungs.

Ricky maneuvered Bernice into position for the next image.

After completing the x-rays, Dawn drew some of Bernice's blood and Ricky took the dog back down to his office where he waited for what seemed like hours before Dawn completed the blood tests and all the rest and came in with her findings.

"X-rays look good," she said. "No pulmonary issues as far as I can tell. Heart enzymes are normal. Histamine enzymes don't indicate an allergic reaction. But she's utterly exhausted. My best guess is anxiety. It's consistent with her symptoms. Does she have a history of that?"

Ricky glanced at Bernice sleeping soundly at his feet now. "Not that I'm aware of, but I can't say for sure because I don't speak dog."

Dawn laughed. "Okay. Well, is there anything else I should know? Anything that might have happened to bring this on?"

Ricky laughed too. "Some of Levi's goons gave her a bath today. Maybe that stressed her out."

Dawn chuckled. "Yeah maybe. Well, for now I recommend just keeping an eye on her and avoiding putting her in any stressful situations. I'll go ahead and prescribe some tranquilizers in case she has another episode."

"Dawn?"

"What?"

"About that thing with Gabriella and the accident. I can't imagine what you must think of me."

Dawn wrapped an arm around him. "Ricky, we've all made mistakes. It was an accident. And it was a long time ago. Look at all the good you've done since then."

Ricky buried his face in his hands. "It's not a long time ago for Gabby. She has to live with the consequences every day for the rest of her life... Unless we get the artificial eyes to work."

Dawn massaged his shoulders.

"Dawn?"

"Yeah?"

"I don't suppose you'd consider..." Ricky stubbed his toe at the floor. "Do you have an evening gown?"

Dawn smiled. "Do you have a razor?"

Chapter 29

Friday evening, Ricky sat silently, tugging at his bowtie and staring out the windshield of Dawn's self-navigating government issued Toyota Prius as it buzzed along the frozen road toward the fundraiser dinner at the Dodge House. His breathing became difficult as dusk gave way to nightfall. He wished the strangling suit and tie was all that was causing that. But he knew better.

Dawn studied Ricky's face, trying to decide whether the sprouting beard made him look rugged sexy or just unkempt. "You're awfully quiet tonight. Everything okay?"

"Fine," Ricky said, though he didn't feel fine at all. In the past few days, the narrow path of his mechanical existence had opened up into an expressway of hope – however tenuous – that dead-ended into something like a purgatory. With his future now as dead as his past apparently was, that headstone at the ranch with his name on it seemed oddly on-point. Seeing Gabriella again could only aggravate the feeling that life had taken a sharp turn, slinging him aside as it did.

"It's Gabriella, isn't it?" Dawn said.

"I don't want to talk about it."

"Well, I think we should." Dawn directed the car to pull to the side of the road. "What is it you see in her besides... You're in love with her, aren't you?"

"I wish it were that simple. I owe her. And it's a debt I'm starting to doubt I can ever repay."

"You borrowed money from her?"

"Not that kind of debt."

"Oooh. Of course. I'm sorry."

"I told you I don't want to talk about it."

"Fine," Dawn huffed. "It's your life. If you want to waste it wallowing in self-pity or guilt or whatever this is, then go right ahead." She directed the car back onto the road and fifteen minutes later they arrived at the Dodge House where Gabriella and Josh were waiting for them out front with a pair of harmonizers.

The valet attendant took Dawn's keys and handed her a parking slip.

"Ricky. Dawn," Josh said, dutifully acknowledging them.

"Josh. Gabriella," Ricky returned the acknowledgment.

Dawn forced a smile, doing her best to conceal any evidence of the unjustified animosity she felt toward Gabriella. Gabriella's nervous body language seemed to swell with the same desperation Dawn saw in Ricky's eyes. "Good evening to you both," Dawn said, and shook Josh's hand and then Gabriella's.

"And to you as well, Doctor," said Josh.

Gabriella stood silently, biting at her lower lip and fidgeting. She had reminded herself repeatedly over the past couple of days that the revelation of Ricky's role in the accident did not make her any more blind than she had been when she thought she was responsible for it herself. She told herself it didn't really change anything at all and that she should continue on with her life as it had been. But it did change something. It changed her image of Ricky as a good man, a man who loved her even if fear had prevented him from fully showing it. Being in his presence now made her tense, off balance. But Ricky, as a liar and a coward who destroyed her life and then left her to suffer alone in the darkness – that just didn't fit. Was she flirting with denial?

One of the harmonizers held the door open and Josh took Gabriella by the arm and guided her into the dining hall with Dawn and Ricky at their sides.

"Screw you, asshole," Ricky muttered beneath his breath to the harmonizer.

Inside, the place hummed with conversation and flatware clinking against fragile plates. Ricky gazed around at the white linen tablecloths set with fine china and crystal glasses. It seemed a bit overdone for an event where the hors d'oeuvres were jalapeño poppers and deep-fried steak fingers, with BBQ as the main course.

"The planners felt a touch of pretentiousness to go with the local cuisine was in order since most of your guests are the who's whos of the cosmopolitan billionaires club," Josh said as though reading Ricky's mind. He called Ricky's attention to the half dozen eighty-inch television screens and the *Vizion Inc. for President* banners hanging between them. "The screens are mounted strategically around the hall so that after introductions and a bit of self-congratulating, the guests can easily view the third episode of the Citizens United series from their seats without straining their billion dollar necks."

"Nice," Ricky said.

Josh scrubbed his hands together. "I better announce you now. The donors are getting restless. Ladies and gentlemen," the dining hall quieted, "please welcome the man of the hour, CEO of the next President of the United States, Mr. Ricky Santana and his lovely guest, Dr. Dawn Wise."

Lovely was an understatement. In her elegant open-backed black evening gown accessorized by a triple-tiered pearl necklace, Dawn was nothing short of stunning. Almost as stunning as Gabriella who had worn a nearly identical dress and a similar strand of pearls. Ricky thought that simple silver necklace he had given Gabriella in college would have looked better.

The guests stood and applauded as Josh and Gabriella escorted Ricky and Dawn toward the table to join Levi. Ricky scanned the room to see who all was in attendance, and nodded and waved acknowledgments. He recalled many of the faces from the meeting in a Wall Street office where Levi had pitched the deal to take Vizion Inc. public several years earlier.

The applause trailed off and the guests settled back into their seats after Ricky and company reached their table. Josh, Ricky, and Dawn each shook Levi's hand.

Gabriella marched impressively sure-footed to the bar and downed a scotch and returned to the table with another one. She raised the glass and said, giggling, "To the election. May the best man…or woman…or corporation, or whatever, win."

The others at the table raised glasses of water, and Levi said, "Hear, hear."

Gabriella guzzled down her drink, then said, "Joshua, would you please go and get me another Dewars. Make it tall and neat." She turned to Ricky. "Maybe you ought to go with him to make sure he doesn't botch the order. I hear after a few decades sabbatical from your drinking career you're back in full swing so I'm sure you'll get it right."

Ricky felt the blood vessels in his forehead begin to pulsate. "Whatever, Gabby." He got up and shoved his chair in forcefully and he and Josh went together to the bar.

"I'm not sure she needs anything more to drink," said Ricky as they waited in line.

Josh sighed. "You're one to talk."

After a moment of silent tension between the two men, Ricky said, "I don't guess I could expect a friend who stole my girl to understand."

"Your girl?" Josh said incredulously. "You've had more than thirty years to make your move. How many more years did you expect us to wait."

"Oh now it's *us*. Like Gabriella had anything to do with it."

"Don't be stupid, Ricky. I asked her to marry me but it's not like I forced her to say yes."

The bartender interrupted. "What can I get you gentlemen?"

"A Dewars," Josh and Ricky said at the same time. "Neat and tall," Ricky added.

"So is that one or two Dewars?"

"Make it three," Ricky said.

The bartender nodded and after pouring the drinks, Josh and Ricky went back to the table where Gabriella was grilling Dawn about the nature of her relationship with Ricky.

"Um, he's my employer," Dawn said to Gabriella, a touch of annoyance in her tone. "We share a common vision so it's a good fit."

"I'll just bet it is." Gabriella drew in a healthy whiff of Dawn's perfume, wondering if she looked as good as she smelled. "May I touch you?"

"Pardon me?"

"I said may I touch you? It's how I see. I'm blind, remember?"

123

"I suppose so." Dawn spread her arms.

Gabriella placed her hands on Dawn's shoulders and traced from there across her arms to her hands, all the way to her manicured nails, and then moved to the sides of her breasts and down to her waistline and back up, exploring her facial features last. Unless Gabriella's sense of touch had failed her, Dawn was near perfectly proportional, if a bit large in the bosoms. Most likely extraordinarily attractive. "How old are you?" Gabriella said.

"Thirty-six."

Younger, of course, Gabriella thought, and abandoned the inquiry there.

Josh settled into his chair, and Levi leaned over and whispered in his ear, "I think you'd better give Gabriella a sedative or something."

Dawn glanced at Ricky, smiled, and shrugged her shoulders.

Ricky winked at her, then sat down with his two Dewars and took a sip from one.

"Ladies and gentlemen," a young lady from the event planning team announced over the PA system, "the third episode of the *Citizens United* series with award-winning talk show host, Gabriella Meir and Attorney Joshua Horowitz is about to begin. Ms. Meir, Mr. Horowitz, please stand and be recognized."

Josh stood, giving Gabriella a hand that managed to make her intoxicated stumble appear an intended curtsey synchronized with his bow. The guests applauded and Gabriella and Josh lipped *thank-yous*, then Josh sat and quickly pulled Gabriella back down into the seat next to him.

Citizens United and the Future of Associated Candidacies, Part Three appeared in bold white letters across the black background on the television screens and remained for ten seconds before dissolving into the set with Gabriella and Josh seated across from one another at the quarter-moon chrome and glass table.

Onscreen Gabriella said, "Good evening viewers and thank you for joining us for our third segment with Attorney Joshua Horowitz, a leading first amendment expert and a man who may rightfully come to be known as the father of associated candidacies." She turned to Josh. "Welcome back, counselor."

"Thank you for having me," Josh said and smiled into the camera.

"Now," Gabriella said, "in the previous segment you gave us a history of sort of the metamorphosis of campaign finance regulation which in some respects came full circle with the *Citizens United* decision. In your view, that decision revealed a corporate right to seek electoral office – a right which you say had been implied all along in the first amendment. But what about substantive qualifications for candidacy? How do you respond to the argument that because corporate entities are not really people it is impossible for them to satisfy the age, residency, and citizenship required by the Constitution?"

"Thank you for the question," said Josh. "So, let me begin by saying that the basic premise that corporations cannot satisfy the qualifications for candidacy because they are not people is flawed if for no other reason than because the Supreme Court has said repeatedly that corporations are people – as well it should have. And here's why:

"In the declaration of independence the founders reaffirmed English philosopher John Locke's proclamation of three unalienable rights that all people are endowed with by their creator, independent of whatever rights or privileges their government may grant them. Those rights include life, liberty, and the pursuit of property. The drafters of the declaration substituted *pursuit of happiness* for *pursuit of property* because slaves, while technically property, were also people, people endowed with the same unalienable rights as all others, and in due time slaves' right to liberty should be and would be enforced. Hence, pursuit of happiness has long been understood as pursuit of property exclusive of slaves.

"Enter the Bill of Rights and the fifth and fourteenth amendment prohibitions on government depriving any *person* of life, liberty, or property without due process and equal protection under the law. Then, consider the first amendment proscription against abridging the right of the *people* to peaceably assemble. Now, think about what a typical corporation is in its most basic form, and what it does. It is a group of people, sometimes in the form of other corporations, who have chosen to assemble, commonly, though not exclusively, for the purpose of doing business – that's pursuit of property. Right?

"But if corporations are not people they have no rights. The government can seize a corporation and/or its property on a whim. The right of the people to peaceably assemble is thus effectively thwarted because no sane persons will assemble if doing so requires them to forfeit their rights. So, as you can see, the concept of corporate

125

personhood is essential to the rights of the individual. Individual and corporate rights are indivisible.

"The Supreme Court first confronted this issue in the 1819 case of *Trustees of Dartmouth College v. Woodward*. The situation in that case was that the State of New Hampshire had attempted to alter the corporate charter of Dartmouth College and appoint the state's own board of trustees without the college's consent. Dartmouth argued this violated the constitutional prohibition against laws impairing the obligations of contracts. The state countered that, because corporations derive their existence from government they are in essence public *property*, not people, and as such are not entitled to constitutional protections.

"The Court disagreed with the state's position and in so doing established the foundation for the three theories of corporate personhood that the Court uses to this day in analyzing questions involving corporate constitutional rights. Those are: The artificial person theory, the aggregate person theory, and the natural entity theory.

"The artificial person theory is premised on the notion that corporations are fictional entities, dependent upon the state for their existence, and that they are created for some public good – charters for educational institutions or municipalities, for example. Under this theory, corporations' classification as people is merely a tool of economic and judicial convenience. In the *Dartmouth* opinion, Chief Justice Marshall summed up the corporate person as, 'an artificial being, invisible, intangible, and existing only in contemplation of law.' But the Chief Justice also acknowledged that, artificial beings or not, corporations are formed by people to benefit people in some form or fashion – an unavoidable truth that resulted in the aggregate person theory of corporate personhood.

"The aggregate persons theory is simple: Corporate entities are an aggregation of people joined together for some common purpose. The fact that corporations cannot be formed without the action and agreement of natural persons and no corporate acts can be undertaken without those natural persons taking them is of far greater importance to corporate character and rights than the limited role of the state in granting their charters.

"This theory also recognizes that in many instances the public good corporate activities serve may be only incidental to the private interests of the individuals who form corporations for their own mutual benefit. Hence, there is no per se public interest in corporations; but there is an obvious and critical public interest in assurances that the government will not require individuals to check their rights at the corporate door should they choose to exercise their right to assemble in the form of a corporate charter.

"The crux of the matter, as far as aggregate persons theory is concerned is that a corporation's identity is not distinct from the natural persons who own, manage, and administer it because a corporation's acts and interests are manifestations of the acts and interests of those natural persons. It follows that a corporation's rights are coextensive with the rights of the individuals of whom it is comprised.

"Justice Field put it this way in the 1886 case of *Santa Clara County v. Southern Pacific Railroad Co.,* the first case to recognize a corporate right to equal protection under the fourteenth amendment: 'Wherever a constitutional provision guarantees the enjoyment of property...a means for its protection, or prohibits legislation injuriously affecting it, then the benefits of the provision extend to corporations.' Justice Field added, 'The courts will always look beyond the name of the artificial being to the individuals whom it represents.'"

The camera focused in on Gabriella. "We'll be back with more on corporate personhood after these brief messages."

The set dissolved into a video clip of a white flag embroidered in red, white, and blue with the words *Vizion Inc.* waving in the wind above the old Whitehouse. After a five-second delay, a voiceover deriding corporate dominance of the government began: "My fellow Americans, what you just heard was silence – the silence of Congress, the silence of the Senate, and so far even the silence of the Supreme Court in the face of Vizion Inc.'s campaign to complete the corporate conquest of our government..."

Levi fumed. Whoever allowed this to run would find himself unemployed by morning, never to work again in broadcasting. He cast a suspicious glance at the very amused-looking Cole brothers two tables over while making a hand gesture across his neck, signaling the media control booth to mute the audio. "Cut it."

The unexpected but welcome effect of Levi's signal was a silent image of the Vizion Inc.'s flag fluttering victoriously above the

127

Whitehouse. Yes, victoriously. The silence transformed the clip into a powerful promotion of the company. He rose to his feet, seizing the opportunity, and clapped a couple of lonely claps, and then a few guests clapped. Finally, everyone at the event joined in until the walls vibrated with applause. Levi raised a glass and shouted, "To corporate political leaders. Long live the corporation."

Soon glasses rose throughout the hall, everyone chanting fervently, "Long live the corporation, Long live the corporation."

Ricky shivered. He glanced at Dawn, Gabriella, and Josh, all of them mesmerized.

"Volume on," Levi lipped, signaling to the control booth again as the clip neared its conclusion. The audio resumed in time to catch the tail end of the voiceover. "We are Citizens United and we approve this message."

A Leviathan PR spot announcing the rollout of the harmonizer 3.0 ran next: "The new harmonizer will enable the final phase-out of human police officers and DHS troops, and ultimately even GTP free trade enforcement officers, eliminating the need to place humans in harm's way," Levi's onscreen image boasted with a confident smile.

The near hypnotic moment of corporation worship faded into a buzz of conversation and mingling among the guests that continued with scant attention to the Leviathan clip.

Gabriella's image reappeared onscreen and the segment resumed. "Welcome back," she said. "We began today with Josh explaining the legal basis for corporate personhood and the various theories our courts employ to describe the corporate person." She turned to Josh. "So far you covered the artificial person theory and the aggregate person theory. Tell us about the third theory."

Josh nodded onscreen. "The natural entity theory. It's the theory of corporate personhood that most supports the legitimacy of associated candidacies because it recognizes corporations as full-fledged living realities with real personalities, separate and distinct from the natural persons of whom they are comprised. Although natural entity theory does not dispute that corporations are artificial persons, it emphasizes that they are no more artificial than, say, artificial lakes – which are nevertheless undeniably real lakes.

"Similarly, natural entity theory concedes that corporations are aggregations of natural persons, just as natural persons are aggregations of biological cells; and like a natural person, a corporation is more than the sum of its individual parts. The corporation then, is an individual, the offspring of the natural persons who form it, just as a child is the offspring of its natural person parents. And the corporate charter is the corporation's birth certificate, documenting the date of its coming into existence and endowing it with the responsibilities and the rights of any other person.

"By the way, society does not merely recognize that corporations have the same sorts of moral and social responsibilities as any other citizen, it insists upon it and it demands that corporations honor those obligations. That insistence and those expectations are powerful evidence of the natural and individual nature of the corporate entity. Add in perpetual life and it's difficult to imagine a workable relationship between corporations and natural persons – certainly between corporations and the people's corporate manifestation as government – if the corporation is viewed as anything but a singular and natural entity.

"For example, corporations can persist for several generations without losing their fundamental identity as distinct units even though all members at some point come to differ from the original ones. So how is society to interact with them if not as individual and *real* entities unto themselves? How is a government to extract taxes from them? And how is the corporation to fulfill its responsibilities to its investors, employees, creditors, consumers, vendors, and to the community in which it operates without the individual rights necessary to do so? And how could a corporation have those rights if it is not individual and not real? The natural entity theory resolves these issues."

For a while Levi ignored the cell phone vibrating in his pocket as Josh continued on but he eventually gave in to the caller's persistence.

"Levi Baxter...I see...I'm on my way."

He slipped the phone back into his pocket and stood. "My apologies, but I've got to go," he said to the others at the table. "Max is in the emergency room."

"Why? What's happened?" Gabriella said.

Levi said, "I don't know the details," and rushed out.

Gabriella took a sip of scotch and returned her attention to herself onscreen where she asked Josh, "But isn't one of the reasons the *Citizens United* decision was so controversial because corporations do not have the same rights as natural persons?"

129

"To the contrary," Josh said, "although the courts initially expressed a reluctance to recognize corporate rights beyond those necessary to protect property interests, in due time, as we discussed, they had to accept the unavoidable fact that natural rights whether property rights or liberty rights are interdependent. So, the real issue is not so much a distinction in the rights of individual persons versus corporate rights as it is a distinction between activities commonly engaged in individually versus activities routinely engaged in collectively – that is, corporately.

"Let me explain: The absoluteness of rights becomes a bit murky when one right bumps up against another, irrespective of the identity of the holder of those rights. With that in mind, the scope of constitutional rights are dependent upon context, specifically, the presence of conflicting constitutional provisions or conflicts between rights and between holders of rights.

"For example, we're all familiar with the rule that freedom of speech does not give one the right to falsely yell fire in a crowded theater because the resulting stampede would likely result in a violation of others' right not to be gravely harmed or killed. One's right to be secure in one's person is logically more important than the right of another to play a practical joke. It's a matter of balancing burdens against harms when rights collide.

"*FCC v. AT&T* is one case demonstrating this principle in the corporate context. In that case, the Court held that a statutory personal privacy exemption under the Freedom of Information Act (FOIA), which covers law enforcement records, the disclosure of which could reasonably be expected to constitute an unwarranted invasion of personal privacy, does not extend to corporations.

"Although the Court refused to rule on the constitutionality of precluding corporations from the exemption, instead framing the question as one of statutory interpretation, one might soundly speculate from that refusal, that the Court, at least tacitly, reasoned that the people's interest in awareness of AT&T's criminal conduct, if there was any criminal conduct, outweighed AT&T's right to privacy. And here's why: The threat posed by an individual with a history of nonviolent criminal misconduct is negligible in comparison to the far-reaching financial devastation a multi-billion dollar corporation with millions of customers and stockholders, and tentacles deep in the economy could inflict on members of society – think Enron. Burden on corporate right of privacy versus potential harm to the public's property rights.

"There are literally tens of thousands of situations in which corporate entities are seemingly required to abide by a different set of rules than individuals – violations of privacy as in the *AT&T* case as well as other cases where reporting of sensitive information is required by anti-trust provisions and such. Other examples are warrantless searches of corporate property – more commonly known as *inspections* – for corporations dealing in firearms, hazardous materials as in chemical factories and nuclear power plants, and so on. What do all of these have in common? The potential harm to others is presumably far greater than the burden on the corporations' fourth amendment right against unreasonable searches. Alternatively we might say those searches are reasonable.

"The simple fact is that individuals are, with few exceptions, more capable and more likely to engage corporately in the types of activities that strain the boundaries between their own constitutional rights and the presumed responsibility of the government to protect others from any harm they might do. If an individual were to engage in his individual capacity in pervasively regulated enterprises such as those previously mentioned, that individual would find his rights no less burdened than those of a corporation engaged in such activities. Hence, as I said earlier, corporations' rights are not limited because of what corporations *are* but because of what they *do*."

"So, you're suggesting that corporations are entitled to *all* the rights that individuals have except where their activities dictate otherwise?" Gabriella said.

"Entitled to them? Perhaps. There are only three constitutional rights the Court has explicitly denied corporations – the right to vote, the fifth amendment right against self-incrimination, and privileges and immunities. An additional two constitutional rights remain somewhat open questions with respect to corporations – the second amendment right to keep and bear arms and the eighth amendment proscription against excessive fines. Even so, I contend that these anomalies are not because of the corporate identity, but rather, because of impracticability or impossibility of the application or exercise of these rights in the corporate context. So, no bearing on the question of corporate personhood.

"Privileges and immunities are a bit beyond the scope of this discussion so we'll skip it, and begin with the fifth amendment right against self-incrimination: The logic behind the Courts refusal to recognize this right in the corporate context is that it is a liberty interest. Because a corporation cannot be incarcerated, its liberty cannot be at stake in a criminal trial. Thus, because a corporation cannot be subject to the harm the right protects against, the right is essentially moot as applied to corporations.

"Then there's the right against excessive fines. So far, the appellate courts have avoided the issue, viewing it as a question of the reasonableness of punitive damages which courts of general jurisdiction are in a better position to evaluate in light of the fact that incarceration of a corporation is not an available deterrent to corporate misconduct.

"The right to keep and bear arms is even murkier. The courts have upheld all sorts of firearm regulations both corporate and individual, but it is not clear to me that there is any meaningful distinction between the effects. I'll leave further comment on that to the law professors.

"And finally, the right to vote. A North Carolina Court of Appeals case, *Texfi Industries., Inc. v. City of Fayetteville* is demonstrative, though not controlling outside of that state. The issue in that case was whether the City of Fayetteville wrongfully denied a corporation a right to vote in a referendum regarding annexation of the corporation's property by the municipality. The Court upheld the City's right to prevent the corporation from voting, reasoning that, unlike natural persons, corporations could multiply their voting power by merely creating additional subsidiaries, thereby diluting the strength of a natural person's vote to give greater weight to corporate interests.

"The dissent in the *Texfi Industries* case had quite a different view, finding that the right to vote should not be predicated upon the fear of potential abuse because such abuse can be prevented by appropriate legislation. I think this is a common sense view that should be applied to any similar concerns that might arise regarding corporate candidacy."

Gabriella held a hand up as though it were a white flag of surrender. "Okay okay, corporations are people and they have almost every constitutional right *actual* people do. But that still doesn't mean they're qualified to hold electoral office and certainly not the

132

presidency. You know? Being legally a person doesn't make a corporation or even a...person person a citizen. And citizenship is required for candidacy. At least it is for Congress and the Senate and the presidency. As are the minimum age and residency qualifications."

Before Josh could respond, the camera moved in on Gabriella for a close-up. She smiled and said, "That's all the time we have tonight. Tune in to our final segment next week when Josh will answer these remaining questions and offer a few last thoughts on the case for the first corporate president of the United States. As always, thank you for tuning to GABN."

The guests rose to their feet and applauded. Off-screen Josh cupped a hand between his mouth and Ricky's ear and said, "That's your cue to say a few words."

Ricky nodded, and slammed the rest of his scotch. He held a hand up. The hall quieted. "Ladies and gentleman," he said and belched, "thank y'all for coming and for donating to the cause. I'll do my level best see to it y'all get your money's worth." He raised his glass. "See y'all at the Whitehouse!"

A second round of applause followed, this one less than enthusiastic. Then the crowd began to mix and mingle. "Ricky, I've got to run," Josh said. "The president asked me to stop by after we wrapped up here." He nodded toward Gabriella. "Would you mind –?"

"We'll take her home," said Ricky.

Dawn said, "We will?"

"Yes, we will," Ricky said firmly.

Josh nodded something less than a Thank-You and hurried out the door.

Ricky turned when he felt a tap on his shoulder. "Hi, I'm Tom Cole," one of two men standing there said, extending a hand for a handshake, "and this is my brother, Don Cole."

"Good to meet y'all," said Ricky.

Dawn cleared her throat, and elbowed Ricky.

"Oh. And this here is Dr. Dawn Wise."

"Pleasure to meet you, Dr. Wise," the Cole brothers both said.

Tom Cole went on, "Ricky, we just wanted to reintroduce ourselves. We're minority stockholders in Vizion Inc. You probably don't remember us from your company's initial public offering. It's been a long time."

Ricky's eyes began to glaze over from all the booze, and his memory was even foggier than his sight.

Tom slapped him on the back warmly. "I know it's been a long night so we won't keep you but I would like to discuss your policy positions sometime in the near future. I was particularly intrigued by your comment at the news conference about issuing Vizion stock to the public. You might be on to something with that. Sounds a little like a federal version of the concept behind the Texas miracle." He handed Ricky and Dawn both a business card. "Call me."

Chapter 30

After dropping Gabriella off at her apartment, Dawn drove Ricky to Vizion to check on Bernice. Ricky had decided and Dawn had concurred that keeping the dog there where she could be more closely monitored was for the best. Dawn headed to the breakroom and Ricky went to his office where the dog laid in her crate pawing at the goggles strapped around her eyes. "I know those things are a pain." Ricky said, peeling off his suit jacket. Then he reached into the crate and scrubbed her floppy jowls affectionately. "But until I figure out a way to shrink the equipment down to size where it fits into your retinal implants, you've got to wear them to see."

He led the dog into an exam room and unbuckled the goggles and slid them back on Bernice's head. She looked really tired, but something more than that was different about those eyes. "Dawn?" he called out.

"I'll be right there," Ricky heard her say from the breakroom.

Dawn appeared in his office a minute later with a steaming cup of hot cocoa. "You sure you don't want some of this? It'll help you sleep later."

Ricky tapped the side of his bourbon glass. "I've got all the help I need with sleeping right here." He tugged his bowtie off and tossed it on the counter.

"You keep on with the drinking and it's going to put you out permanently," Dawn said. "So what do you need?"

"I'd like you to take a look at Bern's eyes. Something doesn't look right."

Dawn switched on the overhead lamp.

Ricky leaned against the examination table while Dawn got down on a knee and pried the dog's right eyelid up, and then the left. "There's definitely a lot of redness. Other than that, I don't see anything out of the ordinary," she said. "She's probably just tired but I'll call in some antibiotic drops in the morning to be on the safe side. And just so you know, it wouldn't be an issue with the retinal implants after this many months if that's what you're worried about."

Ricky nodded his appreciation and his relief. "So, after that fundraising shindig are you convinced that it's time for a corporate president?"

"If it's Vizion Inc., I'm all in. Assuming our fearless leader can sober up." Dawn laughed. "You know I'm only partly joking. I'd support you in anything you do and I think Josh has made a great case for the candidacy so far. But unless he can magically turn Vizion Inc. the corporate person into Vizion Inc. the *natural born* thirty-five year old corporate American *citizen*, I don't see how the Supreme Court can allow it. Whether it does or doesn't, you're going to have to pull it together if you plan to keep this company going." She leaned against the exam table next to him.

Ricky searched her eyes, whether to measure her thoughts on the candidacy or something else entirely, he was not quite sure. He felt woozy suddenly and almost slipped off the table, but Dawn broke his fall.

Not every day an opportunity literally falls into your arms, she thought as their lips met. "Mm," she breathed, "I always imagined you'd be a good kisser." She shoved him down on the exam table, straddled him, and ripped his shirt open. Buttons bounced across the floor.

Ricky felt even dizzier than before now and his double vision as Dawn leaned over for another kiss caused him to see four breasts that her evening gown could barely contain barreling down at him.

She stopped suddenly. "Did you hear something?" she whispered.

Josh stepped into the exam room. "Whoops." He did a quick turnabout.

Dawn leapt off Ricky and straightened her dress.

Ricky swung his legs over the side of the exam table and tumbled off it, then picked himself up from the floor, tripped over Bernice, then picked himself up again. "Could you take Bern back to her crate?"

"Uh-huh." Dawn nodded.

Ricky staggered down the hall to Josh's office, holding his buttonless shirt together.

"Sorry about that," Josh said, "I didn't realize you and Dr. Dawn were –"

Ricky waved a hand in a downward motion like he was swatting at an invisible insect. "It's not what you think," he said through short and choppy breaths.

"You sound like a cheating lover caught in the act." Josh chuckled. "Hey, it's none of my business what two consenting adults do. I'm just sorry I interrupted." He couldn't wait to review the security tape for that exam room. One could always find a purpose for a scandalous tape.

Ricky was too drunk to explain. But heck, he didn't owe Josh any explanations for this or anything else. If he owed him anything at all after Josh's engagement to Gabriella, it was a swift kick in the rear, or better yet a termination notice. No. Firing him would be a bad idea. As both an engineer and a lawyer, Josh's value to the company was substantial – especially the legal part in light of the Attorney General's new challenge to the company's candidacy. Rick doubted any other lawyer on the planet would risk his reputation defending Vizion in that. "What are you doing here this time of night?"

"I thought you'd want to hear about my meeting with the president," Josh said.

"I assumed that was confidential."

"It is." Josh grinned. "He wanted my advice on the new Texas developments."

Ricky raised an eyebrow. "New developments? What kind of developments?"

"Apparently the Texans have created a new border patrol sector in the annexed territory extending all the way up to south Dodge City; at least on paper they have. And there's rumors they're actively preparing to move that sector off paper and onto the ground in the near future."

"You're kidding."

"No, sir. According to the president's sources, the plan includes building a wall partitioning Dodge City at the Arkansas River. A fellow by the name of Juan Rodriguez, the new Texas border patrol chief, will be overseeing the construction personally."

Ricky's face paled and he leaned against the wall to steady himself.

Josh tapped him on the shoulder. "Are you alright?"

"Fine. A little too much to drink maybe. So what does it mean?"

"Actually, this is very good news for Vizion. The president wants twenty battalions of the new 3.0 harmonizers for DHS. At two eyes per unit, that translates into a massive order of our camera eyes. Vizion Inc.'s economy is about to boom like never before, my friend."

The news of Juan, a man like a brother to Ricky, on the opposing side of what could well become the frontline made the prospect of an armed conflict between the U.S. and Texas all the more troubling. "So war, then?"

"War's illegal, an impediment to commerce," Josh said. "And the DHS brass seems to think that even the domestic equivalent of war might be averted by a large enough show of force. That's why the harmonizer deployments along the Red River and the order for so many new harmonizer 3.0s. We've got a problem though, a technical problem. You got a minute to take a look?"

Ricky checked his watch, pleased that his vision had returned enough to normal that he could actually read it. Almost midnight. "It's late."

"C'mon, it won't take long." Josh pulled a flash-drive out of the center drawer of his desk. "This is a video demonstrating the problem I mentioned. Let's go to the conference room."

Ricky ignored the cell phone ringing in his pocket as they made their way down the hall.

Josh inserted the flash-drive into the computer in the conference room and moved the curser on the monitor to select the video file. Then he and Ricky both swiveled their chairs toward a viewing screen encompassing an entire wall from floor to ceiling.

The video appeared on the screen in three distinct sections. The section on the left depicted a company of human DHS troops wearing goggles and marching in formation in desert terrain. The section next to it showed a snow-covered field where a company of marching harmonizers' movements exactly mimicked those of the troops. The far right section contained hundreds of images, each of them confined to a small square frame of its own.

Ricky scratched his chin. "Levi showed me this, but not on such a massive scale. It must take a good bit of computing power to accomplish all that."

"That it does." Josh nodded. "But it's Cloud based so the serious crunching is done at the mainframe, not in the harmonizers themselves."

Ricky's eyes widened. "That's it!" He jumped from his chair and began to pace.

"What?" Josh followed him back and forth across the conference room, almost at a jog to keep up with his brisk pace. "That's what, Ricky?"

Ricky stopped suddenly and Josh bumped into him. "Sorry."

"The retinal implants I designed work well," Ricky said, his speech forced with excitement, "but obviously those are of no help where the entire eye is damaged or destroyed. So, as you know, I'm confident the software I created for that kind of situation will replicate the neural code required for sight. Of course it still needs to be tested and probably some bugs worked out but that can't happen as long as that ban is in place –"

Josh interrupted. "You're rambling. What's the ban got to do with the Cloud?"

"Nothing. I'm just thinking out loud," Ricky went on. "So, the problem with the neural code software is that it requires so much disk space that it isn't really mobile. Artificial eye transplant recipients would be forced to spend their lives sitting at a computer. At least to see they would if... I contemplated a scooter setup with a battery powered computer compartment on it or something along those lines. That would give them some mobility, but they couldn't ...The point is, by using Cloud technology, digitizing the code and distributing it by satellite, none of that would be necessary. And no new infrastructure would be needed either because I could piggyback off our harmonizer sight system. With a small microcomputer implant to act as a client for the wireless connection, artificial eye transplant recipients could live full lives with one hundred percent mobility."

"Good," Josh said less than enthusiastically. "So, about that problem I mentioned. The technology works fine except for –"

"That's it?" Ricky said. "I tell you we're a giant leap closer to curing the blind and giving them a hundred percent mobility and all you can say is, *Good*? Are you thinking about what this could mean for Gabriella?"

"Sure I am, Ricky but if we don't solve the problem I'm trying to show you, Vizion could be out of business and that would mean an end to everything including the artificial sight project." Josh aimed a laser pointer at the section of the screen with the small frames. "Now, these images represent what each of the harmonizer pilots – in this case, the troops on the left – see through their goggles. As you know, the images are collected by the cameras – the harmonizers' eyes – or by satellite cameras in the newer models. Then they're bounced back to the server, modified as needed with overlays and so on, then routed to the pilots' CPUs via the network where they're viewed on monitors or through goggles, depending on the model.

"What should happen is every pilot should see what's within the field of vision of the harmonizer he's operating, right? But that isn't the case here. Note that each of the images is the same. Every pilot is seeing the same thing. That tells us that we have a distribution issue. All of our pilots except for one may as well be blind."

"That is a problem," Ricky said. "Must be an issue at either the server or the router, or both. Unless there's some sort of interference in the wireless transmissions. I assume these are 2.0s since they are relying on line of sight. Are you having this issue with the 3.0s?"

"Only when they're on line of sight backup," Josh said.

Ricky's thoughts reverted to remotely processing neural code using the Cloud.

"Could be a connection issue with the 2.0s' cameras," Josh said. "Or a technical glitch with the signal somewhere, as you say. But there is one other possibility. The system could have been hacked. Ricky, are you listening to me?"

"Yes. Sorry. What did you say?"

"I said the system could have been hacked, sabotaged."

"Yeah, I guess it could have," Ricky said, trying to show interest.

Dawn appeared in the conference room, avoiding eye contact with either of the two men, but otherwise acting as if the incident in the exam room had not occurred. "Ricky, Levi just called. Max passed away."

"Oh no," Josh said, his sympathetic tone clashing with the relieved expression on his face.

Dawn said, "Apparently he went into the ER complaining of a severe headache, and an hour later, he was dead. They won't know the exact cause until after an autopsy."

"I suppose Levi will want a state sponsored funeral for him," Ricky remarked coldly.

Dawn glared at him, incensed at his callousness. Considering his obnoxious performance at the fundraiser earlier, she shouldn't have been surprised and she regretted her earlier moment of weakness in the exam room. "Levi also asked me to tell you that he scheduled a virtual visitation session for you with Chick tomorrow morning." She stormed out of the conference room.

"Thanks," Ricky hollered after her.

Josh said, "I'll let Gabriella know about Max."

Chapter 31

Ricky's excitement about using the Cloud to distribute the neural code from a mainframe kept him awake all night in bed staring at the ceiling and thinking. Assuming he could get any existing kinks worked out of the software, the next job – one bordering on impossible so far – would be persuading Dawn to violate that ban and perform artificial eye transplants on one of the lab animals. There had to be a way to convince her. Hmm. Brutus? Despite being by far the most temperamental and generally obnoxious of all the research animals, Brutus was a model ape with Dawn. Watching him interact with her was like watching a child with a loving mother. Might she bend the rules if he suggested Brutus for the procedure? If it meant a chance to give Brutus the gift of sight?

He checked his watch. 8:30 AM, a half hour until his appointment to see Chick. He glanced at the half empty bottle of bourbon on his nightstand, then attached his lower legs and went to the kitchen and chugged a cup of rancid coffee from several days ago before hiking over to the visitation center.

Ricky examined the sign on the glass door:

Global Video Visitation Inc.
Keeping the World Connected
A subsidiary of Leviathan Corp

Inside, an attendant directed him to a cubicle with a computer monitor and a headset. "Thank you," Ricky said, and followed the login instructions.

A minute later Chick appeared on the monitor, wild-eyed and gaunt with a Band-Aid on his right temple and a gray cinderblock wall behind him. "Man, am I glad to see you," he said.

Ricky said, "I'm sorry I got you into this mess, Chick, but –"

"Don't be sorry. This is something I been needing. I mean, the first couple days was rough, but I ain't never felt so good since they gave me that harmonization vaccination. Makes you see the world in a whole new way. Everything is more colorful, sort of tinted like, and it's –"

"Harmonious?" said Ricky, wondering what in the heck a harmonization vaccine was?

Chick's wild eyes went distant like he was looking at Ricky but seeing someone or some thing else entirely. Maybe there was a problem with the video connection. Ricky thought about the harmonizers he and Josh viewed last night and how they all saw the same thing – something in another's line of sight.

"Yeah, harmonious," Chick said too agreeably. "That's a good word for it."

Ricky felt concerned creases tightening across his forehead.

Chick's demeanor suddenly changed. And so did his eyes again, as if Ricky were coming back into focus. "Hey I got you-know-who's you-know-what."

"What? Who? Chick, you're not making any sense," Ricky said.

"You know who," said Chick.

"Yeah, you already said that, but who is you-know-who?

Chick rolled his eyes. "You know who you-know-who is. Who is it got me in here?"

"Jeez, I feel like I'm stuck in an old *Abbott and Castello* episode,'" said Ricky. "Ooh. You mean Max?"

"Dang it, Ricky, why'd you have to go and say it. You know they're monitoring every word." Chick shook his head violently as if he was trying to dislodge something stuck solidly in his ear canal. "Hey what happened to the harmony?" He was clearly not talking to Ricky now.

Whatever's in that harmonization vaccine must be potent, Ricky thought. He decided not to risk aggravating the situation by telling Chick Max was dead. "Who is they?"

"Big brother, who else?"

Ricky sighed. "Listen, you need to pull it together or they're going to keep you in there."

"I need to pull it together?" Chick shook his head. "You one to talk."

"Let's focus on you for now," Ricky said.

"Be better if you focus on getting yourself over to wherever they towed my ice cream cart and grab what I got for you," said Chick.

A timer appeared onscreen, counting down from ten.

"What? Oh. Are you saying you got the DNA sample?" Nine, Eight.

Chick's eyes went distant again. "Oh, now that's better. Such a pretty pretty world."

Seven, Six, Five, Four, Three, Two, One. The screen went blank and a computerized voice that sounded eerily like a harmonizer said, "Your session has expired."

"Dang it." Ricky rubbed his face, thinking. Where would they have taken Chick's ice cream cart? …The impound lot. Of course.

Chapter 32

Ricky walked the mile and a half from the visitation center to the impound lot, counting dozens of harmonizer patrol units along the way. The government must have been serious about phasing out human police officers.

In the impound office a wide-bodied towering six-foot tall woman with a triple chin, beer gut, bad hair, bad tats, a nametag that said *Sis*, and long fake fingernails painted lime green leaned on a counter shielded from unhappy customers by a bulletproof glass window. She had just taken a drag off a cigarette. Behind her, a *Helen for President* campaign spot blared from a television, Helen declaring, "If I'm elected president, my first act in office will be to sign an executive order banning the American flag. No longer will the citizens of the world be subjected to that symbol of slavery, bigotry, oppression, homophobia, xenophobia, and corporate greed."

Helen has lost her mind, Ricky thought.

Sis dropped the cigarette when she saw him in suit and tie. Regulators always wore suit and tie. She quickly ground the burning cigarette out under the toe of her army style boot and waved both hands frantically to clear the smoke. "Sorry, burnt my lunch. You know." Her face turned ripe red. "It's not what it looks like. I wasn't smoking."

Ricky seized on the opportunity for a little humor. It had been far too long since he'd had a good laugh. "I'll take your word for that, but," he pointed to a black-market soda pop can on the counter, "I'm afraid I'm going to have to confiscate that and have the fructose content tested."

Sis's eyes widened with panic.

Ricky laughed.

A look of relieved annoyance swept Sis's face as she realized who he was. "Say, you're no regulator, you're that corporation candidate or whatever. Aren't you?"

Ricky grinned.

"And a comedian, to boot." She lit another cigarette. "What can I do for you?"

"I'm looking for an ice cream cart."

Sis pecked at a computer keyboard one key at time with her cumbersome long nails and after five or six minutes she looked up at Ricky. "We got one. I need five-hunerd-forty-five dollars and proof of ownership." She took a long drag off the cigarette.

"Five forty-five!" Ricky said. "How long has it been here?"

"Long enough so's the bill's five-hunerd and forty-five dollars. Sorry. I just work here, I don't make the prices."

"Fine." Ricky reached into his pocket for his cash clip and peeled off six one-hundred dollar bills and slid them into the stainless steel payment slot beneath the window.

"And how about the proof of ownership?" Sis said.

Ricky slipped another hundred into the slot. "That proof enough?"

"That'll do it, Mr. Franklin." Sis smiled, and tucked the bill into her bra and put the rest in the cash register, then pushed a button on the wall.

Ricky heard a gate creaking open outside.

"Past the office here, first row to your right," Sis said. "You'll find that ice cream cart near the rear."

"Thanks," said Ricky.

As soon as he reached the cart, he opened the refrigeration compartment and pulled out a cigar butt. "Hmm. This must be it." He dropped the butt into a plastic baggy and stuffed it in his jacket pocket.

If Ricky's hunch was right the DNA on that butt would prove dearly departed Max's involvement in the unsolved rape cases, including the one that drove Gabriella's sister to kill herself. Not that that would fix everything. Ricky was all too aware that exposing yet another betrayal to Gabriella would not exonerate him from his role in the accident. But hopefully it would give her some level of closure on the issue of her sister's death.

Although not complete closure.

That would require learning the identity of the source of the other DNA recovered from the victims. Ricky thought about that for a minute. According to Gabriella, the other party was a relative of Max's, assuming Max's DNA matched one of the samples from the victims like he expected. Yet Max had no living relative besides Levi. Well, whatever the case, this was a start. And if Ricky could convince Dawn to test the artificial eyes on Brutus, and if they actually worked... He squeezed in behind the steering wheel of the ice cream cart and pedaled out of the impound yard.

Chapter 33

"Chick was right," Ricky muttered to himself through teeth clattering in his head so violently that even his thoughts rattled by the time he got to Gabriella's apartment. "It's definitely too dang cold to be tooling all over town in this ice cream cart."

He knocked on the door. "Gabby, it's Ricky."

Gabriella sat up on the sofa where she'd slept, and massaged her temples, her head throbbing like a burly lumberjack had landed an ax between her eyes. "Oh God that hurts." She remembered now why she'd never been much of a drinker.

"Gabby, open up. I got something for you," she heard Ricky's muffled voice say from outside the door.

"Go away, I don't want anything from you," she yelled back and when she did it felt like that imaginary lumberjack landed another blow. "Why don't you run along and go play with your sexpot doctor girl and leave me alone."

"Don't be ridiculous, Gabby. Dawn's just a colleague. And if it makes you feel any better, I don't think she even likes me anymore."

"That makes two of us," Gabriella yelled back.

144

Ricky blinked as fuzzy visions of what happened in the exam room last night trickled into his consciousness. If Gabriella was this bent out of shape about him bringing Dawn as his guest to the fundraiser he could only imagine how she would react if Josh told her about that. Or had he already? "Gabby, did Josh say something to you?"

Still nothing.

Ricky dropped the subject. "Gabby, I got the DNA sample."

A few seconds later he heard the deadbolt unlatch.

The door slowly opened and Gabriella appeared in plaid flannel pajamas, her hair pulled back tight in a ponytail revealing a few strands of silver that had cropped up only recently at her hairline. Shadowy half-moons swelled beneath her eyes. Her eyebrows were perfect like always.

She held an open hand out but didn't say a word.

Ricky handed Gabriella the baggie. "I hope this helps," he said, his teeth still clattering, "that's a cigar butt from Max's ashtray." He wanted desperately to tell her that his artificial eyes would be tested soon even though he wasn't sure that was true. And he wanted to share his idea about using the Cloud to give transplant recipients one hundred percent mobility. "Gabby, there's something else."

"I don't need to hear any more of your BS, Ricky. Go lie to someone else." She closed the door, then pressed her ear against it and listened until the clickety-clack of Ricky's boots faded to silence as he shambled down the steps. "This is where the cowboy rides away," she whispered to herself. She swallowed a couple of Tylenols, returned to the sofa, and sat and fiddled with the baggie that presumably contained the evidence to finally bring at least one of the monsters responsible for her sister's death to justice. But Max? Why did it have to be Max? And how would this be justice given that Max was dead now.

Chapter 34

The mileage from Gabriella's apartment to Vizion to pick up Bernice and then back to the cottage had been close to thirty miles. Ricky glanced at the chopper tied down in the yard, imagining the heat from the engine coursing through the cockpit and thawing his brittle fingers.

On his way up the driveway he stopped at the mailbox and scooped the contents out with the balls of his frozen hands and tucked it under an arm. Then he went inside and sat at the dining table. He tore open his carbon credit statement with his teeth and it pleased him to see that he had enough credits left to legally burn a few more logs in the fireplace this winter. Just the thought of that seemed to encourage the feeling back into his fingers.

Bernice laid at his feet and pawed at her goggles.

Next, Ricky opened a notice from the Department of Health and Human Services informing him that failure to submit proof of having received the new harmonization vaccination upon filing the current year's tax return would result in a hefty noncompliance penalty along with a two-year commitment to a harmonization center. That disturbed him, especially after seeing what that vaccine had done to Chick. He set the notice aside and perused the monthly grocery rations flyer – Leviathan Farms advertised a special on eggplant for $39.99 a pound.

Last in the stack of mail was a legal-sized envelope from the Law Office of Joshua Horowitz. Ricky figured it must be something about the Attorney General's lawsuit against Vizion's run for the presidency. He unclasped the envelope and fished out a fancily embossed postcard:

PLEASE JOIN US FOR OUR ENGAGEMENT PARTY
Joshua Horowitz
And
Gabriella Meir
FRIDAY, APRIL 1, 2028
6:30 PM
THE DODGE HOUSE, DODGE CITY, KS
RSVP to Joshua Horowitz@Horowitzlaw.com

Ricky's chest tightened. Gabriella was really going through with this? He felt something else in the envelope. He shook it, and the silver necklace jingled out onto the table. The pain in his chest worsened. "Oh, Gabby." He shuffled to his bedroom and reached for the bottle of bourbon on his nightstand there…No. No. He grabbed the keys to the chopper. "Come on, girl," he called to Bernice. "Let's go to the office and see if we can't persuade Dawn to our way of thinking on testing those artificial eyes. Sitting around here sulking ain't gonna help nothing."

Bernice stumbled along behind him and he hoisted her up and buckled her into the copilot seat. Then he did his preflight inspection and climbed onboard and fired up the engine. He scanned the gauges and instruments. Everything looked good, except the oil pressure. He tapped a finger on the gauge. He'd have maintenance take a look at it when he got to Vizion.

"Here we go." He lifted off and after a relatively smooth ten minutes in flight at an altitude of fifteen hundred feet AGL he began his descent to the helipad at Vizion. At seven-hundred feet, he saw the windsock flapping erratically around the pole, and decided to take the chopper back up to give the gust a minute to clear. He shoved the throttle in.

The engine sputtered and the descent continued.

"Crap." He glided in over the helipad.

The stall horn blared as he worked the throttle pointlessly.

He glanced at the altimeter – three hundred feet. Smoke seeped from beneath the instrument panel.

Nose down, but not too much.

Three-hundred feet.

A burst of wind strafed the tail, spinning the chopper around. "Hang on, Bern!" The helicopter slammed sideways into the helipad.

Chapter 35

Few attended the private memorial Levi arranged for Max at the Baxter mansion.

The two harmonizers stationed there stood motionless behind the casket with artificial eyelids shut, temporarily deactivated in the interest of privacy.

Helen and Gabriella approached, arm in arm.

"Such a pity," Helen said. She pulled back her black veil and leaned over and kissed Max's cold forehead.

Gabriella dabbed at a tear, mixed emotions coursing through her like adrenaline.

"I guess he's all yours now," Helen told Dr. Shultz, who appeared to be in charge of the paid pallbearers waiting impatiently to load the casket into the hearse for transport to the crematorium.

"My condolences, Madam." Shultz closed the lid.

Helen took Gabriella by the arm and guided her into the den where Levi and Josh sat solemnly across from one another smoking cigars in silence. Flames roared in the fireplace.

The two men stood and hugged the women.

"Would you mind taking Gabriella home?" Josh said to Helen. "Levi and I need to discuss Max's estate."

"Of course," Helen said.

"Thank you."

"Could we go by the hospital along the way to see about Ricky?" Gabriella said.

"Gabriella darling, he's in a coma. There isn't anything to see about."

"I know, but –"

Josh intervened. "Don't be an idiot, Gabriella. You're blind because of him. Let karma have its way."

Helen wrapped an arm around Gabriella's waste. "Josh is right, dear. Ricky got what he deserves and it's just fortunate he didn't harm anyone else this time. Now come along, I'm taking you home."

Josh noticed a slight moistening in Levi's eyes after Helen and Gabriella left. Tears? Was it possible the old man was capable of feeling? No. Must be a reaction to the cigar smoke.

"It could have been prevented," Levi said. "An aneurysm is easily detectable by an MRA. But the fool was too stubborn to seek my assistance with a waiver to get around the new age limits on such tests." His eyes transformed back to their familiar cold blue steel. "Arrogance can be lethal."

"That it can," said Josh.

After a protracted blink, contemplating the conviction with which Josh agreed with his comment on arrogance, Levi said, "You don't suppose my supporting Vizion in the election struck such a blow to Max's ego that he'd rather died than asked me for help, and that's why he never told me about the headaches?"

"Doubtful," Josh said.

"Was it my supporting Vizion that made him hesitant to let me know about his problem? Surely Max knew that whether he won the election himself or Vizion won, either way the presidency would still be his – or ours, rather. His and mine, I mean. The business end will be mine as always but the frills and the glamour, that sort of thing would have been his."

"How would the presidency have been Max's if he lost?" said Josh.

Levi said, "He'd have had a position on Vizion's board of directors, that's how. I'd have seen to that."

Dr. Shultz appeared in the den and said, "The body's ready for transport."

Levi exhaled something just short of a defeated sigh. "Well, I suppose under the circumstances it's time I met my other heirs."

"Now?" Dr. Shultz said.

Josh gnawed nervously on his half-smoked cigar.

"Yes, doctor, now," said Levi sternly.

"Right this way then." Dr. Shultz shuffled out of the den with Levi following curiously.

"They're here?" Levi said when they came to the cellar door. "They certainly must be very quiet."

Dr. Shultz nodded and they continued down the steps.

At the bottom, the doctor twisted the dial to the combination lock on a walk-in cooler tucked beneath the cellar stairs. The door hissed open, releasing a frosty cloud. He slipped a pair of insulated gloves on and went inside, and a minute later reemerged with a steel container that looked similar to a safe deposit box. "Here they are." He handed the container to a decidedly puzzled looking Levi.

Levi lifted the lid and peered through the haze rising off the liquid nitrogen at the dozen or so vials inside, each of them labeled "Human Eggs," along with a donor's name – except for one marked sperm/Levi Baxter. His eyes narrowed to slits. "What is the meaning of this?" He heard footfalls.

"The existence of a qualified naturally conceived, if somewhat unconventionally delivered, male heir to your bloodline rendered fertilization of the eggs unnecessary, sir."

Josh stepped off the stairs onto the cellar floor. "Why the long face, *Father*?" I thought you would be pleased to have a full grown ready-to-go descendent to perpetuate your gene pool and your business interests."

Levi's gaze shifted from Josh to Dr. Shultz, then back to Josh again. "I am not at all amused by whatever game you two are playing." He closed the container and tucked it under his arm.

"This is no game," Josh said. "Helen had it wrong when she told you I was female. And as you can see for yourself, you all's attempt at exterminating me didn't quite succeed."

149

"Pardon me?"

"Forcing a Catholic doctor to perform a late term abortion and not following up wasn't one of your brighter moves, *Father*," Josh said tauntingly.

"You mean –"

"Yes. I survived the procedure. And after delivering me, my would-be executioner raised me, saw to that I got a fine education. When I was old enough, he told me the truth."

Levi held a hand to his chest. "Well then, as a child of Helen, there would be no question your royal bloodline goes all the way back to our beloved evil Queen Jezebel." He chuckled. "Undoubtedly of far better breeding than those handpicked for me by Max and Dr. Shultz here."

"Whatever you think of my genetics, it'll have to do," Josh sneered. "I'm the only game in town now."

Levi nodded. "So you've known all along about the egg collecting?"

"Don't play coy with me. I had no choice and you know it."

"You're mistaken ol' boy. This is the first I've heard of your involvement."

Josh frowned. "Do you expect me to believe you didn't know Max blackmailed me into helping with your sick scheme? Well, I don't believe that any more than I believe you didn't know what else Max was doing to those girls."

"Blackmailed you? Whatever for?" Levi said. His thoughts shifted from the current allegation back to Max as a teenager, how he'd been forced to have young Max sterilized after he molested a neighbor girl. Levi had also paid the girl's parents a handsome sum to keep it to themselves. Without a son capable of siring children, Levi had no alternative but to see to it himself that his bloodline continued and that his seed wasn't wasted on subpar genetic mates.

"I won't say I wasn't aware of Max's propensity for acting upon his compulsions," Levi admitted, "but I certainly did not approve of it. Nor do I approve of unwarranted blackmail. Well, whatever you've done, it doesn't matter. If you are indeed my blood, we should be discussing your future, not the past."

Josh reached into his pocket and pulled out a Glock nine millimeter and snapped the slide back, dropping a round into the chamber. "I'm tempted to send you into the afterlife right now."

Levi sighed. "That's a smart-gun, Josh, and it's been deactivated. The government deactivated all of them before the ink dried on the twenty-eighth amendment granting citizens the right to be free of gun violence. Didn't you get the memo?" He calmly eased the pistol out of Josh's hand. "Now, if it's as you say, you have my assurances that I will make it up to you. Perhaps I'll start with making you CEO of Vizion. I assume you're aware that I've acquired controlling interest."

Josh smiled. "That would be a good start, but I'm not sure how Ricky will feel about it. When he recovers, I mean."

"Do you suppose he will recover?" Levi said.

Chapter 36

Dawn waited in Ricky's room in the intensive care unit at Leviathan General Hospital until medical staff wheeled him back in after yet another CT scan. It encouraged her to see that he no longer required a ventilator. "So, how's he doing?" she asked the nurse on duty.

"The swelling in his brain has gone down. But he's obviously still unresponsive. The hospitalist will be in after while. He'll give you details about what to expect going forward."

I'm a neurosurgeon, Dawn thought, I don't need some hospitalist to tell me what to expect with a brain trauma patient. What I need is information. She scanned the various monitors until the staff left, then she fished her stethoscope out of her satchel and listened to Ricky's chest. He seemed to be breathing normally. That was good. She pried his eyelids open one at a time and shined her keychain flashlight into each eye. Nobody home.

"Ricky, if you can feel this, wiggle your toes or blink." She ran a fingertip down his left arm, then his right. Nothing. She moved to the end of the bed to repeat the stimulus on his feet. "Oh yeah, titanium. So much for wiggling toes."

Dawn settled into the chair at his bedside. "Ricky, I didn't mean to be so nasty the last time we talked. It's just that, well, you were being such a jerk," she said to him. "You've been acting badly ever since that news report about the car accident came out. And, I guess this is probably not the best time to tell you, but I understand how you feel about Gabriella and I'm sorry if what we almost did made things even worse between you two. I was lonely. It was a mistake. And I don't love you... What I mean is I do love you, but not like that."

She picked up the television remote and scanned through the channels to GABN. The last segment of Gabriella and Josh's series on the Citizens United case and corporate candidacy had just begun. If that didn't stimulate a response out of Ricky, nothing would. She turned the volume up as loud it would go – which was not very loud at all.

Judging from the befuddled expression on Gabriella's face on the television screen, Dawn assumed Josh must have just ambushed her with another of his multifarious legal enigmas.

"So you're saying that the age, residency, and citizenship qualifications in the Constitution violate a corporation's first amendment right to free speech...which is... also in the Constitution?" Gabriella said. She looked like she might start pulling her hair out in bunches any minute now. "You're saying the Constitution violates itself?"

Josh chuckled. "Actually, yes, in this situation. And that's one reason why, in my view, the Supreme Court cannot rule on the case against Vizion. It's a political question."

Gabriella rubbed the back of her neck, fatigue clearly setting in. "So if the Supreme Court doesn't sort this out, then who will?"

"Congress," Josh said.

Dawn thought she heard Ricky murmur.

"Ricky!" She jolted up from her seat and cupped his face in her hands.

"And if Congress determines that corporations must satisfy the same substantive qualifications as an individual to hold office?" Gabriella pressed.

Ricky's neck fell limp in Dawn's hands. She eased his head back onto the pillow, then whispered in his ear, "Ricky, you're missing Josh and Gabriella's last segment on corporate candidacy."

No response at all.

Josh continued confidently, "If Congress were to decide corporations must satisfy the qualifications, I believe Vizion Inc. can do it. Let me explain: The qualifications for president are natural born citizenship, age of at least thirty-five, and U.S. residency for at least fourteen years. Right?"

Gabriella nodded. "Right."

"Okay," said Josh. "Before I go any further, I'd like to point out that these three qualifications do not describe what one must *not* be to hold the office, nor do they specify any particular identity requirement. Rather, they simply refer to three attributes one must possess. So, in analyzing whether a corporation is capable of possessing these attributes, I looked not only at the literal text of the qualifications, but also at the purpose of them."

Dawn settled back into the chair, one eye on Ricky, the other on the television, her interest piqued as Josh proceeded.

"Let's take age first. Literally, for an individual natural person this is calculated as thirty-five years from the day of leaving the mother's womb, as noted on a birth certificate. In corporate terms, the charter is analogous to a birth certificate, so its qualifying age for president should be calculated literally as at least thirty-five years from the date of incorporation.

"As for purpose, it's believed that the drafters of the Constitution had two objectives in prescribing age qualifications. One, to prevent royal-like succession by minor children of wealthy office holders – no boy kings, in other words. And secondly, to exclude those who lack the wisdom and leadership qualities presumably attainable only through a certain number of years of life experience. Well, royal-like succession is no less constrained by a thirty-five year age minimum for a corporation than for an individual, so nothing more need be said about that.

"On the second point, however, the wisdom and leadership qualities the typical thirty-five year old corporation has to draw from without reaching beyond itself far exceeds what an individual can access in and of him or her self. Consider Vizion Inc., for example. The age of any one of Vizion's senior managers or directors surpasses thirty-five years. Collectively, they possess centuries of knowledge and experience in planning, execution, and management. Talk about wisdom and leadership qualities.

"Moving on to residency – the purpose of this qualification is to increase the likelihood that office holders are familiar with the interests of the people they represent. As we saw earlier, for president one must have been a U.S. resident for at least fourteen years. Remember that at the founding of the nation most men of English decent – the only men with any real prospect of becoming president – thirty-five years old or more would not have been natural born, so U.S.

citizen at the time of the adoption of the Constitution and resident of at least fourteen years sufficed. But I digress. For House of Representatives, the requirement is twenty-five years old or older, seven years as a U.S. citizen, and an inhabitant of the state chosen from. For Senate, it's thirty years old or older, U.S. citizen for nine years or more, and an inhabitant of the state chosen from.

"Notice that for the legislative offices, residency of a particular state is not required, only habitation. According to the Supreme Court, it appears little more than an address in the state from which one is chosen will suffice – see the 1995 case of *U.S. Term Limits, Inc. v. Thornton.*

"Getting back to residency – according to the federal rules of civil procedure, a corporation is a resident of any jurisdiction in which it is subject to personal jurisdiction, including but not limited to its place of incorporation or its primary place of business. Without splitting legal hairs here, this means a domestic corporation will definitely be a resident of some state, and a resident of any state within the United States is a resident of the U.S.

"So, is there any reason a domestic corporation with the requisite number of years as a resident would be less familiar with the interests of the people than an individual natural person? I think not.

"And that brings us to citizenship. The presidential qualifications clause requires natural born citizenship, whereas the qualification clauses for House of Representatives and senate require only citizenship, without qualifiers. Hence, we know that in the U.S. at least two types of national citizenship are possible.

"Based on historic documents, it is believed that the core purpose of the citizen qualifications is to ensure that office holders have sufficient allegiance to the jurisdictions they represent. Representatives and senators for example, owe their allegiance to the district or state they represent. The president's allegiance, however, must be to the entire nation. So, the natural-born requirement for the presidency is believed to be an attempt to bolster that broader allegiance to the highest degree possible.

"Because allegiance and a literal understanding of what it means to be a citizen are inextricably intertwined, we'll examine them together. Broken down to its lowest common denominators, the concept of the citizen refers to a four-way relational contract between the citizen

154

attribute, the self to whom the attribute is attached, the government, and the other selves within the society and the body politic.

"Under the classical conception, a citizen possesses not only the rights of the whole, but the virtues necessary to fulfill the responsibilities owed to the whole and to himself in exchange for the individual citizen's protection. This conceptualization – which has survived into modernity – dates all the way back to ancient Greece.

"Aristotle saw the state, or nation, as a composite, like any other whole made up of many parts; those parts being the citizens who compose it. He likened political and social citizenship to the communitarian structure aboard a sailing vessel – all sailors (citizens) are specialized in their tasks aboard ship; as such, they are indispensable members of a whole without which the community cannot function.

"This construction deeply influenced contemporary philosophers such as John Locke who in turn profoundly influenced the founding fathers of the United States – perhaps most notably, Thomas Jefferson, who drafted the Declaration of Independence. The continuation of this concept into the American idea of a citizen is also evident in the courts. For example in *Afroyim v. Rusk*, Supreme Court Justice Black, following Aristotle's language, declared, 'the citizenry is the country and the country is the citizenry.'

"So, what am I saying? I'm saying that Aristotle's timeless concept of the citizen as one part of the whole entitled to protection of itself *from* and *by* the whole in exchange for its indispensable contribution to that whole is fundamental to the American concept of the citizen.

"But the American construction of citizenship broadens this concept to equal membership and incorporation into the body politic – citizens as equal members of the society are also equal members of the political community.

"Note, as I said before, that the attribute of citizen does not describe any particular type of identity, but, rather, represents a contract between a community and a member of that community. The contract doesn't describe any particular identity either, it describes the member's relationship to the community.

"Summing up in the simplest of terms, it might be said that to be a citizen is synonymous with being a shareholder, a shareholder in the community or the state – in the case of the U.S., a state which exists only by the consent its shareholders, shareholders from whom and by whom, the managers and directors are chosen.

"How, then, does one acquire the citizen attribute in the United States?

"According to the fourteenth amendment of the Constitution, all persons born or naturalized in the United States and subject to the jurisdiction thereof are citizens. So, here we see two ways the citizen attribute attaches – by birth or by operation of law.

"An alien – without getting into the weeds, a noncitizen of the U.S – acquires the citizen attribute in the United States by operation of law through the process of naturalization as set forth by the Naturalization Act which was created by Congress pursuant to article one section eight of the Constitution, which empowers Congress to establish a uniform process for granting citizenship to those who are not citizens by birth.

"Although there have been several versions of the Naturalization Act since the first one in 1790, they all have three things in common: One, a requirement that an applicant first reside on U.S. soil for a prescribed number of years. Two, a requirement that an applicant demonstrate good moral character – or, as Aristotle put it, *virtue*. And lastly, a requirement that an applicant pledge allegiance to the United States and in some instances denounce allegiance to any other sovereign. All of this, of course, is consistent with the purpose of the citizen qualification.

"Now, unlike naturalized citizens, a *natural born* citizen – a citizen by birth – must be born within a place where the sovereign is at the time in full possession and exercise of his power, and the party must also at his or her birth derive protection from, and consequently owe obedience or allegiance to, the sovereign. Here, we see the purpose again, as well as an overview of the relationship.

"Those born on U.S. soil to foreign ambassadors or enemies of the United States are not natural born citizens because they are not subject to U.S. jurisdiction. A presumptive conflict of allegiance exists at birth also. So, this tells us that one born in the United States and under the jurisdiction of the United States without allegiance to another sovereign is a natural born citizen.

"But is this the only way to acquire the natural born citizen attribute? Probably not.

"While neither Congress nor the Supreme Court has officially defined 'natural born citizen,' the weight of legal and historical authority indicates that natural born citizens also include those born abroad to at least one U.S. citizen parent.

"Turning now to the corporation. Domestic corporations are citizens – at least they are for purposes of Article three federal diversity jurisdiction purposes. In that context, it is settled law that domestic corporations are citizens of the state in which they were incorporated, as well as the state in which their primary place of business is located. But are they national citizens?

"I say they are, because I'm not aware of a citizen of any state in the U.S. ever not also being a citizen of the nation with the exception of *Dredd Scott*, a former slave whom the Supreme Court determined was apparently a greater part property than person. And it isn't clear that the Court thought Mr. Scott was a state citizen either. Regardless, it's moot because that horrendous decision has long been overturned.

"So exactly what type of citizen is a domestic corporation, then?

"It seems to me that a corporate citizen is a natural born citizen because even though it is created by law, it cannot ever have been an alien. Moreover, it is not created by the naturalization process, but, rather, by state incorporation statute. Additionally, a corporation comes into being – is *born*, if you will – within the jurisdiction of the state in which it is incorporated, and, again, a state which must necessarily be within the jurisdiction of the United States.

"Lastly, with respect to the purpose of the citizen qualification – it is difficult to imagine any individual satisfying the purpose of the citizen qualification, natural born or otherwise, more soundly than a domestic corporation can. Domestic corporations depend on the states of their incorporation for their very existence, for police and fire; they depend on the federal government for military protection and interstate infrastructure. There is much more, of course – the judicial systems, federal and state, and so on.

"Similarly, both federal and state governments depend on corporations for a variety of goods and services, including but certainly not limited to police and military hardware. Vizion Inc., for example, is the primary supplier of surveillance technology components used by the Department of Homeland Security. Domestic corporations also provide vehicles, software, and the labor and material that go into that interstate infrastructure I mentioned. The list is virtually endless and I would be remiss if I failed to mention the hundreds of billions in revenues remitted to state and federal government by domestic corporations. This is precisely the interdependent relationship and unshakable allegiance citizenship connotes, and it more than satisfies the purpose of the citizenship qualifications both natural born and otherwise."

Josh took a moment to catch his breath and Gabriella used the opportunity to press him on what effect the Supreme Court ruling in *Paul v. Virginia* might have on his theory. "If you'll recall," she said, "in that case the Court said corporations were not citizens within the meaning of the article four privileges and immunities clause."

"I don't think it matters," Josh said.

The hospitalist came into Ricky's room and Dawn powered off the television and met him at the door.

"Hi, I'm Doctor Dawn Wise."

The hospitalist looked at her skeptically, in the same way some medical doctors look at liberal arts college professors who refer to themselves as *Doctor*. He nodded as he flipped open Ricky's medical chart. "Doctor Powell," he introduced himself.

Dawn rolled her eyes. Mr. personality, I see. "So, what are we dealing with, Doctor Powell. And by the way, I'm a neurosurgeon. In case you were wondering."

"Um-hmm." Dr. Powell thumbed through the pages of the chart. "No more swelling. No bleeds. No obvious brain damage." He slapped the chart closed. "I don't think we'll be needing a neurosurgeon." He moved over to Ricky's bedside and went through his own iteration of the tests Dawn had performed on Ricky's arms and noted the same unresponsiveness. Then he took out his reflex hammer and pulled the sheet away from Ricky's lower legs. "What have we here?" He gave the titanium a couple of taps.

Dawn chuckled. "So what do you think?"

"Psychological," Dr. Powell said coldly. "If he's unresponsive after a couple of days, we'll have a feeding tube inserted and send him to a long term care facility. We're short on beds here."

Chapter 37

Josh sat in the throne toying with the Levi's chess set, then Levi came in with Dr. Shultz and cleared his throat. "I'm afraid your time for that seat has not yet come, Josh," said Levi. "But you'll be pleased to know that I've spoken with Vizion's board of directors, and in accordance with the promise I made you, as of today you're no longer simply acting CEO of Vizion." He turned to Dr. Shultz. "And as for you, you can thank me later for not firing you. You'll take your orders from Josh until further notice."

"Yes, sir," Dr. Shultz said.

Josh said, "You mean –"

"Yes," Levi finished for him, "the CEO position is yours permanently now...well, permanent until or unless the board should decide otherwise in the future."

"That's a good start," Josh said as he vacated the throne.

"Provided a DNA test confirms what you've said," Levi clarified.

Dr. Shultz brandished a blood-draw syringe. "Either arm will do."

"Why not just a swab?" Josh said as he rolled up his right sleeve. He held his arm out.

Dr. Shultz jammed the needle into Josh's arm. "The man in charge insists upon blood."

Levi lifted his chin and watched Josh's blood dribble into the vial.

"The results won't be long," Dr. Shultz said. He taped a small piece of gauze over the puncture wound. "We have a very efficient lab here."

Levi took Josh by the arm after Dr. Shultz left for the lab. "While you're here, I'd like to show you some other things Leviathan Corp is working on." He aimed his remote, and the doors in the wall concealing the large screen behind it receded. "Make yourself comfortable." He gestured to the not-throne, then opened a PowerPoint presentation.

The first slide featured a video clip of the Earth from the arctic region with ice caps and vegetation advancing and receding rhythmically.

Josh watched with fascination. "Wow. It looks like –"

"Respiration," Levi completed the thought. "I give you Mother Earth. What the several years in time-lapse reveal here is that the Earth isn't merely a glob of inorganic matter spinning mindlessly while people exploit it. Rather, it is a living breathing organism comprised of untold multitudes of cells, of which humans are far from the majority. Which isn't to say that humans – at least some humans – are not

159

among the most important cells. Naturally, those superior human cells derive from impeccable bloodlines.

"When we look more closely, we see a self-regulating system, a collection of feedback loops, if you will, in which the Earth by way of the interlinked organisms that inhabit it is constantly working to optimize life on the planet. And all of this without a conscious thought. Rather like the autonomic system in the human body, wouldn't you say? From the many comes one."

"I've heard of this," Josh said, continuing to watch. "I think they call it Gaia."

Random spouts of vapor oozed sporadically here and there from the surface of the planet onscreen, forming a carbon dioxide blanket in the atmosphere that in time lapse dissipated almost as quickly as it had formed. "Volcanoes," Levi explained. "Phytoplankton multiply in the oceans in response to the carbon dioxide emissions from volcanic eruptions to absorb the excess into the water; nitrogen is generated from bacteria, oxygen from photosynthesis – processes stimulated to counteract instability and optimize conditions for the living.

"You might think of these processes as something of a global immune system. The magnitude of the power of this organic self-regulation, utterly independent of human intervention, is all the more astounding when you consider carbon dioxide once dominated our planet's atmosphere."

Josh considered the implications of what Levi said. "Are you suggesting that climate change science is a hoax?"

"I'll leave it to you to draw your own conclusions about that," said Levi, "but the presence of a common threat of annihilation, real or no, is essential if mankind is to achieve a unified world."

"So it is a hoax, then," said Josh. He'd suspected as much since academia and big media began assigning blame to climate change for everything from actual weather phenomena to terrorism to obesity, dirty diapers, racism, and bad attitudes. But he frankly didn't give a damn. Everyone had an angle and if others were stupid enough to fall for it, so be it.

Levi shook his head. "Not at all. The climate is continuously changing and no one can dispute that. And that's the beauty of it, denier's are automatically discredited – dissent is quashed from the outset. What role humans play and whether there's anything humanity can do to alter the climate's ultimate course is an open question. But

160

like any potential global catastrophe, we must try to prevent it. The people demand it."

Josh chuckled.

"Just so you know," Levi went on, "regardless of whether or not the solutions we've implemented will ever have any effect on climate, they've certainly been beneficial in countless other ways. We've redistributed untold trillions to the world's poorer nations through climate regulation and the carbon credit scheme. And of course the banks receive a transaction fee on every credit traded. Naturally, the wealth ultimately flows to those properly equipped to manage it, which certainly is not any of the nation states.

"Really?" Josh said. "Redistributed trillions?"

"Of course," said Levi. "Surely you don't think it's fair that governments representing two percent of the people in this world should be allowed to continue to hoard the vast majority of the wealth." The fact was Josh couldn't care less about that, and Levi knew it, but there was a point to be made and an agenda to be forwarded. "Well now, when we're talking in the context of the global community, the United States and its primary constituency, the American middleclass is that greedy two percent. Never mind the one-percenters politicians are always babbling about. That propagandized one percent is the tiny few among us capable of managing things, and you will note that that elite class maintains its position at the top under every economic system – capitalist, communist, totalitarian, all of them, and for our purposes, capitalism is the least efficient of them all."

"Fine," Josh said. "Whatever. Tell me about the redistribution."

Levi nodded. " It's quite simple, actually. The global climate change agreement requires that any person or entity that consumes energy produced by burning fossil fuels pay a fee correlating with the volume of emissions required to produce the amount of energy consumed. The fees must be paid in carbon credits purchased on the carbon credit exchange. Incidentally, I expect before long, trading on the carbon credit exchange will dwarf New York Stock Exchange trades.

"We began this process with a finite number of carbon credits, a number which coincides with the presumed maximum amount of carbon that can be safely emitted annually without further altering the climate. That fixed number of credits was distributed among nations, which regulate distribution to private sector users under their jurisdictions. But because the wealthiest and most industrialized nations gained their advantage over the others under the unrestrained carbon emissions paradigm, it was only fair that the underdeveloped nations, including China, Russia, and India, among others, received the vast majority of the carbon credits from the initial disbursement. The wealthy industrialized nations, of necessity, are purchasing most of those credits from the underdeveloped nations on the Exchange or watching as their manufacturing base flees to less developed nations where a better deal can be cut on credits."

"Clever," Josh said. "Very clever."

Levi smiled. "Isn't it, though? There have been complications though. National militaries, for example. Prior to banning them, manufacturers had to also include the cost of security in weaker unstable nations in their calculus. Now they must deal with that cost wherever they go. The other problem was renewable energy. But thanks to our close relationships with governments around the world, Leviathan Corp. is positioned to monopolize global renewable energy production. Of course, the Cole brothers participation in the Texas miracle is less than helpful.

"But there's a great deal more to this climate change business than redistribution and selling renewables. One might rightfully think of climate change as a public policy tool; a tool which enables the few among us who are competent enough to do so to guide humanity for the greater good."

Josh raised an eyebrow. "How so? I mean, other than using it to monopolize the energy market and make the largest transfer of wealth in human history?"

"Let me show you." Levi pointed to a new image onscreen, this one of the western hemisphere facing away from the sun. "Look. It's obviously nighttime in the west here. If you'll pardon the contradiction, darkness can be most illuminating. Note the glowing hotspots."

Josh scrutinized the image. "I assume those are city lights in industrialized regions."

"Indeed they are," Levi said. "But your observation is overly simplistic, misses the real significance. These are the brains of the world as it currently exists – where the real action takes place, where important decisions are made, where orders are transmitted to the rest of the world. The plurality is the problem.

"Let us consider this using the human organism as an analogy. The closest condition to multiple brains in a human organism is schizophrenia. Of course one suffering from schizophrenia doesn't really have more than one brain, though he or she may think and act as if that were so. Just as a human cannot function properly with unaligned or misaligned thought, neither can the Earth. So, what we see here is an illness, a cancer that can be every bit as devastating to the Earth as schizophrenia is in an individual human organism.

"The solution is to wipe out the cancer of independent thought so that the Earth is of one mind, one very powerful centralized mind from which all of the many cells which make up the whole receive their instructions and act upon them. Those who do not conform to the will of that central power must be destroyed, just as the rogue cells in a cancer patient are destroyed for the good of the whole."

"To what end?" Josh said, his mind awash in fanciful thoughts of himself at the top of the cells that would comprise this all-powerful central mind.

Levi shifted in his throne. "You mentioned you are familiar with Gaia. So you are undoubtedly aware of the one supposed flaw in the theory."

Josh nodded. "The argument is that the Earth cannot be a living organism because it doesn't reproduce."

Levi leaned back and drew in a deep breath. "But what if it could reproduce? What if the mixed signals from humanity in all its ignorance have prevented it from doing so? What if the all-powerful central control system of which I've spoken were able to mute all the noise preventing the Earth from hearing the calls of her mate?"

That didn't make any sense at all to Josh. He had always known Levi was eccentric. How could he not know that about a man who thought producing a royal bloodline in test tubes from involuntarily confiscated eggs of young women was a good idea? But now he had to seriously consider the possibility that the old man was not merely eccentric but insane. What was it people said, that the only difference between crazy and eccentric was a large bank balance? He glanced at his watch. "Listen, Levi, this has been very enlightening, but I've got a meeting to make."

163

Levi leaned forward, glaring. "Yes, I suppose your new position as CEO of Vizion keeps you quite busy."

"It does," Josh said, and after he left, Levi gazed at the chess set on his desk. His eyes narrowed. "Once I've firmly reinstituted the BCRA, this is what's in store for all of you arrogant would-be business barons," he muttered, and thumped a pair of rooks off the chessboard, "including you and you, brothers Cole." He raked off the rest of the pieces except the king, which he placed at the center and smiled. "There now, that's much better." He grabbed a handful of pawns from the pile of pieces. "Perhaps it would be useful to save a few of you."

Chapter 38

The director of harmonization at the Lawton facility discharged Chick in the midst of a mid-April deluge and ordered him transported by bus back to Dodge City. "Sonsabitches could've been decent enough to give me an umbrella," Chick muttered as he stepped off the bus at the Santa Fe Depot Transit Center. "Dang it's chilly." He shivered. "At least it ain't snowing." He sloshed down half-flooded Wyatt Earp Boulevard, soaked to his toes, to the AA meeting place.

At straight up noon he walked into a session in progress. A full house – standing room only, a lot more lively than the one-on-ones he and Ricky had had at five AM for so many years.

Arnold, a bankrupt former banker turned recovering alcoholic landscaper, stood at the bright yellow podium. And Frederick – a physicist whose membership was purely preventative, based on some calculation he'd done that indicated an unacceptable distance from the highpoint of the probability of becoming an alcoholic curve – sat in a foldout metal chair next to him. Chick didn't recognize any of the several others. He smiled and said, "Hey hey hey, you bunch of drunks, I'm Chick and I'm not just any old alcoholic, I'm a *free* alcoholic!"

Everyone in the room turned and stared at him.

"Excuse me," said Arnold, as he stepped away from the podium. He gestured at Chick to meet him in the back office.

Chick followed him in there and Arnold closed the door behind them.

"What's up?" Chick said.

"About this AA group," Arnold started. "You see it's," he heem-hawed. "Well, it's changed since you've been gone. We're a part of a sort of national...well, international if you include the Texas chapters...uh, network."

"Yeah, so?"

Arnold said, "The feds demanded our membership list. You can just imagine what they could do with that. I mean, we were called alcoholics *anonymous* for a reason."

Chick raised an eyebrow. "That ain't constitutional, is it?

"I don't know, but we decided not to risk it. Instead we disbanded. This is not AA anymore. We hold TEA Party meetings here now."

Chick threw his arms apart. "You ain't making no sense."

"Look, the purpose of this group now is to sober up the government. In case you haven't noticed, the America me and you grew up in is all but gone. You surely ought to see that after what they just put you through. Harmonization camps, forced adult vaccines, euthanasia, micromanagement of our daily lives, violations of our first amendment, the second, and heck, the whole bill of rights. Healthcare and food and energy rationing. Kicking Texas out. That ridiculous GTP agreement that handed over our sovereignty and our national wealth to an unelected board of foreigners. And these God-awful machines patrolling our streets.

"And as if all that wasn't bad enough, now our dictator president is flirting with world war three and vigorously promoting the idea that it's un-American to be pro-American. The whole political establishment is drunk on power and we've got to sober them up or replace them. We meet to discuss ways to do that. I think one way to start is to vote for that corporation, Vizion Inc., if Congress lets it run. Otherwise I don't know. I guess we roll the dice and write someone in. If Emperor Farnsworth gets another term, we're finished. Same if Helen wins. And we gotta do something about Congress too."

"Can't argue with that," Chick said. He pointed to the cell phone clipped to Arnold's belt. "Say, can I borrow that?"

Arnold tossed him the phone.

Chick dialed Ricky's cell phone number.

It went straight to voicemail so Chick called Vizion.

"Vizion Inc.," the receptionist answered.

"Hello there," Chick said. "Can I speak to Ricky Santana?"

"I'm sorry but he's...not...in. Would you like to speak with Josh?"

Chick thought about that. Josh was not only a scrawny little persnickety creep, he was a lawyer, and as a general rule Chick thought as much of lawyers as he did spiders, snakes, pedophiles, and bankers. Well, Arnold was alright for a banker. "Nah, that's okay. How about Dr. Dawn, she there?"

"I'll check. Who may I say is calling?"

"This is Chick."

"Oh, hi Chick. Are you out?"

"Just got out today."

"Good for you. One moment, please."

After a few minutes of elevator music, Dawn came on the line. "This is Dr. Wise."

"Hey, it's Chick."

"Who?"

"Chick, part-time sanitation director there at Vizion. You forget me already? I thought me and you had a good thing going on."

Dawn chuckled. "I know who you are. How could anyone forget that big grin and the gold tooth. I thought you were in a harmonization camp."

"I was. They cut me loose. You busy Friday night?"

"Pardon me?"

"I said, are you busy Friday night? A man been locked up needs some loving when he gets out. We could go to a movie, dinner, or just skip all that and get right down to business."

"Listen, Chick, I'm very busy –"

He interrupted. "Alright then, if you're busy Friday, how about Saturday?"

Dawn thought about hanging up on him but instead she asked if he knew about what had happened to Ricky and after he indicated otherwise, told him all about it.

Chick choked. "He at the hospital?"

Dawn sounded exhausted suddenly. "No. He's been moved to the long term care facility on Frontview."

"The what? Oh, you mean the nursing home. That's clear on the other side of town. You don't know if Ricky got my ice cream cart out of hock before all that happened, do you?"

"I believe I did see a pedal cart in the driveway over at the cottage when I went to pick up Bernice's stuff."

"Alright then. I'm going to go on ahead and walk to that nursing home and see Ricky. Any chance you could take me over to get my wheels later on?"

Dawn said she would, reluctantly, and that evening she did, and for the next three and a half weeks she and Chick took shifts at Ricky's bedside at the nursing home. During that time, they learned a lot more about one another than either ever imagined they would want to know.

For example, they weren't two people from opposite sides of the tracks. They both grew up in a poor single parent home in an Area four public housing project just a stone's throw from ritzy Kendall Square in Cambridge, Massachusetts. After losing her father in Iraq, Dawn immersed herself in her studies, and went on to medical school, then dual residencies in ophthalmology and neurosurgery.

After losing his father in a drug deal gone bad, Chick immersed himself in booze and car theft, and got an education in computer programming during the ten year stint he did in prison for grand theft auto.

Dawn was an accomplished doctor now. Chick, an ice cream street vendor, supplementing his income with the janitor job at Vizion, and hacking into others' electronic business as a hobby.

"Besides all that, we're just two peas in a pod," Chick recalled Dawn saying and laughing. But she'd yet to go on a date with him. It made him smile thinking about her as he sat passing the time at Ricky's bedside. It had been almost two months since the crash. How much longer would it be before Ricky came to?

Chick looked over at him, at the sweat beads forming on his brow. Sure is hot for May, he thought. They ought to up them carbon credits for these kind of places so they can keep them a little cooler. He nudged Ricky. "Come on, brother man, wake up. According to that cold-blooded creepy doctor in here, they gonna kill you in a minute if you don't snap out of it."

The phone at the bedside rang.

"Hello?"

"Hi, Chick, it's Dawn. How's the patient?"

"Same as he has been for the past three and half weeks. Just lays there. Don't move. Don't say nothing. Don't do nothing. Just sleeps."

"Has the doctor been in to see him today?"

"Uh-huh."

"And?"

Chick felt a churning in the pit of his stomach. "He said Ricky ain't gonna make it. Said sixty days is the max allowed by DHHS for feeding tubes on comatose patients and it's been like fifty-six already."

"Oh my God. Is the doctor still there? " Dawn hung up without waiting for an answer, and a half hour later Chick heard her down the hall sparring with the attending physician, who happened to be none other than Dr. Shultz.

Chick poked his head out into the hallway and he chuckled when he saw Bernice hobbling toward Ricky's room with those crazy looking goggles on. She woofed and went into a stumbling gallop when she saw him. "Come on, girl." Chick patted his thighs. He was amazed the old dog had survived the crash unscathed. A shame Ricky hadn't.

Bernice followed Chick into the room and plopped down on her hindquarters beside the bed and pawed at Ricky's arm, whining as she did.

"Hey, buddy, look who's here," Chick said to the unresponsive shape of a man that had been Ricky a few short weeks ago.

Dawn came in. "That Dr. Shultz is a real ass, you know that," she huffed.

"No kidding," Chick agreed. "I wonder how he'd like it if somebody was fixing on starving him to death."

Dawn cupped a hand over Chick's mouth and pulled him out into the hallway. "Don't talk like that in front of Ricky," she whispered.

Chick blurted, "Why? It ain't like he can hear us."

"Shh. Maybe not, but you never know. Now listen, we've got to figure a way to get him out of here before that sadistic Dr. Shultz has that feeding tube removed."

Chick's trademark grin appeared again. "What you got in mind?"

"I said, keep your voice down." Dawn frowned. "I don't have anything in mind. I've always played by the book. I was hoping maybe you might have some ideas."

"I don't get what it is with you straight-laces that a man can't swipe a few automobiles without being labeled a jack-of-all-crimes – not that I don't appreciate the confidence."

"You're right," Dawn whispered. "I shouldn't assume. You've obviously changed your ways, but....What I mean is. I don't know what I mean, but I'm sorry if I offended you."

"Hey, maybe Ricky's lawyer man can help. Get him a compassionism waiver or something."

Dawn chuckled. "I think I know what you mean, and it's worth a try. Assuming it's Josh your talking about. But we better have a backup plan."

Chick scrubbed his chin. "Let me think on it. I'll come up with something."

Dawn hugged him. "I'm counting on it."

Chick slid his hands down her backside. "Mmm-mm, you sure do smell pretty."

Dawn pried his hands off her buttocks. "Settle down, Rover."

Chapter 39

Thinking about Chick hitting on her all the time took some of the edge off Dawn's anxiety over Ricky's situation as she rode the Prius into the south side on the way back to Vizion. Chick had no concept of subtlety and he didn't have a hint of sophistication or grace or any redeeming quality of any kind that she could think of. But he was sweet, in his own way. And there was a certain charm in his childlike innocence – an innocence not unlike Ricky's, only it was … Innocence? Wait. What was she thinking, the man was a felon? She slapped herself on the cheeks. "Wake up, girl." She tried to be disappointed in herself for not being furious with that criminal for pawing at her like that.

The Prius's brakes applied heavily when the car in front of it screeched to a sudden stop. Dawn lowered her window and hung her head out to see what was going on. A smoky haze and throngs of people filled the road ahead – some of them shouting obscenities, others chanting *hey-hey-ho-ho, corporations are not people, no no no*. Still others stabbed the sky with picket signs bemoaning corporate greed, corruption, America's racist past, homophobia, Islamophobia, various other o-phobias, and income inequality. Another demonstration with a patchwork of ineffective messages – most prominent among them, that these people had nothing better to do. But this demonstration was much larger than similar events in recent years, and more intense.

As the Prius crept forward again, Dawn saw an American flag ablaze and a dummy of the Chief Justice of the Supreme Court hanging in effigy from a lamppost. A sign pinned to the dummy's chest said: *Overturn Citizens United.*

"That harmonization vaccine is working real well." She chuckled, trying to modulate the fear she felt creeping into her. She had searched medical journals to no end hoping to learn what that peculiar vaccine was and how it worked, but so far all she had discovered was that everything about it was top-secret – except for the fact that it was now mandatory, was administered exclusively at harmonization centers, and compliance would be monitored by the IRS.

A Molotov cocktail soared over the hood of the Prius and exploded into flames when it struck the sidewalk on the other side of the street. Dawn let out a frightened little yelp. "Where are all the harmonizer patrols when you need them? Not here. None!"

She raised her window and locked the doors.

A pair of F-16s with the lonestar symbol on their tails crisscrossed the skies at low altitude. The thunder of their powerful engines rattled the Prius, reminding Dawn that the cold war with Texas was inching closer to erupting into a hot one. She clasped her hands together and squeezed her eyes shut. "Please Lord, don't let them drop any bombs on me. And please wake Ricky up from his coma so he can talk some sense into his Texas brethren before all this gets out of hand. In the name of Jesus. Amen."

"Public prayer is forbidden," the Prius's compliance system warned.

"Damn." The last time this happened, it cost her a hefty fine. "God only knows how much it'll be for a second offense," she complained out loud.

"Verbal invocation of a deity in public is forbidden," the compliance system responded.

Dawn muted the system and growled. "Leave me alone."

A menacing face appeared in the passenger window, beating on the glass.

She screamed and kicked her door open and bolted from the car and crashed into a pair of powerful arms. "Let me go," she shrieked, struggling to free herself.

"Baby, it's me."

"Chick?" Dawn's heart pounded so hard that she thought it might fly out of her chest. From the corner of her eye she saw a thug with a billy-club lunging at them. "Chick, look out!"

Chick caught the swinging club with one hand and landed an uppercut on the goon's chin with his other, laying him flat on his back.

"Wow. Who knew?" Dawn said. But it was too soon to relax.

Chick hoisted Dawn off the ground as another thug rushed toward them. "Hang on, baby, my sled's just around the corner." He ran into a nearby alley with her dangling over his shoulder and dropped her into the seat of his ice cream cart. Then he slid in beside her, sandwiching her between himself and Bernice, and started pedaling furiously.

"Oh, oh, oh." Dawn pressed a hand against her chest as the cart zoomed around the corner and bounced up onto the sidewalk where they bumped along for a half mile or so before dropping off the curb, crossing a side street, and bounding down into a dry creek bed.

They hit a dip and Dawn's rear end rose eight inches or better off the seat, then dropped back down, slamming her tailbone into the hard metal surface. "Ouch."

Chick slipped an arm around her. "You got to hold on better than that, baby."

Dawn grimaced. "Easy for you to say with that steering wheel holding you in place so your tuckus isn't battered every five seconds. And stop calling me baby."

Bernice's long slobbery tongue lapping at Dawn's face made her giggle. She glanced over at Chick and saw the grin again, that gold tooth shimmering in the sunlight. "That was some punch you laid on that reprobate back there," she said, hoping the compliment wouldn't overload his already unjustifiably inflated ego.

"I can hold my own." Chick kept pedaling, and didn't say more.

Maybe she had underestimated his humility, although she doubted it. "So where exactly are we going?"

"I'm taking you to Vizion." The cart approached another deep rut, and Dawn threw her arms around Chick to brace herself.

Bernice bounced out into the creek bed, and Dawn found herself eyeball to eyeball with Chick, her lips just inches from his. They were nice lips, full and smooth. And his eyes were prettier than she'd noticed before.

Chick stopped the cart and pulled her closer and pressed his lips to hers.

171

Their tongues tangled together.

Dawn's her heart raced. Chick tasted good. Wait. What in the world was she doing! She pulled back, shoving off his chest with both hands, then slapped him. "You shouldn't have kissed me. And by the way, you could slow it down. We lost those thugs way back."

"I shouldn't have kissed you?" Chick said. "You kissed me."

"Did not."

"Did too."

"Okay, well, can we agree we kissed each other?"

"Alright then."

"And it's not going to happen again." Dawn sighed, and glanced at Bernice parked in the dirt on her haunches, panting. "So, are you going to get the dog so we can go or are we going to just sit here all day?" she said.

Chick hopped out and helped Bernice back into the cart, then wiped the sweat from his brow. "Shoo-wee, sure is a scorcher today. I wish them regulators would hurry up and get this global warming fixed."

"We're all holding our breath for that," Dawn said. "Now come on, let's get going."

Chick started pedaling again, this time slower. "That better?" he said.

Dawn nodded. "It'll do. But I just thought of something. What about my car? We can't just leave it back there."

"Dang, you're high maintenance, woman. Ain't that one of them cars that goes where it's s'posed to with or without nobody in it?"

"It is a smart-car, if that's what you mean. And I did set Vizion as the destination, but –"

"If that car's so smart," Chick interrupted, "let it prove it by getting where its s'posed to on its own."

"Fine." Dawn folded her arms across her chest. "God only knows what will happen to it in between with that bunch of vandals rioting in the streets. Not to mention the warplanes swarming overhead. It could be hit by a bomb or something."

Chick stopped the cart. "I'll turn around if that's what you want."

"No no. Keep going."

Chick nodded. "Whatever you say, lady."

"How much further?" Dawn said after Chick had been pedaling for a couple of more miles. "I've never taken this back alley creek bed route before."

Chick cocked his arm out in front of him to check his watch, making sure Dawn got a good look at the imitation Rolex. "About another fifteen minutes or so," he said, and after more than twice that many more butt-busting bounces, they tacked up the creek bank at the backside of Vizion. He stopped for a minute to catch his breath, then pedaled around to the entrance gate.

"Warning, you are approaching a restricted area," said the harmonizer at the guardhouse.

"No shit, robot," Chick said.

Dawn displayed her Vizion badge. "Make way. I'm Dr. Dawn Wise, in case you've forgotten. This man is Chick, our uh, sanitation director, in case you've forgotten him. And I presume you recognize the dog." She felt herself beginning to despise harmonizers as much as Ricky did.

Chick waved his fist in the air. "You heard the lady, make way before I bop you one."

The harmonizer raised the crossbar. "You are cleared to enter," it said, and they passed through and went inside the building where they found Josh leaning back in Ricky's chair with both feet propped up on the desk, a cigar jutting from his mouth.

Dawn felt a twinge of resentment. She hadn't completely resigned herself to the fact that Josh was the boss now, and she hoped things could go back to normal when...if... Ricky got well before the government starved him to death. Josh might have been a very capable attorney but he wasn't a businessman and he didn't seem to share her and Ricky's vision for curing the blind either – even though he was engaged to a blind woman... or maybe because of it. She couldn't imagine Gabriella being much interested in Josh if she had the benefit of sight to remind her what a scrawny little dork runt he was.

"Hey, Dawn. You look stressed," Josh said.

Something as much a growl as a sigh escaped her throat. "Stressed is an understatement." She rubbed her sore bottom. "Do you have any idea what's going on out there? There's rioting in the streets. People burning things, throwing things. Oh and I'd be remiss if I didn't mention the Texas warplanes."

"The Texans are just testing the president's resolve. All the rest I'd guess is a response to the Supreme Court's announcement this afternoon that it's invoking the political question doctrine on our case. Nothing to worry about."

Dawn rubbed her sore bottom again. "That's easy for you to say. You didn't just have your entire body jarred silly for twenty miles through a bumpy creek bed on an ice cream cart to escape that bunch of maniacs. Lord only knows what they've done to my car by now. What's a political question doctrine?"

"It means them black-robed geniuses is too cowardly or too corrupt to answer the question the lawsuit's about," Chick said.

Josh shifted his cigar to the side of his mouth. "Broadly speaking, the political question doctrine says that the Court may dismiss a case when there is a lack of judicially manageable standards to decide it on the merits, when judicial intervention might show insufficient respect for other branches of government, or when a judicial decision might threaten the integrity of the judicial branch. With respect to our case, the Court concluded that whether a corporation can satisfy the qualifications to become president is a question for Congress not for the Court."

Chick mumbled, "Smart ass."

Josh ignored the slight. "So where were you that you wound up in the middle of the protests anyway? I've been looking for you."

Bernice growled.

"Behave yourself, dog," said Chick.

Dawn said, "I went to see Ricky. Why were you looking for me?"

"The animals. They're out of control, especially that big male monkey. They're cages are filthy and –"

Dawn folded her arms across her chest. "If you're referring to Brutus, he isn't a monkey, he's an ape, and in case you've forgotten, counselor, I'm a doctor, not a zookeeper."

"I see." Josh puffed his cigar. "Then you won't be disappointed to know that I've decided to terminate the medical research projects and refocus Vizion's efforts exclusively on our security products. We'll have no further need for the animals."

"What!" Dawn's shout rattled all three of them.

"Vizion is not a non-profit," Josh said coldly. "My responsibility is to protect the interests of our shareholders. And that interest lies in the new contract with Leviathan – a contract that's worth billions, unlike Ricky's fantasy of curing the blind, which has been nothing but a parasite feasting on this company's profits from the beginning."

Dawn's jaw dropped. A cure for the blind would also be worth billions, and she – and Ricky too, she assumed – was far more concerned with helping people at least see *something* than helping the government see *everything*. "I don't believe this. Apparently you've forgotten that Vizion's founding mission was to find a cure for the blind, not to enable the government to spy on everything that moves. And what about your *fiancé*? What about your responsibility to her?"

"Yeah, what about that?" Chick chimed in.

"Why don't you go sell some snow cones. You certainly aren't doing your sanitation job here," Josh said to him, then turned back to Dawn. "My decision won't make Gabriella any more blind than she already is and I doubt your research was going to make her any less blind either."

Dawn elbowed Chick in the side when she noticed his nostrils flaring. She changed the subject to the more urgent matter at hand. "Let's talk about Ricky," she said to Josh.

"I sell ice cream, not snow cones," Chick clarified, "something folks want, and that's more than I can say for what you're selling."

Dawn elbowed him again.

Josh took his cigar out of his mouth and pointed it at Chick. "I'm losing my sense of humor with you." He slipped his other hand beneath the desk and pushed a button alerting security.

"Let's focus, please," Dawn said.

"Okay. So what about Ricky?" said Josh.

"He's got less than a week before they pull his feeding tube. I was thinking you could use your legal skills or your connections or whatever to get an extension."

Josh stuck the cigar back between his teeth and bit down hard on it. "Dawn, you know that no one would like to help Ricky more than I would, but the timing is terrible. Not five minutes after the Supreme Court announced its decision, the president ordered Congress to schedule a special session to address the issue. They meet tomorrow morning and I've been asked to appear. I just don't have the time to deal with Ricky's issues right now."

"Are you serious?" Dawn shrieked. "You'd put the election ahead of your friend's life? Jesus, have you forgotten it's Ricky's company that's running for president? What difference will any of this make if he's dead?"

Josh laid his cigar in an ashtray and took a deep breath. "It *was* Ricky's company. Before it went public. Anyway, my failing to appear

175

could have far more serious repercussions on me and Vizion than merely costing us an election."

"Repercussions on you?" Dawn said. "What about the repercussions for Ricky? They're going to starve him to death! Don't you get that?"

"You no good," Chick began, and a harmonizer marched up behind him and lifted him off his feet.

"What kind of man are you?" Dawn's voice turned guttural.

Chick thrashed as the harmonizer lugged him toward the exit. "Let me go before I do something you're gonna regret, tinman."

Bernice stumbled after them, growling and nipping at the harmonizer's titanium ankles.

"Wait up, Chick, I'm going with you," Dawn called after him, and started out of the office.

Josh cleared his throat. "You're forgetting something?"

"And that is?"

"Your Vizion badge." Josh held his hand out. "Call me next week so we can discuss your severance package."

Dawn slapped the badge into his hand and ran out the exit to catch up with Chick.

"So, any ideas on that backup plan I asked about?" she said as she and Chick piled into the ice cream cart.

Chick smiled. "How about another kiss?"

"Come on, I'm being serious."

Chick folded his arms across his chest and scrubbed his chin as though carefully weighing a slate of options. "I guess we bust Ricky out."

"Brilliant. And just how exactly are we going to do that?"

"By ambulance."

"Okay. But how are we going to get one of those?"

"Let me worry about that," Chick said. "What I need you to do is send over whatever paperwork we need to get that nursing home to release Ricky to us, and meet me there tomorrow night at, say" – he cocked his arm, showing off the Rolodex knockoff again – "seven o'clock."

"Tomorrow night? But where are we going to take him?"

"His folks got a ranch down in Texas. I was thinking that'd be the best place."

176

"Texas!" Dawn tugged at her hair. "Is it even legal for a U.S. citizen to travel to Texas?"

Chick sighed. "Well if it ain't, all I can say is, welcome to the felon club."

The Prius buzzed up beside the ice cream cart. It pleased Dawn to see it still ran. She wasn't thrilled about the cracked windshield though, or the *corporations are not people* spray-painted on the hood, or the *corporations* are *people* spray-painted on the rear hatch. It's amazing how easily people can be divided over the most ridiculous things, she thought.

Chapter 40

Today was the big day, the day that Josh would make his final pitch for a fundamental transformation of America that would make even former president Barack Obama blush. The limo pulled up in front of Gabriella's apartment, trailed and preceded by several self-navigating black Chevy Suburbans, each of them transporting a team of heavily armed security harmonizers.

"Your insistence that I ride along with you is shortsighted," Levi said from the rear seat next to Josh. "Openly fraternizing with a man of my enormous wealth and power can only weaken the narrative of Vizion as the people's corporation, a corporation now headed by an orphan child who through hard work and sheer determination made it to the top in America."

"I couldn't agree more," Josh said, and straightened his tie. "But right now we've got to persuade the members of Congress, not the people. Without Congress's stamp of approval on corporate candidacy, the voters will never have an opportunity to hear that narrative. And, as you well know, Congress only understands two things – money and power. I think your accompanying me to the session will speak volumes on both."

"Perhaps you're right," Levi conceded, still adjusting to the idea that he had an adult son at all after Max's death – much less a son with an impressive acumen and a sharp political instinct. A blessing sprung forth from colossal failure. Sooner or later he'd have to tell Helen about this.

Josh dialed Gabriella from his cell phone. "Honey, are you ready yet? It's almost seven-thirty."

"This may come as a surprise to you, but I can read my brail watch just fine," she snapped, frazzled in anticipation of covering the special session – the biggest story of the year, the biggest story of her career, and possibly even the biggest story in the entire history of the nation. She was well aware of what a privilege it was to have been chosen to cover it live. But she had so much on her mind right now. Josh having replaced Ricky as the face of Vizion had zapped her enthusiasm about this corporate candidacy business. "I'll be out as soon as I can," she said.

Josh said, "Honey, please hurry."

"I could hurry better if you'd let me off the phone." Gabriella hung up. She sighed as she fluffed her hair. She had had it with Josh's impatience, his constantly push push pushing her – not to mention his having dismissed out of hand as some sort of mistake the fact that the DNA sample taken from the cigar butt out of Max's ashtray matched the DNA profile of one of the serial rapists. And not to mention the fact that the other DNA sample taken from the victims indicated the other perpetrator must be a close relative of Max. Another inexplicable mistake? As difficult as any of this was to accept, Levi being Max's only living relative could mean only one thing, and she wondered if Josh was covering for the old man. She never should have told him she was looking into this. But who else did she have to turn to now?

Gabriella's cell phone rang again. And again it was Josh. Of course. "Coming, coming," she hummed. She misted herself with perfume, grabbed her camera bag, unaware how obsolete the camcorder in it was, and hurried out to the limo.

Josh stepped out and held the car door open for her – a small act of courtesy, rare for him. She appreciated it until she found herself squeezed between him and Levi in the backseat of the limo. Now she wished that Josh had let her open the door and help herself to a window seat like he usually did these days.

"Good morning, Gabriella," Levi said as the motorcade departed for the capitol. He took her hand and kissed it. "You look absolutely ravishing."

She shuddered, and eased her hand back into her lap, hoping her apprehension wasn't obvious. "Good morning, Levi," she said with a forced smile.

The thud of something slamming into a side window startled her.

Josh patted her on the knee. "It's alright, honey. Just a tomato."

"Seems to me if these protestors can afford to use vegetables to deface corporate property, their rations need a bit more tightening," Levi said.

Despite the near soundproof windows, Gabriella's keen sense of hearing detected the muffled sound of dozens of sirens, and shouts, jeers, and chanting of crowds massing along the roadway. "It's the police, isn't it?" she said. "They're protesting being replaced by harmonizers, aren't they?" She handed Josh her camcorder. "Would you mind getting me some footage?"

Levi shook his head and silently lipped *no* to Josh.

Josh fumbled with the camcorder, feigning ignorance of its operation.

"Never mind, I'll do it myself." Gabriella yanked the camcorder back from him and crawled over his lap to the window. "Lower it please."

Josh gazed out at the chaos in the streets. Hundreds of harmonizers roved among the crowd apprehending protesters, mostly police officers they had displaced, and hauled them away to box trucks that would transport them to harmonization centers. He recalled the words of former President Barack Obama at the first hints of the nation's crumbling – *This is what change looks like.*

"I'm afraid I cannot allow the window to remain lowered," Levi intervened. "It isn't safe."

"Some things are more important than safety," Gabriella balked before climbing off of Josh's lap. She fell back against the seat and brooded for the next hour while the limo slowly churned through block after block of street mobs venting outrage at all things corporate until the motorcade arrived at Capitol Hill. The makeshift capitol building was domeless and as unimpressive as the temporary Whitehouse. The presidential limo pulled up beside Josh's, and Farnsworth lowered his window and curled his index finger. "Josh, I'd like to have a word with you," he said.

Levi said, "I'll see Gabriella in." He waved to Farnsworth. "Nice to see you, Mr. President."

A secret service agent in a chauffeur's uniform ushered Josh into the backseat of the presidential limo. "So," Josh said, "what's on your mind?"

"What isn't on my mind," said Farnsworth. "I've got the Texans trying to bait me into a hot war, the GTP central bank threatening to raise interest rates, a democrat opponent soaring in the polls on a platform of more or less nothing besides abolishing the flag, and then there's you…my protégé pulling this crap."

"Mr. President –"

Farnsworth pounded the seat between them. "Spare me the feigned respect. I want you to go in there and put an end to this corporate candidacy crap. And do it tactfully."

"If you're asking me to throw the proverbial ballgame, I'm afraid I can't do that."

"Why not? Your client is as good as dead. A shame. I thought highly of Ricky. May his soul be freed from the bondage of his vegetative state."

"My client is Vizion Inc., not Ricky," Josh said.

The veins in Farnsworth's forehead began to bulge to the point Josh thought they might explode right then and there. "Stop. Stop this now. You've not only started believing your own bullshit, you've got half the world believing it too. Corporations are not people. Vizion Inc. is not a person. It's nobody!"

Farnsworth paused to let his blood pressure settle. "Look, Josh, why don't you join me. I could make you my running mate. My current VP is just dead weight anyway. You think Vizion is doing well now? Imagine the new government contracts, the subsidies, the loan guarantees, the tax credits, with you and I running the country together. Just name it and it's yours."

Josh grasped Farnsworth's hand. "Listen, I owe you a lot. But the fact is you're the establishment poster child. That's a political death sentence in this election."

"The people's rebellious mood will blow over and the race will boil down to a choice between the lesser of evils like it always." Farnsworth sighed.

"I'm sorry," Josh said.

Farnsworth snapped his fingers. "Get out, you backstabber." The secret service agent opened Josh's door and ushered him out.

Josh went inside and sat at a table at the front of the chamber until the ceremonial timewasting concluded and the chairman said, "The honorable members of the House and Senate have unanimously agreed to conduct these proceedings in the form of an open hearing." He banged the gavel down. "The hearing is now in session. The floor's yours, Mr. Horowitz."

"Honorable Senators and Congresspersons, I am Joshua Horowitz." Josh scanned the room making eye contact with as many of the legislators as he could in the span of a few seconds. He knew most of these career politicians from his work as a staffer under Farnsworth when the president was in Congress and as unofficial lobbyist on behalf of Leviathan Corp for years after that. "I'd like to begin with some prepared remarks that I hope will address your concerns."

"Please proceed," said the chairman.

Josh adjusted the microphone in front of him. "I understand that you all unanimously concluded that first amendment protection of domestic corporate entities' political speech does not exempt such entities from the qualifications clauses in the Constitution. With that in mind, you asked me here today to assist you in determining first, whether it is possible for a corporate entity to satisfy those qualifications. And, secondly, if so, to share my views on what the rules should be, and to address some other related technical matters.

"Let's start with the first issue: Undoubtedly, you all know I believe emphatically that domestic corporations can satisfy the qualifications clauses. I laid out how and why in detail in the last segment of the four-part series I did with Gabriella Meir so I won't reiterate that here.

"The sticking point seems to be the mysterious privileges and immunities clause in article four section two of the Constitution, and more specifically some troublesome language in the 1869 Supreme Court case of *Paul v. Virginia* in which Justice Field reasoned that corporations were not citizens for purposes of the article four privileges and immunities clause.

"We'll revisit *Paul v. Virginia* in due time, but first let's take a look at what the privileges and immunities clause actually says: 'The citizens of each state shall be entitled to all the privileges and immunities of citizens in the several states.'

"Well, now that that's cleared up, let's move on to crafting the rules for associated candidacy."

The chamber broke out in laughter.

Josh smiled. "Glad I'm not the only one."

After a little more chuckling from the legislators, Josh continued, "Not to disappoint, I'll begin with a little history on privileges and immunities and how the concept evolved before its incorporation into the U.S. Constitution.

"Privileges and immunities date back to the fall of the Roman provinces and the Anglo-Saxon king's subsequent grant of large tracts of land to spiritual leaders for remission of sins. Most of these land grants went to churches, but later kings granted lands to individuals without a spiritual purpose – we generally know these nonspiritual recipients from the feudal periods as lords.

"The king would receive revenue or services from these individuals – these lords – in exchange for the land grants. But in some cases, the king granted *immunities* from the required services or revenues. By revenues, we are, of course, talking about taxes and tolls. Services would be military service, that sort of thing. So that's immunities one-oh-one.

"Now, understand that in addition to the lords, any other occupants of the land – peasants for example – were also required to render revenue and service to the king. But the lords were generally responsible for collecting what the peasants owed and forwarding it on to the Crown.

"So, later, during the Middle Ages, the lords' immunities were sometimes extended to the peasants' requirements with the understanding that the peasants' tribute would still be collected by the lords. It just wouldn't be remitted to the king – at least not all of it. This was known as a *privilege* for the lords to retain that tribute unto themselves.

"It's fair to say that as a recipient of a land grant with privileges and immunities, a lord stood in place of the king for all that the king would have received from the occupants of the land the king had granted. The privileged lord would then remit to the king some agreed upon portion of what he collected from the occupants.

"Over time, privileges and immunities became more or less a commodity that could be purchased from the Crown. Under this arrangement, the lords were in a position similar to that of the tax collector in Israel under the Roman Empire where the highest bidder purchased the right from Rome to collect taxes from the local population at the legal rate and keep it. The benefit to the Crown under this model was that it received its compensation upfront rather than later. It also spared the Crown the administration of tax collection, and diverted some of the ill will associated with taxation onto the collector rather than the king, or in the case of Rome, the emperor.

"The concept of privileges and immunities later developed into grants for the purpose of promoting trade and governing – first, the governing of manors, and later, the governing of colonies. These entities – among them, the colonies of Massachusetts and Virginia – and those administering on their behalf would enjoy freedom of travel; in other words, exemption from tolls. They also enjoyed exemption from taxes, and a host of other benefits.

"This was the Crown's latest greatest way of contracting out governance, revenue generation, and revenue collection. The privileged merchants created the basis of taxation by selling their wares to subjects and foreign sovereigns, and the privileged governing entities collected taxes from the subjects and non-privileged competing merchants.

"During the colonial period, the merchant grants began to be replaced by corporate charters for joint-stock companies in which the various commercial interests could buy shares. These corporations received limited liability, limited taxation, and often, the privilege of governing themselves as though they were their own sovereign.

"When doing business abroad, these corporations needed privileges and jurisdictional rights beyond their homeports. They also needed protection from other commercial interests infringing upon their trade monopolies, and some form of authority from the king to travel and trade in foreign lands.

"The Crown granted these entities with privileges and, yes, immunities, in exchange for services – services such as maintaining order in colonies, constructing infrastructure, and collecting taxes, to name a few. These corporations also required and received privileges and immunities from foreign states with which they traded.

"So, in this context, we might think of a privilege as access provided a corporation by governments to land and natural resources at a reduced rate or even free of charge; and an immunity as a reduced tax rate or an exemption altogether from taxes and tolls. Or the other way around. Or these advantages might be lumped together under a single heading of privileges *and* immunities.

"No matter how they are categorically parsed, privileges and immunities dramatically reduced the cost of doing business for corporate recipients of them during the period.

"As you might imagine, this became quite contentious among the non-privileged and non-immune local colonial and British mainland proprietors who could not compete because of the cost disparity it created. The British Parliament responded by invoking the right to free trade and free use of labor against the Crown's monopolies. And this is where the concept of privileges and immunities for the individual subject – the citizen here, after the American revolution – began to develop.

"During the English revolution of 1640 to 1649, Leveller's writings in opposition to royal, parliamentary, or monopolistic forces championed birthright liberties, privileges, and immunities for freeborn Englishmen. It was within this context that Sir William Blackstone – an eighteenth century English jurist, judge, and politician whose *Commentaries on the Laws of England* profoundly influenced the drafters of the U.S. Constitution and American jurisprudence as a whole – expressed his view of the privileges and immunities of the individual.

"According to Blackstone, private immunities spelled out in the Magna Carta were the residuum of natural liberty not required to be sacrificed to society. Alternatively, he suggested that immunities were privileges – privileges that society had chosen to provide in lieu of natural liberties given up by individuals. These, he said, consisted of the right of personal security, the right of personal liberty, and the right of private property.

"Blackstone underscored the importance of recognizing these privileges, or immunities – or, if you prefer, these *privileges and immunities* – as the inviolable rights of individuals in his assertion that there is no other known method of abridging man's natural free will than by infringement or diminution of one of these rights. Hence, Blackstone's insistence that these individual liberties, these individual privileges and immunities, must be preserved in their largest and most extensive sense.

"By large and extensive, Blackstone meant, among other things, that within these individual liberties was the right of free men to travel freely throughout the territories of the sovereign. To be clear, this was not a positive right, but rather, a negative liberty – a domain of noninterference consisting in an individual power of acting as one thinks fit without any restraint or control unless by the law of nature. In other words, governing entities should be restrained from imposing tolls or tariffs and that sort of thing on individuals and the property they carried with them when traveling within the English territories.

"It is from this concept that the drafters of U.S. Constitution and its predecessor, the Articles of Confederation, are presumed to have drawn their vision of privileges and immunities. Their intention was not to create a federal fundamental rights redundancy. Instead, it was to ensure that under a federalist system, states would not interfere with the rights of citizens of other states by treating them differently than they treat their own citizens under their state laws. Not only would this help in the preservation of those inviolate individual liberties, including the unhindered travel Blackstone wrote of, it would also promote interstate trade through a level playing field, and a sense of unity among the citizens of the several states.

"The Articles of Confederation's privileges and immunities clause states this intention quite clearly." Josh pulled out his pocket Constitution which also contained the earlier Articles, and read it aloud.

> *The better to secure and perpetuate mutual friendship and intercourse among the people of the different States in this Union, the free inhabitants of each of these States, paupers, vagabonds, and fugitives from justice excepted, shall be entitled to all the privileges and immunities of free citizens in the several States; and the people of each State shall have free ingress and regress to and from any other State, and shall enjoy therein all the privileges of trade and commerce, subject to the same duties, impositions, and restrictions as the inhabitants thereof respectively.*

"Now," Josh continued, "although our current version of the privileges and immunities clause – the one contained in the Constitution – does not include this more descriptive language, courts have interpreted it to mean the same thing.

"For example in *Corfield v. Coryell*, the Court struck down a state's attempt to limit the harvest of oysters to state residents only, finding that the limitation violated the aggrieved non-resident party's rights under the privileges and immunities clause. So there you see the equal treatment requirement enforced.

"And consider this excerpt from the Court in the *Slaughterhouse cases.*" Josh read from his notes:

[The article four privileges and immunities clause'[s] sole purpose was to declare to the several States that whatever those rights as you grant or establish them to your own citizens, or as you limit or qualify or impose restrictions on their exercise, the same, neither more nor less, shall be the measure of the rights of citizens of other States within your jurisdiction.

"Now that we all have some understanding of what the article four privileges and immunities clause is all about, you must be wondering what it has to do with a corporation's ability to satisfy the citizen requirement in the qualifications clauses. I say it has nothing whatsoever to do with it.

"Why then did the Supreme Court in the post-civil war case of *Paul v. Virginia* feel the need to specifically exclude corporations as citizens within the meaning of the privileges and immunities clause?

"First, let me say that, in my view, the answer to that question is irrelevant because the qualifications clauses don't say anything at all about a requirement that a candidate be construed as a citizen within the meaning of the privileges and immunities clause. If anything, the qualifications clauses might require citizenship as set forth in the first sentence of the fourteenth amendment, a sentence which is commonly referred to as the *citizenship* clause. Recall that sentence states that, 'All persons born or naturalized in the United States and subject to the jurisdiction thereof are citizens of the United States and of the state wherein they reside.' And recall that the question of corporate personhood is well settled. But in the interest of completeness, I'll address the citizenship controversy created by the Court's comments in the *Paul V. Virginia* case anyway.

"So, the issue in that case was whether a state's imposition of licensing and bond requirements on an insurance company chartered in another state more onerous than those required for in-state insurance companies violated the privileges and immunities clause.

"As we know, the Court held that it did not.

"Now, although the Court did engage in some almost metaphysical rambling about corporations being late-comers and by-products of the social compact upon which society was instituted, the more logical part of its rationale seems to have been based on a need to reconcile the old concept of privileges and immunities with the modern one applied to individuals. This was necessary because, to this day, a corporation's charter does in fact confer upon it something at least akin to privileges and immunities that are not necessarily afforded individuals. Limited liability is one example of that. And note that the advantages conferred by corporate charters vary from state to state.

"As we discussed earlier, corporations under the old charter paradigm had privileges and immunities that quite often exceeded the rights of individuals and often even operated to impede individual rights. No doubt keenly aware of this, the Court averred that corporations of one state could not demand another state recognize the special treatment granted by its state of incorporation and at the same time demand the other state grant it rights equal to those of its own citizens. This, in the Court's view, amounted to requiring states to gives corporations chartered in other states superior rights to those of its own citizens.

"So, rather than identifying a disqualifying distinction in personhood or citizenship generally between a corporation and a natural person, the *Paul v. Virginia* Court's decision appears to have been just another example of the Court grappling with the difficulty of practical application of a constitutional right complicated by corporate entities' unique characteristics.

"Hence, the article four privileges and immunities clause does not imbue state citizens with federal citizenship or any other type of citizenship. Nor does lack of citizenship under the clause terminate citizenship, federal or otherwise. The citizenship clause and legislation by Congress in accordance with the naturalization clause are the domains for determination of citizenship. All the privileges and immunities clause does is constitutionalize the several states' reciprocal agreement to treat citizens of all other states equally under their particular state laws. It is therefore irrelevant with respect to the qualifications clauses whether or not a corporate citizen is a citizen with the meaning of the privileges and immunities clause."

After an extended round of applause, Josh said, "I'll take your questions now."

"The Senate majority leader spoke first. "I'd like to thank you for appearing today, Mr. Horowitz. You've made quite a case for citizenship for a domestic corporation and I'm inclined to agree with you on that point. My concern is that the corporate form might nevertheless still be used to circumvent the qualifications. For example, what's to stop a foreign national individual or a foreign corporation from taking control of an office by purchasing a substantial interest in an elected domestic corporation? In a similar vein, what's to prevent a thirty-five years in existence corporate presidency from being hijacked by a day-trading teenage prodigy trust-fund baby?"

"Excellent questions," Josh said. "I believe this sort of chicanery could be easily prevented by appropriate legislation – a rule, for example, that all officers, managers, directors, and shareholders must be of qualifying of age. On citizenship, you might draft a rule that all of them must be U.S. citizens, or in the case of president, natural-born U.S. citizens."

"The gentleman's time has expired," the chairman said. "The chair recognizes the Senator from Minnesota for five minutes."

"Mr. Horowitz," the senator said, "I'd like to preface my question with the understanding that I don't have any objection in principle to corporate candidacy. It might very well be a good idea. On the other hand, maybe it isn't such a good idea. But my personal feelings on the matter are not the issue. As you know, I'm a strict constitutionalist, which means I believe the Constitution means nothing more nor anything less than exactly what it says. And it says nothing about corporations being able to hold any of the three prestigious electoral offices we're discussing here today. How do you respond to that?"

Josh nodded. "Thank you for your question, Senator. And I'd like to preface my response, as well, by pointing out that the Constitution also does not prohibit corporations from holding office. In fact, I submit that the reason corporate inclusion is not discussed in the Constitution is because the drafters of that document didn't find it any more necessary than speculating on the identity of any other would-be office holders except to say that they must meet the minimum age, citizenship, and residency requirements.

"There is ample evidence in the federalist papers to suggest that the founders of this nation would have wholeheartedly embraced the idea of corporations as officer holders had corporations been as abundant and versatile as they are today. For example, in Federalist number thirty-five, writing on democratic representation, Alexander Hamilton dismissed as impractical, the idea that members of every class would

188

be, or should be, chosen as representatives. He proposed that the members of all classes are best represented by leaders from three discreet classes – merchants, learned professions, and the landed class.

"Now, Hamilton did acknowledge that each of these representative groups would pursue its own interests, but he embraced that. He embraced it because first, in pursuing their own interests, the ruling classes would keep one another in check. The second reason he embraced these self-interested classes was because the interests of those classes – especially the merchants – were inextricably intertwined with the interests of the masses. Hence, the masses would realize the benefit of the merchant's decisions.

"Hamilton wrote:

> *Discerning citizens are well aware that the mechanic and manufacturing arts furnish the materials of mercantile enterprise and industry. Many of them, indeed, are immediately connected with the operations of commerce. They know that the merchant is their natural patron and friend; and they are aware that however great the confidence they may justly feel in their own good sense, their interests can be more effectively promoted by the merchant than by themselves...We must therefore consider merchants as the natural representatives of these classes of the community.*

"I'd say those words are very compelling when you consider that the merchant class was the equivalent of most of today's business corporations. Hamilton drew a similar connection between the landed class and its constituency among the masses, and the landed classes were analogs of today's corporate agriculture and perhaps real estate investment interests. Of course, the modern manifestation of the learned class – doctors, lawyers, and clergy primarily – is most commonly a professional corporation.

"So, if Hamilton's choice for political leadership by the early post-independence cousins of today's most common corporations is any indication of the founders' views – and it obviously is – they would not have objected to corporate candidacy had they considered

189

corporations in the modern context. In all likelihood, they would have encouraged it."

The senator nodded. "Thank you. I yield back the balance of my time."

"The senator from Minnesota yields back. The chair recognizes the senator from Ohio."

"Mr. Horowitz, it seems to me that Attorney Miller got it right when he said that this idea of corporate rulers was a violation of the constitutional guarantee of a republican form of government that could lead us back to feudalism with a cartel of corporations lording over the former citizens that will have been reduced to serfs. By the way, any word on Mr.Miller's condition?"

"My understanding is he is well on his way to a full recovery," Josh said.

The senator nodded. "Glad to hear it. Now, can you explain how corporations and their shareholders would be prevented from using the power of government offices to pursue their own interests and the interests of others that hold sway with them – financiers, for example – at the expense of We the People."

"Thank you for the question, Senator," said Josh, "and I believe I answered part of it already in my response to the senator from Minnesota. But I'll take it a step further. My suggestion is that influence and interest be balanced by issuance of a share of stock to the president, as well as each and every member of the Supreme Court, the House of Representatives, and the Senate, in any corporation elected or appointed to any one of these positions. That way an interest in government offices will always be held properly within the realm of government."

All but a handful of dissenters stood and applauded, dollar signs gleaming from their eyes.

Chapter 41

Farnsworth glared at the television in the not-so-oval office. "This is as ridiculous as Texas thinking it can get by with absconding with half of my capitol," he complained to himself as he watched the chamber full of applauding politicians on Cspan. He jerked the telephone receiver from its cradle and dialed the Texas presidential mansion.

"Put Ms. Grant on the line," he demanded when the aide answered.

"Pardon me?"

"Something stuck in your ear, young lady? This is John R. Farnsworth, president of the United States of America. Put the governor...er, uh President, Grant on the line. And do it right this minute or I'll send a heat-seeking missile to Austin and up your hot little fanny so fast you'll be evaporated before you feel the first hemorrhoid sizzle."

"One moment please," the aide said politely.

Farnsworth sat on hold less than a minute before Grant came on the line. "What's this about heat-seeking missiles and hot fannies?"

"Just educating your aide on one of the many conflict resolution tools at my disposal," said Farnsworth. "Listen, I'm calling to see if we can't find a way to settle our little border dispute peacefully before things get out of hand."

"What do you have in mind?" said Grant.

"I was thinking maybe I could recognize Texas' historic borders and then buy that land back from you. That way we can put this silliness behind us and both save face in the process." Farnsworth ground his teeth. It was not his nature to be reasonable, and the charade he just proposed was nothing if not reasonable.

Grant sighed. "Mr. President, Texas is not for sale. Not so much as a centimeter of it."

Farnsworth tightened his grip on the phone receiver. "What about a land swap then? Say, California in exchange for the territory you're illegally encroaching upon. I'll throw New York in as a sweetener."

"California? So you've alienated the moon-bats too now, have you? Wow. You really are becoming quite the *moderate*."

"You'd get New York too," Farnsworth grumbled.

Grant laughed. "Thanks for the offer but I'm afraid I've got to decline."

"You'll regret this," Farnsworth said, and slammed the receiver down.

Chapter 42

Thursday evening, Dawn wrote up Ricky's transfer order and drove to the nursing home. She wished she could have at least one more day to prepare her nerves for this insane undertaking – or to talk herself out of it. It wasn't every day one threw away a lifetime of accomplishment to become a potential felon. But Ricky only had twenty-fours left. It was now or never.

Bernice nuzzled her head into Dawn's lap as she waited in the parking lot in the Prius.

Dawn glanced at her watch. 7:45 already. "Where in the world is Chick?"

Her cell phone rang and tears gushed from her eyes when she saw it light up with Ricky's number. A miracle had happened and he'd woken up. Just in time. "Ricky!"

"What?" said the caller's familiar voice.

Dawn's heart sunk. "Chick?"

"Yeah baby, it's me. Sorry I ain't there yet. I'm over at Ricky's place getting his address book and such so we know where we're going. I got his cell phone too, obviously. Anyway, it turns out that ranch is close to Wichita Falls, not too far from that harmonization place they sent me to in Lawton, Oklahoma. So we got to decide whether to go the interstate thirty-five to forty-four route or cut through the annexed territory. Which do you think would give us more trouble, them Texan rebels or U.S. po-lice?"

Dawn pressed a hand to her forehead, still reeling from the letdown after a powerful five seconds of believing Ricky had miraculously recovered. "Well, I…I don't know."

"Alright, we'll decide later. Go on inside and set things up. Me and my friend Arnold will be there shortly."

"Wait," Dawn said, but Chick had already hung up.

A half hour later, Chick whipped into the parking lot in a stolen ambulance and paramedic uniform. Arnold pedaled up on bicycle. They rushed inside with a stretcher and found Dawn occupying the receptionist at the front desk with small talk. "What took you so long?" she said as they whizzed past.

Chick yelled back, "Had a little trouble finding an available ambulance."

Arnold and Chick hoisted Ricky onto the stretcher and wheeled him down the hallway.

"Wait, I've got some paperwork here for you to sign," the receptionist called out as they rolled past her station.

"Sorry, I ain't got time. My shift ends in five minutes," Chick hollered over his shoulder.

Dawn said, "Nice chatting with you, Miss," and fell in behind Chick and Arnold as they barreled through the door and out to the ambulance.

"Good luck to you," said Arnold, then he climbed on the bicycle and pedaled away.

Chick climbed into the ambulance and shifted it into gear. "Follow me," he hollered out the window to Dawn.

As soon as they cleared the parking lot, a police cruiser zoomed up behind them with overhead lights flashing and siren blaring. "Yield," Dawn directed the Prius. It pulled to the side, and the cruiser sped past her, continuing in pursuit of the stolen ambulance.

Chick made a quick left turn and then a right, and another left and right, his gaze shifting back and forth between the dazzling strobe lights in his rearview mirror and the road ahead. The cell phone rang and he answered it.

"Where are you?" Dawn said, frantic.

"Hey, baby, I'm a little busy right now. I'll get back to you." Chick hung up, then made another quick left and then a right into a residential district. He glanced at the rearview mirror again. No lights behind him, but he could still hear the siren, actually multiple sirens now. A half a block up, a car backed out of a driveway, the driver leaving the garage door open. Chick killed the ambulance's headlights, slammed on the brakes, and jerked the wheel. The ambulance titled up onto two wheels, then dropped back down onto all four as he whipped it up the drive and into the open garage. He quickly pulled the garage door down, then hoisted Ricky over his shoulder and darted into the house.

A middle-aged woman in a nightgown with hair up in curlers screamed.

"Pardon me, Miss." Chick dashed out the back door and made his way around the side of the house where he dropped Ricky on the ground and crouched behind a shrub and watched as a pair of police cruisers crept slowly down the street scanning the area with searchlights.

Chick dialed Dawn's cell phone. "It's me," he whispered.

"Where are you?" Dawn whispered back.

The woman in the house bolted out the front door and ran down the street, waving her arms and screaming after the cruisers.

"Oh no." Chick shoved the cell phone into his pocket, heaved Ricky back over his shoulder and ran the opposite direction down the street.

The woman screamed again and when Chick looked back he saw her running away from the cruisers. "Them police cars been taken over by androids," she shrieked.

Chick shook his head. Apparently she missed the news about human police being replaced by harmonizers.

A few seconds later, the Prius rolled up. Chick wrestled Ricky into the back seat and piled in next to Dawn. "Scoot over, dog." He nudged Bernice, then said to Dawn, "How'd you find me so quick?"

"I followed the cruisers, how else" she directed the car to make a u-turn.

"I'm impressed," said Chick. "You might make a decent felon yet."

"Funny," Dawn said. "Where to?"

"South."

"Could you be a little more specific?"

A cruiser pulled out from a cross street, blocking the road ahead.

"Reverse!" Dawn screamed at the Prius's navigation system.

Chapter 43

Josh peered out at the twirling lights of police cruisers crawling all over town. Virtually all of Dodge City could be observed from the balcony of the Leviathan building penthouse.

"It was thoughtful of Levi to loan us this place for the evening," Gabriella said to him. "I just wish I could take in the view. It must be lovely."

"It certainly is." Josh poured some wine into her glass. "Amazing architecture going up everywhere." It was a dramatically different scene than the rest of the nation which had rapidly disintegrated since the Deep Freeze. "It's hard to believe this was just a podunk use-to-be cowtown not so long ago."

Cowtown – the word made Gabriella think of the Santana ranch. She drew in a deep breath, imagining the smells of horses, leather saddles and leather boots, of barbeque and corn on the cob, Isabella's hot rolls, cedar trees, bluebonnets, and hay, and Ricardo's cherry tobacco.

The scents kept coming, flooding into her head and swirling, mingling with other senses until she thought she might faint from sensory overload. She imagined her cheek warming against Ricky's chest, the softness of his skin stretched tautly over the hardness of all that muscle. Her fingers tingled as she imagined them running through his hair and her nose twitched at the distinct scent of his closely-cropped mane after having been under his Stetson hat all day. And dog smell. She wondered if Bernice was doing okay without Ricky.

The garbled voice of Ricky's accuser over a staticky transistor radio intruded into her mind. The romantic images of Ricky were just cruel fantasies fueled by loneliness and unsatisfied desires. Now he was where she was, where she'd been for so many years – a prisoner within himself. But unlike her, he deserved it.

She plied herself back to the present moment. No matter how horrible Ricky was, there was nothing wrong with her having feelings for Bernice. Bernice was just a dog, an innocent dog that depended on Ricky; and a dog that like her, Ricky had almost killed and then left to the mercy of others. "Any change in Ricky's condition?" she asked Josh. "I bet his dog really misses him."

"No change," Josh said, and didn't elaborate. It irritated him that she seemed to be identifying with that damn dog.

"Where is the dog now?" Gabriella wondered aloud.

"As far I know, Dawn's got it."

Josh's reference to Bernice as *It* angered Gabriella as much as the idea of that sexpot doctor woman playing guardian to Ricky's trusted companion. *It* is a pronoun for inanimate objects, not beloved pets. She decided to let it go. "So, you had something you wanted to talk about?"

"Yes." Josh took her hands in his. "I was thinking we should set a date."

His cell phone rang, interrupting the moment, and he apologized and answered it.

No need to be sorry, Gabriella thought. If anything, she'd like to thank the caller for delaying the conversation she'd dreaded since the night she'd been foolish enough to let Josh put that ring on her finger. Why had she said yes? That was the question she should have asked herself the last time he proposed, instead of, *why not say yes*. But *why not* was a good question too, maybe even the best question, all things considered, and when she thought of it like that, *yes* seemed as good an answer as any.

195

A squadron of Texas F-16s glided across the sky south of the river. Josh pressed a finger to his ear. "They did what?" he yelled into his phone over the roar of the powerful jet engines. "Has law enforcement been notified?" ..."I can't hear you. I'll have to call you back."

A flurry of leaflets streamed from the aircraft. Josh snatched one that fluttered onto the balcony:

> To the Residents of Dodge City
>
> In the coming hours, Texas will deploy troops to the south of the city below the Arkansas River to reclaim that territory for the Republic of Texas and to liberate those within the territory suffering under the tyranny of the U.S. occupiers. This operation is a response to President Farnsworth's rescission of the 1845 annexation resolution in which Texas retained the right to this and all other land within its borders, and in accordance with the agreements signed between Texas and the States of Oklahoma, New Mexico, Colorado, and Wyoming. Henceforth, all residents of the territory shall be under Texas's jurisdiction.
>
> President Cassie Grant, Republic of Texas.

Chapter 44

Dawn saw the deceptively cool blue glow of the low-flying Texas F-16s' afterburners reflected in the Prius's rear window as the car sped backwards. The automatic anti-collision system turned the car sharp left onto Central Avenue, narrowly avoiding an oncoming police cruiser.

"Accelerate," Dawn directed, and the car zoomed down the street, still in reverse.

Chick hung his head out the window. "I think we lost them."

"Forward now," Dawn ordered the Prius. It spun around. She yelped when a leaflet powered by the wind flattened against the middle of the windshield.

Chick reached out and peeled it off. "It says Texas is invading."

"Oh my God," Dawn screamed.

196

A block up they entered Wyatt Earp Boulevard.

Chick wrestled Ricky's cell phone out of his pocket and yanked Dawn's off her belt clip.

"What are you doing!" Dawn said.

"Getting shed of these," said Chick. "We ain't never going to lose the law with these trackers onboard." He tossed both phones out the window.

Dawn frantically rattled off directives to the car. "Turn right. Full power."

The tires chirped and the Prius lurched forward, then suddenly it sputtered and the engine shut down. "Come on, come on." Dawn punched in her engine activation code. The car did not respond.

A couple of cars blocked in behind them honked and several others swerved around the stalled Prius. Impatient drivers displayed middle fingers and shouted obscenities as they passed.

Dawn tried entering the code again, slowly this time to make sure she made no errors.

Still nothing.

The honking grew more intense and the two cars behind them became a line of cars.

Dawn banged her sweaty palms on the steering wheel. "What now?" She glanced up and saw a glob of cruiser lights in the rearview mirror bunching up behind the traffic. "Cops behind us. Warplanes above us. We are so screwed."

Chick said something and pointed but Dawn couldn't hear him over the blaring whistle and rumbling from a freight train chugging along the tracks across the street. "What?" she yelled.

Chick's pointing looked more like jabbing now.

"Oooh," Dawn said. They jumped out. Chick heaved Ricky over his shoulder and grabbed Dawn by the hand and they ran for the train, dodging oncoming cars. Horns blasted from every direction.

A cruiser managed to maneuver out of the traffic jam.

"We're almost there," Chick said through labored breath as he and Dawn approached the slow-moving train.

The cruiser screeched to a stop behind them and a harmonizer stepped out. "Stop immediately," it said as it marched swiftly toward them.

"You go first," Chick told Dawn when an open boxcar approached.

"Me? Why do I have to go first?"

Chick gestured his chin at Ricky dangling over his shoulder.

"Oh yeah." Dawn took a deep breath, "One, two, three." She leapt onboard.

Chick jogged alongside the train and Dawn reached out and tugged Ricky off him and into the boxcar.

The harmonizer edged closer to Chick. "Stop at once or lethal force will be used against you." It raised its arms and engaged its weapons.

"Uh-oh." Chick jumped and found himself clinging to the edge of the open boxcar, his feet dragging the ground.

Bullets pinged off the train's iron wheels.

Dawn grabbed his arm and wrenched him up.

Another bullet whizzed past Chick's feet as he wiggled the rest of the way in.

"Thank God," Dawn panted.

Chick rested a minute, then poked his head out of the boxcar, his chest heaving, and saw the glow of the harmonizer's eye-lights as it swung from the caboose.

Chapter 45

Farnsworth shifted in his easy chair in the den of the temporary presidential mansion's residential wing. His anxiety over his crumbling odds in the upcoming election had lessened some after reflecting on Josh's recommendation to Congress that the president and all members of the three branches of the federal government receive a share of stock in any corporation elected to federal office.

A share in any of them in office would undoubtedly be worth a considerable amount of money. If that office happened to be the presidency, a single share would be worth a fortune. He'd have to make some calls in the morning. Assuming Congress approved corporate candidacy and moved forward with Josh's recommendations on the rules, Farnsworth would need to persuade them to give the stock-granting provision retroactive effect. Losing the election to a corporation under those circumstances would be less than tragic.

He turned on channel three evening news. The anchor reported, "Despite Ricky Santana's prolonged coma, Vizion Inc.'s stock continues to soar amidst predictions that Congress will approve Vizion's candidacy for the presidency. In other election news, with both the republican and democrat parties' candidates running unopposed after the untimely death of Max Baxter, the RNC and DNC have agreed to move general election debates up to the period usually reserved for primary debates. Having met the threshold of fifteen percent in the polls, Vizion Inc. – the only independent on the ballot – will also participate if Congress allows its candidacy to move forward. The first debate could take place as early as June."

The anchor clutched his earpiece, "We've got breaking news coming in. Dodge City Chief of Police reports that moments ago, a squadron of Texas warplanes overflew the south side of Dodge City dropping leaflets warning of an imminent invasion of the city's south side."

"Sonofabitch!" Farnsworth jumped out of his chair. "An invasion is underway and I have to hear about it on the evening news?"

He dialed his Chief of Staff. "I want you to round up the National Security Advisor, Secretary of Internal Defense, Secretary of State, DHS Secretary, and Chairman of the Harmonization Department, and meet me in the Situation Room in a half hour. Oh, and Levi Baxter, see if he's available. And call our communications people in too. I'll need a statement and talking points prepared for a press conference."

"Yes, Mr. President, right way," the Chief of Staff said.

Farnsworth hung up and sighed. For as long as he could remember, Josh had been at his side in times of crisis, steadily and methodically transforming chaos into political fortune. But Farnsworth was on his own now. He began to laugh, then picked the phone back up and dialed the Texas presidential mansion. "Working late tonight?" he said when the aide answered.

"Always," the aide said, irritatingly cheerfully. "How may I help you?"

"This is President Farnsworth. I'd like to speak with Grant."

"Oh, hi, Mr. President. President Grant said you might call. Unfortunately she's unavailable, but she asked me to pass a message along to you."

"And that is?"

"She said to tell you Texas has hemorrhoid sizzlers too and one of them has your name on it."

Farnsworth hurled the phone and stomped downstairs to the Situation Room where he paced until his cabinet members arrived. They huddled around the conference table debating amongst themselves while Farnsworth stomped back and forth.

A few minutes later, Levi arrived.

Farnsworth planted his hands on the table. "Alright, now that everyone's here, let's get to it. I trust you all know by now that an invasion of the south side of Dodge City is under way. I'd like to hear from each of you on this, one at a time, and keep it brief. Whatever we decide, we're going to have to do it quickly. Let's start with you, Mr. Secretary of Internal Defense."

"I say we meet aggression with aggression."

"What about the political fallout?" said Farnsworth. "Once it's over they'll argue it wasn't aggression because it's legally their territory under the treaty of, uh…or the resolution in the 1800s making Texas a state, or, ah…whatever it is they're arguing."

"You have my answer, sir."

"Fine, and you?" Farnsworth pointed to the Chairman of Harmonization.

"Mr. President, I'm afraid I have to agree with the secretary."

"So what are you suggesting then?" Farnsworth pressed, "We send DHS infantry into South Dodge, drop paratroopers behind the Texans' line? Or are you saying we should go into Texas proper and teach them a lesson? Roll in some tanks? Bomb Austin? What exactly?"

"I thought you wanted us to keep it brief, sir."

Farnsworth slapped himself on the forehead. "What does it take to get a straight answer out of you people? Never mind, how about you?" he said to the Secretary of State, whose one word answer was, "Diplomacy."

Farnsworth pointed to the National Security Advisor who said, "I'd need to study it further."

"Fine you do that… And you?" Farnsworth said to the DHS Secretary.

"Well, it's a little late for preemptive action so I suggest we fortify the north side of Dodge City and take the matter, the entire matter including the issue of the other annexed territory to the GTP and ask for sanctions. My guess is it'd be an easy sell given Texas' defiance of the GTP embargo against Israel, and sooner or later Texas will have to give in and withdraw."

"That's the first answer even close to sensible that I've heard," Farnsworth said. "Although I'm not inclined to just sit on my laurels and wait to find out how long the Texans can hold out through sanctions while they burrow in on the south side of our capitol. Okay, you're all dismissed. I'll let you know what I decide."

"But, Mr. President," the Chief of Staff protested, "we haven't –"

"Go!" Except for you," Farnsworth pointed to Levi and the DHS Secretary, "and you."

The other cabinet members shuffled single file out of the Situation Room and Farnsworth slammed the door behind them and took a deep breath. "Gentleman, now that we've narrowed the input pool down to the serious-minded is there anything else?"

Levi held a hand up. "If I may, Mr. President."

"Go ahead."

"First, let's not make more of this than it is," Levi said calmly. "And what this is is nothing more than an attempt to shore up political support by the woman you transformed from duly elected governor of the State of Texas to acting President of the new Republic of Texas."

Farnsworth's eyebrows pulled together. "Think so?"

Levi drew in a deep breath. "Sure. You sucked the proverbial wind out of her sails both locally and nationally when you so brilliantly wiped her off the presidential ballot by preemptively ejecting Texas and along with it, her and every other Texan's U.S. citizenship – and voting rights – in the face of her secessionist rhetoric."

Farnsworth folded his arms across his chest. "If you're suggesting I'm at fault here, save it. I'm looking for a solution, not a lecture."

After a protracted single blink, Levi said, "Yes well, solutions require an understanding of the problem. And the problem, as I was explaining, is that you've set up a potentially disadvantageous political dynamic for our friend in the Texas presidential mansion. Although her public investment program – the so-called Texas miracle – has unquestionably given her a significant boost in popularity, she's a cautious woman. She's covering her bases by attempting to lure you into a conflict, and she's using this business about historic borders to set it up. If you take the bait, she'll be perceived as a hero, defending the Texas homeland, as it were, against you, the big bad bully, regardless of the outcome. Hero Grant, just as she was in the Red River conflict."

Farnsworth grimaced. "That crafty wench. So its checkmate then? She wins?"

Levi smiled. "Hardly. You simply refuse to play his game. Be the reasonable leader, rising above it all."

Here we go with the reasonableness bit again. Farnsworth cringed. "So just let Grant keep the ten percent or whatever it is of U.S. territory and do nothing but hope Texas will buckle under GTP sanctions? That could take years." He kneaded his forehead, the throbbing veins there giving him a massive headache. He glanced up at the DHS Secretary and said, "Is that what you meant by your recommendation?"

The DHS Secretary scratched his head. "Essentially, yes. But I would add one thing."

"And that is?"

"Don't just ask the GTP for sanctions, ask them to back it up with enforcement."

"As in military enforcement?" said Farnsworth. "Why not cut out the middleman and use DHS forces if it comes to that?"

"Because that could be construed as a violation of international law," the DHS Secretary said. "This is no longer clearly domestic. Besides I think we'd have a bit of trouble getting DHS troops to fire on Texans."

"Right," said Farnsworth. "And that's why we have the harmonizers."

The DHS secretary held a finger up. "True. And a limited operation executed by DHS harmonizers might pass as domestic."

Farnsworth turned back to Levi. "Any thoughts on that?"

"I tend to concur with the secretary," Levi said. "And that limited action should be the taking of the disputed Red River land that started all of this nonsense. That would send a strong signal to the Texans that we mean business. We could augment the forces already in the region with additional harmonizers to ensure the operation goes smoothly. I expect the Texans will withdraw from the annexed territory, including south Dodge City after that. But assuming they don't, its fearless leader will indeed be perceived as the aggressor, a bully herself, a radical wacko-bird who's destabilizing the world, destroying unity to serve her own selfish political interests. You'd be in the clear. And the global community acting through the GTP would be morally and legally bound to put Grant back in her place."

Farnsworth closed his eyes for a moment, considering the recommendation. "Very well." He turned to the DHS Secretary. "Coordinate with Levi here to expedite procurement of as many additional harmonizers as DHS needs. I'll expect deployments along the north side of the Arkansas River here in Dodge City to begin immediately. And get those along the Oklahoma border ready."

"Yes, sir, Mr. President."

"Oh, and gentlemen," said Farnsworth, "what about timing for the Red River operation?"

"I'm glad you asked," Levi said. "It seems the delusional talk show host, Mr. Ben Black has applied for a permit to hold a unity rally July fourth in Boston where undoubtedly what he really intends is to stir up dissent among our citizens. He's asking that Texans, including Grant, be guaranteed safe passage for the event. I think you should accommodate him."

"So while Grant and her entourage are bogged down in the fog of civil unrest at Ben Black's event in Boston," Farnsworth grinned, "we strike."

"Correct," said Levi.

"Good." Farnsworth clapped his hands together. "Meeting adjourned."

Levi's cell phone rang. He held a finger up. "Excuse me." He answered, "Levi Baxter."

"Levi, it's Josh. Ricky's been kidnapped."

"Oh has he now?" Levi said coolly. "So the plot thickens."

Chapter 46

As a matter of principle, Josh ending his and Gabriella's dinner at the penthouse abruptly and without explanation infuriated her. She'd had enough of the oh-so-important random phone calls that always took priority over her. And the secrecy – if something was more important than her, she deserved to know what that something was. On the other hand, she had to admit that she was far more comfortable here alone in her familiar apartment than with Josh in a luxurious penthouse. And principles aside, she felt tremendous relief at having avoided the wedding date debate. She tried to imagine the big day, but she couldn't.

Josh, conversely, had no problem imagining their wedding day. He'd been thinking about it since Gabriella was Ricky's fiancé back at Harvard. The question on his mind right now though was, *where is Ricky?* He leaned back in his chair in Ricky's former office at Vizion, confident that he knew who the abductors were. The nursing home receptionist's description of the suspects matched Chick and Dawn to a tee."

A harmonizer ushered in Dr. Shultz, who tugged a reluctant Bernice along on her leash.

"Isn't every day a comatose patient escapes," Dr. Shultz said with a chuckle.

Josh's eyes narrowed.

"Police recovered the dog from the Prius after remotely shutting down its ignition system," the Doctor explained.

"Take that mutt and put it in a cage," Josh ordered the harmonizer. "But not in there with those damn monkeys. I don't want them going ape-shit again." He chuckled at his pun as he gestured to Dr. Shultz to take a seat.

"Before you start in on me, I am not a jailer –"

Josh said, "But you are a doctor, and as a doctor you were in a position to prevent this."

"I won't be blamed for your sorely lacking skills as a helicopter saboteur," Dr. Shultz countered.

"You could have prevented this," Josh repeated.

Dr. Shultz exhaled heavily. "Expediting Ricky's demise by complying with government healthcare mandates is one thing," he said, "but intentionally overdosing him is quite another. If that's what you're suggesting I should have done. I won't commit murder for you or anyone."

"You mean you won't commit murder for anyone except the government, as you just admitted," Josh pointed out. "All I asked was that you have some compassion for a friend, make it quick and painless. But no. You'd rather he die a slow miserable death by starvation so long as it's the government requiring it. So, what do you think? Any chance Ricky's coming out of the coma?"

A look of puzzlement washed across Dr. Shultz's face. "Quite honestly, I'm not sure why he hasn't already. Any word on his whereabouts?"

Josh nodded. "It seems Dawn and Chick managed to hop a southbound freight train with him. But according to my sources at the Dodge City PD, a harmonizer patrol officer is also onboard. It shouldn't be long before Ricky's returned to the facility and Dawn and that felon are locked up in harmonization."

Chapter 47

"Chick, what is the matter with you?" Dawn tried to shake him out of the trance.

The train chugged slowly along toward highway 56 and the old Santa Fe Trail.

"Isn't it all so beautiful?" Chick said dreamily. The expression on his face made him look like a happy lunatic.

Dawn slapped him. "Come on. How are we supposed to get all the way to Texas with you and Ricky both out of it?"

Chick shuddered and after a series of rapid blinks, seemed to come back to his senses. He peeked out at the caboose. No harmonizer.

"What was that all about?" Dawn said.

"I don't know. It just happens every now and then since I got that harmonization vaccination. All the sudden the whole world just gets colorful and happy, kind of tinted like or something. Then it goes back to normal."

Dawn contemplated the mysterious vaccine again and whether Chick's spell might have been some sort of side-effect from it. Then another thought entered her mind. "Chick?"

"Yeah?"

"We forgot Bernice."

Chick's eyes widened. "We dang sure did." He crawled to the open boxcar door and prepared to jump.

"Wait!" Dawn grasped his arm. "What are you doing? I can't handle this alone. I don't even know where I'm going. And even if I did, I can't lug Ricky around all by myself. In case you haven't noticed, he's not a small man."

"Just stay on the train. I'll catch up to you." Chick kissed her and then jumped.

"Dear God!" Dawn slumped back against the boxcar wall and closed her eyes, trying not to think about what might happen if Chick didn't come back – or what might happen if he did. But more than anything else, she found herself worrying about his safety. She felt like crying but she wouldn't let herself. And just how did Chick plan to catch up with a train anyway? ...Oh. He'd steal another vehicle she supposed. He was obviously good at that. She slapped herself on the forehead for feeling relieved that her coconspirator was a talented car thief.

After the train had chugged along for another twenty minutes or so, Dawn began to worry again. Where is he? She crawled over to the side to look out. "Oh my God," she gasped, and cupped a hand over her mouth when she saw a stream of headlights from a convoy of trucks and armored personnel carriers with Texas flags flapping in the breeze above them. The convoy halted and an officer with a handlebar mustache and a gigantic cowboy hat hopped out of the lead vehicle and pointed. He seemed to be pointing at her.

She scrambled into a corner out of sight and peeked around the open door. The officer continued pointing, only now more vigorously. He yelled something, but she couldn't hear him.

A pair of robotic arms swung down from atop the boxcar. Dawn screamed, and scooted away, kicking violently at the harmonizer.

The pointing officer rushed the train, and several other soldiers piled out of trucks.

Sparks flew and iron wheels screeched against the tracks as the train clunked and clanked to a jerky stop, almost dislodging the harmonizer from its perch.

The officer drew his side arm as he neared the train in a swift jog. "Get down from there immediately and keep your hands where I can see them," he yelled.

The harmonizer continued swiping at Dawn.

Another soldier kneeled and raised an RPG launcher to his shoulder while several other troops converged on the train.

"This is your final warning," the officer shouted.

The harmonizer stood and extended an arm, deploying its weapon.

The officer gave a nod to the soldier with the RPG launcher.

"Oh no." Dawn squeezed her eyes shut.

The soldier trained the barrel of the RPG launcher at the top of the boxcar above her.

Several other soldiers climbed into the boxcar and dragged Dawn and Ricky out and rushed away with them to the convoy.

The soldier with the RPG launcher fired. Whoosh!

Chunks of harmonizer rained down alongside the tracks.

Dawn clung to the officer while a couple of other soldiers heaved Ricky's limp body into the back of a truck. "You won't be having any more trouble out of that robot," the officer told Dawn with a satisfied grin. He shined a flashlight onto the face of the man laid out in the truck. "Ricky?"

The officer turned back to Dawn. "What happened to this man?"

Dawn explained about Ricky's helicopter crash, the coma, that she was a doctor, how she and Chick had rescued Ricky from the nursing home, and all the rest. "We had to do something," she finished, "or they would have starved him to death."

The officer scrutinized her face skeptically.

"Why are you looking at me like that?" Dawn said. "And why are you so concerned about Ricky anyway? Isn't your occupation of south Dodge City or whatever this is you and your troops are doing here enough to keep you busy?"

"My name is Juan Rodriguez, Texas border patrol chief. These men are here to secure the area so we can begin construction of the new border wall. And that man laying in the truck happens to be like a brother to me. We grew up together on the Santana Ranch."

Dawn's eyes popped open wide. What a stroke of luck. Or was it?

Juan ordered one of the troops to zip-tie Dawn's hands.

She thrashed. "What are you doing?"

"Give her some water and make sure she don't go anywhere," Juan told the soldier binding her hands. Then he snatched his cell phone off his belt and started up into the cab of the truck. He turned back to Dawn. "I'm going to check out your story and if it's true, I'll arrange transportation for you to the Santana ranch. If it turns out you're lying to me..."

A few minutes later, Juan hopped out of the truck. The driver got out next, tied a white handkerchief to the antenna, then climbed back onboard. The diesel engine rattled to life and black smoke spit from the stack.

"I just got off the phone with a Mr. Joshua Horowitz who's apparently filling in for Ricky at Vizion, and his story is quite a bit different than yours," Juan said. "He's having a medical transport team sent to meet my driver to pick up Ricky and return him to where he can get proper care. The Dodge City police are on their way for you."

Dawn squirmed and thrashed, trying to free her hands from the zip-tie. "Look, if you want to turn me over to the police, go right ahead but you can't let them have Ricky. He'll die."

The driver shifted the truck into gear and it lurched forward, bouncing Ricky out the back and splatting him onto the ground. The driver continued onward unaware.

Juan ran to Ricky.

Dawn hobbled after him like a penguin with hands bound behind her back.

They both dropped down to their knees.

Ricky moaned.

Juan glanced at Dawn and said, "On second thought, I think I'll take him back to Wichita Falls."

A Dodge City police cruiser approached with blue lights activated.

Chapter 48

It took all of the strength Ricky had to sit up.

Isabella reached over from the bedside chair and squeezed his hand. "Hijo, it is good to have you home again."

He looked at her wonderingly.

"How are you feeling?" she said.

"I'm…ah, well, I'm…" He shifted his body a centimeter or two.

Juan barged in with Dr. Daniel Langford, an old friend of Ricardo's and also the Santana family's physician since Ricky was a young boy.

Isabella smiled at the doctor. "Did you and Ricardo get to visit a minute?" she said.

Juan wrapped his hands around Ricky's and Isabella's hands.

Dr. Langford took off his Stetson and bowed his head slightly and said, "It's hard seeing Ricardo like that. And I don't mean to be harsh, but it's unwise of you to leave him unattended. Folks with his conditions might wander off or worse." He pulled his shoulders back, attempting a more optimistic posture and smiled at Ricky. "And how are you doing, young man?"

"Ricardo never goes far," said Isabella.

Dr. Langford let the comment go, though he knew it wasn't true. He'd come to examine Ricky, not to discuss the obvious catastrophes that might arise from allowing a bipolar Alzheimer's patient with PTSD, among other things, to do just whatever he pleased, including flying aircraft.

Ricky examined the doctor's face and said weakly, "Do I know you?"

"Only since you was knee high to a jackrabbit, son." Dr. Langford glanced back at Isabella and then Juan. "I'll need a few minutes alone with Ricky here if y'all wouldn't mind."

"Not at all," Isabella said, and she and Juan left the bedroom.

A few minutes later, the doctor came out to the den where Juan told Isabella, "I hope it was the right thing to do, turning that gal over to the Dodge City police. But I just don't know. Maybe she really was a doctor. I've got an uneasy feeling about the whole thing. And did I tell you they wanted me to turn Ricky over too? Came mighty close to a shootout over that."

"Doctor?" Isabella said to Langford, her eyes pleading for a positive prognosis.

He fiddled with the hat in his hands and said, "Physically, Ricky appears to be fine. Muscles have atrophied some from a few weeks without use but a good physical therapy regimen will take care of that. No neurological issues so far as I can tell."

"What about his mind?" Juan said bluntly.

Langford said, "Retrograde amnesia, I'm afraid. It happens sometimes with head trauma. The good news is the memory loss is usually temporary. The bad news is it isn't always."

"What can we do to help?" said Isabella.

Ricardo came in and he smiled at the doctor with surprise as though he hadn't just visited with him a short while earlier. "Buenos tardes, doctor. What brings you out to the ranch?"

"Just came to look in on that fine boy of yours. You must be mighty proud of him, despite that unfortunate...well, we've all made mistakes, especially in our youth."

"Yes, I am very proud of both of my sons," Ricardo said, and lit his pipe.

Dr. Langford returned to Isabella's question, with a look of grave concern as much for Ricardo as for Ricky. "There's cognitive therapy, hypnosis, and a couple of other treatments for amnesia, but the effectiveness of any of them is questionable." His tone expressed no more confidence than his words. "For now I'd say just immerse him in life as it was before the crash as best you can."

"But I know nothing about what his life was like for him for the past many years," Isabella fretted.

"Don't let that trouble you," said Langford. "Reminders of earlier life experiences often work better than more recent ones anyway. In fact, early childhood is the best. If you can reconnect him to those memories the rest will likely follow in short order."

Isabella nodded her understanding.

"Well, I best be going." The doctor put his Stetson back on. "I'll be out next week to see how he's doing." He shook Ricardo's hand. "It was great seeing you again, my friend. You take care of yourself now, you hear."

"Thanks for coming out," Juan said.

"Yes, thank you," said Isabella. She reached for Ricardo's hand and led him toward the kitchen. "Come along, Papa, it is time to take your medicine."

Juan kissed Isabella on the cheek, then put his hat on. "I've got to get back to Dodge City. We've got a wall to build."

Isabella hugged him and said, "You be careful, Juan."

Chapter 49

Chick held his arms up and sniffed at his pits. "Shuwee. Another night in this creek bed and I won't be able to stand to be around myself," he muttered. He ducked instinctively when he heard the rumbling of a diesel engine as another semi docked at the warehouse next to Vizion. Trucks had been coming and going from there all night. Strange, considering the place had been abandoned for several years. Curiosity got the best of him and he slipped around back and peeked through an open bay door. "Wow, old-timey robots." There must have been hundreds of them strewn about haphazardly.

Two silver-headed men were looking down at them and talking. Chick cupped a hand around his ear to listen. One of them squatted and lifted a robots' foot, and then another's foot, and another. "Looks like they all came from the same line," Chick heard him say. "Manufacture date stamped on them is Nov. 2, 2001. Pretty old."

"Too bad they aren't even older," the other man said. "One of them could run for president. But any of them is old enough to run for the House of Representatives."

They both laughed.

"Maybe they could be refurbished," said the first man. "I've always thought it would be a good idea to make these things available for household use. For everybody. Like cars and dishwashers used to be. Imagine how much individuals could increase their productivity by leveraging the work of one of these."

The other man nodded. "Empowering individuals, now you're talking. Couple a personal robot and semi-industrial scale 3-D printer

210

with basic education in engineering, agriculture, and home-economics like they're doing in Texas, and presto, every household could do its own manufacturing and grow its own crops. The only thing that'd be left standing between the people and darn near total self-sufficiency would be water and energy."

"And regulation," the first man added. "I hear the new water and energy program down in Texas is going well so far. We ought to take a trip down there and check on the progress."

The other man's cell phone rang. Chick couldn't hear what he said when he answered it but he could tell by the fade of the enthusiastic glow from the man's face that whatever the caller had to say was not good news. The man held the phone down for a minute and told the other man to get their legal department on the line. Chick thought he said something about a rescue mission.

Chick could have stood there and listened all morning. He liked the way these men seemed to think. Plus, that call had his curiosity on overdrive. But, he reminded himself, he had a mission to accomplish. He crept back over to Vizion and flattened his body against the ground behind the row of low-profile shrubs along the chain-link security fence.

The office door creaked open. Right on time.

Josh stepped out into the parking lot with Bernice. "Go do your business, mutt."

The old dog growled, then stumbled out into the lot sniffing around, and Josh went back inside, presenting Chick the opportunity he'd waited for.

Chick pulled up the severed electrical conduit he'd unearthed the night before and snipped the wires, then held his breath, squeezed his eyes shut, and poked at the electrified fence. His breath rushed out in a wave of relief. He had neutered the correct wires. He clamped onto the fence with a pair of bolt-cutters and chopped methodically, then whistled. "Bernice."

Her ears perked up and she twisted her head. Chick chuckled. "Dang dog looks like a four-legged hairy alien with them goggles on." She sniffed at the air, and after picking up Chick's scent galloped over to the fence, tongue dangling and tail wagging. He reached into the opening he'd created and helped her wiggle through. She lapped at his face with her long slobbery tongue and he scratched her ears. "Good to see you too, ol' gal." He tugged at her collar. "Come on, we got to go catch up with Dawn. She's probably having a real hissy by now."

Chick turned to look when he heard another vehicle passing slowly – a *Cole Brothers Industries* cargo van, a relic with a driver. Vizion's alarm screeched like an air raid siren. "Oh no." He hoisted Bernice over his shoulders and ran for the van. He jerked the door open. "I got an emergency, I need to borrow this." He pulled the driver out and took his place behind the steering wheel. Bernice tumbled into the floorboard and the driver rolled over to the side of the road. "Sorry about that," Chick yelled out, and floored the accelerator.

Inside Vizion, Josh turned the alarm off and rewound the surveillance tape to review it. He laughed out loud as he watched the video of Chick chopping the primary wires to the electrified fence. The idiot would have fried if Josh hadn't shut down the backup power to ensure he would be able to make a clean getaway with that mutt. He switched to a live feed of Chick's right shoe on the gas pedal transmitted from Bernice's goggles. He laughed again. The microcomputer and transmitter Dr Schultz had had installed during the dog's grooming session at Leviathan worked fabulously. He switched to map view to verify that the GPS chip was also functioning correctly.

"And now for the fun part. Another overlay test," Josh whispered as he picked up the telephone. He dialed Leviathan. "Yes, this is Josh Horowitz," he said when the switchboard operator answered. "Connect me to station ten-ninety-seven in harmonization, please."

"Doghouse," the pilot answered.

Josh laughed. "This is Josh Horowitz, deharmonize test-animal number one for sixty seconds, please."

"Right away, sir." The officer flipped the switch.

Josh looked back at the live feed from the mini-camera in Bernice's goggles and chuckled as he watched the dog yelp and dive over into the floorboard on the driver side, hooking her collar on the accelerator pedal.

Chick swerved wildly, almost crashing the Cole Brothers van.

"Dang, dog. You trying to kill us?" Josh heard Chick say.

Chapter 50

A miserable night on a concrete floor in a packed holding cell at the Lawton, Oklahoma harmonization camp frazzled Dawn to the bone and she couldn't have been more relieved when the Cole Brothers showed up with a high powered attorney and a court order for her release.

"I can't thank you enough for getting me out of here," she said to Don Cole. "I would have called someone else but I've never been in any kind of trouble and I didn't know really who to call." She hugged him, then his brother Tom. "They had me scheduled for that harmonization vaccine this afternoon and from what I've seen of others who've gotten it…" She glanced over at a long line of people waiting their turn to go into a door with a sign above it that said: *Harmonization Vaccines, Get yours now, It's mandatory!* "Let's just say it's hard to know whether they'll be zombies or normal from one minute to the next."

"I'm glad you had my card handy to call," Don Cole said. "We would have gotten here sooner but we had a little incident at the warehouse we just acquired next to Vizion. Someone stole one of our vans. Unfortunately, it was one of the few manually operated ones in our fleet so we couldn't reroute it remotely. Anyway," he gestured at the attorney, "don't thank us, thank him."

The lawyer stepped forward and shook Dawn's hand. "Attorney Miller. It's a pleasure to meet you, doctor. I've heard about your work at Vizion and it's not only impressive it's commendable. Sorry I can't say the same about Vizion's determination to pervert our system of government."

"Did," Dawn said.

"Pardon?"

"I *did* work at Vizion. That backstabber, Joshua Horowitz terminated the artificial eye project and fired me."

Miller shook his head. "Josh, huh? So *he's* in charge now?"

"Did you say Josh terminated the artificial eye project?" Tom Cole said. "That project is the reason we invested in Vizion at the IPO. It's also the reason we approved the grants from the Cole Brothers Foundation. And frankly, it's one of the main reasons we contributed to Vizion's campaign – although there were certainly other considerations for that."

Dawn nodded. "I'm sorry. There was no way Ricky or I could have known something like this was going to happen." She could see the wheels turning in Tom Cole's eyes as he glanced over at Miller.

213

"We could bring a shareholder derivative suit to force that imbecile to rethink it," Miller said, "but that could take a while and there's no guarantee we'd win."

Tom Cole paced. "Dr. Wise, might you be willing to consider continuing the project under the banner of Cole Brothers Industries?"

"I'd agree to that in a heartbeat if it were up to me," said Dawn, "but the patents for the artificial eye are in Ricky's name. Plus, the neural code technology requires too much computing space. And the testing ban has basically brought us to a standstill. And the research animals are… " She slapped herself on the forehead. "The animals are still at Vizion!"

"Hmm. Ricky still in a coma?" Tom Cole continued to pace.

"Actually, I don't know," Dawn said. "As I explained to you on the phone, he moaned for the first time in two months when he fell off that truck, but I don't know if he's regained consciousness."

"Miller, can you get the court to appoint a guardian for Ricky that would be friendly to us?" Tom Cole said.

"I'm sure Josh would oppose anyone we propose," Miller grinned, "but I'd welcome a rematch. I eat snot-nosed little turds like him for breakfast."

Dawn laughed at that, turds for breakfast. Miller obviously knew Josh and apparently thought even less of him than she did. She examined Miller more closely. Miller…where had she heard that name before? It came to her. "Mr. Miller, aren't you the attorney that represented President Farnsworth and the Baxters in the lawsuit against Vizion's candidacy?"

"One and the same," Miller said proudly if less boisterously than he might have before the heart attack slowed him down. "And I assure you we would have prevailed if the Supreme Court hadn't lacked the courage to take the case on."

Dawn nodded tentatively. "I guess we'll never know. But for what it's worth, I had very mixed feelings about this corporations-for-president business until Josh took over for Ricky at Vizion. Now I am adamantly opposed to it."

"Good girl." Miller held a fist up to his mouth and coughed. "Experiencing the reality of the slippery slope first hand has a funny way of clearing the cobwebs from one's thinking."

That irked Dawn. She wanted to tell him that her thinking already functioned just fine, but instead she said, "Working on any exciting new cases?"

"Other than yours?" He chuckled through another cough. "Actually, maybe. I'm on my way to Austin to discuss legal options with President Grant on the threatened GTP intervention matter."

"Really? I don't suppose I could ride along with you?"

Miller raised an eyebrow. "To Austin?"

"No. To the Santana Ranch. Should be along the way. It's supposed to be by the Red River."

"I know right where it is," Miller said. "Ricardo Santana and the other ranchers retained me to defend their land from confiscation before that BLM matter got settled the way it did. The old man ever get a telephone installed?"

Dawn said, "I wasn't aware they had no phone."

"No matter," said Miller. "I'll have my pilot radio ahead on the unicom. It's not more than a twenty minute flight from here in my Citation jet."

"Tom and I will follow you to the ranch in our plane and see you in Austin tomorrow?" Don Cole said. "We've got some business to discuss with President Grant as well."

"What sort of business?" said Miller.

"Oh, some old robot business."

The ground rumbled and an eerie breeze blew in. Dawn covered her mouth and gasped. Harmonizers, thousands of them, marched in formation.

Miller placed his hand firmly in the center of her back. "We should go before we get caught in the middle of something."

Chapter 51

Six hours later, the stolen Cole Brothers Industries van's headlamps lit up the Santana Ranch sign at the entrance to the property. Chick lowered the window and took in the scent of a campfire.

The Cole brothers sat around the fire pit with Miller and Dawn discussing the deal they'd made with Josh to buy the research animals from Vizion and how to proceed with the project. Although the temperature outside was just short of sweltering, the smoke helped to ward off mosquitoes. "Dr. Wise can commence animal testing as soon as you get the articles of incorporation filed for the new company here in Texas, can't she?" Don Cole said to Miller.

"I don't see why not. There's no ban on testing here in Texas that I'm aware of." Miller stood when he saw the headlights.

Tom Cole stood up as well. "That looks like our van."

"Sure does," Don Cole said.

Miller reached for his cell phone. "I'll call the police."

Chick hopped out of the van.

"Wait." Dawn grasped Miller's hand. "It's Chick."

"Who?" The Coles and Miller said simultaneously.

Dawn ran to Chick and he gathered her up in his arms and twirled her.

Tears of relief streamed down Dawn's face.

Chick put her down and she pulled away, her fingers gliding from his shoulders down his arms to his hands. She locked her fingers in his and gazed up into his eyes. "Oh, Chick. I was afraid something bad had happened to you."

He bent down and kissed her.

"Did you find Bernice?" Dawn said after that.

"Yeah, she's conked out in the van." Chick kissed her again.

"Okay. Okay. That's enough of that," said Dawn.

Chick smiled. "Whatever you say, baby. You get Ricky here okay?"

"Yes. Well, actually his friend, Juan did and the cops got me and..." Dawn's weary eyes flooded with joy. "Ricky's regained consciousness. But –"

"Halleluiah!" Chick pulled her close again and squeezed her tightly.

Tom Cole cleared his throat.

"Oh, sorry." Dawn turned back to the others. "This is Chick. He's the one that's been helping me with Ricky. Chick, these are some new friends. This is –"

"Attorney Miller," the lawyer said for himself, "and that van belongs to –"

Tom Cole broke in and shook Chick's hand. "I'm Tom Cole and this is my brother, Don, and the van you're driving is the property of Cole Brothers Industries."

It took a minute for Chick to recognize them in the firelight as the two silver-headed men from the warehouse. "Oooh. Yeah. Well, I can't tell you how much I appreciate you letting me borrow it. I'm all done with it now if you want it back."

Miller raised his cell phone again. "That sounds like a confession to me. Shall I call the police now?"

"That won't be necessary," Tom Cole said. "We've got it back now. No harm no foul."

Chick let out a relieved sigh. He'd had enough running for one night. "Can I see Ricky?"

"He is sleeping," a small voice said, startling them all.

Dawn held a hand to her chest, then smiled at the frail woman who had slipped quietly though the darkness to the other side of the fire pit. "Good evening, Mrs. Santana, I didn't realize you were up still."

"I came to ask if you all need anything before I go to bed," Isabella said.

"Got any water?" said Chick.

Isabella pointed to a tin cup dangling from the hand crank on the well. Then she planted her cane in front of her and limped back to the main house.

Chick gulped down three cups, then rejoined the others around the fire. It was quiet now except for crickets chirping and the occasional snap and crackle of the burning logs.

"Ricky looks pretty good, all things considered," Tom Cole said, "besides the shaggy hair and beard." All of them except Chick had visited with Ricky earlier in the day.

"Yes he does," said Miller, shaking his head. "It's a shame about his memory though. That could be a problem in the future if he were to change his mind about allowing his artificial eye to be used in continued research."

"You think he'd challenge his own signature authorizing that?" Tom Cole said.

Dawn sighed. "He won't change his mind. He's a good and decent man whether he remembers he is or not." That sounded odd to her even though she was the one who had said it. "If you should worry about anything, it's Josh changing his mind about selling you the research animals. Not that he has any purpose for them now, but lately he seems capable of just about anything to undermine Ricky."

"Oh now don't you worry about that," Tom Cole said. "I wired Josh the money right after I received his electronic John Hancock on the agreement by email." He gave Dawn's shoulder a squeeze. "The animals have already been loaded on a Cole Brothers Industries big rig and they're en route to the ranch as we speak."

Dawn hugged him. "Thank you so much." She hesitated a moment before asking a question that had been on her mind since she met the Cole Brothers for the first time at Vizion's Dodge House fundraiser. "Mr. Cole?"

"Please call me Tom."

"Alright, *Tom.* I hope this doesn't come off as rude. But I've got to know why you and your brother are so famous for being evil greedy corporatists. You don't seem like that to me."

Tom Cole chuckled. "What, we don't strike you as men interested in pooling our money and talents to earn a profit producing goods and services that benefit humanity?"

"That isn't what I mean," Dawn said.

Tom Cole said, "I'm playing with you. That garbage you hear is misinformation pedaled by competitors with a different business philosophy than ours. Their view is that success requires gigantic barriers to entry. And they won't hesitate to pay off politicians to create those barriers through strategic regulations, tax loopholes, mandates, subsidies, and that kind of thing. It's all about monopoly. And if they can't get an absolute monopoly, they'll settle for a cartel."

"And that's accomplished by regulation?" Dawn said curiously.

Tom Cole nodded. "Yes, regulation and the other things I mentioned. For example, in the energy industry, a good case in point, it costs millions of dollars to comply with the regulations required for approval to *explore* a natural gas field. Needless to say, that's an enormous barrier to entry that narrows the playing field to only those with seriously deep pockets. So, that's how the proverbial little guy is squeezed out from the very start.

"Throw in a subsidy or a tax break to one company or industry and that winnows it even further because lowering the cost of doing business for one effectively increases the cost to competitors that don't receive the same tax breaks or subsidies. That cost increase is a barrier to entry few can overcome."

Dawn took a moment to absorb what he'd said. "I see. So is it true that your companies get subsidies and tax breaks like I hear on the news all the time?"

Tom Cole's one word answer – "Yes."

"So you're a monopolist yourself then," Dawn scoffed. Despite the kindness the Cole Brothers had shown her, she was starting to rethink whether it was a good idea to associate herself, much less Ricky's artificial eye project, with these kind of men.

"It's a matter of necessity," Tom Cole explained. "As things stand currently, subsidies and tax loopholes are a fact of life. Cole Brothers Industries is forced to fight for its share, not to gain an unfair advantage but to level the playing field. Otherwise, we'd be out of business." He sighed. "Don't think for a minute that we wouldn't rather this ugliness be eliminated altogether. This never-ending pursuit of favor from politicians is exhausting and expensive, and the cost is ultimately passed down to the individual."

"Is that so?" Dawn said incredulously.

"Well, sure," said Tom Cole. "We spend twenty percent of our revenues and probably fifty percent or better of our time on lobbyists, politicians, and lawyers to deal with regulations and tax code legislation. All of that expense goes directly into the price of our products and services. Add it up. Eliminating those costs would create a huge savings to the individual. If you can explain to me how individuals benefit from paying higher prices, I might rethink my views."

Dawn looked like she was going to start pulling her hair out in globs. "But isn't the idea behind subsidies to *lower* the cost to individuals?"

Tom Cole scrubbed his hands together over the fire. "That's the pitch. But messing with all this can cost a business as much as the subsidy itself. Plus, think about who pays for a subsidy. That comes from tax dollars, right? So it's a double-whammy against individuals."

"Right." Dawn had him cornered now. Or so she thought. "Which is why we should have higher taxes on corporations," she said. "So *they* can pay for the subsidies *they* receive."

"Sure, and then as I've said, that cost is added by the corporation back into the price to the individual for the product or service."

Dawn rolled her eyes. "Government regulation of prices would solve that."

"Maybe you ought to run for office," Tom Cole teased. "I suspect it wouldn't be hard to convince the other numbskulls in Congress to go along with you on an idea like that."

"Maybe I will run." Dawn couldn't believe she said that. She wasn't serious. But she had to admit she had fantasized about being the president's medical research director when she was employed by

219

Vizion. And that would have been like being partly president, something maybe on par with being a congresswoman. But now, this corporate candidacy thing was just plain crazy.

"You'd make a fine congresswoman if you had any idea what you were talking about," said Tom Cole.

"Pardon me?"

"Your comment on price fixing," Tom Cole said. "We don't have to wonder whether it's a good idea because it's been tried by almost every country in the world – including the U.S. during FDR's presidency – and without exception, the result is always the same. Rather than a reduction in prices, there's a reduction in available goods and services. When companies can't make a profit producing something, they stop producing. But I was serious about you making a good congresswoman."

In less than a minute he'd promoted her from village idiot to hypothetical congresswoman. She let it go. "So that's it? We the people," *we the people*, jeez, she was starting to sound like one of those wackadoodle Constitution worshippers, "are just stuck? There's nothing we can do?"

Miller stepped forward. "Of course there's something we can do," he said. "And if we do it, we'll eliminate ninety percent of the country's problems virtually overnight and the economy will boom like never before."

Dawn's eyes darted from Tom Cole to Don Cole to Miller. "What? Do what? What do we do for that to happen?" She glanced down at Chick, who'd fallen asleep with his head in her lap.

"We demand our elected officials permanently terminate all subsidies and replace the current two-hundred-thousand plus page income tax scheme with a one line flat consumption tax," Tom Cole said. "If our elected officials refuse to implement these two simple reforms, we throw the bums out."

Dawn said, "Consumption tax, huh?"

"Yes," said Don Cole. "You might recall Governor Mike Huckabee of Arkansas urging passage of the *fair tax*. It's similar to what I'm suggesting. One rate that every person and entity pays on every purchase. And before you say it, no, a consumption tax does not burden the poor disproportionately. The opposite is true because the largest corporations and the richest among us purchase far more than the poor. No purchase, no tax. Big purchase, big tax. Moreover, that kind of tax system results in far fewer poor people because it penalizes frivolous consumption and rewards productivity and saving. And that probably explains why we haven't had such a policy in the U.S. for over a century. For politicians running as champions of the poor, less poor people equals less votes. You see what I'm saying?"

Dawn looked at Don Cole skeptically. "If all the nation's ills could be solved just that easily, then why hasn't it been done already?"

Tom Cole reclaimed the lead of the conversation. "It has been done, here in Texas. I can only speculate that the U.S. politicians' insatiable appetite for money and power is why it hasn't been implemented there. If the people in the U.S. took away their representatives' power to use the tax code to decide who can prosper and who must live in poverty, they'd also be taking away the incentive for those with deep pockets to pour money into campaigns.

"You see, the way it works is this, corrupt elected officials coordinate with lobbying firms and corporations to rig the business game through legislation – subsidies, tax code, and regulation, primarily, as we've been discussing. Those same corporations and lobbying firms reciprocate by contributing generously to the democrat and republican parties and their candidates as well as super PACs. That virtually guarantees reelection for incumbent politicians.

"In the odd event an incumbent loses an election, he's rewarded with a lucrative job at one of these corporations or lobbying firms. It's a revolving door, and a multi-billion dollar enterprise. That's billions upon billions of dollars in favors bought and sold. And nothing whatsoever is produced for all of that money. Tell me what value it adds to society when billions of dollars are directed away from production of anything useful and into the influence pedaling industry?"

Dawn went almost cross-eyed from information overload. "Well...I...none, I guess."

"Right," said Tom Cole. "Yet we the people keep reelecting bought and paid for republican and democrat party incumbents. Why? Because they're good at carving us up into warring tribes, democrats and republicans, who'll vote for any crook that can convince them he can beat the other team's crook. Ironically, these clever politicians are just as skilled at a variation of the strawman game, turning us against their corporate masters. But it's a shell game.

"Here's an example: The incumbent blasts so-called big oil for being heartless and greedy, etcetera. Then after the incumbent has gotten the people's ire up, he promises to make big oil pay its *fair share*, to tax big oil to the edge of oblivion. Now he's a hero standing up to the corporate oil monster. So, we elect the heroic incumbent, and he proceeds to keep his promise – or so it appears – typically in one of two ways: By a show-vote with assurances his colleagues will vote to defeat the proposed tax, or by discreetly inserting a subsidy amendment that offsets or even exceeds the tax. After the math is done, it's usually a gift to big oil disguised as punishment for the crime of making a profit.

"That's the game – show votes, accounting gimmicks, smoke and mirrors. It's one of the reasons we see two-thousand page legislation for measures that should require no more than a paragraph or two. And by the way, your legislators don't draft the tax code or any other legislation. Heck they don't even read it before they vote on it. Corporations, lobbyists, and think-tanks are the real legislators. The politicians merely rubberstamp them – after their aides pretend to review them, of course.

"The Dodd-Frank legislation to supposedly reform the banking system after the fraud that shifted the downfall of the United States' economy into high gear is one of the more notable examples of regulated entities writing the rules themselves – in this case, the entity was the central banking cartel. True to the game, the legislation did not restrain the big banks that perpetrated the fraud. Instead, it punished community banks and individual financiers who had nothing to do with it, ultimately, forcing a great many of them out of business; thus, further diminishing individual's financing options and moving the central banking cartel one giant leap closer to the monopoly it's always been after."

Dawn scrubbed her tired eyes with the heels of her hands. "Wow. If politicians don't even make the laws, then what do they do?" She yawned.

"Work on getting reelected mostly. If we ever implemented term limits, I suppose they'd have nothing to do at all." Don Cole paused. "Doctor, as much as I'd like to see a man or woman of the people or even a corporation of the people in the Whitehouse, I don't see it happening this time around. But that's not as tragic as it seems. The real prize is the House of Representatives. If we had an overwhelming

222

majority in the House – representatives with a heart for the people, like you have – we could get the United States back on track in no time. Of course it takes more than heart. You have to have the right mind for it too, and a backbone of steel."

Dawn yawned again. "Are you suggesting I have a deficient mind?"

"Actually, I'm suggesting you have an extraordinary mind, if you'll use it," Don Cole said. "Why don't you consider running for Congress in your district."

"I'll think about it," Dawn said, although all she could think about right now was getting some sleep. She shook Chick awake when she heard Bernice whining from the van.

Tom Cole glanced around at the others. "I don't know about you all, but I'm bushed. Shall we call it a night?"

Miller's and Don Cole's tired nods signaled their answer.

Chick got up and stumbled sleepy-eyed to the Van to let Bernice out.

The dog squatted and did her business.

"I do have one last question before we turn in," Dawn said to Tom Cole. "Why do you suppose this political con-job isn't common knowledge? It seems like the media would report it."

Tom Cole yawned again. "Who do you suppose owns the media?"

The Cole Brothers Industries big rig carrying the research animals rumbled up the drive.

Chapter 52

Miller and the Cole brothers departed for Austin a few minutes after sunrise, right about the time that Ricky shuffled out on his walker into the dining room. Ricardo sat at the table there reading the morning paper, his AM radio spitting out staticky gurgling about an upcoming early presidential debate.

Outside, the apes whooped and chattered at pounding hammers and whining power saws. Startled chickens cackled, pigs oinked and snorted, and the half dozen goats from Vizion bleated.

"Your friends are turning this ranch into a zoo," Ricardo said, his eyes still glued to his newspaper.

"Is that so bad?" Ricky stroked his long beard.

Isabella scampered in and topped off Ricardo's coffee and handed Ricky a cup.

"We have always had animals here," Ricardo mumbled. "I do not guess a few more of them will hurt anything as long as they are not imbedded with spy cameras."

Isabella shook her head sadly and set Ricardo's pill organizer on the table. "It is time for your morning medicine, Papa."

The pounding of hammers and whine of power saws continued.

Ricky said, "What are they doing out there?"

"They are building pens for your zoo," said Ricardo. "Why don't you go and help them."

Isabella clutched Ricky's arm. "You must not push yourself too hard, hijo."

"Pushing myself is exactly what I have to do," Ricky said, and grabbed his hat. "Thank you for the coffee, ma'am." He headed outside and the spring-loaded screen door clapped shut behind him.

"Hey, Ricky," Dawn called out, waving from her perch on a ladder leaning against the frame of a new lab. Francisco's boys stopped their work on the project and turned to look.

Chick set his saw down on a sheet of plywood laid across a pair of wooden sawhorses and pulled off his work gloves and shook Ricky's hand. "You lookin' good, brother man," he said.

Ricky nodded, a distant look in his eyes. "Thank you, I guess."

Dawn climbed down and ran to Ricky. She looped an arm through Chick's and kissed Ricky on the cheek. Bernice squirmed out from under the front porch and hobbled out and slurped at Ricky's hands. He reached down and scrubbed her between the ears. "Well ain't you a pretty dog. What you got those silly goggles on for?"

Chapter 53

Josh watched the episode at the ranch transmitted live from Bernice's goggles to his computer at Vizion, amused by the budding romance between Dawn and Chick. "Didn't see that coming." He chuckled. Then Ricky came into view. "Well, hello. So that's where you are." Seeing Ricky conscious and apparently in good health disappointed him, but didn't surprise him. A problem maybe. But not one Josh couldn't manage. He, not Ricky, was Vizion's CEO now.

Gabriella stepped into Josh's office. "Who are you talking to?" she said.

Josh jerked, banging his knees on the underside of the desk. "Ouch! Gabby, you startled me." He shut down the live feed.

"Sorry," said Gabriella. "I was out familiarizing myself with the new car Helen gave me. The brail controls are terrific and the autopilot system works very well. You up for brunch?"

Josh's phone rang and he held a finger up out of habit. "Excuse me."

Gabriella grimaced. Here we go again. "Really?" she heard him say. "I'll let the staff know and we'll kick the campaign into high gear." He hung up.

"Let me guess, something urgent has come up and you've got to go," Gabriella said.

Josh got up and took her by the hand. "Right you are and you're coming with me."

"What? Where?"

"To brunch, like you said. At Levi's penthouse, to celebrate. Congress sent the corporate candidacy rules to the president's desk last night. And he signed them into law, just now. Can you believe Farnsworth actually signed them? Must have been a doozy of a behind the scenes negotiation."

Gabriella wished she could share Josh's enthusiasm but the news just brought back memories of her and Ricky on the campaign tour; how they'd kissed for the first time since college; how his lips, his mouth, his tongue tasted just like it had before; how they'd fallen asleep in each other's arms with classic movies playing.

Images flooded into her head – Sally chomping gum at the truck stop, Ricardo and Isabella fussing at the dinner table at the ranch, and her and Ricky rocking side by side on horseback through an aromatic sea of wildflowers. All Vizion winning the presidency meant to Ricky was a chance to make her see all those things instead of only imagining them. Or so he had said. But sometimes imagining things was better than seeing them for what they really were.

"So what's the latest on Ricky's condition?" Gabriella said, biting at her lower lip.

Josh suppressed his instinct to plead ignorance. The truth would be more useful in this instance. After all, it would be far easier for Gabriella to keep a grudge going against Ricky if it wasn't watered down with sympathy. "He's recovering well back at his family's ranch."

Gabriella choked. "He's conscious?'"

"Yes." Josh nodded. "Shall we go now?"

"Wait. When were you going to tell me?" She planted her hands on her hips.

"Does it matter? Doctor Dawn is there too. I'm sure she's taking very good care of him."

Gabriella's stomach churned. "I'll just bet she is."

Josh took her by the arm. "Come on, we shouldn't keep Levi waiting."

She pulled her arm away, her stomach pains worsening for a completely different reason now. "I'm not going anywhere near that man until I get some answers about that DNA sample."

"Don't be ridiculous, Gabriella."

"Ridiculous? It's undisputable that that sample came from Max, that it matches one of the samples from the victims, and that the other sample from the victims suggests the other perpetrator was a very close relative of his. So, unless you can prove to me that Max had some other living relative besides Levi, I have no choice but to assume..."

Josh glared. "Go ahead. Go ahead and say it, Gabriella. Levi's a rapist. You can't say that, can you? You can't say an elderly man is a rapist because you don't believe it yourself."

"Look, I'll admit it is hard to swallow. But what's harder to swallow is that three independent tests were all erroneous. That's how many tests were performed, Josh. Three." Gabriella held up three fingers. "Count them, three. I'm going back to my apartment. Enjoy your brunch."

Chapter 54

Josh arrived at the Leviathan penthouse at 11:00 AM.

"Welcome," said Levi and waved him in.

"We've got a problem," said Josh, pacing anxiously as soon as he passed through the door. "Gabriella's had the DNA sample from the cigar butt retested. Same results, of course."

"Oh? Speaking of DNA," Levi strolled over to his writing desk and pulled a file folder out of the center drawer. "Your results." He laid the folder on the desk and smiled. "Welcome to the family."

Josh rolled his eyes. "Did you hear what I said? Gabriella doesn't believe there's been a mistake."

Levi folded his arms across his chest. "Then what does she believe?"

"She believes you are the other party involved in the egg collection."

"She knows about the egg collection?"

"No. No. You know what I mean."

Levi rubbed his chin. "Hmm. I trust you'll find a way to deal with it."

They walked together out onto the balcony. The table there was set with champagne, freshly squeezed orange juice, and a spread of various hors d'oeuvres. Josh was surprised to see Helen leaning on the rail looking out over Dodge City. A thick layer of hairspray kept every strand of her hair glued perfectly in place despite a heavier than usual late morning breeze.

"I asked Helen to join us," Levi whispered to Josh. "I hope you don't mind, but I felt we should get everything out on the table." He raised his voice, "Helen dear, Josh is here."

"She knows?" Josh whispered in Levi's ear.

Levi nodded. "Yes."

Helen hesitated before turning to face them, tension tugging at the corners of her mouth. "Hello, Joshua dear, and congratulations on your new position."

Levi pulled a chair out for Helen and they all sat.

After a moment of uncomfortable silence, Levi planted his elbows on the table, clasped his hands together, and said, "I suppose there isn't any advantage in beating around the bush."

"How could you?" said Josh, glaring at Helen.

She pressed a hand against her chest. "You're being incredibly unfair, Joshua darling. It was the only appropriate thing to do under the circumstances. Had that incompetent doctor – whom I'm told took it upon himself to deny you your rightful station all these years – been able to tell the difference between a vagina and a penis on a sonogram it never would have happened. So blame him, not me. I'm delighted you made it. Proves you've got spunk. You're a survivor. And now that we've gotten that out of the way, let's talk about the election. Shall we?"

Josh glanced at Levi, then back at Helen, as awed as annoyed by the efficiency with which she dismissed the issue of aborting him and pivoted to the election.

"Helen has a proposition," Levi said. "In light of the rebellious mood of the people reflected in our latest internal polls, she believes we should anticipate the possibility of a radical independent entering the race."

"You mean Ricky, running in his individual capacity?"

Levi folded his arms across his chest. "That's one possibility, yes, and if he or anyone else were to have any success at all, it could split the vote such that no one achieves a majority. The House of Representatives would then decide who the next president will be. I don't think any of us wants to gamble on how that might turn out."

Josh cast a skeptical glance at Helen. "So what's the proposal?"

"I was thinking if Ricky or anyone else of consequence should enter the race, Vizion could join me," she said. "We'd be on the ticket together rather than opposing one another. We could combine Vizion's voters with mine."

Josh hadn't seen that coming. "You mean you join the Vizion ticket?"

"No. I mean Vizion join my ticket."

Levi held a hand up. "Please. Let's not argue over semantics."

"But she's a democrat," Josh said. He paused. "Well, I suppose a democrat and independent on the same ticket wouldn't reek quite as badly of establishment conspiracy as a democrat/republican ticket would."

Levi shook his head. "Actually, I was thinking all three on the ticket. We'd advertise it as the unity presidency. Democrat, republican, and independent; all three working in harmony for the greater good."

"There's only room for two on a ticket, President and VP," Josh pointed out. "Besides, Farnsworth would never agree to something like this."

The doorbell rang.

"Speaking of the devil," Helen broke in.

"Excuse me." Levi got up to answer the door.

He returned a moment later with Farnsworth.

Josh and Helen rose from their seats. "Mr. President," they both said.

Farnsworth nodded to the two of them. "Josh. Helen."

Levi resumed the discussion. "Vizion will be our presidential nominee so that leaves vice president and chairman of the board to be decided on."

"You can't expect me to be the VP nominee," said Farnsworth. "Wouldn't look right for an incumbent president."

Helen adjusted her hair even though it didn't need adjusting. "Surely you don't think I should take the number two position."

"Well, Vizion certainly will not be VP," Josh said.

"If I may." Levi slid two stacks of Vizion stock certificates across the table – one to Helen, one to Farnsworth. "As shareholders, each of you will share the presidency."

"Not enough power," Helen protested.

Levi sighed. "I'm thinking the VP nominee would also receive a seat on Vizion's board of directors. Does that help?"

Helen nodded. "That's a little better."

"Very well then," Levi said. "By a show of hands, who thinks Helen should be the VP?"

Farnsworth and Josh both raised a hand.

"Two thirds," said Levi, "That settles it. Should we need to resort to the unity ticket, Helen will be VP and a member of the board. Farnsworth, you'll be Vizion's chairman of the board. Josh, you'll continue as CEO. And Vizion Inc. will continue as our presidential nominee. Shall we eat now?"

Farnsworth's eyes narrowed as he gazed out at the hundreds of Texas troops standing guard over the busy construction site across the river. That wall was going up fast.

Chapter 55

After finishing up a teleconference with Miller and GTP board attorneys regarding the sanctions and enforcement order, Grant took the Cole brothers up in a DPS helicopter for a tour of what had come to be known as the Texas Miracle.

"So how'd it go with the GTP board?" Don Cole said through his headset as they lifted off from the helipad at the Texas presidential mansion.

Grant gave him a thumbs down. "Those jerks said they've made up their minds and that we are not entitled to a hearing on the matter because we're not GTP members. We can either comply or face the consequences."

"By the same logic, Texas shouldn't be bound by GTP determinations," Don Cole said. "They have a novel concept of due process over there. So what are you going to do?"

"Well, we sure as heck aren't going to comply. No way we're forfeiting Texas land to the U.S. or throwing Israel under the bus. I guess we'll wait and see how the U.S. elections turn out. With some decent leadership there, this whole thing could be easily resolved. I can't imagine the GTP making a move prior to the election anyway."

Don Cole nodded. "That's probably right."

Tom Cole gazed down as the helicopter cruised over Austin. It was still odd seeing the lonestar flag flying over the state capitol building unaccompanied by an American flag.

Don Cole observed all the construction under way, including a number of tubular bridges being erected across the Colorado River that snaked its way through the capitol city.

President Grant's voice came over the headsets again. "Those will serve as local surface arteries branching off of the statewide subsurface high speed pneumatic train system. By creating a vacuum in the airtight tube and levitating the train magnetically, drag is reduced to close to zero, allowing the train to travel at speeds as high as four thousand miles per hour. When it's completed you'll be able to get virtually anywhere in our territory from Austin in twenty minutes or less. That's lightning-speed considering it can take up to ten hours to traverse Texas by car."

"That's really something," Don Cole said.

President Grant added, "We plan to extend a line up to south Dodge City as well. Modern technology is amazing."

"A good technology is a good technology whether it's modern or not," Tom Cole commented, "and this system is anything but modern. If you'll recall, an enterprising fellow by the name of Beach had a short line up and running in New York in the 1800s with plans to extend it throughout the city and beyond. Unfortunately for him and the public, the old-style rail barons had more clout with the politicians. Explains why well over a century later antiquated rail still dominates mass ground transportation. Opposition to the pneumatic system from the airline industry in more recent times hasn't helped either."

The helicopter flew east and as the miles passed below them, Don Cole noticed numerous reservoirs. "I don't remember there being so many lakes in Texas," he said.

"We've added several since you were last here," said Grant. "I'll show you how we managed that shortly."

Don Cole pointed to a small town below that looked like a green and silver checkerboard. Virtually every home had a small-scale rooftop windmill.

"That's sunlight reflecting off of solar panels creating that silver glimmer," Grant said. "As y'all know, since we put an end to tax code rigging, discriminatory energy subsidies, and corrupt regulation, competition among energy technology manufacturers has boomed, resulting in a robust industry for household wind and solar systems. Prices have dropped so dramatically that we estimate every household in Texas could be energy independent within five years."

Tom Cole smiled. Cole Brothers Industries was doing well in the Texas wind and solar market. "And because of the increased demand," he said, "price drops haven't hurt profitability one bit. The money's made on volume. One more example of the benefits of a genuinely free market."

Grant pointed out the side window of the chopper. "The green squares you see are homework. They're the result of your influence on some backward thinking school administrators since we opened up the education system to competition. Administrators have incorporated basic agriculture into the curriculum as you suggested, beginning in kindergarten. So, in helping the children with their ag homework, families are working together to grow their own crops and finding out for themselves what some of us already knew – that you can easily produce enough food to feed a family in the average backyard if you know how?

"That's what I mean by backward thinking. As you pointed out earlier, newer ideas are not inherently better ideas. Most people nowadays don't know it wasn't all that long ago that people weren't hostage to corporate farms. Not that there isn't value added by corporate farms. Without them, food choices would be limited by local climate, weather, soil conditions, and so forth."

"That's a fact," Don Cole said, "and one that cannot be overstated. Some things just aren't doable without a large scale operation."

A short while later the helicopter approached the sprawling metropolis of Houston. "A ton of new construction under way here too," Tom Cole commented.

About a half hour later, they approached the coastline and as the helicopter proceeded out over the water more than two dozen buildings extending a mile or better out into the Gulf of Mexico off Galveston Island came into view. "The desalinization plants," Grant said. "Your filtration systems are our answer to all that nonsense about freshwater scarcity."

Don Cole slapped Grant on the back. "Glad we could help."

"We've built an extensive water pipeline system deep into the heart of Texas," Grant continued. "They're modeled after the old Roman aqueducts. That's how we filled the new lakes. We're also recharging the aquifers regularly so anyone so inclined can drill for his own water without limitation. I expect lifting restrictions will spur competition in the water drilling industry and drive down prices so that personal wells will soon be affordable for most anyone. I can't wait to show you the impact the new freshwater infrastructure has had out in the desert regions."

"I guess this explains all the pipe orders from Cole Brothers Industries." Don Cole winked. "Must take an enormous amount of energy to desalinize that much water."

"A little less than twice as much as it takes to treat waste water," said Grant, "just as you estimated. But we've solved that problem with our new tidal energy system. It stretches all the way down to the southernmost tip of South Padre Island. As y'all know, it works on the same concept as fossil fuel systems except rather than burning fuel to generate steam to spin turbines, the tides turn the turbines directly twenty-four seven and every day. Talk about sustainable.

"The system generates enough energy to power every square inch of Texas all the way up to Dodge City and beyond with plenty to spare. And for the most part it works fine with the existing distribution lines. But we're updating those lines with buried cable anyway, for national security purposes and to protect them from storms. We'll be making additional modifications to service electric vehicle recharging stations as well."

The helicopter banked around to a southwest heading.

"Looks like you're well on the way to making Texas completely independent of fossil fuels," Don Cole said.

"You know better than that." Grant grinned. "We'd be foolhardy to put all our energy eggs in one basket. Especially with this GTP business brewing. For obvious reasons, most of our military vehicles are still powered the old-fashioned way. We've also backed up the grid with fossil fuel powered generators in case a missile strike or natural disaster of some sort were to damage the tidal system. And of course oil is still used for lubricants and other chemicals and in plastics for medical devices and technological equipment and a gazillion other products. Your oil and gas interests are in no danger of going obsolete anytime soon."

Tom Cole smiled. "Just so you know, we would have invested more in fossil fuel alternatives sooner if the subsidy structure and tax code hadn't made it a losing proposition."

Grant squinted at the sun's glare reflecting off the cockpit window and said, "You're too modest. I know very well that the Cole Brothers Foundation has given millions in alternative energy research grants."

"We try to do our part," said Tom Cole. "But government tying our hands from doing more has been frustrating." He paused a minute. "Listen, about those household energy systems we talked about earlier; what's the point of those now that you have a tidal system that generates far more energy than everyone in Texas could possibly use?"

"National security for one," said Grant. "Individual empowerment for another. If you think about it, those are one and the same thing because an enemy does not defeat a nation without defeating it's individual citizens. That's why Afghanistan's known as the graveyard of empires." Grant readjusted the mic on her headset and explained what she meant by that. "Countries have been invading Afghanistan for thousands of years, and so far not one has been able to hold it. Why do you suppose that is?

"Well, I'll tell you why. Because beyond a couple of urban centers the people of Afghanistan live in villages where they provide for themselves and manage their own affairs. An invading army has to fight door to door, one household at a time, across the entire nation. It can't just chop off the head of the snake in one fell swoop the way it could a centrally planned society where everyone is dependent on distribution from central power grids and water supply stations, centrally controlled defensive units, central food supply, central decision-making, and all the rest. And not to change the subject, but

233

that's one more reason why we're so adamant here in Texas about protecting the individual right to keep and bear arms.

"A society with a central control setup is also vulnerable to the stupidity and corruption of its own policy makers. You don't have to look any further than up north and what happened during the Deep Freeze when the politicians cut off coal to the east coast power plants to see that."

Tom Cole nodded appreciatively, although the question had been a rhetorical one.

"Tom and I have some ideas of our own about ways to empower the individual," Don Cole chimed in. "For example, individual households with their own personal water, energy, and food supply – all of which appears to be well underway here in Texas – will be nearly a hundred percent self-sufficient. If, on top of that, all individuals could leverage the work of a personal robot and a semi-industrial 3-D printer for manufacturing from home, they could produce well beyond subsistence and be truly free, if not wealthy. They'd have time for family, worship, for advanced learning, art, community service, and God willing, time to participate in their government. Or maybe just more time for fun. Who's to say. It's just a matter of letting the free market work to drive prices down on those technologies so they're affordable for individuals."

Tom Cole could see the wheels turning in Grant's mind.

"Tom, you're a genius!" said Grant.

Tom Cole blushed. "Let's not get carried away."

"Don't you see?" Grant said. "You've arrived at an idea that could render the whole socialism versus capitalism debate moot. Because working outside of the household would be a choice rather than a necessity, big business and labor unions could no longer exploit individuals. Individuals would be in the driver's seat. The labor market would be authentically free."

Tom Cole wrapped his arms across his chest and smiled proudly. "You're describing a society where individual liberty is the highest priority. And that, Madam President, is the concept upon which the United States was founded. In fact, I would argue that this we're discussing was the U.S.'s natural destination had our representatives followed the course set by the founders in the Constitution rather than subverting the law and selling out the people to satisfy their own gluttony for easy money and power."

The helicopter landed in very cosmopolitan San Antonio for refueling and a late lunch. Afterwards, they flew North, mostly silent as their lunches settled, until they cruised over the formerly scrub-brushy and fairly desolate region outside the town of San Angelo.

"Amazing what can be done with a useless chunk of dirt when you add a little water," Don Cole said as he gazed out at the greenway miles and miles wide of flourishing crops and orchards that Grant said extended all the way to the border with Mexico.

They flew northwest from there and over the Midland-Odessa area where the Cole Brothers' vast oil and gas interests had been slowed considerably by the multifarious climate change regulations before the United States ejected Texas. "Ah the memories," said Tom Cole, smiling at the oilrigs dotting the landscape below. His company had made a lot of money out here and employed thousands of men and women who provided fine lives to their families on the wages it paid. After years in the unemployment line, most were back to work now. Seeing the wells churning again felt good.

They landed again a half hour later at a solar power plant situated about seventy-five miles outside of El Paso in the desert region of Hudspeth County. "This is one of the backup generators I mentioned," Grant said. "It's actually a hybrid system. When it's sunny out – which is most of the time in these parts – it runs off solar. The rest of the time it runs off fossil fuels.

"How this works," Grant pointed at the several rows of enormous mirrors, "is that the sunlight is redirected at the water towers." She pointed again. "That heats the water, generating the steam to spin the turbines that generate the electricity. A little different than household solar systems and it takes a lot of water. But," she grinned, "like I said, we've got oceans full of that stuff. So, as they say in Mexico, no problema." She paused to give the Cole Brothers a minute to take it all in. Then she scrubbed her hands together. "So what do you think of the Texas Miracle?"

Tom Cole and Don Cole both nodded approvingly and Tom Cole said, "As impressive as it all is, the part I appreciate most is how it's financed."

Grant said, "And I appreciate Cole Brothers Industries' help in starting what we hope will become a new trend in public private partnerships – doing right by the shareholders."

Chapter 56

Despite the menacing harmonizer buildup just across the river from the Santana ranch, for the next three weeks, life there went on as usual – plus a little zoo keeping. By June 15th, Ricky completed his physical therapy and recovered completely – except for his memory – and he spent his days working the ranch again, much the same as he had as a boy.

Chick had transformed into something of ranch-hand himself, working cattle and keeping the aging farming equipment running. When he wasn't busy with that, he helped Dawn with the research animals and just about anything else she asked, including the critical task of acting as her surgical assistant when she performed the artificial eye transplants on Brutus the ape a week and a half ago. He was mostly getting in Isabella's and Dawn's way at the clothesline where they were hanging freshly laundered lady things when Dawn said, "Well, today's the big day."

Chick saw Ricardo coming. "Uh-oh," he said, and dropped a women's undergarment and ducked behind a hanging dress.

"What are you doing?" said Dawn. "You got dirt all over that."

"Hiding from that crazy old man," Chick said. He poked his head around the dress and planted a quick kiss on Dawn. "Today's the big day for what?" He ducked back behind the dress.

"Brutus's eyepatches come off today," said Dawn.

Ricardo flung the dress aside. "You cannot hide from me," he said to Chick, laughing.

Chick said, "I done scooped all the poop out the stalls, Mr. Santana. What you want now?"

Ricky watched with amusement from the corral. He scooped a pitchfork full of hay into a trough, and after the horses nibbled a while, he saddled up the Palo Pinto mare and started out to mend a downed section of fence in the northeast pasture where a bull had ripped through the barbed wire in pursuit of a heifer in heat. Isabella caught Ricky before he rode away. "Take this with you, hijo," she said, holding up an old battery powered transistor radio small enough to fit in his shirt pocket. "It is the one you always listened to when you were a little boy."

It disappointed her when Ricky said, "Thank you, *ma'am*" yet again, instead of *Mama*.

Ricky tuned to an AM talk radio program as he rode.

"Well, hello Texas and welcome to the Ben Black radio show," the host said enthusiastically. "Buckle up, we've got a lot to get to today."

Ricky recognized the host's voice but could not quite place it.

After a short burst of canned upbeat music, Ben Black began the show. "Well it's hardly breaking news that we're on the brink of world war three or that every nation on the planet is preparing to gang up on Texas under the auspices of the GTP. I've been predicting this for years. But I have to say I am a little surprised by the particulars."

"Whoa, what do you mean every nation?" Ben Black's cohost Mike objected. "Israel isn't supporting this and neither are the Kurds."

"The Kurds aren't a nation," Ben Black said.

"Yes they are. Okay, they aren't a nation *state* but they are a nation. They should be a nation state. The GTP ought to recognize a Kurdish state instead of trying to un-recognize Israel."

"I agree on both points. But we're getting off into the weeds. Now, what was I saying?"

"You were saying world war three isn't breaking news."

"Right right. The real story here – the one the fake news is ignoring – is the quiet takeover of Vizion Inc., the corporation that might well become the next president of the United States."

"Why do you think the media's ignoring it?"

Ben Black did his famous imitation evil laugh. "Because Levi creepy dude is behind the takeover and creepy due controls the fake news cartel."

"I thought that lawyer dude, Josh was pulling the strings at Vizion now," said Mike.

Ben Black said, "He's a creepy dude puppet. How about we call him mini-creep. I can't wait to see what happens when Ricky Santana comes back to reclaim his company."

"You think he will be back?"

"I'd bet the farm on it because God is obviously using him for his purposes. I mean, who else do you know who's committed practically their whole adult life to curing the blind? It's God stuff, and it's admirable."

Ricky's body swayed with the graceful movements of the Palo Pinto mare beneath him. He held the transistor radio closer to his ear, amused by the discussion about the man he was purported to be.

"Your fondness for a man exposed for blinding Gabriella Meir seems a bit misplaced even if he did start a crusade to cure the blind after," Mike said.

"It does?" Ben Black sounded surprised by Mike's assessment.

"Yes, it does."

Ricky frowned. What was that about him blinding somebody? He listened intently.

"You ever heard of redemption?" Ben Black said. "Recall the Apostle Paul was a murderer; Apostle Peter a coward; doubting Thomas a doubter. And so on. Anyway, I can relate to Ricky Santana."

"How so?"

"For starters, I know what it's like to be a booze-fueled human tornado spinning out of control and ripping everything and everyone in my path to pieces."

A booze-fueled human tornado? With every word, Ricky grew more troubled by Ben Black's assessment of him, albeit Black's self-deprecating inclusion of himself in the drunken tornado category did make the blows less personal somehow.

"But you never blinded anyone?" Mike said.

"Didn't I?" Ben Black pressed on.

"Did you?"

"Haven't we all?"

"I don't follow."

And neither do I, Ricky thought.

"The single greatest impact we have on others is the way we live our own lives," Ben Black explained. "When we screw up, we legitimize screwed up living, blinding people to the truth of what a good life is. Throw in a big megaphone like our platform here and on my television network, and the lie is amplified a gazillion times over."

"Dude, that's heavy," Mike said. "Makes me nervous about saying anything at all. Which is awfully inconvenient since I make my living spouting off."

Ben Black chuckled, then said, "It's an awesome responsibility, no doubt about it. And each and every one of us owes it to everyone else to live a life worth emulating and we also have a responsibility to know what we're talking about before weighing in on things of importance, lest we lead others astray. That's especially true with the internet now where one tweet or Facebook post or whatever can go viral and infect hundreds of millions of people overnight."

"Infect?"

"Yes. Not all infections are bad. Can you imagine a world infected with truth?"

"I wish I could imagine it," said Mike.

"And I don't want to imagine it," Ben Black said. "I want to make it reality. That's why the goal of this network is and always has been to create an epidemic of truth."

"Lofty."

"Yes, lofty. But worthy."

After a short pause, Mike said, "So, you'll be making an exciting announcement on the television program tomorrow night."

"That's right," said Ben Black. And I'll also have a special guest on – President Grant…"

The sun had settled to just above the horizon by the time Ricky returned from mending fences. He unsaddled the Palo Pinto and began brushing the horse down, then Dawn rushed out to the stables, the tails of her lab coat flapping in the warm evening breeze. She dragged a little red Ryder wagon behind her with a computer and Brutus the chimpanzee in it with gauze patches over both of his eyes. She looked Ricky up and down. "Well, aren't you a sight to see in those wranglers, big belt buckle, and Stetson." She still couldn't get used to the shaggy hair and beard.

Ricky nodded and continued brushing the horse.

Dawn pointed at the ape in the wagon. "Remember Brutus?" she said, "the critter that used to pepper you with poop all the time? The one you pushed me to do the transplants on?"

Brutus peeled his upper lip back, showing off his teeth, and woowooped what seemed to Ricky like a chimp version of a greeting. Ricky took his hat off and wiped the sweat off his brow. "You threw poop at me, did you?" he said to the ape. "Lucky I don't remember that."

"You don't remember Brutus at all?" said Dawn.

"No, ma'am." Ricky tugged a little chain that switched on the light dangling from an overhead cedar beam.

Dawn tossed out a more important question. "What about the artificial eyes, do you remember inventing those? Anything come back to you about that yet?"

Ricky shook his head. "Afraid not, but they were talking about that on the radio today."

"Who was?"

"A fella by the name of Ben Black. He says my company's been taken over and some corporate mogul that helped me get it started's behind the hijacking."

Dawn shook her head. "Ben Black's a nut-job."

"Why do you say that? He sounds pretty sensible to me."

"Because." The truth was she didn't have any good reason for believing that about Ben Black, she'd just heard others say it. "I don't know. But what I do know is Levi Baxter is a very wealthy and powerful man and I'm sure he has much bigger fish to fry than taking over little ol' Vizion Inc. Although I can't imagine the board bumped you off and appointed your former friend, Josh as CEO without Levi's approval."

"Little ol' Vizion?" said Ricky. "I thought you said Vizion was a billion dollar company."

"Well, yes, but compared to Levi's Leviathan Corp…"

Ricky said, "Seems to me a snow cone stand would be worth billions if it became president of the United States."

Dawn giggled. "I'll be sure and tell Chick you said so."

Chick stepped into the stables just as Dawn said that. "I don't s sell snow cones, I sell ice cream," he said. "At least I used to before Ricky went and crashed that helicopter and all."

Brutus woowooped again and slung his arms.

Ricky said, "I was just telling Dawn –"

"Ricky, stop," she interrupted. "I came to show you something. Is there a power plug out here?"

"Sure." He pointed to an electrical outlet on the support post beside him.

Dawn tossed the end of the computer cord to him. "Plug it in, please."

Ricky did as she asked, then pointed at the computer, "What's that for?"

"It's got the neural code processer on it," Dawn said. "Thank goodness the remote access password for your drive on Vizion's system was in the address book Chick got from the cottage before our great escape from Dodge City so I could download the program." She powered on the computer and plugged a cord from it into a mini-port to the microcomputer embedded a centimeter from Brutus's right eye.

"If them transplants work on the monkey, you ought to get Gabriella down here and let Dawn fix her up," said Chick.

Dawn said, "He's not a monkey, he's an ape."

"Who's Gabriella?" said Ricky.

"The woman you've been in love with practically all your life," Chick blurted.

"Actually she's that despicable Josh's fiancé," said Dawn.

"That's only because somebody spilled the beans about the accident," Chick began."

Dawn cut him off, "Chick would you Shut Up. Hold Brutus, gently, please, and try to keep him calm while I peel the patches off."

"Sorry," Chick said, and rested his hands on Brutus's shoulders.

The ape jerked his head up and down and chattered when the patches came off.

"So Gabriella's her name," Ricky said contemplatively.

Dawn looked into his distant eyes and saw that he was searching for a memory. She reached inside her lab coat and pulled out her ophthalmoscope and shined the light into Brutus's eyes. The ape responded with a squint. She shifted the instrument slowly from left to right, then right to left. Brutus's new eyes followed the light in each direction. Dawn clicked the light off. "I...ah." She held a hand to her forehead, "It, uh." She looked like she was about to faint. "I think it worked."

Chapter 57

Dawn put Brutus through a series of additional vision tests the following morning, all of which confirmed that his sight was substantial if not perfect. If only Ricky had his memory back so she could have him rig up that Cloud technology idea of his. With the mobility that would provide, Brutus could be disconnected from the computer and turned loose in the chimp enclosure so she could observe how he responded to his surroundings in a less controlled environment. A test of that kind would be reasonably definitive. She secured Brutus back in his cage and stepped out of the newly constructed lab for a breath of morning air.

Ricky trotted up on the Palo Pinto and tipped his hat. "Morning, Doctor."

"Good morning to you, cowboy." Dawn cupped a hand above her eyes and squinted at the morning sun and saw Chick racing up on the mustang.

"Whoa," said Chick, his eyes wide as he pulled back on the reins, bringing the horse to an abrupt halt beside the Palo Pinto. Dust swirled in the air around him.

Dawn clutched his hand. "Chick, what's wrong?"

He pointed toward the northern pastures. "It's…ah, …there's a…"

"What, Chick? What?" She caressed his fingers, trying to calm him.

"The hay bailer quit," Chick started again, "and I was on my way out to the field to get it running, and I saw it, a headstone under that big ol' oak tree down by the river. It's got Ricky's name on it."

"What?" Ricky's brows crumpled together. "Show me." He tipped his hat to Dawn again. "Doctor." And he and Chick rode off together.

"Right there," Chick said as he and Ricky trotted up under the oak's sprawling canopy.

Ricky slipped his boots out of the stirrups and hopped off the Palo Pinto. "It's a headstone alright." As he gazed at the name engraved on it, memories began crashing into his mind in reverse order like a waterfall rushing up a cliff to the trickling mountain stream it originated from. He felt the slam of the Vizion corporate chopper into the helipad; heard the wisp like a sword slashing as the detached rotor blade whipped away; saw Bernice tumbling terrified.

Ricky held his hands against his head and squeezed his eyes shut, trying to suppress an awful pain as the images continued to flow: Gabriella kissing him on Vizion's campaign bus; him and Chick in the Suffolk county jail; then nothing, nothing at all; and suddenly, dim lights, music, a drink in his hand at the Green Dragon Tavern.

He opened his eyes and saw the headstone still there, his name on it staring back at him. The pain in his head intensified. Then an image of himself as a young boy standing beneath the oak tree, barefooted in denim overalls, clinging to a much younger Ricardo's leg appeared in his mind. "Papa, why are you crying?" he heard the young boy him say.

Ricky jerked his head, shaking himself out of it.

"You alright, brother man?"

"No, I am not alright." Ricky yanked a branch off the tree, snapped it in two, and chucked the pieces to the ground. "I've got a blind gal to heal and I don't know how many fences to fix. This ranch is falling apart. But before I do anything, I'm getting to the bottom of this here."

Chick's jaw dropped. "You're back."

Ricky kicked the headstone with his boot heel, loosening it from the soil, then gripped it and heaved, grunted, pulled, and heaved again until it came up out of the ground.

"Ricky?"

"Yeah?"

"What you figuring on doing about Vizion and the campaign and all now that you got your memory back?"

Ricky said, "I don't know. I'm gonna find out what this here is all about and then I've got to get that remote neural code processer fine-tuned. I'll worry about the rest after that." He tugged at the loose headstone.

"Let me help you, brother man." Chick and Ricky hoisted the grave marker onto the back of the saddle and tied it down. Then they rode back to the main house where Ricardo sat on the porch-swing puffing on his pipe.

"Papa, we've got to talk," Ricky said.

Chick wrapped the horses' reins around the hitching post.

"Is this what you want to talk about?" Ricardo said, pointing to the headstone.

Ricky nodded.

Ricardo took a deep breath. "I did it for you, hijo, so you could be an American citizen."

Ricky shook his head. He knew his parents entered Texas illegally when they were young and that they hadn't become citizens until they were naturalized under President Reagan's amnesty program years later. But he also knew that Isabella gave birth to him on American soil and he had a Texas birth certificate to prove it, so there was never any question about his citizenship. And even if there was, what the hell did that have to do with this?

"You were born in Mexico," Ricardo continued. "When your younger brother who was born here died I gave you his name and his birth certificate because I did not know then if any of us would ever be granted citizenship."

"Oh my God." Ricky held a hand to his forehead. He wasn't born in the United States? "You're saying I had a brother and he's buried beneath that tree?"

"Si." Ricardo wept. "I should have told you."

"Wow." Ricky's head was spinning. He couldn't imagine the grief of losing a child. And to have the presence of mind at a time like that to think of your other son's future. He rubbed Ricardo's shoulder, regretting more than ever now having let so many years pass between them.

Ricky glanced at Chick and saw tears welling up in his eyes.

"I'm real sorry to hear about your other son, Mr. Santana," Chick said.

The front door creaked open and Isabella stepped out with coffee. "Papa, what is wrong?" she said. Then she saw the headstone. The cup slipped from her hand and shattered at her feet. She dropped to her knees and laid her head in Ricardo's lap and wept with him.

Ricky said, "Maybe you could shed a little light on all this, Mama."

Isabella lifted her head and gazed through soaked eyes. "Hijo, you called me mama."

"Yes, I got my memory back. Now, what about all this?"

"It is true you had a brother," Isabella said. She dried her eyes on her dress sleeve and then she stood and embraced Ricky in a hug that seemed to last for hours. She stepped away then and took Ricardo's hand. "Come, Papa. It is time for your medicine."

Chick nudged Ricky in the side. "Don't seem like your mama wants to talk about it right now, brother man."

"I reckon not," Ricky said. "Say, Dawn has a computer with internet access out in the lab, doesn't she?"

Chick said, "Mm-huh."

"Good," said Ricky. "I've got some modifications to make on the artificial sight software. I think if I can link it to the harmonizer sight-system, the neural code can be transmitted from the satellite network. I'll need to log in remotely to Vizion's mainframe to do it."

Chick started, "But what about the headstone –"

Ricky cut him off. "Like you said, Mama don't seem to want to talk about it right now."

Bernice crawled out from under the porch.

"Come on, Bern," Ricky adjusted his Stetson, "we got work to do."

Chapter 58

Two days later, Ricky sat at the picnic table with Dawn and Chick, the midday summer sun searing. Bernice laid on the ground next to them, panting and drooling.

Dawn patted Ricky on the hand. "How you doing?"

"Hot." He wiped the sweat off his brow with his shirtsleeve. "Some reason y'all didn't have AC plumbed into that lab?"

Dawn sighed. "AC wasn't in the budget. So, besides hot, how are you?"

Ricky squinted at the sun. "Honestly, I'm a little shell shocked still. Or maybe bewildered is a better word for it. You'd think I'd remember having a brother. But I don't."

Chick said, "You sure do have a lot of trouble remembering stuff, brother man."

"I reckon that's so." Ricky chuckled.

Dawn fidgeted. "But you haven't forgotten the remote neural code processing technology, right? Or, what I mean is, you will be able to get it working, won't you?"

Ricky smiled. "I've done my part, doc. The ball's in your court now."

"What do you mean by that?" said Dawn.

"I'm done," Ricky said. "All you've got to do is hook the wireless receiver up to Brutus and see if it works. While you're doing that, I'm going into town and pick up a ceiling fan for the lab."

"You're finished with the remote neural code?" Dawn gasped, her voice crackling with excitement.

"Yes, ma'am." Ricky slipped his hat on.

"Mind if I ride along?" Chick said. "I could use a break from this place."

"I reckon a little company wouldn't hurt. Come on, we'll take Ricardo's work truck."

"So, what you figuring on doing about Vizion now that you come back to your senses?" Chick said as they drove into Wichita Falls.

Ricky shoved his hair to the side of his face. "I don't rightly know, but I'm not so sure it's a good idea to let my company get elected president with Josh in charge."

Chick pointed to a hardware store in the strip center on the left. "I bet they got fans."

Ricky turned into the parking lot and noticed a TP sign in the window of the establishment to the left of the hardware store. The sign to the right said, *Cyber Saloon.*

"I'm going to check that cyber place out while you're fan shopping," Chick said. "I ain't checked my email since Dodge City. Dawn won't let me near the lab computer. She's worried I'll hack into something, I guess."

Ricky laughed. "You, hack? No. Okay, I'll see you over there when I get done fan shopping."

Country music blared inside the Cyber Saloon. Chick gazed around at several couples two-stepping on a dance floor surrounded by tables with desktop computers on them. He sat down at one of them and went online.

Ricky came in a few minutes later. "Got the fan," he yelled over the music, "and a go-phone too since you tossed my cell."

"Sorry," Chick yelled back, his gaze stuck on the computer monitor in front of him. "I had to get rid of Dawn's too on account of them harmonizers was using them to track us."

Someone lowered the volume on the music a couple of notches.

Ricky said, "That's better. So what are you doing there?"

Chick glanced at him. "I was just poking around on the internet, then I got to thinking, seems like with your company running for president without you and all we ought to study up on how they done all this corporate candidate stuff in case we need to file some kind of new lawsuit. Let's look up *Citizens United.*"

Ricky nodded. "I tried that back when Levi first mentioned the idea of Vizion running, but all I got was blogs about how the Court's decision in the case let loose a stampede of gigantic corporations to buy elections and such."

A middle-aged waitresses that Ricky thought resembled Sally from the truck stop stopped by the table and asked if they wanted beer.

"No thank you, ma'am," Ricky said

"Nothing for me neither," said Chick. "I been sober probably long as you been alive. Well, maybe not that long."

The waitress batted her eyelashes sarcastically. "I bet you say that to all the girls. Probably why there ain't no wedding ring on your finger." She moved on to the next table.

Wedding ring? That gave Chick an idea. He saw what looked like a gumball machine up against a wall. "Excuse me a minute."

Ricky finished the internet search that Chick had started.

Chick came back with a plastic toy ring in his hand. "Find anything?" he said.

Ricky pointed to the search results and clicked on *CitizensUnited.org*, and began to read:

> *Citizens United is an organization dedicated to restoring our government to citizens' control. Through a combination of education, advocacy, and grass roots organization, Citizens United seeks to reassert the traditional American values of limited government, freedom of enterprise, strong families, and national sovereignty and security. Citizens United's goal is to restore the founding fathers' vision of a free nation, guided by the honesty, common sense, and good will of its citizens.*

"Wow." Ricky glanced at Chick. "This non-profit was the plaintiff in *Citizens United*? The media talks like the case was about some evil greedy corporate monster that got its panties all in a wad and sued because Congress passed a law to try and stop it from gobbling up the working class and eating the people's government for dessert." Ricky got up from his chair. "Come on, let's go find a law library and read that opinion for ourselves."

Chick pulled him back down into his seat. "You ain't got to go to no law library. You can read it right here online. Go to *supremecourt.gov* and click on the link for *opinions*."

Ricky perused the Supreme Court website until he found *Citizens United v. Federal Elections Commission*. This is the case we're looking for, ain't it?"

"That be the one," Chick said.

"Alright," Ricky stroked his beard, "says here that Citizens United produced an unflattering documentary about democrat candidate Hillary Clinton and they wanted to make it available by Video-on-demand shortly before the primaries. Trouble was the BCRA campaign finance law made it illegal to do that on account of Citizens United spent its own money to make the film, and the law prohibited corporations from using their general treasury funds for speech that constitutes electioneering communication. The law defined an electioneering communication as:

> Any broadcast, cable, or satellite communication that refers to a clearly identified candidate for federal office and is made within thirty days of a primary election, and that is publicly distributed, which in the case of a candidate for nomination for President means that the communication can be received by fifty thousand or more persons in a state where a primary election is being held within thirty days.

"Apparently the law did provide an exception for certain non-profit corporations," Ricky went on, "but Citizens United was afraid it wasn't one of them, so rather than risk getting it's people fined and jailed, it filed suit seeking a declaratory judgment that the provisions of the BCRA in question were unconstitutional, at least as applied to Citizens United." Ricky paused. "We already know all this."

Chick sighed. "Yep, just like Josh said on that program he done with Gabriella. And we know the Supreme Court agreed that those provisions was unconstitutional, and not just to Citizens United. Keep reading. There's bound to be more to it than just what Josh said."

Ricky read silently for a while. "Okay, right here they're talking about that three-part test the Court used for figuring out whether a corporation could be exempt from the law."

"Remind me about that," Chick said.

"Alight. The test asked first, whether the corporation was formed for the purpose of promoting political ideas, and not engaged in business. Secondly, whether the corporation has shareholders that have any economic reason to remain affiliated if they disagree with its political activity. And thirdly, whether the corporation accepts any funding from for-profit corporations such that it could act as a conduit for for-profit corporate electoral spending."

Chick closed his eyes and thought about that for a minute. "Hmm. So, basically a nonprofit created to spread political opinions was exempt unless any organization that made any money donated to it. Well, how in the world's a nonprofit supposed to get any money to do what it does then? That's stupid."

"No kidding," said Ricky. "And, of course, no exemption for any corporation in the business of making money – which was the point of the law. Except for media corporations on account of first amendment freedom of the press."

"Well that don't make no sense," Chick said, scratching his head. "They saying if a business makes money, unless it makes it as a media business it ain't got no first amendment rights?"

Ricky nodded. "That's about the size of it. The thing is, according to this here, the freedom of the press exemption was actually written directly into the BCRA law itself already, but there was no exemption for freedom of speech for anybody else written into the law." He laughed. "I reckon the law would have been completely pointless if there had been."

Chick shook his head. "Bottom line is the BCRA never did apply to media corporations then? They put that freedom of the press exception in there on purpose. Maybe they ought to just take that part out."

"Oh, they would take it out if the dissent had its way," said Ricky. "Right here the dissent says the courts ought to determine who can speak and who can't on a case by case basis. Judges would decide what's a fact, what's an opinion, what's truth, what's a lie. I reckon that might work for companies with hundreds of millions of dollars to throw around for legal fees. But the average corporation would have to weigh the prospect of financial ruin and imprisonment of its people before saying anything politically. Talk about chilling speech."

Ricky thought about that as he read further. "Hey, here's another interesting wrinkle. Although for-profit corporations were banned from electioneering communication expenditures from their general treasuries, they could spend as much as they wanted to so long as they funneled it through a super PAC…But look at this." He pointed to the text on the computer monitor. "Apparently after lawyers and accountants and filing fees and what not, it costs so much to form and maintain a super PAC that only about two thousand of the more than three million U.S. corporations can even afford to have one."

Chick folded his arms across his chest. "Looks like free speech wasn't all that free under the BCRA. Crooked ass politicians."

"Right." Ricky slid his finger down a few paragraphs. "According to this, more than seventy-five percent of all corporations in the U.S. have less than a million dollars in receipts per year. Knowing a little something about how expensive it is to run a business, I can tell you that after operating costs most of those companies probably make less than fifty-thousand dollars a year, if they make any profit at all.

"We're talking landscapers, bakers, real estate agents, mechanics, contractors, cooks, hair stylists, sole practioners in law and medicine, delivery drivers, farmers, mom and pop shops of every kind. You know? These aren't exactly evil greedy multinational corporations. And Congress along with half the Supreme Court is worried these tiny businesses are going to buy the government away from the people? These are the people. Something ain't ringing true here."

Chick scooted his chair closer. "I knew there had to be more to this than that weasel, Josh was talking about on that program he done with Gabriella." He reached for the mouse. "Let me look at that." He scrolled down, scanning the text as he silently read. When he got to the end of the opinion, he slumped back in his chair and sighed. "You getting what I'm getting out of this?"

"Damn sure am." Ricky's face erupted with anger. "Congress sold the BCRA to the public as a way to keep corrupt gigantic corporations from buying the government and dominating political discourse. But what the law really did was shut down the ability of small business owners and others to combine their voices through the corporate form to compete in the political process. It ensured that the very humongous corrupt corporations it supposedly aimed to restrain maintained a virtual monopoly on political speech – specifically, those corporations with deep enough pockets to maintain super PACs and those that own or *are* media corporations."

Chick closed out the Supreme Court website and returned to *CitizensUnited.org* for a second look. "Man, these folks got it going on," he said. "Look here, *Hillary* ain't the only film Citizens United done made. There's a bunch of others here," he pointed, "like this one; says it's about how corrupt corporations buy up all the politicians. Tell me that ain't ironic."

"Our so-called representatives are full of crap and so is the major media, that's what it tells me." Ricky stood up and kicked his chair away. "Where the hell did that waitress go? I think I could use a drink after all."

Chick grabbed him by the arm and said, "How about a meeting instead? "

"You mean an AA meeting?" said Ricky.

Chick said, "I was thinking TEA Party meeting.

Ricky raised an eyebrow. "I thought the TEA Party was dead."

"Not by a long shot," Chick said. "They got one next door. You see the TP sign in the window?"

"Here and I thought they were advertising a sale on toilet paper." Ricky chuckled.

Chapter 59

Chick pushed the door open and the restless crowd of a hundred or so seated in front of a projector screen quieted. "It's Ricky Santana," several whispered.

Ricky and Chick slipped into the back row just as a man stepped in front of the screen. "Welcome to the Wichita Falls TEA Party and our daily showing of the Ben Black television program" the man said. He dimmed the lights.

"Hey, I like that Ben Black," Ricky whispered to Chick. "I've heard him on the radio a couple of times. But I didn't expect to be viewing his television program at any TEA Party meeting."

Chick said, "Shh."

The attendees whistled and applauded when Ben Black appeared onscreen, arms folded across his chest, sitting on the edge of his desk. "Well, hello Texas," he said, "and thank you for watching the Ben Black show, the streaming TV network that you are building. We're doing something different tonight. We're combining limited live coverage of this year's first U.S. presidential debate with an exploration of who these candidates are when they're not actors on a debate stage. We're also going to take a look at the new corporate candidacy rules. And later in the program, Texas President Grant will be with us."

Ben Black clapped his hands together. "So let's get to it." The studio camera followed him across the set to two freestanding chalkboards where he stopped and said, "Yes, it's chalkboard time again. What we have here to my left is the abbreviated version of the new candidate rules. On the right, the three U.S. presidential candidates and some very revealing associations. But before we get into that, let's cut to the debate where the two admitted establishment candidates and one representative of a corporate candidate posing as an independent are about to say a lot of nothing in their opening statements."

The debate moderator introduced the candidates, Helen first. She smiled from her podium and babbled something about unfair carbon credit distributions and evil greedy corporations paying their fair share, then vowed to appoint Supreme Court justices that would overturn the *Citizens United* decision. She ended with a rehashed promise to ban the universal symbol of racism, bigotry, homophobia, xenophobia, abuse of women and children, exploitation of the poor, climate change, and everything else that plagued humanity – the American flag. The live debate audience applauded. The TEA Party audience as well as Ben Black's studio audience booed.

Next, President Farnsworth bragged about the deal with the GTP to use sanctions and GTP free trade enforcement forces to bring the rogue Republic of Texas to its knees militarily if it didn't cut ties with Israel and return the occupied territories by some unspecified date. He would also strengthen the unity of the nation by abolishing statehood and the electoral college so that United States citizens would at long last think and live as one. "Oh and uh, I too would appoint Supreme Court justices that would overturn *Citizens United*," Farnsworth added.

"Bring it on!" Some cowboy at the TEA Party meeting hollered. Several others joined in.

The live debate audience responded with less enthusiasm when Josh spoke. "As CEO of the next president of the United States, I will not only unify this nation, I will unify the world in harmony…"

The segment cut back to the studio where Ben Black with hands pressed over his ears said, "Enough! Enough! We'll wait for closing statements before we cut back to the debate again. I can't stand a solid hour of that nonsense." He paused. "By the way, did anyone notice anything missing on the debate stage? Of course not, because we've been conditioned by the republicrat partnership not to see the obvious. He pulled a piece of paper out of his shirt pocket and waved it in front of the camera. "This is a list of the twelve viable U.S. candidates not invited to the debate. Believe me, their exclusion was no accident and not a one of those three who were invited gives a crap about the American people. I'd like to draw your attention to one in particular – Vizion Inc., and the new election rules that made this farce of a candidacy possible."

Ben Black tapped the board with the tip of a chalk stick. "These are the rules Congress passed for how a corporation can establish natural born citizenship as required by the Constitution. Basically what it says is that a corporation is a natural born citizen as long as every shareholder, manager, director, or whatever is a natural born citizen." He chuckled. "I still can't believe the U.S. is allowing this. It seems like the whole world – except for Texas – has gone totally mad.

"Buuuut, as I was saying, Vizion Inc. has apparently satisfied the requirements to run. So, *who is* Vizion." He turned to the other chalkboard, which had some stick-on photographs incorporated into a flowchart linking numerous people, companies, and various other entities, including non-profits and charitable foundations. "This man is Vizion Inc." He tapped on one of the photos. "Levi Baxter, known more commonly as the big boss of global giant, Leviathan Corp. Around here, we call him *creepy dude*.

"I know, I know. On the surface, there's no sign that creepy dude or Leviathan Corp have any interest in Vizion besides that tiny little detail of almost half of Vizion's stock being pledged as collateral for several million dollars in loans from Leviathan. Of course there's that other little detail, the one about ownership of the other half of Vizion's stock. Which gets really interesting." Ben Black traced the linking lines with his chalk stick. "Each of these companies owns a small minority of stock in Vizion Inc., but together, they own a majority. Everybody with me so far? Good, because guess who owns controlling interest in every one of these minority Vizion stockholder companies? Yes! Creepy dude. The remaining shares are predominantly held by three people – Ricky Santana, and…wait for it… fellow republicrats, Helen Baxter and President John Farnsworth."

"But wait, there's more." Ben Black traced more lines on the chalkboard linking Levi to numerous other companies. The lines from all of those converged on four of the largest global media companies. "Creepy dude uses the same MO to control at least four of the big six global corporations that own more than ninety percent of the media worldwide. He might even control all six. We're still researching.

"And the last piece of this little puzzle is this." He laid the chalk stick down and washed his hands together, sending a cloud of chalk dust into the air. Then he pointed back at the board. "Enormous amounts of money flow from every one of those companies to the democrat and republican parties, their candidates, and to all manner of super PACs and charitable foundations that promote the republicrat agenda. That being the case, it's hardly surprising that Congress passed the BCRA – a fraud on the American people which gave truly evil men like creepy dude a monopoly on political speech by criminalizing competing viewpoints from small businesses and individuals who combine their voices in the corporate form." Ben Black paused, then said, "We'll get Texas President Grant's thoughts on this and other matters after a commercial."

Several TEA Party attendees got up to stretch their legs during the break.

Ricky seethed. "We were right about that BCRA being a con-job on the people," he said to Chick. "But I never suspected the devil was lurking so close to home."

"A shame what them crooks in Congress be doing?" Chick said.

"It's a bigger shame the people can't put two and two together and end this nonsense." Ricky fumed. "Remember the TEA Party demanding an end to government corruption? And the Wall Street occupiers demanding an end to corporate corruption? "Thinking back on it now, it's clear that each side correctly identified half the problem, but they bought into the media's diversions and wound up feuding with each other instead of joining forces. The occupiers crapping on cop cars and trashing cities and all that, of course, didn't help endear them to their tidier and better behaved TEA Party counterparts."

"Ladies and gentlemen, the program is resuming," the leader of the TEA Party meeting called out. "Please return to your seats."

Grant appeared onscreen, seated in a chair next to Ben Black on the set.

"President Grant, welcome to the program," Ben Black said.

Grant shook Ben Black's hand. "Thank you for having me, Ben."

"Madam President, I want to talk about the saber rattling from the U.S. and the GTP. I'd also like to discuss the Texas miracle. But first, I'd like your thoughts on this corporate president madness that's grown out of the *Citizens United* case."

Grant nodded thoughtfully. "Ben, only God knows how things are going to turn out between the U.S. and Texas and you know no one would like to see us reconcile our differences more than me. But one thing I can tell you for sure is that we are absolutely not bowing down to the GTP and we are not turning our backs on Israel.

"Now, as far as *Citizens United*, you said it right when you described the law at issue in that case as a fraud perpetrated on the American people. Laws like that are exactly what the establishment and the corporate cronies that own them depend on to perpetuate their

254

monopoly on the people's government so I'm not at all surprised that they've perverted the Court's ruling to justify corporations running for office.

"I am, however, encouraged that in doing that they provided the American people the opportunity to finally see for themselves that their government has been hijacked and their country all but destroyed, not by free market capitalism but by centrally planned monopolies created by cartels of corporate crooks, promoted by cowardly journalists and financed by central banks in cahoots with corrupt politicians and lobbyists who get rich pedaling influence while producing nothing of any value."

Grant took a deep breath, then went on, "Unfortunately, the BCRA is just one of many frauds the people's representatives have perpetrated on U.S. citizens. Take Medicare, for example, and social security. They sold Medicare to the American people as old age health insurance. The people would pay premiums all their working lives for that coverage. Similarly, they sold social security as a retirement program the people would contribute to all their working lives so that they would have that as a source of income in their old age.

"Both of those programs could have worked had Congress not spent all the money the people paid in for those benefits. Adding insult to injury, Congress then colluded with the Federal Reserve to devalue the currency – to print money, in other words – to replace the stolen retirement funds, which effectively reduced the value of social security payments by more than half. And how did they handle the shortages in Medicare? By jacking up copays and deductibles and denying treatment. Most people don't realize that Medicare, not private insurance, was number one in denying treatment to patients.

"Now, after Congress figured out it couldn't print its way entirely out of social security payments or deny its way out of providing treatment under Medicare, they came up with another brilliant idea – illegal immigration. Remember that little problem so many people were up in arms about during the Trump administration?

"What the politicians did was make legal immigration dang near impossible while at the same time virtually eliminating border security. The initial result was millions of low-skilled workers illegally flooding in and paying into social security and Medicare under fake social security numbers. And just like that, the trust funds were solvent again because those immigrants were not eligible for the benefits they paid for. Problem solved. Until legislation and court rulings mandated taxpayer funded education, healthcare, and a variety of welfare benefits that far exceeded the unclaimed contributions into social security and Medicare for those immigrants.

"At this point, several members of Congress did something unheard of in politics – they told the truth. They admitted publicly that both programs were a sham from the start. Specifically, they pointed out that when these programs were created, the average life expectancy was such that few who paid into them would live to benefit from them.

"So they proposed two new solutions: One, to raise the retirement age so that, once again, few who pay in will get what they pay for; and two, to make the benefits unavailable to people who attain to some arbitrarily chosen level of wealth, even though those 'rich' people would still be required to pay the premiums – again, ensuring the people will not get what they pay for. Of course, all of this is moot now that the U.S. has instituted the euthanasia program which creates an absolute certainty that no one will benefit from these programs. It's odd that no one's asking why they're still required to pay for them. I guess that harmonization vaccine is working good."

Ben Black shivered. "It's just plain evil," he said. "Many of us warned that euthanasia would be a natural outgrowth once widespread acceptance of abortion on demand desecrated the sanctity of life. All that nonsense about a war on women, sure, big threat. Ladies run for cover, we're under attack by unborn babies! Of course they'll say unborn babies aren't people.

"Not that disregard for human life under the premise that certain people are not human enough is anything new. Recall proponents of slavery and the genocide of indigenous Americans justified their evil deeds with the same argument. In fact, abortion is an extension of the ideas of those who despised black people and other minorities. I mean, does anyone even know who Margaret Sanger was? The mother of Planned Parenthood whose highest priority was to exterminate the African race first through forced sterilization and then by persuading them to terminate their own offspring by abortion. Margaret Sanger knew and slave owners knew the truth. I mean, seriously, how does one not know a person is a person?

"So here we are again, few among us willing to openly declare what abortion is. The butcher drills a jagged metal bit into the baby's tender scull or crushes it in the name of 'women's health,' turning a mother's womb, the safe place, the sanctuary of life, into an execution chamber that muffles the baby's screams. So long as we don't hear those screams it isn't the murder of innocence, it's a constitutional right. It was only a matter of time before all human life would be reduced to lines on a spreadsheet on some government accountant's desk."

Ben Black moved along to a lighter subject. "So, tell me about the Texas miracle, how Texas manages healthcare and retirement."

Grant scrubbed her hands together. "Well, as a government, we don't manage either. Our responsibility is to protect our citizens' life, liberty, and property from infringement by others. Government has neither the responsibility nor the right to protect individuals from their own choices, nor to make choices for them. And history shows that every attempt by governments to do either has ultimately led to the severe decline of those societies.

"Having said that, Texas takes individual empowerment very seriously because it's key to addressing all social issues. So we educate. We suggest wise choices but we don't mandate them. For example, the healthcare you asked about: We encourage the young and healthy to purchase only catastrophic health insurance or to join private cooperatives that cover only major surgeries, complex diseases, serious injuries, that kind of thing. The cost for this coverage is minimal.

"The rest, pay-as-you-go. It's a lot cheaper than paying premiums for full coverage insurance because doctors compete for the non-catastrophic business and they're not contractually obligated by insurers to artificially inflate prices to cash-payers. Local communities also form cooperatives that work similarly to how Medicare was supposed to work to care for the elderly. Individuals can participate in those or purchase advanced aged insurance through a private insurer whose managers would be jailed should they convert the people's money and deny them benefits as was done with Medicare."

Grant paused for a minute, then said, "Ben, do you rely on an insurance company to pay your rent, your food, your clothes, your fuel, your car, your bus ticket, your shampoo, your cable television, phone, utilities, entertainment, vacation, education…anything like that? Obviously, the answer is no. You pay as you go and you save up to manage things during an income interruption. That savings is insurance. So then why do we falsely believe healthcare requires insurance? Because it costs so much? Not here in Texas. Maybe the question our brothers and sisters in the U.S. ought to be asking is why they're allowing the government to make healthcare uncompetitive. You'd be surprised how many healthcare facilities are owned by insurance companies, but that is a much longer conversation."

"I'll just bet it is," said Ben Black.

Grant said, "So leaving that conversation aside for now, what we've done here in Texas is allow churches and other non-profits to do what they do. Part of that is caring for the chronically-ill poor with donations and volunteers just as they did in the U.S. before the government got involved. That's something we didn't even have to suggest. There's a reason virtually all of the county hospitals where the poor are treated is named saint this or saint that. It's because these hospitals were all started by churches. The way it works is this: If you show up at a church-run hospital – or one run by a synagogue or mosque or whatever – in need of treatment and you have no money, the treatment is free. If you show up and you have modest resources, you pay a little. If you show up needing treatment and you're rich, I hope you brought your gold MasterCard. Sliding scale, in other words.

"It's a blatant lie that poor Americans died in the streets for lack of healthcare before the government stepped in; just as it's a lie that poor Americans starved to death before food stamps. The same private institutions that provided healthcare for the poor also provided food and clothing. So, here in Texas, we've simply gone back to what works. With all due respect to so-called progressives, progress isn't scrapping everything that ever worked and starting over with something that never did. It's about discarding what doesn't work, continuing what does, and adding to that and improving upon it. Getting out of the way of voluntary service has dramatically reduced the cost of healthcare and other services and increased availability without denying recipients the opportunity to personally know and be grateful to the people that sacrifice to help them.

"Grateful people pay it forward. The government run system where morally bankrupt imbeciles pat themselves on the back for running around demanding one's resources be confiscated and given to someone else was an utter failure both ethically and financially. The responsibility to look after the needy is not a collective responsibility, it is an individual responsibility, and if each of us does just a little, no one is left behind. And individual responsibility does not prevent individuals from *voluntarily* working collectively to assist others

258

either. Texans do that through religious, as well as secular, institutions, all the time."

"Amen!" Ben Black nodded his head enthusiastically. "And when we fail to do our part as individuals, we kick open the door to a government 'solution,' paid for not only in mad money but also in the loss of freedoms. Every positive right created by government infringes upon our naturals rights because one's government created right to something is paid for by taking that something from another's natural right to keep what is his."

Grant smiled. "That's right. Like this business of government mandating what you can eat or drink and what kind of lifestyle you can live. Think of it. If I'm paying for your healthcare, shouldn't I have the right to demand you don't give yourself diabetes by eating doughnuts? Shouldn't I have the right to demand you exercise regularly?"

"Of course you should," Ben Black said, "if you're paying my healthcare bill."

"And by the same logic," Grant pressed on, "I should also have the right to demand you refrain from, say, playing football or snow skiing because those activities have a higher risk of injury than others, and I'm the one stuck with the bill if you hurt yourself. And you can just imagine what rights I should have regarding your mental health. I mean, mental health treatment can be very expensive, so surely I have the right to require you to divorce your high-maintenance wife or quit your job if I think either of those might cause you too much stress.

"And child birth, my goodness, that can be expensive too, and so can the kids that result. So, if I'm on the hook for your medical bills I should be able to prevent you from having children even if it means forced sterilization. You get the picture. When one steps on another's right to keep what one has earned – and that's exactly what occurs when the 'government' pays for anything – the one receiving the fruit of the other's labor forfeits the right to make his own decisions. Under this paradigm, the poor's choices in life are dictated by those who are better off financially. And frankly, that's *fair*. But it isn't *right*."

"I couldn't agree more," Ben Black said. "And every government solution inevitably creates a hundred new nightmares. But besides encouraging personal responsibility, common sense, and good will among men – and women, to be politically correct – what else is Texas doing? Not to diminish those things. I've always believed that compassion for others begins with taking care of yourself and your family so that you and yours aren't competing with those less capable for resources."

Grant sighed. "Honestly, Ben, that takes care of ninety-nine percent of it, but as you know, we've undertaken a couple of macro level reforms that have been a shot in the arm to the economy. And by the way, when I say the economy, I'm talking about the economy that matters – that of each and every individual, not formulaic measurements of GDP, unemployment rates, inflation rates, and all of that easily manipulated macro data nonsense.

"Remember the 4.9 percent unemployment rate reported in early 2016 when employment was well below eighty percent? Below sixty percent if you figure under-employment. That's just one example of why we don't use U.S. government style accounting. Our kindergartners here in Texas can do math better than the leadership in Dodge City.

"And we sure as heck don't use rising stock markets as evidence of growth. Because, all other factors equal, that's not evidence of anything but currency devaluation – an illusion of growth. When the value of a dollar is reduced to fifty cents through quantitative easing – which is a fancy way of saying printing money backed by nothing – a dollar's worth of stock costs two dollars. There's no real increase in value. Yet the U.S. government used exactly this sort of data to try and convince people the prolonged mini-depression after the economic crash in the early 2000s was a recovery while that coal miner at home in West Virginia had a 100% unemployment rate.

"So, the Texas Miracle: What we did was look at a number of projects that are typically in the public domain, such as transportation infrastructure, utilities, and so on – the stuff the failed U.S. 'stimulus packages' were made of. You'll recall the government sold those frauds to the public as," she held her fingers up in quotes, 'investments.' Well, I thought about that word,' and it occurred to me that it implies a return on investment – a profit. So, we put a massive public works project on a ballot initiative as a *real* investment, complete with a return, and the people voted for it overwhelmingly.

"The way it works is this: We started with the premise that there is no free lunch here. If you want to use a new roadway, a train, or utilities in Texas, you have to pay for it. Public services should run as

260

efficiently, effectively, and as profitably as any purely private sector enterprise.

"But, as a taxpaying Texas citizen, you're not merely a potential customer, you're also an investor, a shareholder, entitled to monthly dividend checks from the profits of the investments you make with your tax dollars. And by the way, because free markets have made it possible for individuals to supply most of their own household water and energy, the majority of the revenues from the utility investments come from big industries, not individuals. The same is true of the revenues from roadway and train use which is billed by the mile. Big businesses tend to use a lot more mileage, for shipping and so on, than individual commuters, and they pay for those miles. No one pays more for earning more, they pay more for *using* more.

"The idea was to create a system where individuals and businesses alike pay proportionally for benefits received from public investments. It's a fair system that allows everyone to make their own choices. For example, as I said, most individuals will choose home energy and water systems rather than pay their entire lives for public water and energy service. Some will choose to commute by rail at a lower cost than purchasing and maintaining a personal motor vehicle and paying for road usage. Still others may choose to avoid either of those costs and simply walk or ride a bicycle. And by the way, we also incorporated an impressive system of walking and cycling paths into the new infrastructure. That's another thing that's doing wonders for the health and quality of life of our citizens. You get the idea.

"As long as individuals make wise choices about use, this system provides a lifetime of financial security through the dividend payments. And did I tell you that two of our best energy customers are countries? The United States and Mexico. Very profitable contracts."

Ben Black raised an eyebrow. "Sounds a little Fabian."

Grant grinned. "And yet it's not. Individuals don't get to make their own choices in socialist societies. And individuals are routinely cheated out of their return on investment under crony capitalism, socialism's ugly cousin. The Texas miracle is free market capitalism at its finest with just a dash of realism."

"Right," Ben Black said. "So, what about the really poor, and the homeless?"

Grant said, "I'm glad you asked, Ben. First of all, private charities provide food and clothing and healthcare to the poor, as I pointed out already. As for the homeless part, well, public land is just that – public. So with some exceptions, people are free to pitch a tent. The idea that living in a tent is cruel is just plain nonsense. You know, my grandparents lived in a tent during the great depression and it didn't hurt them one bit. Both of them lived to be nearly a hundred years old and they did well enough financially to leave a small fortune to their children. And I know I don't have to tell you that before Europeans arrived on this continent many native Americans lived in tents all their lives and preferred it that way.

"Having said that, I do recognize that most people nowadays prefer to reside in a permanent fixed dwelling. And the investment dividends alone make that achievable for anyone if they properly manage that income. So, speaking generally, there's no reason for anyone in Texas to live transiently if they don't want to, certainly not for an extended period of time."

"Come on, Madam President," Ben Black shook his head, "those dividends aren't that big."

"They aren't huge, no. But they aren't small either. Plus, have you checked the prices of housing since the Texas government got out of the business of guaranteeing mortgage loans with taxpayer dollars? You may have to save up and pay cash for a house now – and that might even require living in one of those tents for a few months – but for ten thousand dollars you can buy the same house that would have cost a couple hundred thousand or more under the government guaranteed mortgage paradigm and you won't owe a single payment after the purchase. Not great for big banks and speculators, but terrific for Texas families.

"That, my friend, is the magic of a free market, and by free, I mean really free – free from government intervention and manipulation. Funny thing is, until I read *Free Market Revolution* by *Yaron Brook* and *Don Watkins*, it hadn't dawned on me that none of us alive today has ever experienced anything close to a free market. No wonder so many got sucked into the false promise of socialism. They didn't realize that the socialism democrats were pushing was nothing but different packaging on the crony capitalism republicans tried to pass off as a free market; the same rigged game in which the politically connected prosper at everyone else's expense.

"*The Road to Serfdom* by *Friedrich Hayek* is a great book for anyone who wants to understand why socialism never has and never

262

will work, how it inevitably leads to poverty and unthinkable atrocities for everyone in the society besides a small group of political elites."

Grant took another deep breath and continued, "You've probably noticed the downward trend in the cost of college education here as well. Any Texas student can pay for a four-year degree with a part time job since we privatized universities and got out of the financial aid business. It's the same logic that resulted in dramatic reductions in housing prices.

"The thing is, taxpayer backed student loans and home loans provided instant gratification, but in the bigger picture all that debt made our citizens lifelong slaves to the central banking cartel and their coconspirators in government. And I don't have to tell *you* about central banks. You practically wrote the book on that legalized counterfeiting and Ponzi scheme. As you might imagine, the big bankers are awfully upset with me for abolishing the fractional reserve scam and phasing out paper money."

Ben Black chuckled. "I *read* the book on the central banking cartel, I didn't write it. *G. Edward Griffin* did. And since we're plugging books now, I may as well plug that one – It's entitled *The Creature from Jekyll Island* and I strongly recommend it. So, anything else you want to share with the audience about the Texas miracle?"

"Certainly," said Grant. "We've not only reverted to a sound currency backed by gold, we've also eliminated the income tax altogether and instituted one flat rate consumption tax. I'll see your last book plug and raise you one – *The FairTax Book* by *Neal Boortz* and *John Linder*. That book covers everything you need to know about a corruption-resistant tax policy that promotes massive economic growth. The other thing we did on tax is amend the Texas constitution to require a war tax in the event of any military conflict. No borrowing for wars of choice. The idea there is that the people will restrain their representatives from unnecessary foreign entanglements if they feel the immediate burden of it."

Ben Black squirmed in his chair. "That's pushing it, isn't it? I mean with the U.S. and GTP threatening –"

Grant shook her head. "Not at all, Ben. No doubt in my mind that the good citizens of Texas will step up to the plate and pay whatever it takes to defend the Republic. That's entirely different than sacrificing to finance regime change and other foreign meddling to benefit some politically connected multinational corporation jockeying for better terms on another nation's natural resources or whatever.

"But, getting back to your question on the Texas Miracle, we've also pared regulation to a minimum and instituted tort reform so that professionals have considerable immunity from liability when providing charitable services. That's one reason we now have an overabundance of volunteers providing free healthcare and other services to the poor. Another reason is that we don't have many poor people anymore. That's the real achievement."

"Tell me about the Dodge City wall," Ben Black said, "I'm not sure how I feel about a wall between us and other Americans."

Grant sighed. "That wall is symbolic – a symbol of the economic and psychological wall that Farnsworth erected between us when he ejected Texas from the United States to improve his reelection odds by shutting out freedom loving electors. Not that border walls can't serve other purposes. Take the wall on our border with Mexico, for example. That one has done an amazing job of preventing noncitizens from entering without an invitation. It's indispensable for national security. Plus, as you know, it's a recreation and commerce mecca with the bicycle lanes and foot paths, and shops and restaurants along the top of it. Not to mention the light rail extending all the way from the Gulf of Mexico to the Pacific. Makes the Great Wall of China look like the fancy fence it is. Our folks and the Mexicans enjoy that wall. And like all of our other public works, it generates a ton of money for the shareholders, the citizens of the Republic of Texas.

"Most of the other problems once associated with immigration are not even factors in Texas anymore because we are a very welcoming Republic for those who respect our way of life. The drug cartels and all that violence coming from south of the border – no more since we decriminalized individuals' ingestion decisions and refused to get distracted from addiction treatment and sucked into a so-called war on drugs by the emotional allure of the problem itself. Incidentally, drug addiction has also dropped since we promote treatment instead of incarceration and interdiction."

Ben Black raised a hand. "Wait a minute," he said. "Do you really think legalizing drugs was a good idea? What about the children?"

"Look," said Grant, "I'm no more in favor of drug abuse than the t-totaling Baptist ladies who led the charge to repeal liquor prohibition were in favor of drinking. As for kids getting drugs, Texas will come down on you like a ton of bricks if you give drugs to a kid, just like we do if you give a kid alcohol. The truth is, under the war on drugs paradigm kids could get crack and heroin easier than they could get a sip of beer."

"Whoa." Ben Black raised an eyebrow. "I think most people are under the impression that well-connected zealous boozers were responsible for overturning the alcohol prohibition. But you're saying it was Baptist church ladies?"

Grant nodded. "That's right. And it obviously wasn't because these devout Christian ladies thought anything good would come from drinking, it was because they saw firsthand how prohibition created a lucrative black market for liquor that primed the pumps of organized crime. As adamantly opposed to drinking as these ladies were, they were more opposed to the poverty, bloodshed, and disproportionate incarceration of the poor resulting from liquor prohibition.

"Those are the same festering cancers that we got from the so-called war on drugs. I mean, there's mountains of documentation that shows that decades after implementation of narcotics prohibition and after trillions of dollars of the people's money being wasted on it, we did not realize any decrease in drug addiction. But we did get far worse carnage and incarceration of minorities and poor whites than we did under liquor prohibition. And, by the way, the war on drugs also unwittingly gave those engaged in the multi-gazillion dollar black market drug business a de facto exemption on both sales tax and income tax. The shooting and killing in urban neighborhoods wasn't because there weren't enough gun control laws on the books, it was because the government created a lucrative tax-free black market for gangbangers to war over?

"But getting back to immigration: Another reason it isn't much of an issue here in Texas anymore is because we provide no individual subsidies – no welfare. Consequently, the presence of foreigners does not negatively impact our national budget like it did when we were part of the U.S. welfare state. So, those policy decisions have helped a lot, but the biggest improvement on immigration comes from the multinational agreement we entered into with the Latin American countries which entitles our people to unimpeded ingress and egress and private property rights in those countries. The free flow of capital and labor both ways has created a net economic benefit to the citizens of the Republic of Texas as well as to our Latin American neighbors."

Ben Black folded his arms. "So the Dodge City wall isn't designed to stop U.S. citizens from coming into Texas?"

"Not at all," Grant said. "If anything, it's designed to attract them by clearly marking the boundary between freedom and tyranny."

"I take it it won't stop more DHS harmonizers from entering either, then."

Grant shook her head. "With Farnsworth in office, I doubt it. I think the only thing that would stop that maniac from doing something stupid is the will of the American people. Unfortunately, I don't believe the people have the will to stop him right now because they don't understand that their own futures depend on their respecting and protecting the futures of others. The guiding principles set forth in the U.S. Constitution have been erased from their consciousness. But we plan to fix that, and strangely, President Farnsworth has approved our plan to do it. Right, Ben?"

Ben Black shook his head now. "I wouldn't say that he's approved our plan, but he has guaranteed Texans safe passage to and from," he looked directly into the camera and smiled, "the Port of Boston! On July fourth, President Grant and I will host the 2028 Boston TEA Party onboard an oil tanker provided by Cole Brothers Industries. All of the citizens of the United States and Texas are invited to join us in a study of the Constitution, prayers for reunification and a return to the values and principles that made our people the greatest nation on Earth. Spread the word!"

The attendees at the Wichita Falls TEA Party meeting cheered and whistled.

"Man, that Ben Black and President Grant are really something," Ricky said as he and Chick shuffled out.

"Where to now?" said Chick.

Ricky tossed his long hair out of his eyes and stroked his beard. "I reckon, it's time I see a barber. Then we better get back to the ranch."

Chapter 60

"It works, it works," Dawn yelled out, waving frantically from the chimp enclosure when Chick and Ricky pulled into the drive. The two men ran to see what had her so excited.

Brutus darted around the enclosure, whooping and chattering, and leaping and climbing, and swinging from branch to branch on the artificial trees. A tear rolled down Ricky's cheek. After all these years, they had done it.

Dawn and Ricky and Chick joined hands and danced around in circles until Ricky pulled away. He reached into his pocket for the go-phone. "There's just one thing left to do." He dialed Gabriella's number.

No answer.

Before Ricky could put the phone back in his pocket, it rang.

"Hi," the voice on the other end said. "Someone just called me from this number."

"Gabby," Ricky choked.

"This is Gabriella Meir. Who's this?"

"It's Ricky."

Gabriella went silent.

"Please don't hang up," Ricky said.

He heard her sigh.

"I, we...uh," he stammered. "The artificial eyes have been proven in an animal test. What I'm trying to say is, we're ready." His voice crackled. "Gabby, come to the ranch for the surgery. Babe, you're going to see again."

The call disconnected.

"Gabby? Gabby, are you there?"

Chapter 61

Two days later at a few minutes before 5:00 AM a big rig rolled into the drive at the Santana ranch, the driver tooting the horn. Chick peeked out the window from the bunkhouse where he and Ricky had stayed since Ricky gave up his bedroom in the main house to Dawn.

"Wake up," Chick shook Ricky who was sleeping soundly with his face buried in a pillow.

Ricky rolled over, groggy, and mumbled. Then his eyelids slammed closed again.

Chick shook him some more, pointing out the window while he did, at the man helping Gabriella down from the cab of the truck. "Look. Your girl's here."

Ricky's eyes popped wide open and he shimmied over to the window and watched JB – the trucker who had helped him and Gabriella detour from Vizion's campaign tour – assisting Gabriella out of the truck. He hurriedly attached one prosthetic, then pointed to the other one laying in the floor a few feet from his bunk. "Toss me my other leg there, would you."

Chick handed the prosthetic to him, said, "I'm going to go tell Dawn," then bolted outside.

Ricky rushed out the door behind him wearing nothing but boxers and an undershirt. "Gabby!" he hollered as he stumbled to the truck.

"Ricky," she greeted him dryly, holding her hand out perfunctorily. She suppressed her excitement about the possibility of being able to see again, determined not to set herself up for another disappointment.

"Thank you for bringing her," Ricky told JB as he took Gabriella's hand.

She reciprocated with a disappointingly stiff handshake.

"Anything I can do to help my fellow patriots," JB said. "Oh and Miss Sally sends her best and she asked me to give you this." JB reached into his pocket and pulled out a coupon: Buy one Country-Fried Steak and Eggs Plate at Sally's Truck Stop and Diner and Get one Free.

Ricky grinned. "You be sure and tell Miss Sally *Thank-you* for me."

Gabriella's nostrils went into high alert when she caught the scent of Dawn approaching with Chick. The smell of that tramp sent a rush of jealousy jolting through her. Gabriella silently scolded herself. It didn't make any sense to suffer this gut wrenching feeling about Dawn and Ricky's relationship. After all, Ricky, her would-be knight in shining armor, was responsible for this nightmare he was now riding in on his white horse to rescue her from. Paying a long overdue debt was hardly chivalry. She thought about the conversations Ricky and his little sexpot must have; pictured them lying in bed after a romp, chitchatting about poor pathetic Gabriella and how oh-so-charitable of them to try and heal her.

"Nice to see you, Gabriella," Dawn said. "Are you okay?"

Gabriella sucked in a deep breath. "Fine," she said.

Chick was not sure what to say to Gabriella. "Congratulations," is what he came up with.

"Pardon?" she answered back.

"Well, you know, I mean in advance for being able to see again," Chick explained. "My girl here done proved them eyes work on monkeys. I know it's going to work for you too."

Dawn elbowed him in the side. "Brutus is not a monkey."

My girl? That confused Gabriella and she did not appreciate being equating with an ape or a monkey either one. "If I didn't have confidence in Dr. Dawn's ability, I wouldn't be here," she said. "It's the *only* reason I'm here."

Dawn forced a smile. "I appreciate the confidence, but I can't do it alone. I'll need some assistance with the procedure. If I'd known you were coming –"

Chick said, "I'll help you, baby."

Dawn patted the backside of his hand. "No offense, Chick, but this time around I need someone trained in ophthalmology or neurosurgery, or at least medicine in general."

Ricky saw the familiar irritated wrinkle bunching up above the bridge of Gabriella's nose. "Listen, if now's not convenient," she began.

Ricardo stumbled up with Isabella on his arm. "Ah, my son's beautiful friend," said Ricardo. "I cannot believe you have come back."

"Who's there?" Gabriella said.

Isabella reached out and touched her forearm gently. "It is Isabella and Ricardo. Remember us from your last visit?"

Gabriella smiled warmly. "Of course. How are you, Mr. and Mrs. Santana?"

"We are well," Isabella said. "And we are very excited about your operation." She glanced reassuringly at Dawn. "I am sure Dr. Langford would assist you, Doctor Dawn, and he should help you with an operating room at the hospital. He does have privileges there."

Dawn lipped a silent thank-you to Isabella.

"Ricky, will you drive Papa and I to the hospital so we may discuss this with Dr. Langford?"

Chapter 62

By 6:00 PM the following afternoon, Dawn had completed Gabriella's transplants. She and Dr. Langford pulled off their skull caps, tossed their rubber gloves, and headed out to the waiting room where Chick was snoring loudly, his head hanging over the arm of his chair.

269

Ricky jumped up, his eyes bloodshot with fatigue.

Dr. Langford shook Ricky's hand, but didn't say anything.

Dawn nodded and her smile answered the question on Ricky's face. "So far so good. Assuming Gabriella remains stable and infection free, she'll be moved from ICU to a recovery room in a couple of days."

"Thank you." Ricky hugged her. "So what now?"

"Now we wait. The bandages come off in a couple of weeks so long as there are no unexpected complications."

"Can I see her?" Ricky said.

"She's heavily sedated," Dawn explained. "And after the anesthesia wears off, she'll still be out of it for at least three days or so with the pain medication and all. The best thing you can do right now is go on back to the ranch and try to get some rest."

Dawn looked more exhausted than Ricky felt. "And you?" Ricky said.

"I'm going to hang round here a while longer. I'll see you at the ranch for breakfast."

Chapter 63

The Cole Brothers landed in their private jet at the Santana ranch the next morning just in time to celebrate Gabriella's operation over one of Isabella's hardy sunrise breakfasts. "Ma'am your cooking is ever' bit as good as Miss Sally's," JB the trucker said through a mouthful of scrambled eggs. He smiled and winked. "But don't tell Sally I said so."

Tom Cole drizzled syrup on his pancakes and smiled at Dawn and Ricky. "I knew you two were going to be a good investment."

"Mm." Dawn swallowed a sip of orange juice. "The credit is all Ricky's," she said. "Now that he got the remote neural code processer working, artificial eye transplant recipients will be able to enjoy one hundred percent mobility. I just hope the sight restoration is as good as it appears from observing Brutus."

"I have every confidence it will be," said Tom Cole.

Chick said chomping on a biscuit, "My Dawn sure is something, ain't she." He draped an arm over her shoulders.

Dawn blushed.

Ricky dipped a buttermilk biscuit into a bowl of gravy. "Thank you for believing in us, Mr. Cole. I hope y'all won't be disappointed."

Isabella rounded the table, topping off everyone's coffee.

Tom Cole thanked her, then he glanced back at Ricky. "I assume you've heard about the Boston TEA Party July fourth. You plan to attend?"

"Well, I don't know," Ricky said. "I reckon it all depends on how things go with Gabriella."

Dawn reached across the table and squeezed Ricky's hand. "You should go. It's going to be a once in a lifetime event. Chick and I will stay and look after Gabriella. You'll be back in time for the bandages come off."

"It is going to be a rather big deal," Don Cole said after swallowing a bite of pancake. "A whole slate of fresh faces will be announcing their candidacies for the House of Representatives. "He gestured at Dawn with his chin. "Including this one, if she can get away for twenty-four hours to be there."

"You're running for Congress?" Ricky said.

Dawn nodded. "I know it sounds crazy, but we can't just sit idly by while our country disintegrates. Besides, Mr. Cole can be very persuasive. Anyway, Attorney Miller offered me a seat on his corporate helicopter so I can fly out to Boston on the 4th, make my announcement, and fly right back. Dr. Langford will keep an eye on Gabriella while I'm gone."

"Any chance I could get a ride with Miller too?" Ricky said, and took a sip of coffee.

Tom Cole shook his head. "Afraid not. Miller, and more importantly, his insurance carrier, seems to think you have a target on your back. He's concerned that if anything were to happen to the helicopter with you onboard it would be treated as an act of war, or whatever they're calling it these days, and the claim denied. It's nothing personal, understand. For similar reasons, the commercial airlines aren't offering flights between Texas and the U.S. either."

Tom Cole clasped his hands together. "But, I'm sure you've heard that we'll be staging the event from the deck of one of our tankers. She's currently docked at the port of Houston undergoing a little reconfiguring. We'll be departing the twenty-fourth. You're welcome to join us on the voyage. The accommodations onboard aren't extravagant, but they do the job."

Ricky nodded. "Alright."

"Woohoo!" Chick said, "I want to make a toast now." He raised his coffee mug. "To Dawn, the prettiest eye surgeon in the world." He reached into his pocket and pulled out the toy ring he'd got at the Cyber Saloon. "Dawn, will you marry me?"

The dining room went silent. All eyes turned to Dawn.

Her jaw dropped and she said nothing.

Chick poked her in the side with an elbow. "Well?"

Dawn looked at the plastic ring and laughed, assuming Chick must be joking.

Ricky watched as the joy drained from Chick's face. It reminded him of Gabriella's first reaction when he'd given her that stupid necklace instead of a ring.

JB said, "Well, I best be getting back on the road. Ain't no telling what kind of grief they're going give me at the checkpoint." He stood up and wiped his mouth with a napkin.

Ricardo pulled a .38 special out and slid it across the table to Ricky and said, "You are going to take your company back, no?"

Don Cole arched an eyebrow. "Well, are you, Ricky?"

Ricky felt a twinge of rage as the betrayal he had learned about from Ben Black's program surged to the forefront of his thoughts again. He had planned to go to the hospital to see Gabriella today. But what was to see? Dawn said Gabriella would be out of it. "It's either that or run for president myself as an individual," he said. "I can't just stand by and let Vizion become president with Josh and Levi in charge."

Don Cole nodded. "I agree, but it's too late to get on all the ballots as an individual candidate. And I don't think there's any chance Levi's going to happily fork over controlling interest in Vizion to you."

Ricky stood up and tucked the .38 into the front of his waistband. "We'll see about that. Would your insurance carrier object to me riding along with y'all to Dodge City?"

"We're self-insured," Don Cole said. "But you're going to need something more powerful than that pea shooter if you aim to save the country." He tossed Ricky a pocket U.S. Constitution.

"What's this? And since when is it my responsibility to save the United States?"

Don Cole said, "Vizion Inc. is about to become the United States now, in a sense. And that Constitution, my friend, is the most powerful weapon in the world against tyranny – a roadmap to maintaining liberty, the first right that makes a nation great. The thing is, it only works if you use it. And you can't use it if you don't know what's in it.

Under the current circumstances, I recommend you start by familiarizing yourself with the parts regarding the power of the purse."

The look on Ricky's face confessed he had no idea what the power of the purse was. He tucked the Constitution in his shirt pocket and laid the pistol on the table.

Don Cole picked up the handgun and looked it over. "I didn't mean to suggest that you shouldn't have personal protection," he said and handed it back to Ricky.

Ricky nodded. "I'll be out at the bunkhouse when y'all are ready to go."

Chapter 64

After an uneventful flight to south Dodge City, a shakedown at the checkpoint crossing into the north side, followed by a short train ride to the Santa Fe Depot transit center, Ricky made the familiar trek down the sidewalk to Leviathan headquarters, dodging the hordes of stumbling zombie-like pedestrians that had become commonplace. The empty eyes and distant expressions were as bazaar as they were annoying. Was it the harmonization vaccine causing that?

Ricky slapped the harmonizer at the entrance to the Leviathan building across its face with the pocket Constitution and high kicked it to the ground before it could begin its predictable obnoxious interrogation. "Don't screw with me," he barked as he rushed to the elevator.

Levi eased up from his throne when Ricky stormed into the office.

"Well well, if it isn't the prodigal Vizion CEO. I must say you're looking rather well for a man who a few short months ago wasn't expected to survive."

"No need to slaughter the fatted calf," Ricky said. "I'm just here to take my company back."

"Take it back? Whatever do you mean? You've as much interest in Vizion as you've had since the IPO."

Levi had a point. Albeit a purely technical one. Before, Ricky's thirty percent of Vizion's stock had given him a substantial plurality of interest. But that was no longer the case now that Levi had reshuffled the shareholder deck. "I know all about your covertly linked strawman corporations, how you've used them to conceal your hijacking of Vizion. And I know you've done the same to control the major media.

"All that hooey about *Citizens United*," Ricky went on, "and how the case opened the floodgates of big corporate money to corrupt the government; how Vizion Inc. as president would return the government to the people. Your real intention all along was to restore the monopoly on power that you and your politician cronies had before the Court struck down that ban so cleverly woven into the BRCA on political speech by small businesses and individuals who combine their voices in the corporate form.

"Tell me something, Levi, did you really think your corrupt media companies could get by indefinitely with misleading the people about the *Citizens United* case? That no one would ever read the opinion and discover the truth of how that freedom of the press exemption written into the BCRA actually created a legalized monopoly on political speech for the largest most powerful – and obviously most corrupt – corporations, those that own the media or are the media? Your politicians and your media sold that law to the public as a means of accomplishing just the opposite. Have you no shame?"

Levi settled back into his throne and folded his hands together. "If you've read the entire opinion then you must be aware that the dissent took issue with the freedom of press exemption. The solution was simple; regulate the press as well, prohibit propaganda and force the press to report only news. But the right-wingers on the Court were having none of that."

"Gee, what could possibly go wrong with making the courts arbiters of what's news and what's not?" said Ricky.

Levi said, "We'll agree to disagree on the wisdom of the dissent's proposal. As for the rest, don't be such a prude. It's strictly business."

"Business? Business ain't about buying the government and using it to further your own interests at everybody else's expense. It's about producing goods and services or *cures* that people want and need and competing in the marketplace to sell them. That's what I founded Vizion on, remember? A worthy goal of creating a technology to cure the blind. And the market saw a heck of a lot of value in that pursuit. But we're getting off track here."

"Ah, yes. Still the bleeding heart. The miracle man who won't give up until he makes the blind see. But tell me, Ricky, what shall they see when their eyes are opened? What will Gabriella see? A return to the same old world in decay after all the strides we've made? Men

274

trampling progress beneath their self-interest as they scurry greedily about like cockroaches?

"It seems to me that you, Ricky, are the one who is truly blind, blind to this historic moment when at long last collective enlightenment, with or without the consent of the individual, is within our grasp. We have the technology to do it you know. And we owe much of the credit to you. A new age has dawned, my friend, and your refusal to accept it will not make it any less so. The ship has sailed, as they say – the good ship Vizion. The only question remaining is who shall captain it to the final destination. I had hoped that would be you. Pity you aren't up to it."

Ricky shook his head in disgust. "Funny thing is, without individuals there couldn't be any collective. So it seems to me the real question is who's going to stand up and defend the rights of individuals against the collectivist Frankenstein you and your corrupt politicians are making of this nation."

"Let me guess." Levi laughed mockingly. "You? What do you intend to do, challenge Vizion for the presidency as an individual candidate?"

"Maybe," Ricky said.

Levi laughed again. "Surely you're aware it's too late to get on all the ballots."

"That may be so, but it ain't too late to disqualify Vizion," Ricky countered. "If I understand the rules correctly, for a corporation to establish natural born citizenship, all of its stockholders have to be natural born citizens. Right?" He paused. "Well, I may not own controlling interest in Vizion but I am still a stockholder. And guess what, I was born in Mexico to Mexican parents, and I may be a naturalized American citizen, but I'm not natural born."

Levi leaned forward, his eyes bulging. "Listen to me!" He banged his fist on the desk. "You were not born in Mexico, your older brother was. You, my friend, were yet in your mother's womb when your brother slipped from her arms and drowned as she struggled across the Rio Grande. The river swept him away. The poor child never set foot on U.S. soil, alive or even dead. You, on the other hand have never seen the southern side of the border."

Ricky shook his head. "No. No. My brother was younger than me. And he's buried on our ranch. I've seen his tombstone."

"Is that what Ricardo told you? In case you haven't noticed, your father is insane."

Ricky was speechless, stunned more by Levi's apparent intimate knowledge of a past foreign to Ricky than the alternative version of it he offered now.

"By the way, in case you have any other foolish ideas in mind, Josh asked me to extend his apologies for being unavailable to meet with you while you're in town."

"Unavailable? How did Josh even know I would be in town?"

"You're predictable," Levi said.

"Whatever." Ricky got up, rushed to the elevator, and quickly descended to the lobby.

"Have a nice day, Mr. Santana," the harmonizer there said as Ricky exited the building.

Chapter 65

The crickets' sudden silence awoke Isabella a few minutes past 10:00 PM. She peeked out her bedroom window and saw Ricky's shadow pass the main house on his way to the barn.

Ricky grabbed a shovel and a flashlight, saddled up the Palo Pinto, and rode quietly out to the gravesite beneath the old oak tree. The horse whinnied and pawed at the ground, agitated as Ricky hacked at the ground. The first several jabs were like shoveling into concrete, but once he pierced the parched crust of the surface, the digging became easier.

Within a couple of hours Ricky's hands had begun to blister with nothing but a four foot heap of dirt to show for it. He squatted down in the hole and wiped his brow. Apparently, Levi had it right – his brother wasn't buried here. He rammed the shovel into the ground and heard a pinging thud. There *was* something here. He poked the shovel around randomly, reproducing that thud each time. A chill ran down his spine. He got down on his knees and scraped off the last layer of dirt with his hands, little by little uncovering the rotting lid of a tiny wooden coffin.

Ricky found Isabella rocking on the front porch swing. The dim glow of the kerosene lamp beside her flickered in her weary eyes.

"Mama?" Ricky said.

She held a finger to her lips and continued to rock. "Shh. Do not wake your papa."

Ricky sat beside her, clutching a badly soiled doll. He didn't say a word.

A tear trickled down Isabella's cheek. "You did have a brother," she said softly, "an older brother. Your Papa has it all mixed up."

"I know," Ricky whispered. "Levi told me."

"Did he also tell you that it is my fault your brother is dead? And that it is my fault that your papa is loco?"

Ricky closed his eyes and let Isabella talk.

She wiped away her tears and straightened her back. "Your papa was not always like he is. When we met in the village outside Monterrey, he was young and strong and handsome and very competent. I remember how he tried to impress me doing barrel rolls in the sky above my house in that old plane after a day of crop dusting. And I was impressed. Although he did not know it. I made him prove he loved me as much as I loved him by pretending I was not interested. And he did prove it. He proves it every day, still – in his way.

"A year after we married, I gave birth to your brother. As much as we loved him, it was so hard to care for him with the ten dollars a day your papa made working cattle and crop dusting. I begged him to take us to Texas. Everyone said a flying vaquero could get rich working there.

"A terrible storm erupted the night we crossed the Rio Grande, and the water was rushing like crazy." Isabella took the doll from Ricky's hands and held it to her bosom. She began to weep again. "Little Ricky was holding this doll when the river swept him away. I waited in the brush along the bank for what seemed like an eternity while your papa searched for him. Papa returned at sunrise with this doll. I will never forget how he smiled as he clung to it. 'I am so glad I found you, Ricky,' he kept repeating. He never accepted that little Ricky was gone."

Ricky cradled Isabella's head to his chest and wiped the tears from her face. "I'm so sorry, Mama."

"We wandered across Texas for days until we ended up here at the ranch," Isabella continued. "At that time, an old man, a widower with no children and no family, owned the place. The poor lonely old soul. Papa went to work for him as a vaquero, handyman, crop picker, crop duster – whatever the old man needed, your papa did it. I did the

277

housework for the old man. Every night after dinner, Papa would tuck the doll in in a bassinet beside our bed in the bunkhouse. Until he volunteered for Viet Nam a couple of months later. I cannot imagine the horrors he saw there. He never talked about it.

"You were born a little while later, and I named you the same as your brother for Papa's sake. The army gave him leave to come home and see you after his first tour. That is when he buried the doll under the tree. I think it was his way of finally letting your brother go. Or maybe it was some kind of confused reaction to the war. I do not know for sure. No one knows – maybe not even Papa himself. Dr. Langford says it is a brain disease worsened by PTSD and the new doctors in Houston agree. That is why they put him on the medicine. But I do not know if they are right."

Ricky rubbed Isabella's back. "You and Papa have been through a lot. I wish you would have told me. So what happened to the old man?"

"He died a few months after Papa got out of the army and he left this ranch to us in his will." Isabella smiled weakly as they stood together. "You should get some sleep, hijo."

"I am worn out," Ricky said. "But before I hit the hay, I gotta know about Gabriella. How is she?"

"Dr. Dawn says that she is still mostly sleeping from the pain medication."

Ricky Kissed Isabella on the cheek. "Goodnight, Mama."

Chapter 66

The darkness when Gabriella awoke terrified her. "Ricky?" she cried barely audibly when she felt the body heat of someone sitting next to her.

An icy hand covered hers and a man said, "It's alright, honey."

The voice drove her spirits deeper into the endless night that had been her world for so very long. It was happening all over again. "Josh?"

Josh released her hand and slipped out of her recovery room when he heard commotion in the hallway growing closer.

"Thank you for all you've done," Gabriella heard Ricky tell Dawn outside the door. Her heart sunk as she imagined he would kiss Dawn now.

Ricky went in and sat at Gabriella's bedside. "Gabby, are you awake?"

Gabriella rolled over on her side, facing away from him. "Go away," she whimpered.

Ricky rubbed her back. "How are you doing?"

"I said, go away."

Chapter 67

June 27th, the Cole Brothers ship departed the Port of Houston bound for Boston. Ricky hated leaving Gabriella at this crucial time, but he'd been to the hospital every day since the surgery, and every day she had rejected him. What choice did he have anyway, with nothing less than the fate of the United States and possibly Texas at stake? He would be back, right by Gabriella's side when the bandages came off, whether she wanted him to be or not.

Ricky's cramped cabin onboard the ship contained a small bunk, tiny shower, a tall narrow cabinet imitating a clothes closet, and a built-in dresser with two shallow drawers. No frills, just as Tom Cole had said. But it did have a porthole with a great view of the open sea – a view that became somewhat monotonous after a couple of days, except at sunset and sunrise.

Ricky gazed out over the vast expanse of the glittering Atlantic as the third day at sea came to a close. He reckoned they must be somewhere off the coast of the Carolinas. The sun seemed to explode as it dipped into the horizon, intense flames of crimson, gold, and translucent white steaking across the water.

Deep hollow bellows from the ship's whistle vibrated the cabin walls, summoning him to dinner.

Don Cole greeted Ricky as he passed a line of fidgety people snaking down the hallway on his way to the mess hall, several stamped in place, holding their groins. "Evening, Ricky."

"Evening, Mr. Cole." Ricky pointed at the line. "What's that all about?"

"They're waiting to use the restroom," Don Cole said. "We converted all of our facilities to single toilet unisex and added locks in response to the gender neutral bathroom law."

Ricky shook his head. "The United States is coming apart at the seams and our representatives are micromanaging bathrooms. It's insane."

"Their priorities certainly are a bit misplaced," Don Cole agreed. "Come with me. There's someone I'd like you to meet." He rested a hand at the center of Ricky's back as they entered the mess hall, and steered him to a table next to a soft ice cream dispenser. The man there looked up from the bowtie he was wiping ice cream dribbles off of and smiled warmly. A pair of binoculars dangled beneath the tie. "Ben Black, I'd like you meet Ricky Santana."

Ben Black jumped to his feet, taking a quick last dab at the ice cream dribble, and reached across the table and grasped Ricky's hand. "It's a real honor to meet you, I think."

Ricky chuckled nervously while they shook hands, embarrassed for being star struck. So this was the man who had described him as an alcohol-fueled human tornado in the context of what otherwise might have been interpreted as a compliment. "I think it's good to meet you as well."

The grin on Ben Black's face expanded. "Hey, how about you two join me for dinner." He angled his thumb at the ice cream machine. "Best table in the house."

Don Cole pulled a chair out. "Glad to. Thank you."

Ricky sat next to him.

Ben Black scooped another spoonful of ice cream out of his bowl. "I'm sorry. No no, I'm not sorry. I will never be sorry for my love of ice cream. It's how I keep up this irresistible Pillsbury doughboy physique. He rubbed his tummy and shoved the spoonful into his mouth.

Ricky laughed.

A waiter stopped by the table. "Drinks for you gentlemen?"

Ricky answered first. "Coffee, please."

The waiter scribbled that on his order pad and turned to Don Cole. "And you, sir?"

"Ice water, thank you."

"And I'll have a chocolate milkshake," Ben Black said. He held his hand up. "Wait. Make that a *diet* chocolate milk shake."

"Pardon me, sir?"

"Just joshing. I'll have a Coke, a real one. Not a Pepsi, not an RC."

"Yes, sir."

"So you're Ricky Santana," Ben Black said after the waiter left for their beverages.

"Yes. Yes I am," said Ricky timorously as if confessing to a crime.

Ben Black pointed at Ricky's shirt pocket. "Say, what's that?"

"This?" Ricky pulled out the Constitution and handed it to him. "A gift from Mr. Cole."

"Ah, the U.S. Constitution." Ben Black flipped through the pages. "My favorite book, or book-let, besides the Bible."

Ricky nodded. "Say, Mr. Cole here suggested I study up on the power of the purse in light of everything that's happened with Vizion. Do you know anything about that?"

"Sure." Ben Black drug his chair around beside Ricky's, licked his thumb and turned to Article one, section nine, clause seven. It says here, in part: '*No money shall be drawn from the Treasury, but in consequence of appropriations made by law.*' What this little blurb does is require appropriation of funds be passed separate from the legislation to be funded. Which means whatever laws or programs Congress passes, if there's any money needed for them – as there always is – it has to go to the House of Representatives for funding. And the House doesn't need the Senate's or the president's approval to decline."

The waiter brought the drinks and set them on the table. "We'll be serving the main course shortly. Will there be anything else in the time being, gentlemen?"

"No thank you," said the three men, one after another.

Ben Black took a sip of his Coca Cola. "So, the bottom line is the government can't spend a single dime from the federal treasury without the House's approval," he said. "Or I should say, the *people's* approval, because the House is comprised of the people's direct representatives. Basically, if the people don't like something their government is doing, all they have to do is demand their representatives in the House refuse to fund whatever it is."

"No kidding?" said Ricky.

Ben Black nodded. "Sure. It's simple. Here's an example of how it works: Say the people finally get sick enough of the Supreme Court legislating from the bench rather than interpreting and applying the law fairly like it's supposed to. One thing the people could do about it is demand the House cut off funding for heat and air conditioning to that Courthouse. Of course Congress would have to have the spine to actually do it."

Ricky laughed out loud. "Could get mighty hot in them black robes in the summer time."

Don Cole laughed as well.

"Hey, you gotta do what you gotta do," Ben Black said with a big smile.

"Or better yet, cut off the IRS's air conditioning," Ricky suggested.

Ben Black said, "The House could have and should have gone one better and cut off funding entirely to that cesspool of corruption the minute they found out about the IRS persecuting citizens based on their political views. It's unconscionable that the people's representatives would fund such an agency, but they did, along with the IRS director's exorbitant pension."

"That's pathetic," Ricky said.

Don Cole nodded. "You're starting to get the picture."

"I think am." Ricky folded his arms across his chest. "I remember when there was all that talk by the republican majority in the House about defunding that *Planned Parenthood* outfit when the whole world learned they were carving up babies and distributing their body parts. But I didn't realize the Republicans in the House could have actually done it on their own without approval from the Senate or the president. Why in the world didn't they?"

Ben Black's face flushed with something like anger. "Because most of them were self-serving cowards," he said. "Same reason they continue to fund the national joke of a healthcare system and the euthanasia program and the myriad of executive orders that exceed the bounds of presidential power. All of which they could bring to a swift end whether the Senate or the president like it or not.

"And then there's the national debt," Ben Black went on. "Remember how the republicans in the House carried on about President Obama doubling the national debt? Well, those same republicans were the majority, which means they had to appropriate that debt. And that means the blame for doubling the debt should have been placed squarely on their shoulders.

"Same with this threat of war against Texas. It takes lots of money to wage war. The House could stop any possibility of that simply by refusing to fund it. If it doesn't refuse…well. And, again, the House does not need approval from the Senate or the president to cut off funding to that or anything else. That, my friend, is the power of the purse.

"And, as I said already, it's no accident that that power belongs exclusively to the one branch of government whose sacred responsibility is to directly represent the will of the people within the confines of the Constitution. In the Federalist Papers, James Madison described the power of the purse as, 'the most complete and effectual weapon with which any constitution can arm the immediate representatives of the people, for obtaining a redress of every grievance, and for carrying into effect every just and salutary measure.' Powerful, huh?"

Ricky nodded. "I'll say."

"It's also no accident that the whole House goes up for election every two years as opposed to every four years for president and every six with staggered election years for Senate," Ben Black added. "Makes it easy for the people to promptly replace representatives who won't get with the program. The people could replace every single member of the House every twenty-four months if they wanted to. And that wouldn't be a bad idea. The people should replace them all at least every four years. Term limits, you know. Public service was never intended to be a lifelong welfare program for used car salesmen types who can't hack a real job."

Ricky leaned back in his chair and closed his eyes, digesting how incredibly simple the check on out of control government actually was. Out of several million Americans, was it really that hard to find a few hundred who weren't corrupt or stupid or both to represent the people? He opened his eyes, and asked the obvious question, "Why isn't Congress using this power?"

"Well," Ben Black said, "several House members claim using it would upset the senators or the president or both and then they wouldn't be able to gain cooperation to gets things done. But that's a bunch of poppycock. With the exception of providing for a common defense, preventing obstruction of commerce amongst the states, preventing government infringement on individuals' civil liberties, and a couple of other matters, it's not the job of the feds to," Ben Black held his fingers up in quotes, " 'get things done.' That's primarily state and local business.

"In fact, Congress originally only went into session briefly every two years. And with the exception of national emergencies, those sessions were more a matter of representatives appearing to ensure things did *not* get done, because when things get done in Congress those things are almost inevitably a fleecing of the people, violations of individual liberties, grants of unfair advantage to one industry or corporation or state over others – or recently, even advantages to foreign nations over our own. They say these are unintended consequences.

"Call me cynical, but I have my doubts whether the consequences of legalized corruption are unintended. I believe the founders were every bit as cynical, seeing as how we fought a revolution over exactly this sort of abuse of centralized power. But, to your question, the other argument our representatives make for not using the power of the purse is that us little people don't want them to shut down the government or default on the national debt.

"First of all, as one of the *people*, I can tell you that most of us are not as averse to shutting down an out of control federal government as the media suggests we are. The very idea that people cannot get on with the business of their day to day lives without the federal government operating at full tilt should make it obvious to anybody with a brain that the government has injected itself where it does not belong.

"Secondly, selectively defunding certain departments or programs does not require shutting down the entire federal government like the politicians always suggest it does, and it certainly does not require the government to default on the national debt like the politicians say. The truth is the government is constitutionally bound to service the national debt. So, that's all nonsense too. Having said that, these default scares should, however, call our attention back to another question – why doesn't the House of Representatives use the power of the purse to reign in out of control spending and to shut down the Federal Reserve Ponzi scheme that crippled the nation with debt."

The waiter appeared with the main course.

"That smells wonderful," Don Cole said.

"Sure does," Ben Black agreed.

After arranging the steaming plates around the table, the waiter refilled the three men's drinks, and they each thanked him, then dug into their meals.

"Mm-mm, this is delish," Ricky said through a mouthful of grilled seabass dripping with garlic butter. "Now, what was that you were saying about a Ponzi scheme?"

"Mm." Ben Black swallowed a bite. "Central banks, purveyors of the root of all evils. I'll start with a brief lesson in the history of banking. So, once upon a time, money was in the form of precious metals. Gold coins, for example. Why? Because unlike paper money, precious metals have intrinsic value. Anyway, keeping gold coins at home made one's home a prime target for robbers. This was particularly true if one happened to be wealthy. The solution? A Bank. Well, actually a Goldsmith, because goldsmiths had secure gold vaults.

"For a fee, the goldsmiths would allow others to store gold in their vaults. And the owner of the gold would receive a paper receipt with which he could redeem the gold at any time. Later, gold owners began transferring their right to redeem to third parties by simply endorsing the receipts, rather than withdrawing the gold itself and physically transferring it. Still later, the arrangement evolved such that goldsmiths provided owners with a series of smaller receipts equaling the total for all of an owner's gold on deposit instead of just one receipt. These receipts could be used more or less like currency is today, making it possible to conduct several transactions without making an actual withdrawal. So here we see the birth of paper money, backed by gold.

Ben Black took a sip of his Coca Cola, then continued, "Now, because owners of transferred redemption rights also needed the gold secured, the gold seldom left the vault after transfer. Naturally, the opportunity to capitalize on this by lending out and collecting interest on someone else's gold did not go unnoticed by our crafty goldsmiths-turned-bankers. And, because these loans could be made in the form of paper receipts, again without the gold ever leaving the vault, these *bankers* often loaned far more than there actually was in gold in the vault to back it. The modern day *fractional reserve* system – the system ours is loosely modeled after – is based on this very concept, and it's legal for bankers. The rest of us would be sent to prison for life for running a Ponzi scheme like that.

"The idea behind a fractional reserve system is this: Absent a largescale financial crisis, gold redemptions in a given bank will not exceed, say ten percent; so, as long as the bank maintains that ten percent – that *fraction* – in reserve, it may loan out the rest. So far so good, except today the reserve is not required to be gold and even if it were, what happens if more than ten percent of the depositors do demand their money?

"Let's look at the first half of that, the part about reserves not required to be gold. If not gold, then what, you might ask, is used for reserves? The answer to that is Debt. In the U.S., that starts as depositors' dollars, which represent debt obligations payable by the government in…well, nothing, to the depositor…Ok, I shouldn't say payable in nothing. Actually, because the government bound itself to accept dollars for payment of taxes, it's more accurate to say that dollars are redeemable for a reduction in tax liability. But I digress. Those initial dollars in reserve are just the start, the seed, if you will, from which the Ponzi tree grows. Additional reserves are created in the form of notes payable to the bank from borrowers after the bank loans out the depositors' dollars.

"So, let's say a bank starts out with a million dollars. Then, let's say the bank loans out nine hundred thousand, keeping the ten percent or a hundred thousand in reserve. Is that all the bank can loan now? Nope. Because the notes for the nine hundred thousand dollars owed by the borrowers become nine hundred thousand in additional assets. So leaving ten percent of those assets in reserve as required, the bank can now loan another eight hundred ten thousand. After deducting the ten percent of this eight hundred ten thousand in new notes for reserve, another seven hundred twenty nine thousand can then be loaned out. And so on. So after just three rounds – and believe me, it doesn't end there – the bank has loaned out over two and a half million dollars when it never ever had more than a million dollars on hand. That will change drastically, of course, as the bank collects the hundreds of millions in principal and interest owed by borrowers for money the bank never had for lending to them in the first place.

"If that doesn't piss you off, wait until you see how this plays out on a national level. The infamous 2008 financial system bailout is instructive. That deal went down something like this: Federal reserve dude goes to the U.S Treasury and says, 'We gotta have a trillion dollars or the worldwide economy is going to collapse and life on Earth as we know it will end.'

" 'Gee, we'd love to help, but we don't have any money,' says Treasury.

"Federal Reserve dude says, 'No problem. We'll loan it to you in exchange for a treasury note,' then prints out a piece of paper – a trillion dollar check payable to Treasury.

"Treasury, in turn, prints out a piece of paper – a trillion dollar treasury note payable to Federal Reserve.

"Then Treasury deposits the check into Federal Reserve bank, and the Federal Reserve dude deposits the treasury note in the Federal

Reserve bank, and presto – a trillion dollar reserve created out of thin air appears, establishing the basis from which the Federal Reserve bank lends several trillions by means of the fractional reserve system. Most of these new loans, by the way, are made to support the federal government's deficit spending addiction.

Ben Black took a breath, "So, what's wrong with all this? Other than the fact that this is how a national debt balloons from under a trillion dollars – a staggering debt itself – to over seventy trillion in the space of just a few presidencies? Or the fact that the Federal Reserve never had any of those trillions that we, the taxpayers are on the hook to pay back, with interest! Or the fact that all of those trillions in loans increased the money supply, effectively reducing the value of our dollars – if you accept the unsupported premise that dollars ever had any value – to pennies. That's called inflation."

Ricky and Don Cole listened intently, neither of them touching their dinner as Ben Black went on, "This isn't quite the end of all of this, naturally. The Federal Reserve attempts to rein in the inflation it causes by raising interests rates to contract the money supply. This then causes chaos for small businesses and occasionally big business too, leading to bursts in the bubbles created by flooding the markets with money backed by nothing in the first place. This mess is the business cycle that the Keynesian economic propagandists on the media manufacturing networks would have us believe are natural and unavoidable patterns, like the weather.

"Except we have documented history of periods when central banks' legalized counterfeiting monopolies were not allowed, and surprise, surprise, no business cycle, no boom and bust. The general state of affair during those periods was always widespread economic prosperity. Incidentally, that prosperity has always been interrupted by a major war; one so expensive and destructive that it creates the excuse to reinstitute central banking and resume the Ponzi scheme. But I'm sure that's just a coincidence. Just as it must be a coincidence that Congress refuses to audit the Federal Reserve's books. Makes me sick," Ben Black concluded, and pushed his plate of dinner way.

Ricky pushed his plate away as well and said, "Me too."

"Shall we go up top now?" said Ben Black.

Don Cole said, "You two go ahead. Maybe I'll join you later."

"It's a beautiful night," said Ricky when he and Ben Black reached the main deck. He could taste the salt in the air as he watched the ship's Texas flag whipping in the balmy breeze.

Ben Black drew in a deep breath. "Mm, the sweet smell of God's creation." He raised his binoculars and peered out over the ocean. He clutched Ricky's arm.

"What is it?" Ricky said.

"Looks like a GTP aircraft carrier, southbound."

"Really?"

Ben Black handed Ricky the binoculars.

"It's enormous," Ricky said. "I have to tell you, the creation of this GTP military to enforce free trade makes me real uneasy. Especially with what's going on with Texas." He saw a ripple in the water, and a photonic mast popped up between the carrier and the Cole Brothers ship. "A sub. What the heck is going on out there?"

"Let me see those again," Ben Black tugged the binoculars back. "It's surfacing. "You're not going to believe this, Ricky."

"What?"

Ben Black grinned. "It's the Peshmerga. And If I didn't know better – which I don't, actually – I'd say they're escorting us. Or maybe they're trailing that carrier. I don't know."

"The what?"

"The Kurds," Ben Black said.

Ricky's eyes widened. "Seriously? The Kurds have submarines? Hey I don't know about you, but I'm suddenly not feeling great about being out here in the open."

Ben Black said, "The Kurds are the good guys. Their society is seriously democratic, inclusive, complete with individual liberties, freedom of religion, free markets, and all the rest. It's basically the early United States, less the slavery. Much more American than the U.S. these days."

"I thought the Kurds were Muslim," said Ricky.

"The majority of them are, but not the radical jihadi kind, not political Islamists, and there's a considerable minority population of Christians, Jews, and other religions, and even agnostics and atheists. They get along fine, for the most part. The government is not Islamic. Freedom of religion, like I said. You can't have that in a theocracy. Individual rights are the highest priority in Kurdish society. Even for women, who, incidentally, comprise more than fifty percent of their armed forces. Fierce fighters, those ladies, but hey, there's no greater cause than freedom, right?"

Chapter 68

Thousands of harmonizers patrolled the swelling mass of humanity gathered at the shoreline when the Cole Brothers ship steamed into Boston harbor on the morning of July 4th. Ben Black peered through his binoculars at the dense air traffic. "Mostly U.S. military drones and media choppers, except for –" He tracked a low-flying helicopter. "Ricky, I think that's Marine One. The drones must be escorts."

Ricky cupped a hand above his eyes, blocking the sun's glare over the swirling aircraft. "Looks like trouble," he said as his gaze settled on the U.S. presidential helicopter.

"You think so?" Ben Black lowered the binoculars. "Maybe Farnsworth decided a show of solidarity with the people might improve his incredibly terrible odds in the upcoming election."

"A U.S. president supporting the people instead of manipulating and coercing them would be pretty darn remarkable." Ricky sighed. "I ain't holding my breath. Politics these days ain't about unity, it's about divide and conquer."

"I hate to say it, but I think you're right," Ben Black agreed.

The ship docked a half hour later and a sense of pride came over Ricky as he gazed out over the millions of cheering people, Texas flags waving, and the hundreds of thousands of picket signs jutting into the air.

Ben Black read a few of the signs aloud: "Muslims for America, All lives Matter, TEA Party Patriots, Gays and Lesbians for Religious Freedom, Unity, Unity, Unity." He chuckled as he read one that said, "We are All Americans, Even us Texans." Tens of thousands of people wearing TEA Party t-shirts were sprinkled throughout the crowd.

"Here," Ben Black said as he handed Ricky the binoculars. "You can hang onto them. I've got to go get ready to speak."

"Thanks." Ricky held the binoculars to his eyes and laughed when he saw several signs that said, *Write-in Rebel Ricky for President*. "I didn't expect that," he chuckled to himself.

A severely bleached-blonde middle-aged woman holding a *Throw the Bums Out* sign came into Ricky's view next. "Now there's a lady who gets it." He squinted. The woman, one of those wearing a TEA Party t-shirt, waved frantically, and she seemed to be waving at him.

He raced down several flights of stairs and across the gangplank onto the shoreline, yelling out, "Miss Sally!" He wrestled his way through the packed crowd until he reached her.

Sally looked Ricky up and down. "Well if you ain't a sight," she yelled over all the noise. "You get that coupon I sent with trucker JB? How's your gal? I don't believe a word of what they said about you on the fake news. Media's all a bunch of lairs except for Ben Black and his crew. They tell it like it is. I'll bet that crooked lawyer that stole your company was behind that. Say, wasn't that backstabber a friend of yours once?"

She flipped a hand down. "Well, never mind all that. How you been? You running for president as a real person now? A lot of folks gonna be real disappointed if you don't." She cupped a hand around his ear and lowered her voice a notch. "I hear tell there's a conspiracy underway to take back the House of Representatives for the people and defund them bunch of establishment crooks in Dodge City."

Ricky smiled. "I hope so."

Sally covered her giddily gaping mouth.

One of several men in TEA Party t-shirts behind Sally – all but one of them bearded – cleared his throat. Sally gestured toward them. "Oh, how rude of me. Ricky Santana, these here are my cousins from Louisiana. They's duck hunters, except for that'n without the baby-butt face. He's a pastor. Cousins, this here is Ricky Santana."

"Everybody knows who he is," one of the cousins said.

Sally smiled big. "You hear that, Ricky Santana? You're famous."

A powerful male voice boomed from the loudspeaker system set up for the event. "Welcome, fellow patriots, to the 2028 Boston TEA party!"

The crowd roared, obscuring the whine of engines and slapping of rotor blades as the Texas presidential chopper touched down on the ship's helipad. Seeing that proud lonestar symbol on the tail gave Ricky goosebumps.

Miller's chopper landed next, with Chick and Dawn onboard.

A command rang out over the loudspeakers, "Please join me for the national anthem."

Across the mass of more than three million people in attendance, hands reverently covered hearts as they began to sing – "Oh say can you seeee, by the dawn's early liiiight…"

"Fellow patriots," the same booming voice announced after the anthem, "it is my honor to introduce from Dallas, Texas, the one, the only, Mr. Ben Black!"

Roars, whistles, applause, and cheers reverberated through the crowd when the image of Ben Black smiling and waving from the ship's upper platform appeared on huge viewing screens. "Ben Black, Ben Black, Ben Black," the crowd chanted.

"Thank you, patriots! It's great to be back in the United States!"

Ben Black waited for the crowd to settle, then asked the people to bow their heads and join him in a prayer for unity and healing for the nation, ending with, "God bless America. Amen." After that, he said, "You know, I grew up in different times than many of you. When I went to grade school we leaned basic civics and the story of the original Boston Tea Party. The way I hear it, public schools don't teach civics anymore and if they teach young people about the Boston Tea Party at all, they present it as a riot by some unruly colonists upset because they didn't like paying tax on a cup of tea or something to that affect. Well, that might be true, but the folks most harmed were the exorbitantly taxed smaller scale colonial tea merchants forced out of business by the British government's exemption of the British East India Company from the tax. That exemption effectively granted a monopoly to the largest, most powerful, and most corrupt multinational corporation of the day at the expense of small business. Does that sound at all familiar to the rigged game that's played in the United States today?"

The crowd jeered.

"I thought so," Ben Black said. "So a quick and dirty civics lesson for those of you who attended public school: The U.S. federal government is comprised of three branches – the presidency, the judiciary, and the legislature which includes the House of Representatives and the Senate. The House and the Senate pass laws. The president's job is to enforce those laws. And the judiciary's job is to settle disputes by applying the law. By the original design, senators represent the states, and the House of Representatives – the branch with the greatest power, the power of the purse – directly represents the people. The reason we find the United States in the sorry condition

291

it's in today is because the House has utterly failed to fulfill its obligation to us. But we're going to solve that problem."

Ben Black paused and took in the solemnity of the wave of silence surging from the masses, then he began a call to action in the form of something like a speech loosely modeled after the Declaration of Independence: "When in the course of events, it becomes necessary for the people of the several states to unify in opposition to that political body which was designed from its inception to be comprised of the people's direct representatives, a decent respect to the opinions of one another requires that they should declare the causes which impel them to replace the entire membership of that failed representative body.

"Like our forefathers before us, we hold these truths to be self-evident – that all people are created equal; that they are endowed by their Creator with certain unalienable rights; that among these are Life, Liberty and the Pursuit of Happiness; that to secure these rights, governments are instituted among people, deriving their just powers from the consent of the governed; that whenever any branch of government or any agency or department under any branch's direction becomes destructive of these ends, it is not only within the power of the people's House to force them back into submission to the people by declining to fund them, it is the House's solemn responsibility to do so. And the House has not done so."

Following another prolonged roar from the crowd, this one lasting ten deafening minutes, Ben Black enumerated a list of transgressions that members of the various branches of government had perpetrated against the people, and which the House of Representatives had been complicit in either expressly or through its failure to use its power of the purse to stop it.

"But you know, patriots, it's easy to blame our representatives for not using their power, and they should be blamed. But what about us? What about our responsibility to manage them and the rest of our employees? Does it make any sense at all that out of the several millions of us we can't manage a mere few hundred employees in the House and Senate?

"I mean, these clowns tell us the way it's going to be and tough cookies if we don't like it. They read or our emails and texts, listen in on our phone calls, comb through our financial records, log every website we visit and every search term we enter on the internet and every keystroke on our computers. They track every move we make by tapping the GPS on our cell phones and record us at will by remotely activating our smartphone and laptop microphones and webcams. They enslave us and our children and grandchildren in debt; they force us to accept payment for our labor in the form of worthless Federal Reserve notes that they devalue at will. They tell us what we can and cannot ingest in our own bodies; they decide what type of relationship we can have and with whom; they demand we participate in religious ceremonies that violate our consciences, and now this model global citizen crap. Conform or be sent to a harmonization camp."

Ben Black paused for a breather, then continued, "Let me ask you something, would you take that kind of crap off an employee on your family farm? Off an employee at your pizzeria? Off your plumber? Your accountant? Or the man who mows your grass? Would you let any of those employees get by with any of that?"

"Noooooooooooo," the crowd screamed.

"What would you do?"

"Fire them," the crowd screamed.

Ben Black smiled. "Then you won't be surprised by your homework assignment. When we leave here and go back to our daily lives, the first thing each and every one of us must do is join together with the people of our districts and exercise our own sacred authority, our sacred responsibility, to choose one from among us in each district to replace our current representative with a patriot who will hold fast to the Constitution and not hesitate to use the power of the purse to fend off corruption from the other branches of government."

The crowd began to chant, "Throw the bums out, throw the bums out."

Ben Black raised a hand to quiet them. "In a moment I'll be introducing some independent patriots that I know will represent the people without wavering, patriots who will wield the power of the purse like the sword of righteousness it was meant to be, and refuse to ever ever fund corruption and injustice."

A heckler with a bullhorn yelled out from the crowd. "If we vote for your independents, we'll just bleed off votes so the worst candidates from the major parties will win. We'd be fools!"

Ben Black shook his head. "Oh, the old lesser of evils game. That, sir, is the game the republicrats play and they win at it every time only because we play it with them. Voting for a lesser evil is still voting for evil. Jesus asked, what does it profit a man to gain the whole world and forfeit his soul? And I say what does it profit a citizen to vote one crook rather than another? Remember, we learned after 2016 how the corrupt media uses its platforms to promote republicrat candidates and crush the people's choice. These are the same so-called news organizations that tell us year after year that independents and libertarians can't win. The solution? Don't listen to them. Vote independent, vote libertarian. It really is that simple."

Levi and Farnsworth watched a livestream close-up of the presentation below from Marine One as the aircraft circled above the crowd.

Farnsworth sighed. "I'll do it."

"Pardon?" Levi said.

"I'm in on the unity ticket," said Farnsworth. "I don't see that I've got any choice."

Levi nodded. "I suspect Helen and Josh will concur. But, you know, unless you plan on sharing power with your opponents among the commoners as well, unity will not be enough. You must also ensure that the commoners are *not* unified."

"Are you saying what I think you're saying?"

"I am. And I suggest you do it right away before this gets out of hand."

Farnsworth's hand trembled as he dialed a number from the aircraft's secure satellite phone. "This is the president. Give the deharmonization order."

Grant stood by awaiting his turn to speak on the Cole Brother ship's platform as Dawn hustled out, waving to the crowd. "Fellow patriots," Ben Black shouted, "give a warm welcome to the next congresswoman from the First district of Kansas, Dr. Dawn Wise!" He held her hand up high.

The crowd cheered.

A shot rang out.

Chick, Grant, and Ben Black collided as they all ran to Dawn. After a second to untangle themselves, they rushed her off the platform, ducking, weaving, and shielding her.

Another shot popped.

Grant fell.

Chick swung wildly, almost striking Grant before stumbling backwards and plunging over the side of the ship. Splash!

The unified crowd on the waterfront deteriorated into a brawl.

Sally and her cousins disappeared in the mayhem.

Ricky fought his way through the violent masses, running toward the buildings further inland where it sounded like the shots came from. He turned briefly and saw the roving harmonizers closing in on the rioters like a net tightening around a school of clueless fish.

Chapter 69

Two colonial era brick streets inland, Ricky rounded the corner of a warehouse sandwiched between a long-abandoned mom-and-pop pub and another defunct small business of some sort.

The shooter was nowhere in sight.

Ricky leaned against the wall, taking a minute to catch his breath. His chest pounded.

Although he was some distance from the patriot-fest-turned-riot, he could still hear yelling and screaming as the people who had shown such solidarity beat and battered each other.

He heard the rat-tat-tat of a machine gun, and a stream of bullets whizzed past. "You sonofabitch." He fired a couple of rounds back with his .38 and ran in the direction of the shots.

The incoming fire stopped. No sign of the shooter.

Ricky crept to the side door of the warehouse, his back scraping against the brick exterior, both hands wrapped tightly around the grip of the handgun, his breathing deep and controlled now. "I got you," he whispered, then he kicked the door open and rushed inside, leading with his weapon. "Uh-oh." A harmonizer.

"Surrender your weapon," it said, "human possession of a firearm is prohibited."

"Sure, soon as I'm done unloading it." Ricky squeezed off three rounds, all of them ricocheting off the harmonizer."

It raised its weapon.

Ricky squeezed the trigger again. Click. And again. Click, click, click. He hurled the .38 and fled out the door he'd come in only to see several more harmonizers rushing up the street.

"Whoa." He abruptly stopped, then spun around and ran the other way, ducking bullets whizzing overhead as he rounded the block, circling back toward the bay.

Glancing back over his shoulder as he approached the shoreline again, Ricky saw the harmonizers still in pursuit. Ahead, the rioting masses bunched up, subdued, with harmonizers peeling them off and herding them into cattle trailers. What the heck happened to the unity? And what happened to the fight in these people? He darted into the middle of the packed crowd, blending into the zombie-like collective blob of inhumanity as he thrashed through it.

The harmonizers in-chase flanked Ricky on both sides when he exited the crowd on the harbor side, forcing him out onto the dock. At the end of it, he looked to the left, the right, straight ahead, and saw nothing but a few fluttering seagulls and the Cole Brothers tanker well on its way out to sea. He looked back at the harmonizers pouring onto the dock now. He pinched his nostrils, "Here goes," held his breath, closed his eyes, and jumped. "Oh-oh-oh-oh-ohhhhhhh."

The sixty odd seconds of freefall felt like an hour, and the panicked struggle back up to the surface of the water seemed even longer. Ricky gasped and choked, spewing salty water out and sucking oxygen in simultaneously. He grasped blindly for the supports beneath the dock, the salt searing his eyes.

"Glad you could make it, brother man."

Ricky lurched away, startled by Chick's voice, and his head dipped beneath the water again. He bobbed back up, spitting out another mouthful of sea water. "Jeez, you scared the crap out of me, Chick." Ricky clung to the supports with one hand, steadying himself against the ebb and flow of the tide slapping at him, and wiping the salty water out of his eyes. "What are you doing down here? Why aren't you on the ship?"

"Long story," Chick said.

They heard the clanging of harmonizer feet on the dock above them.

"Shh," said Ricky.

Chapter 70

"I feel like a human prune," Ricky said through clattering teeth after hours of soaking in the frigid seawater beneath the dock.

Chick shivered. "You and me both." He rolled his head around to work the kinks out of his neck. "Ricky?"

"Yeah."

"Is it true that sharks mostly eat at night?"

"I don't know, Chick. I'm not a marine biologist. Why're you asking me that?"

"Because in case you ain't noticed, it's dark now, and I just felt something swishing."

Something large splashed not far from them.

They looked at each other wide-eyed, then scrambled up the supports.

Ricky poked his head up and peeked out over the dock. "All clear." He climbed up, then reached down for Chick.

"Brrr. Man, it's good to be out of the water," Chick said as he flopped onto the dock, "but that breeze sure makes it chilly."

Ricky held a finger to his lips. "Keep quiet."

They crept cautiously toward the now abandoned shoreline. Without lights, the Boston Skyline could just as well have been a black hole. "Looks like the harmonizers are gone, and everybody else too," Ricky whispered. "And I do mean everybody."

Chick pulled out a pocket flashlight and clicked it on. "I guess this thing really is waterproof like they advertised." He shined it out into the darkness. "You think there's any place open where we can get something to eat?"

"Boston's closed," Ricky said, and laughed – although it wasn't actually funny. "It's been closed since the Deep Freeze."

"What're we supposed to do about food then?" Chick said.

Ricky shrugged. "A better question is, how the heck are we going to get back to Texas in time for Gabby's patches to come off?"

They wandered around the uninhabited city well into the night, breaking into shuttered restaurants, bars, and convenience stores, hoping to find some canned goods or something nonperishable that had been left behind when the survivors of the Deep Freeze migrated inland.

By 2:00 AM, all they'd come up with was one dead rat and a jug of petrified milk.

Ricky tapped the jug against a wall. "I ain't ever seen milk get hard like that."

They tried one last place, a pub with the front door busted off its hinges. Nothing there either. Chick plunked down on a barstool and pulled his shoes off and massaged his sore feet. "I'm too tired to eat now anyways," he said.

297

Ricky sat beside him. "Me too."

They were quiet for a minute, then Ricky said, "What do you think happened this morning?"

"You mean with the crowd?"

"Yeah."

Chick shook his head. "Man, I don't know. Seems like all them people had a simultaneous episode like the one I had. But that'd be impossible, wouldn't it?"

"Is that what made you swing at Grant? You had an episode?"

Chick nodded tentatively. "I guess so."

Ricky's eyebrows crumpled together. "Tell me about it."

"I already did tell you. I've been having these spells now and again ever since they gave me that harmonization vaccine. But until that'n this morning, they been good spells. Everything gets lighter and brighter, animated you could say. But this time –"

"What, Chick? This time what?"

Chick closed his eyes, retrieving the images from somewhere in his mind. "Grant looked like a monster," he said.

"What?"

"Her face, it looked like a monster. And so did everybody else. I'm talking about eyes on fire, horns and fangs, and hands like claws with jagged blades for fingernails."

"Really? We've got to get you to a doctor when we get back to Texas. If we get back to Texas."

Chick said, "How about Dawn?"

Ricky sighed. "She's not a shrink."

"Oh, so now I'm crazy."

"I didn't say that."

Chick yawned.

Ricky laid his head on the dusty bar and began to doze.

Chick turned off the flashlight and nodded off too, then Ricky sprung back up, shocked wide awake by the sudden awareness of where they were.

"This is the place," Ricky said.

Chick said, "What place?"

"The Green Dragon Tavern, where me and Gabby and Josh were the night it happened. I guess I didn't recognize it now that's it's –"

"The night what happ – ? …Oooh. You're talking about the accident."

298

Ricky closed his eyes, remembering. He'd been sitting on the same stool he was sitting on right now that night. He'd ordered a drink, went to the men's room, came back, took a sip. Then nothing. "I can't be here," he said. "Let's go."

"I feel you, brother man." Chick pulled his shoes back on and groaned.

"Turn that flashlight back on," Ricky said as they stepped into the dark street.

Chick followed him down to the corner, across Union Street, and through the park to Congress Street. "Where are you going?"

Ricky stopped. "I have no idea." He ran a hand through his hair. "Wait a minute, isn't that police station right around here somewhere?"

"That'n where me and you met?" Chick shined the flashlight at the complex across the street. "It's right there. Why?"

"I need to remember what happened that night," Ricky said, "for my sanity. Maybe if I saw the records it'd jog my memory."

Chick nodded. "If the records are still there after all this time."

"Let's go find out."

Chick followed Ricky across Congress to the station. A twisted metal frame and a few dangling shards of glass hung where the main doors had been. "That's convenient," Ricky said.

They took the stairs up to the records department. Chick shined the flashlight around, illuminating overturned furniture and file cabinets, scattered papers, shattered computer monitors, and other demolished equipment. "Good luck, bother man."

They spent the next hour rummaging through file cabinets and turned up nothing.

"Looks like a lost cause," Ricky said.

Chick shined the flashlight around one last time. The beam landed on a doorplate that said, "Archives."

He and Ricky looked at each other hopefully.

"It's worth a try," Ricky said, and twisted the door handle. Inside they found stacks and stacks of dusty file boxes labeled on the ends in alphabetical order by arrestee's last name. Ricky pulled the box out with an alphabetic range that would include his name if it was in there.

Chick pulled another box down.

Ricky tossed the cardboard lid aside and sifted through the files. "Nothing."

Chick handed Ricky a file from the other box.

"What's this?"

"The report you're looking for," Chick said. "It was under Gabriella's name."

"I don't believe it," Ricky gasped as he read the first page. "This says Gabby was the driver." He turned to the next page where he found a mugshot of himself thirty-five years younger along with a police report that contained an entirely different version of the incident.

Chick chuckled as he looked at the mugshot. "I done forgot what a fresh face little punk you was."

Ricky read. "According to this version, when the arresting officer arrived on scene he observed three cars – Max's car, which was parked with hazards on behind the Honda I was in, and a Toyota Camry that was subsequently determined to be stolen. That's the car you were driving before you bailed, I guess. The Honda and Toyota both had front end damage. Appeared to have collided.

"Says, Josh and Max were standing at the rear of the Honda smoking cigars. Josh had a significant, but not life threatening, laceration on his forehead that was bleeding profusely, and he appeared to be in shock. Gabriella was laying in the street approximately five yards in front of the Honda to the right of the Toyota after apparently having been ejected through the windshield." Ricky swallowed hard. "I'm sorry, Gabby," he whispered.

He went on, "It says that Josh told the officer he had been a passenger in the backseat of the Honda. Max reported to the officer that he was driving home when he observed the Honda veer into the oncoming traffic lane and strike the Toyota head on. Max then observed Josh exit the Honda from the right rear passenger seat."

Ricky snapped the file closed. "And the officer found me passed out behind the wheel of the Honda with no apparent injuries. The only other witness to the accident – that would be you, Chick – fled the scene and was arrested a few minutes later and charged with grand theft auto, but could not identify the driver of the Honda."

Ricky turned to the last page, a blood test report.

"So, you remember anything now?" Chick said.

Ricky shook his head. "Nope. Not a dang thing." He rolled up the report and shoved it into his back pocket. "We best get going. It's a long way to Texas from here."

Chick kept the flashlight trained on the dilapidated storefronts as they stumbled aimlessly down the street. "Hey, look at this." He pointed to a cycle shop. He aimed the flashlight into the window, cupping a hand between his eyes and the glass as he did. "There's bikes in there."

"Good find," Ricky said, "but there ain't no way we can get to Texas on bicycles in time for Gabby's patches to come off. It's dang near three thousand miles from here. Beats walking but what we really need is an airplane, or at least a car."

Chick thought about that. "Ricky?"

"What?"

"I don't know where we'd find a plane around here, but I got an old, ah, business associate, in Fall River that could probably hook us up with a car."

Ricky said, "Business associate, huh? I thought Massachusetts was uninhabited now."

Chick smiled. "Not completely. It'd take more than a Deep Freeze to run my buddy, Clep out of his shop. But let's keep that between just me and you."

Chapter 71

Dawn stepped out of the ship's infirmary into the hallway where Tom Cole was waiting for her report on Grant.

"The president's helicopter is fueled up and ready to go," Tom Cole said. "The president is able to fly, isn't she?"

Dawn nodded. "Yes. Thank God the wound is superficial."

"Glad to hear it. So, what about you, how are you holding up?"

Dawn ran a hand across her head and sighed. "I feel terrible about flying back to Texas with Ricky stranded in Boston in the middle of that mess. And Chick. I don't know if Chick even knows how to swim." She tried not to think about that. "But the president said she could send in an extraction team if need be. I just hope nothing bad happens, if it hasn't already."

"Me too." Tom Cole paused. "So, does this change things about your running for Congress?"

"I'd be lying if I said someone attempting to assassinate me wasn't unnerving."

301

Tom Cole squeezed Dawn's shoulder. "I don't blame you for being apprehensive now."

Ben Black rambled up on his way to the mess hall for breakfast. "Good morning, he said cheerfully. "How's Grant?"

"Doing well," said Dawn.

Tom Cole said, "So, Dr. Wise tells me she's reconsidering her candidacy."

Dawn hung her head, embarrassed for preferring to be a coward over being a corpse. But she couldn't imagine she'd be of any use to anyone dead.

"And frankly, I think that's prudent given the attempt on her life," Tom Cole added. "Sacrificing our best and brightest to savagery isn't going to further the cause of liberty. As a matter of fact if things turn ugly we're going to need more doctors, not less of them."

Dawn appreciated the comment.

"I agree," Ben Black said. "The question is, What now?"

Tom Cole nodded. "Right. My brother and I were discussing that last night and we concluded that…Well, this is going to sound absurd, but we've got hundreds of robots that were manufactured in the 90s. According to the rationale put forth for Vizion's candidacy, a rationale accepted by Congress, the robots might could qualify as candidates for the House. Think about it. No wasted energy fending off fraudulent character assassinations, no worrying about potential bloodshed. The establishment destroys one robot, we stand up another just like it."

Dawn snickered.

Ben Black laughed hysterically. "I'm not sure *absurd* quite captures it."

"Any more absurd than corporations running for office?" said Tom Cole.

"Well, no, not really," Ben Black said, more serious now. "Except, at least corporations are people or are made of people or are created by people or whatever. Not that I'm in favor of corporations running for office either. Because I'm not."

"And robots are made by whom?" said Tom Cole.

"Alright, alright, I get the point," Ben Black said. "But I still don't like it."

Tom Cole said, "Why not?"

Ben Black thought for a minute before saying, "Because robots can't think and make decisions for themselves, that's why. Whether manufacturing them is the legal equivalent of giving birth to them or not – aye aye aye –" He chuckled, "they'd always be controlled by someone else."

"I'll let you two sort this out," Dawn said. "I'm going to go grab some coffee before President Grant and I take off for Texas."

Ben Black said, "Nice seeing you, doctor. Have a safe flight."

Tom Cole rested a hand on Ben Black's shoulder. "Listen, you're absolutely right that robots in the House of Representatives would be controlled by someone else. And those someone elses should be the people from the robots' districts. If you think about it, that's the way it ought to be with human representatives too. It's how the system was designed to work. Our representatives are not supposed to go to the capitol and do what they please. They're supposed to do what their constituents tell them to do. Period. As long as what their constituents demand doesn't violate the Constitution, that is. Which is why before assuming office our leaders are required to swear to support and defend the Constitution – that is their responsibility above all else. But I'm not telling you anything you don't already know."

"Hmm. I hadn't thought of elected robots like that," said Ben Black. Still he couldn't help but laugh again. "Wouldn't it be great if we could program robots to strictly adhere to the Constitution."

"It'd be even better if we could train people to do that," Tom Cole said.

"Now, that we can agree on." Ben Black glanced at his watch. "Is it too early for ice cream?"

Chapter 72

The sun had already risen by the time Ricky and Chick got to Clep's place. The screech of a power saw grinding on metal and an odor like burning tires emanated from the workshop as they pedaled up the gravel drive.

They got off the bicycles.

"Ow ow ow." Ricky's thighs burned from the fifty mile ride from Boston.

"Clep?" Chick called out

The sawing stopped, and a pale, boney, middle-aged man in a sleeveless undershirt, safety goggles, and a sideways Red Sox cap held the tool up defensively, his finger on the power button like the trigger on a pistol. "You best back up if you want your arms and legs to stay attached to you."

"Yo, brother, it's me, Chick. And this here's my partner, Ricky Santana."

Clep set the saw down, pulled his goggles off, and squinted. "Who? Ohhh. Chick." He opened his arms and the two men hugged. "Man, I thought you were dead or something. It's been too long. How you been, bro?"

"Been good."

"You still in the transportation business?" Clep said, and winked.

"Nah, I been on the straight and narrow since I got out of prison." Chick looked at the half dismantled car Clep had been sawing on. "I don't guess I need to ask what you been up to."

"Hey, I was recycling when recycling wasn't cool," said Clep.

Chick turned to Ricky. "They used to call Clep the magic man because he could magically transform a whole car into car parts in under an hour and turn them parts into cash just as quick."

Ricky glanced at his watch. Almost 9:00 AM. "How long you reckon it'd take him to magically transform a pile of parts back into a car?"

Clep pointed to himself. "Hey. Mister, I'm right here, if you got something to say to me."

"He don't mean no offense," Chick told Clep. "It's just that he has a sort of an appointment he's running late for. I figured you could help us out with some wheels."

Clep fiddled with the brim of his Sox cap. "Appointment, huh?"

Ricky said, "I've got to be back in Texas in forty-hours or less."

Clep scrutinized Ricky's face. "Texas? You got a long way to go, man. And why would you want to drive straight into a war zone anyway?"

"War zone?" Chick and Ricky said together.

"Yeah," said Clep. "U.S. invasion started last night. All harmonizers they say. Not a single U.S. human troop involved according to the news. You didn't hear about it?"

Ricky and Chick turned and looked at each other.

"Can you help us?" Chick said.

Clep said, "The law's going to come down on me if I do, isn't it?"

Chick nodded. "Most likely."

Clep grinned. He never could resist messing with the law. "Come with me."

Chick and Ricky followed Clep through a door that connected the workshop to the warehouse behind it that housed at least forty cars of various makes and models, all of them caked in years of dust – most of them gas guzzlers. Ricky ran a hand through his hair. "You don't have anything in the way of an economy car?" he said. "There ain't exactly a gas station on every corner in these parts I wouldn't guess."

"Not running," said Clep. He closed his eyes. "Wait. I do have an old Honda Accord that runs. At least it ran when I got it. Front end's smashed up some. Ain't much paint left on her. Interior's a mess, especially the driver seat – coffee stains or something. No radio. Radiator's busted. Tags been expired for thirty-something years. And it doesn't have a windshield. Other than that, it's in great shape." He grinned "And it's low mileage."

Chick said, "Man, I been driving an ice cream cart for the past thirty years. You think I give a crap about a windshield? You care about a windshield, Ricky?"

"Screw a windshield," Ricky said. "But we ain't getting far with a busted radiator."

Clep twisted his Sox hat around backwards. "I got radiators coming out my ears. For everything but a Honda, that is. But I bet me and Chick can make one of them work."

It took a couple of hours to move all the cars out of the way to get to the Honda. And another couple of hours to rig up the wrong radiator in it, change the spark plugs, replace all the dry-rotted tires and belts and hoses, and install a new battery.

The old car ran well.

"Hey," Clep said to Ricky, "don't forget this." He lugged a windshield out – actually, more like half a windshield – and laid it in the trunk. "Maybe you can superglue it back together when you get where you're going."

"Funny," Ricky said.

Clep pulled two envelopes out of his back pocket and handed Ricky one. "This is a map of the black market fuel stops between here and Texas." He shook the second envelope at him. "And this is the registration. Not that thirty-five years expired registration's going to do you any good if the law stops you."

305

Chapter 73

Almost thirty hours later, chick and Ricky rolled past the unattended Texas/Oklahoma border checkpoint on interstate forty-four. "That's strange," Ricky said, clawing at the tiny bugs that had splatted into his eyes along the way. He mumbled, "The next time we do a road trip, let's do it in a car that has a windshield."

Chick gazed out at the *Welcome to the Republic of Texas* road sign as they crossed over the Red River. "Sure is quiet," he said.

Ricky nodded. "Too quiet. You reckon Clep was pulling our leg about the invasion?"

"Clep ain't much of a kidder," Chick said as they drove past the road to the ranch. "Hey, that's our turn ain't it?"

A smoky haze lingered above the countryside.

"I'm going to the hospital first to see about Gabby," said Ricky, and they drove on into Wichita Falls.

The eerie calm ended at the city limits.

Ricky zigzagged his way toward the hospital on side streets to avoid the traffic jams on the main roads. "What the heck?" he said when he saw Ricardo's old chopper on the fifty yard line of the football field as they drove past the high school.

Chick shook his head. "I got a bad feeling all the sudden."

A few minutes later, they pulled into a hospital parking lot that was dotted with tents and a few makeshift triage stations. Dozens of dazed people mulled around. A Medevac chopper landed. Ambulances came and went. Ricky and Chick got out of the car and melded into the crowd of stone-faced people waiting to be tended or to learn a loved one's fate. Doctors' white coattails flapped in the breeze as they rushed from patient to patient.

Ricky saw Dr. Langford. "Dr. Langford?" he called out.

The old doctor looked exhausted when he turned to answer. "Ricky, I'm afraid I've got my hands full at the moment."

Ricky nodded empathy, but pressed him anyway. "Is Gabriella alright? What's happened here? Did the U.S. invade?"

"It's over, Ricky. They got what they came for. Now, excuse me."

"Where's Dawn?" said Ricky.

"Surgery," Dr. Langford said curtly. He gestured with his chin toward the emergency room doors, then went back to tending patients.

Surgery? Did he mean Dawn had been injured and was being operated on? Or that she was operating on someone else? "Come on," Ricky said to Chick, and they pushed through the crowd and into the emergency room where a pair of security guards immediately detained them.

Chick twisted one of the guards into a headlock and Ricky wrestled the other to the ground. Dawn yelled out, "Stop it. Stop it this minute!" They let go of the security guards as she rushed over in blood spattered scrubs, her hair tucked under a surgical cap.

"What is wrong with you two?" Dawn scolded Chick and Ricky.

Neither of them said anything.

Dawn began to cry then. She hugged them, together, her forehead resting against their foreheads. "Thank God you're both alright. I was so afraid." She sniveled. She pulled away and wiped the tears, collecting herself. "I've got to get back to patients."

Chick examined her eyes. Even bloodshot with fatigue they were beautiful.

"Wait," Ricky said when she started to turn away. "Is Gabby –?"

Dawn closed her eyes and shook her head. "Ricky, she's gone."

"Gone?" Ricky pelted her with a barrage of questions. "What do you mean gone? Did you remove the bandages? Did the operation work? Gone where?"

"She left with Josh yesterday," said Dawn. "That's all I know."

"So you don't know if the operation was successful? If she can see?"

Dawn let out a deep frustrated breath. "The bandages were scheduled to come off today, as you know. But she was already gone. That's all I know. I'm sorry."

"Unbelievable," Ricky said, shaking his head. He nudged Chick. "We may as well go on to the ranch now. Nothing we can do here."

Dawn clutched Ricky's arm. "You can't go there."

Ricky's eyes widened. "What do you mean I can't go there? Are my parents alright?"

"They're fine," Dawn said. "They're at the makeshift shelter in the high school gym."

"Come on," Ricky said to Chick again, and they headed for the exit.

"Ricky, Chick, no!" Dawn screamed after them. "It's too terrible."

When Ricky turned onto the gravel road to the ranch, he and Chick noticed that the haze they had observed earlier was rising from the Santana property.

At the entrance, Ricky saw the unthinkable.

He slammed the Honda into park, kicked his door open, and hung his head out and puked profusely. Brutus's mutilated body dangled by the neck from the crossbar.

"Savages," Ricky choked out between heaves.

Chick turned away from the gruesome sight and didn't say anything.

Gravel crunched beneath Ricky's boots when he stepped out of the car. He wiped the drool off his mouth and chin, then fished his pocketknife out and cut Brutus down and cradled him in his arms.

Chick got out and stood there with him. "I'm sorry, brother man. That Brutus was a real special monkey. Specialest monkey I ever known."

Ricky glanced down at a sign planted in the center of the entrance:

NO TRESPASSING
Property of the United States Federal Government

Every muscle in Ricky's face tensed up. He gritted his teeth and laid Brutus's body down gently. Then he yanked the sign out of the ground and hurled it. He proceeded deliberately into the property. Chick followed. The destruction and carnage sickened them both. All of the structures that had been there for more than a hundred years, including the barn, stables, bunkhouse, guesthouse, and main house were now smoldering heaps of rubble. As were the new lab and chimp enclosure. The tractor did not appear to be damaged though. And from what Ricky could tell, the Pitts Special was still in one piece under the collapsed tin roof of what was left of the shed. He gagged, clamping a hand over his nose to block the putrid stench of death while waving his other hand through a cloud of flies.

Chick vomited now.

Slaughtered livestock lay decomposing in the sun, honeycombed with bullet holes.

Chick staggered back to the car to sit down.

Ricky continued, weaving around the rotting carcasses of cows, chickens, pigs, goats. But no horses. He glanced at the mound of ashes where the stables had been a few days ago and shivered at the thought of the Palo Pinto and the mustang being cooked alive in the flames. And the research animals…Had they burned too? …and Bernice.

Ricky squatted on his haunches, queasy.

Chick came back bare chested. "I'm going to hook the bucket up to the tractor and get this cleaned up," he said, his words muffled by the shirt draped around his face.

Ricky walked the rest of the property while Chick dug a ditch and plowed the carcasses into it. The only sign of life was a lone steer from an adjoining ranch roaming the northern pasture where the barbed wire Ricky had repaired was ripped off the fence posts again. Ricky glared at the harmonizer footprints in the soil, "Bastards," then went back and met Chick at the freshly dug ditch and doused the carcasses with diesel fuel. "You find Bernice's body?"

Chick shook his head. "No. I'm sorry."

Ricky felt the blood drain from his face. "Well, let's get this over with." He closed his eyes and bowed his head.

Chick bowed his head too.

"Dear Lord," Ricky cleared his throat, "forgive me for not being here to defend these helpless animals and my family and this land you blessed us with. Amen." He struck a match and dropped it into the ditch. Flames shot up. Whoosh. Sizzle.

They heard whinnying, followed by Bernice's familiar bellow.

Ricky cupped a hand above his eyes and saw the Palo Pinto and the mustang trotting up the gravel road out front, the old dog stumbling along behind them, strings of drool slinging from her jowls. He looked up into the sky and whispered, "Thank you."

Chapter 74

President Grant called all men and women of fighting age to report for military duty and was soon reminded that most every Texan – from toddlers to the elderly – considers himself of fighting age when Texas is threatened. Ricardo and Isabella, Ricky, and Chick and Dawn were among the first to report to the hastily constructed tent city barracks at nearby Sheppard Air Force base.

The day before training began, base commander, Colonel White – a six-foot seven-inch silver headed African-Texan man of steel – introduced himself to the new recruits and ordered them to assemble in the hangar adjacent the taxiway parallel Runway One-five-Right along with a couple of thousand seasoned career military personnel. A gigantic TEA Party banner hung across the wall behind a platform there.

Dawn, Chick, and Ricardo and Isabella stood together on the front row.

"Where's Ricky?" Chick asked Dawn.

"I don't think he's here yet," Dawn said.

The Cole Brothers corporate jet landed, followed by Miller's Citation, then a corporate chopper with TEA Party blazed across the fuselage. A DPS chopper carrying President Grant landed last. Colonel White announced the president of the Republic of Texas, and Grant stepped up to the podium and offered condolences to the victims of the wicked assault perpetrated by so-called harmonizers directed by the U.S. political establishment, and vowed to take back every square inch of the stolen Red River land and return it to its rightful owners – in due time. "I promise you all that this cowardly act will not stand!"

The seasoned troops along with the new recruits roared their eagerness for the fight.

Grant held a thumb up and said, "But if we expect to win this, we've got to be smarter than our opponents. As you've all undoubtedly heard, the U.S. political establishment is conspiring with its counterparts at the GTP to mount an all-out assault on Texas. And they'd like nothing more than to provoke us into an act they can use as a pretext. But we won't take the bait. The first shots fired must be ballots, not bullets."

The troops murmured amongst themselves and one yelled out, "Most of us aren't even U.S. citizens anymore. We can't vote in the U.S. elections. And even if we could, we can't beat the establishment. They're dug in. They're unified. And the citizens are at each other's throats. No way they're going to agree on opposition candidates. We all saw what happened in Boston."

Grant countered, "I firmly believe the establishment can be beaten. And our U.S. friends and family can and will cast the votes to do it. We're going to finish what we started in Boston."

The Cole brothers slipped up behind Dawn and clapped for what Grant had said.

She turned and smiled at them.

310

"We're placing an order with our new venture for a thousand camera eyes for the opposition congressional candidates," Tom Cole whispered in Dawn's ear.

Grant went on to say, "I've invited a man most of you know and respect to explain." She waved to Ricky, who worked his way from the back of the crowd to the platform, hoping his skepticism for the seemingly futile plan he had begrudgingly agreed to endorse last night was not too obvious. "Please welcome Mr. Ricky Santana, the new president of the Republic of Texas TEA Party."

After a round of applause, Ricky said, "Thank you." Then he outlined the latest TEA Party plan to wage a grass roots revolution to retake the House of Representatives. The plan proposed, among other things, starving the mainstream news manufacturers as well as the major entertainment studios out of an audience through a voluntary boycott, a self-imposed blackout. They'll essentially be communicating their deception to no one but themselves then."

The crowd cheered and whistled.

Wow. Their enthusiasm surprised Ricky. He figured, like him, they'd much rather drop bombs on the presidential mansion in Dodge City than engage in political strategies after what the U.S. had just done. When the crowd began to chant, "Ben Black, Ben Black, Ben Black," he turned to see the man himself had crept up onstage behind him. So that's why they're cheering.

"May I?" said Ben Black, and Ricky stepped aside, ceding the podium to him.

Ben Black adjusted the microphone and said, "I believe what Ricky is trying to say is that we can win if we walk by faith and not by sight."

Someone in the crowd hollered, "But where are we going to find the candidates to oppose the establishment this late in the game?"

The hangar rattled with the roar of engines from a Cole Brothers Industries cargo plane.

Moments later, the tires of the aircraft chirped and squealed as it touched down on the runway. Ben Black snickered, and mumbled beneath his breath, "I can't believe the Coles are actually going through with this." He pointed out at Tom Cole and curled his finger, urging Tom to join him at the podium.

Tom Cole hustled up the platform steps and took his turn at the microphone. "I'm proud to announce that our candidates have just landed," he said with a smile. "There's more than enough of them to cover every U.S. district and each of them has an address – a storage unit address, to be precise – evidencing the appropriate district habitation as required by the qualifications clauses in the U.S. Constitution. They're in need of a little work, but with some help from my good friend and expert technician, Chick, I'm confident they'll be ready for the campaign trail in no time."

Chick cocked his head. "Whaaat? ...Oh. They're not –"

The rest of the crowd appeared equally confused.

Chick saw Ben Black cover his mouth to conceal a chuckle.

"You want to let me in on the secret?" Dawn whispered in Chick's ear.

He burst out laughing. "They gonna run them robots."

"What in the world are you talking about?" said Dawn.

Tom Cole went on to explain how the whole thing would work; how the robots' lack of personality or past indiscretions would force their republicrat establishment opponents to debate on issues instead of real or manufactured personal scandals; how TEA Party committees from each district would operate the robots during and after the elections; how the TEA Party would also have a central clearing house of sorts in each state to collect and distribute resources to the district committees; how messaging would be done through word of mouth and alternative media, including social media and internet streaming television such as the Ben Black network, DVDs, free and pay-to-view streaming and electronic print from organizations like *Citizens United, the Blaze, the Ayn Rand Foundation, Circa News with Sara Carter, Matt Kibbe's Free The People, FreedomWorks, CRTV,* the *Cato Institute, Judicial Watch*, and others, with an emphasis on face to face contact – community building; how the robot candidates would be on the frontlines of the revolution to return the government in exile – a government of, by, and for, the people – to power.

President Grant returned to the podium and acknowledged to the skeptical crowd that although he had confidence in the plan, there was no guarantee it would work. "If this doesn't work, we're looking at another crap buffet in Congress come January to go with the triple-decker crap sandwich in the Whitehouse with this unity president nonsense," he said. "That's why it's imperative that the Republic of Texas be prepared for military action." The months of combat training required for that would commence right away.

Grant continued by reiterating her promise that Texas would not surrender a single inch of the annexed territory, including south Dodge City which, in her estimation, was well secured by border patrol troops under the command of Juan Rodriguez. She ended with an admonition to all Texans to respect the U.S.'s territorial claims on the Red River ranchland until after the elections.

The crowd booed.

The new recruits completed their initial training by the end of October. Chick had done his job to get the robots up and running and served now as an airframe and power-plant mechanic on military aircraft. Dawn continued her work as a physician, now at the base medical center. Isabella worked as a line cook in the mess hall, and Ricardo kept busy tending the horses and keeping up the maintenance on his Pitts Special and the Hiller chopper.

Ricky transitioned easily from civilian pilot to a well-rounded combat aviator, qualifying in the Apache gunship; and Colonel White saw to it that Ricky was promoted to the rank of Captain well ahead of schedule and given command of a squadron.

Between his military duties and TEA Party responsibilities Ricky rarely had a moment to think. But when he did, his thoughts always went to Gabriella. He hadn't seen or heard from her since the day he left for the Boston TEA Party, besides watching her on her program. It was impossible to tell from his side of the television screen whether her sight had been restored or not – although the tentativeness in her every gesture gave the impression that she was even blinder than she'd been before the operation if that were possible. The not knowing agonized him almost as badly as the prospect that the procedure had failed; a level of agony that exceeded the nerve-racking uncertainty of the wait-and-see game between Texas and the U.S.

Meanwhile after several delays, the GTP board finally agreed on a date certain to consider the Persian Caliphate's proposal to strip Israel of nationhood, and the sliver of a country on the Mediterranean made an extraordinary appeal to Texas in response.

Ricky sat behind the desk in his office on base with Bernice dozing at his feet as the radio broadcaster reported, "In an unprecedented move, the Israeli prime minister announced this morning that he has petitioned the Republic of Texas for statehood, throwing a last-minute monkey wrench into the GTP board's anticipated approval of a proposal to strip the tiny nation of its sovereignty.

"President Grant expressed enthusiasm for the union with Israel and the rebranding of the Republic of Texas as the United States of Texas. The Israeli Knesset and the Texas legislature have been called into special sessions where representatives of both countries are expected to overwhelmingly approve the union. It is unclear what effect that might have on already strained relations between Texas and the GTP and the U.S. But according to the Texas attorney general, such a union would render the trade embargo against Israel and the question of its nationhood legally moot.

"On the U.S. election front," the broadcaster continued, "the latest polls show incumbent democrats and republicans with wide leads against their independent robot challengers in every single congressional race. No contest in the Senate where all incumbents up for reelection are running unopposed. But a substantial number of ballot write-ins for rebel Ricky Santana indicate the political future of the unity presidential ticket is not quite as certain."

Ricky chuckled. *Rebel Ricky Santana.*

"In other U.S. news," the broadcaster rattled on, "Joshua Horowitz, CEO of Vizion Inc., the company at the top of the unity ticket, confirmed rumors that he and fiancé, Gabriella Meir will wed tomorrow evening. The ceremony will be held on the balcony of the Leviathan penthouse at 7:30 PM, followed by a reception at the Dodge House where a number of politicians, businesspersons, movie stars, and foreign dignitaries are expected to attend."

Ricky washed his hands across his face. News of the wedding should not have come as a surprise but somehow it did.

A Major appeared in his office doorway.

Ricky leapt to attention and saluted.

"At ease, Captain," the Major said. "I'm here about that old wreck of yours."

Ricky lowered his salute. "You mean the Honda?"

"Whatever it is. Colonel White has declared this *base beautification week*. That heap needs to be gone by seventeen-hundred hours. This is a military installation, not a junkyard."

"Yes, sir." After the major marched off, Ricky muttered. "Beautification week. I signed up to fight not to be a damn janitor."

314

This housekeeping nonsense was undoubtedly Colonel White's attempt to keep his restless volunteers occupied with busy work.

Ricky called a salvage yard and the buyer offered him scrap metal price for the car and told him to have the registration ready when the tow truck driver got there. Ricky pulled the police report file from the accident out of his desk drawer, and then the envelope underneath it that Clep had given him with the old Honda.

He peeled the envelope open.

"Jesus," He gasped when he saw the name on the registration.

Chick poked his head into Ricky's office, whistling. "Need your trashcan emptied?"

Ricky didn't answer. His eyes stayed fixed on the registration.

"You hear me, brother man? Colonel White done sent orders down taking me off fixing airplanes and put me on garbage duty. Said it's base beauty week or something.... Ricky?"

Ricky looked up finally, and said, "That Honda we got from Clep was Gabriella's."

Chick's mouth fell open. "You ain't serious?"

Ricky slid the registration across the desk. "Look for yourself."

Chick looked at it. "Sure is. But hey, it ain't like you should've recognized it after thirty-something years. Besides, that ain't the only Honda Accord ever made. Do it match the VIN number on the po-lice report?"

Ricky raised an eyebrow. "Good question." He compared the numbers, then glanced back at Chick. "Yep, matches." He scratched his head. "You know, there's something else in that report that's been eating at me."

"What's that?" said Chick.

Ricky said, "Josh's injury. How is it that he busted his forehead from the backseat?" He got up and Chick followed him outside to the car.

Ricky popped the trunk lid and lifted what was left of the windshield out. "Look at this." He pointed to a shattered section of the glass that resembled a spider web. "That's the driver side. So, if I was the driver, how is it that it broke like that and I didn't have any injuries? I mean, doesn't that look like someone's head bashed into it?"

"Sure does."

Ricky opened all four car doors, then leaned into the backseat.

"What you looking for?" said Chick.

"Blood," Ricky said. "According to that police report, Josh was bleeding profusely. Remember? Well, guess what? There ain't no blood in this backseat at all." He moved up to the driver seat and rubbed a hand over it. "But, what do you bet this big ol' stain here's blood."

Chick took out a pocket knife and chopped out a piece of the stained fabric. "One way to find out. We can have Dawn get it tested."

"One more thing, Chick."

"What's up?"

"You know anything about drugs?"

"Nah man, I don't roll like that. Why?"

"Because according the blood test results included in that police report, the intoxicant in my system wasn't alcohol. It was some crazy concentration of flunitrazepam. I don't guess you know what that is?"

"Never heard of it."

"I hadn't either, so I looked it up on Google. It's ruffies, date rape drug." Ricky kneaded his forehead. "Do me a favor, Chick. If Dawn determines it's blood on that fabric, have her send it for DNA testing as well."

"Alright. Ricky?"

"Yeah?"

"Sure is a lot of write-ins for you in the early voting. What we going to do if you win?"

Ricky laughed. "I don't think we're going to need to worry about that. Now go on and take that to Dawn."

Chick saluted. "You got it, Captain."

Chapter 75

Ricky awoke the next morning to his tent's canvas door flaps slapping in a gusty breeze. He could smell rain bulging in the crisp predawn air. Bernice groaned when he switched on the battery powered lamp. He shimmied over and attached his prosthetics, then said to Chick, who was snoring face down with both arms dangling over the sides of his cot, "Let's go get some chow."

"Ok," Chick groaned

They walked together over to the mess hall.

"Three eggs, please, and a slice of bacon," Ricky said to Isabella.

"Good morning to you too, hijo," she said from the server side of the chow line.

"I'll have what he's having," said Chick.

Ricky said, "Sorry, Mama. Got a lot on my mind."

Isabella set Ricky's plate on the counter and said, "You will go for the girl today, no? If you do not, she will marry another. I heard this on the radio."

"Yes," said Ricky. "Have you seen Ricardo this morning."

"He is at the stables tending the horses," she said, and set Chick's plate on the counter. "The helicopter is fueled and ready for you if that is what you are wondering about."

"And the navigation charts?" Ricky said.

"Papa put them in the door pocket," said Isabella.

Ricky glanced at his watch. 6:00 AM. Exactly thirteen and a half hours before the wedding. The flight to Dodge City would take a good while in Ricardo's old Hiller. Were U.S. airspace monitors to detect him and he got intercepted, he might not get there at all.

Thunder crackled and boomed and the chow hall shook. Ricky gazed out the window at lightening flashing, tree limbs whipping violently in the wind, and rain coming down in sheets.

By early afternoon the storm had not let up, leaving Ricky no choice but to risk a flight that could very well end as badly or worse than the one that had put him in a coma. The silver lining was that the small chopper would be harder to track in this weather.

Ricky kept the transponder off and flew below five-hundred feet AGL using only the ADF and a map of AM radio frequencies for navigation to avoid being picked up by air traffic controllers or flight service. The strategy worked, but sustained winds of twenty-two knots or better with occasional gusts as high as forty along with the heavy rains and frequent lightening made for a rough ride.

The Chopper descended to three hundred feet and Ricky saw the windsock spinning atop the cottage that had been his home. He pitched up and executed a go-around, then approached again and hovered down to the backyard without incident.

Rain continued to pour.

Ricky grabbed his bag and ran up under the eave over the stoop and lingered there a minute. It didn't appear anyone had been here in all

317

the months he'd been gone. "Good evening, Mr. and Mrs. Swanson," he said, smiling at the familiar rusty brass nameplate beside the door.

The musty odor inside made him sneeze. "Achoo, ahhh-choo. Dang." He wiped his nose on the tallit he'd borrowed along with the other orthodox Jewish garb from the chaplain's office on base. The idea of paying the role of rabbi even if only for a few minutes made him chuckle. He stopped at the dining table. The necklace he'd given Gabriella was still laying there. He snatched it up and shoved it in his pocket, then hurried to the bedroom closet and retrieved the wig he'd worn to AA meetings back in the day.

Ricky glanced at his watch. 6:40 PM. He was running out of time.

He slipped the wig on, then a yarmulke, then grabbed an umbrella and rushed off to the train station.

After another twenty-minutes he arrived at the Leviathan building.

A harmonizer stood guard at the entrance, like always. Ricky nailed it with a dropkick, then ran for the elevator and rode it up to the penthouse. The door was open.

A few guests mingled inside. "Good evening, Rabbi," one of them said to Ricky.

Ricky cleared his throat. "Good evening to you. Is the bride here?"

"Not yet. But the groom is." The guest gestured across the room at Josh who was engaged in a conversation with Levi.

Ricky choked. Josh had seen his wig enough times that he would surely recognize him. He needed to get out of sight quickly, and stay out of sight until Gabriella arrived. "Could you tell me where the restroom is?"

The guest pointed to a door beside Levi's writing desk.

Ricky glanced down at the desk and saw a file folder labeled: Joshua Horowitz DNA results. Jackpot! He snatched up the report and hurried into the restroom and locked the door behind him.

His cell phone rang.

He wrestled it off his belt clip. "This is Ricky Santana," he answered in a whisper.

"Hey, cowboy, it's Dawn. I got the lab results back you asked for. You were right about the stain on that fabric, it was blood."

"Man, that was quick," Ricky whispered.

"I've got connections," Dawn teased.

"And a DNA profile?"

"Got that too," Dawn said. "Why did you need that, anyway?"

"Guard it like your life depended on it. I'll fill you in when I get back. If I get back." Ricky ended the call.

He heard a knock at the door.

"Will you be much longer?" It was Gabriella's voice. "I really need to use the facility."

Ricky froze. Took a deep breath. "Showtime," he whispered, then flushed the toilet for no reason at all and slowly opened the door. Whoa. In her flowing white wedding gown, Gabriella was as beautiful a bride as he'd always imagined. Too bad he wasn't the groom. Their eyes met. Could she see? If she could, her distant look suggested she did not recognize him. Her nostrils began to pulse. Ricky heard Levi's voice approaching, saying something about a security breach.

Time to go. Ricky grabbed Gabriella around the waist and hoisted her over his shoulder as Levi's voice drew nearer. "Sorry, Gabby, this wedding's been cancelled," Ricky said, and rushed out the door with her.

Gabriella pounded his back, thrashing as he ran for the elevator. "Put me down," she shrieked.

"Gabby, calm down. It's me, Ricky."

"I know, I can smell you. Now put me down I said."

The elevator doors opened and two harmonizers stepped out.

"Uh-oh." Ricky spun around and darted into the stairwell. "Gabby, you can't marry Josh," he said through labored breath as he barreled down the stairs. "He was the driver."

She stopped pounding on his back after he said that. "What are you talking about?"

"The accident." Ricky cleared another flight of stairs and kept running downward. "I don't know exactly what happened but I was drugged and it was Josh driving. I'm sure of it. It had to be. There's no way I could have even been conscious much less driving with the amount of flunitrazepam they found in my system." Ricky could barely breathe and talk at the same time. He shot through the door onto the twenty-fourth level and into the elevator there. It didn't take but a few seconds to reach the ground floor after that.

"You mean flunitrazepam as in Rohypnol," said Gabriella, "as in ruffies? Date rape drug?"

"Yes," Ricky said as he bolted out the front door and into Wyatt Earp Blvd. The rain had subsided. "Can you save the questions for later so I can use some of this air for breathing?" He glanced over his shoulder as he ran down the block to the transit center, Gabriella hanging on to him tightly. Several harmonizers with Josh running alongside them were closing in.

"All of those girls that were raped had ruffies in their system," Gabriella said.

"Gabby, can we talk about this later?" Ricky said, huffing for air and running as fast as he could.

"Stop or I'll order these harmonizers to fire," Josh yelled out.

Ricky ducked into the transit center and then onto a train car just as the doors were about the close. He plopped Gabriella down on a seat, and the train lurched forward with Josh finally catching up, and running alongside it, banging on a window and yelling.

"Wuwee," Ricky said, "that was close. But we're not out of the woods yet."

"Out of the woods?" Gabriella said frantically. "What woods? Are you going to tell me what's going on?"

Ricky took several deep breaths, then waved a hand in front of Gabriella's eyes. She didn't even blink. But then, he had no idea whether reflexes worked with artificial eyes or not. It was something he hadn't even thought about. "Gabby, can you see me?"

She shook her head.

"Oh no," Ricky groaned. "So the surgery didn't work?"

"Not exactly," Gabriella said. "I can see. I just can't see what I need to see? The really weird thing is what I do see I see whether my eyes are open or closed."

"What?" The train slowed to a halt. Ricky wanted to follow up on what she said, but there wasn't time now. The doors hissed open.

"Come on," Ricky said. "This is our stop." He hoisted her onto his shoulders, piggyback this time, and jogged down the block to the cottage where he dropped Gabriella into the left seat of the chopper and buckled her up.

She reached for the seatbelt and started to unbuckle it. "I'm not flying anywhere with you until you tell me what's going on."

Ricky secured her seatbelt again. "We have to get out of here. We can talk about it once we're airborne."

A few minutes after midnight, they landed at Sheppard. During the flight, Gabriella had told Ricky about her defective sight, how the things she saw bore no relationship to the reality right in front of her.

After assuring her that what she described had to be a technical problem and that it most likely could be corrected, Ricky had explained the revelations about the accident, told Gabriella about how he and Chick had gotten the Honda from Clep, what they'd learned from the police report and a thorough examination of the car, how lab results confirmed Ricky's suspicions about the stain on the seat, and the dumb luck of finding Josh's DNA profile in the penthouse. The only thing left to do was to compare that with the DNA profile prepared from the blood sample from the car.

Ricky led Gabriella by the hand to his tent. Chick was fast asleep with the lamp on and Bernice snoozing on the ground beside his cot. "Here we are," Ricky said. "Home sweet home."

Gabriella said, "Who's that I hear snoring?"

"Chick. We'll see about getting him another place tomorrow." Ricky helped Gabriella onto his own cot and tucked her in, then laid down on the floor beside Bernice. "Goodnight Gabby." He turned off the lamp.

"Goodnight, Ricky," he heard her say softly in the darkness.

Chapter 76

Ricky walked Gabriella to Dawn's office in the military medical complex right after breakfast the next morning. "You promise there isn't anything romantic between you and Dawn?" Gabriella said while they sat in the patient waiting area.

Ricky sighed. "I told you our relationship is and always has been professional. I mean, we're colleagues and, yes, friends. But that's it. Other than that one night Josh was so determined to make sure you knew about, which was…well, nothing happened. And that's the point."

"Okay then. I'm trusting you." Gabriella smiled. "And you can't imagine how good it feels to know I can trust you. It's like a terrible burden has been lifted from my shoulders."

Ricky wrapped an arm around her. "Yours and mine both."

Gabriella cradled Ricky's face in her hands and pressed her lips to his.

Dawn stepped into the waiting room and cleared her throat. "Come on back," she said, and grinned at Ricky's blush.

"Thank you for getting me in so quickly," said Gabriella.

"Glad to do it," Dawn said. "Oh, and Ricky, that DNA profile you brought me...It does match the DNA from the car seat."

Gabriella choked, felt the jagged blade of betrayal twist in the pit of her gut. Even though there hadn't been any serious doubt in her mind about what the results would be, she wished for some other explanation. On the other hand, this was conclusive proof of Ricky's innocence and she could not imagine anything better than that.

"Are you alright?" Ricky said.

"Um-huh," said Gabriella simply and leaned back in the examination chair.

"Say, any possibility Chick can camp with you in your tent until he gets one of his own assigned to him?" Ricky said to Dawn while she examined Gabriella. "It's a little cramped in mine now that Gabriella's here."

"Ricky," said Dawn, "I'm not that kind of girl."

Gabriella perked up and said, "Are you suggesting *I* am?"

"I'm not suggesting anything at all," said Dawn. "I just hadn't planned on Chick or any other male as a roommate. But," she sighed, "I suppose I can handle it temporarily. I just hope Chick can."

"Something tells me he'll be thrilled," Ricky said.

"Right," said Dawn. She pried each of Gabriella's eyelids open. "That's what worries me."

Ricky said, "Thanks. I'm sure it won't be for long."

"Well," said Dawn, and set her ophthalmoscope aside, "all is well with this patient biologically. The ball's in your court, Ricky."

"What do you mean the ball's in his court?" Gabriella fretted.

"She means it's a technical problem, like I thought," said Ricky.

Gabriella slumped her shoulders.

"Hey." Ricky rubbed her back. "Don't worry, we'll get it solved. Come on, let's go see what we can do." He helped her out of the exam chair.

Dawn slapped the file folder containing the DNA profiles against Ricky's chest and said, "You may as well take these with you. I certainly don't have any use for them."

Ricky rolled up the folder and shoved it in his back pocket, and he and Gabriella trekked across base to his office where he pulled up Vizion's login page on his computer and typed in his user name and password.

Gabriella sat quietly in a chair beside him.

A message appeared onscreen: Password Invalid, Please Try Again. Ricky did try again and got the same message, so he attempted to reset his password. ACCESS DENIED.

"Dang it," Ricky groaned.

Gabriella squeezed his hand. "What's wrong?"

"Looks like Josh blocked me out."

Chick appeared in the doorway. "Hey, brother man, why ain't you all listening to the election polling? New ones just come out. Them robots are getting slaughtered. But you still looking good in the presidential even though you ain't running." He noticed the defeated look on both Gabriella's and Ricky's faces. "Something wrong?"

"Something's wrong alright," Ricky said. "Josh has me blocked out of the sight-system."

"Maybe I can help." Chick fished a flash-drive out of his pocket and slipped it into the USB slot on the computer, then leaned over and started punching keys on the keyboard.

"What are you doing?" said Ricky.

"Hacking into Vizion's system, what else? About time I got a chance to make use of that stuff I learned in them computer classes in prison."

Chapter 77

In Dodge City, Josh paced anxiously back and forth across the golden carpet of the not-so-oval office. "You've got to order an invasion into south Dodge now," he said to Farnsworth.

Farnsworth leaned back in his chair behind his desk and sighed. "Seriously, Josh, Gabriella is not the only woman on the planet. Why not just get a new girl? Or practice being presidential and get a few new ones." He chuckled. "Either of those options would make a lot more sense than starting a war prematurely over some silly broad."

Josh banged his fist on the desk. "It's not about that. You know as well as I do that internal polls show we're getting tromped in the House races and just barely leading Ricky – the people's write-in hero – in the presidential contest."

"Control yourself." Farnsworth swiped Josh's fist away from the desk. "As long as I'm president, you will show the proper respect for this office."

"Yeah well, that won't be much longer," said Josh.

There was a knock at the door and Levi stepped in and said, "I'm afraid I have to agree with Josh that the old *our man sucks less than theirs* message does not appear to be working so well this election season. But the situation is not so dire as to justify risking going it alone against Texas. Patience."

Chapter 78

With Chick's help, Ricky penetrated Vizion's sight system, and after two very long days, he finally managed to untangle the technological knots that had tied Gabriella's eyesight to the satellite feed for a harmonizer stationed in St. Louis, Missouri.

Gabriella stumbled backwards to the wall in Ricky's office as he came into focus. Tears gushed down her cheeks as she gazed at the man she had loved for as long as she could remember. He looked different than she remembered but, remarkably, not different than she expected. Time and circumstance had hardened his face, sharpened his already chiseled features even as they seemed to soften now before her eyes. Her *eyes*... The crow's feet at Ricky's temples when he smiled back at her were attractive in a mature manly sort of way. He was not a boy anymore. He was all man. Her man.

They met in the middle of the office and wept in each other's arms. Ricky kissed Gabriella's forehead and her cheeks and then whispered in her ear as they clung to each other, "You still want to get married?"

That caught her off guard. What a cruel and insensitive thing to say. She pushed away from him, and he reached into his pocket and fished out the simple silver necklace.

"Oh. You mean marry *you*." Gabriella nodded her answer – Yes – and turned so that he could put the necklace on her. Then she twirled back to him and he saw the same exotic beauty in her eyes that he'd seen before the accident and he realized that what he was seeing was her soul in all its splendor reaching out to merge with his. They kissed. "Soul mate," Ricky breathed.

Gabriella cocked her head. "What did you say?"

"I said you're my soul mate. And I can't wait to marry you. But I guess it will take a while to get everything arranged," he rambled. "I'm sure you want a big wedding with lots of people there. Should I call a wedding planner or something? I've never done anything like this before so I don't know where to begin."

Gabriella placed a finger on his lips. "All I want is to be Mrs. Ricky Santana, and I'm not waiting another day. Let's go to the chaplain and ask him to marry us right now."

Ricky turned when he heard Dawn's knuckles rap on the frame around the open office door. Chick stood in the hallway next to her. "Hey, sports fans, we just stopped by to see how things are going," Dawn said.

Gabriella's eyes traced Dawn's curvy contours, confirming the striking beauty she had imagined. She braced herself for a jealousy eruption from herself if not Dawn. But rather than jealousy, something much more akin to mutual respect and admiration with a hint of adoration hung in the air between the two women. She reached out and gently stroked Dawn's cheek, taking in the twinkle in her hazel eyes, and said, "You are a lovely woman. And I'm so grateful to you, not just for what you've done for me, but also for sticking by Ricky through everything. I cannot imagine how alone he would have been without you."

Dawn blushed, and touched Gabriella's cheek in return and said, "Thank you."

Ricky and Chick looked at one another and shrugged.

"So," Gabriella said to Dawn. "Are you busy this afternoon?"

Dawn said, "Today's my day off. Why?"

Gabriella smiled. "Because Ricky and I decided we want the chaplain to marry us today, and," she fiddled with her necklace, "I was wondering if you would be my maid of honor."

Dawn's eyes beamed. "Congratulations! Oh of course I will." They hugged.

While the women prattled on about gowns and shoes and bouquets, and all the rest, Ricky said to Chick, "And I'd like you to be my best man."

"I can't," said Chick.

The women stopped talking and stood holding hands and stared at the men when they heard Chick say that.

"Why not?" said Ricky.

Chick glanced at Dawn and said, "Because I can't be a best man and a groom at the same time, and I was thinking a double wedding..." He knelt on one knee and reached for Dawn's free hand. "Marry me, Dawn."

Dawn raised an eyebrow and peered down at Chick doubtfully until she saw that he wasn't kidding. For Heaven's sake. She suddenly realized he'd been serious when he asked her the first time. How could she have so misinterpreted something so very obvious? She urged Chick up and kissed him, then glanced at Gabriella.

Gabriella grinned, and said, "A double wedding sounds wonderful." She looked to Ricky.

"Fine by me," he said.

Dawn wrapped her arms around Chick and bounced on her heels. "Yes. Yes, yes yes."

Chick bounced with her. "Woohoo!"

"Congratulations, you two," Gabriella said.

Ricky took Gabriella's hand and pulled her to him. "Looks like we're at square one for best man and maid of honor." He chuckled. "I wonder if Ricardo and Isabella would mind doing double duty."

"Oh," said Gabriella, "that's a fabulous idea." She reached out and clutched Dawn's arm. "Come on, girlfriend, let's go wedding gown shopping."

Dawn glanced over at the men. "Why don't you boys see about scheduling the chaplain and find something appropriate to wear yourselves."

And late that afternoon, the two couples were married in a quaint ceremony beneath a scrubby mesquite tree on base attended by Isabella and Ricardo, as well as Colonel White who granted them four days leave for a honeymoon on South Padre Island as a wedding gift. "But keep your cell phone on in case I have to call you back early," the colonel said, "Lord only knows what might happen when the election results come in."

Gabriella marveled at the sunrise as she and Ricky strolled hand in hand along the beach the next morning, the sea water sloshing at their feet. "It's sooo beautiful," she said. Her chestnut curls danced on the sea breeze. "And the sound of the waves breaking. It's almost musical."

Ricky smiled at her and whispered, "There ain't nothing in all creation half as beautiful as you, Mrs. Santana, and nothing more musical than the sound of your voice."

"That's quite a compliment coming from the most handsome man in the whole wide world." Gabriella wrapped her arms around him and nibbled teasingly at his lips. "I wonder what Chick and Dawn are up to this morning."

"Probably still in their bungalow doing what people do on their honeymoon." Ricky waggled his eyebrows suggestively.

Gabriella looked up and down the deserted beach, and seeing nothing but a few seagulls fluttering about, slipped a hand beneath her white cotton swimsuit cover. Ricky's breath caught when her bikini bottoms dropped onto the sand. She clenched his hand and tugged him out into the cool water, and his heart began to race.

And race Ricky's heart would time and again over the next three days as they exhausted one another in hour after hour of lovemaking, stopping only long enough to fall asleep with their bodies tangled together, to eat, to take Bernice on occasional moonlit walks along the beach; and on November 8th, the final evening of their honeymoon, to celebrate with Dawn and Chick and a handful of strangers around the fire pit at a beachside tiki hut, basking in the evening breeze as the election results trickled in, district by district, from a flat-screen blaring beneath the thatch roof. Ricky stripped a grilled shrimp off a kabob and tossed it to Bernice. She gulped it down.

Chapter 79

A few minutes past midnight, Josh stepped onstage at the Dodge House where supporters of the unity presidential ticket gathered for a victory party after a race that had concluded with non-candidate Ricky Santana sweeping more than half of the popular vote through write-ins but losing the electoral college.

Josh gave a quick speech, congratulating himself, Helen, and Farnsworth, then thanked the campaign staff and hastily retreated to the restroom where he splashed some water on his face and brooded over reports that had slipped in between the non-stop election coverage that not only had Texas and Israel made their union official, so had Gabriella and Ricky. He glared into the furious slits of his eyes in the mirror. "It's not over, Gabriella," he seethed. "Ricky is not immortal." He began to laugh, a strange and evil laugh. "And thanks to you, his life expectancy just got a whole lot shorter."

Meanwhile, at the Leviathan penthouse, Levi's aides rushed about, packing the old man's things for his hastily planned trip to Dubai. On the television, networks shifted from one celebratory congressional campaign victory scene to another, bookending each clip with commentators pontificating about how the overwhelming number of votes for radical robot independents was evidence of widespread noncompliance with the mandatory harmonization vaccine – and, of course, Texas's medaling – and speculating about what the new unity president would do to correct that.

"Just look at this," one commentator said from his side of a split screen, the other side airing a robot speaking from a Dodge City storage unit, the recharge cord connecting the machine to an electrical outlet clearly visible to the viewers. A small crowd of people there waved tiny American flags and cheered. The lone human winner of a House seat, Republican turned independent, the amazing Andy Biggs waved a Texas flag with one hand and Arizona flag with the other. Libertarian senator, Rand Paul stood next to Biggs, his face radiating with hope.

"I want to congratulate the voters for taking the first step toward breaking the establishment's monopoly on the federal government and retuning it to the people," the robot said in a monotone voice not unlike that of the harmonizers. The small crowd surrounding the storage unit cheered some more, and then the robot continued to outline a plan which included auditing the government from top to bottom for corruption, reinstituting a national military, and eliminating all but a handful of federal agencies, among other things, but first and foremost using the power of the purse to block funding for any DHS action against Texas.

"Well, folks," the commentator sighed, "there you have it. That's what we have to look forward to from the House of Representatives for the next twenty-four months. And we thought we had problems with radicals before." He sighed again. "Ah well, twenty-four months is not that long and we've still got enough sensible and experienced *people* in the Senate to keep these wackjob machines in check."

Levi chuckled. "Indeed we do."

The telephone rang.

"Levi Baxter," he answered.

"Levi darling, I'm glad I reached you," Helen said half-frantic. "What in the world is happening? I thought the congressional elections were taken care of."

Levi sighed. "Calm yourself, dear. Everything will be fine. My sources assure me the lame duck Congress will appropriate more than

328

enough funds to see our objectives through until the new Congress is properly trained. It isn't as though we haven't had a radical insurgency in the House before. Remember the TEA Party? Yes, there will certainly be a few more flies to swat come January, but I'm confident we can depend on the courts to help us with the swatting."

"Yes, well," said Helen, "the TEA Party insurgents captured a few seats but nowhere near a majority and certainly not all of the seats like these robots just did."

"True," Levi said. "But it will all be alright. Now listen, I'm going abroad for a few months. It's best I keep a lower profile until everything is settled. I'll just be a phone call away should you need me...Oh and, let Josh know I'm taking Dr. Shultz along with me."

As soon as Levi hung up, his phone rang again. "This is Levi Baxter."

"Apparently you're not as good at controlling things as you think you are, old man," Farnsworth said mockingly. "What a disaster."

Levi shook his head. He wasn't looking forward to dealing with this arrogance for another four years but at least two others in management on the unity ticket along with a slate of loyal shareholders would dilute its potency. A divided presidency, what a feat. "I suggest you save the insults and focus your efforts on Texas," Levi said.

"Seems to me the Texas thing is not so pressing now that we've won the presidency," said Farnsworth. "Not that I wouldn't like to take Grant down just as a matter of principle."

Levi chuckled. "Well, principle is something and there's also 2030 to think about."

Chapter 80

The newlyweds returned late afternoon November 9th to find security at the base even tighter than usual amidst intelligence reports of harmonizers massing at the south Dodge City border wall. Troops armed with M-4 rifles stood by ominously as the taxi approached the front gate. A soldier stepped out of the guardhouse, saluted Ricky and said, "Welcome back, Captain Santana. Would you and the others gather your luggage and exit the vehicle, please." Another soldier directed them to empty the contents of their pockets into plastic trays and proceed through the body scanner.

Gabriella went through first, and the alarm went off.

"It's the microcomputer for her sight," Ricky said, and the screener waved her through.

Dawn went through next. Then Chick stepped into the scanner and the alarm went off again. The screener at the viewing monitor called another over to take a look. The two of them conversed for a moment, then one of them pulled Chick aside for further screening while Ricky went through with Bernice.

The alarm went off on Ricky too.

"Let's try it without the dog," the screener said.

No alarm this time.

The screeners conversed again, then one of them asked Ricky to walk Bernice through the scanner again, this time without the goggles.

No alarm.

The screener dangled the goggles. "We'll need to hang on to these."

"Like hell you will," said Ricky. "Bern needs those to see."

Colonel White whipped up in a Jeep and leaned out and said, "Give Captain Santana those damn goggles."

Another guard hurried over and waved a scanning wand around Chick's head.

"But Commander," the screener with the goggles protested, "there's something –"

Colonel White glared. "I said give the captain the goggles."

"Yes, sir, Commander."

The scanning wand bleeped with every pass over the right side of Chick's head.

Colonel White hopped out of the Jeep and planted his fists on his hips. He glanced at his watch and grunted, "Is there a problem?"

"Yes, sir," the guard with the wand said, "there seems to be some kind of electronic device implanted in this soldier's right temple area. I'm afraid we have no way of knowing whether it's a security threat or not without removing it, and that would require a surgical procedure, and –"

Ricky raised an eyebrow, thinking about Gabriella's implanted microcomputer for her artificial eyes. But Chick's eyes were one hundred percent all natu-ral…Weren't they?

Chick grabbed the end of the wand and pushed it down. "Get away from me with that, you psychopath," he told the guard. "I ain't got no electronics in my head. What's the matter with you? You leave your tinfoil hat at home so's you ain't getting a good signal from the mothership?"

Ricky glanced over and saw the colonel tapping his boot impatiently. "If y'all want to ride with me back to your tents, you best get this figured out," the colonel said.

"Dawn," said Ricky, "how about we drop you and Chick over at your office and you have a look at his head." He tossed her the goggles, then handed her the end of Bernice's leash. "And give Bern a good once over too while you're at it, if you wouldn't mind."

Dawn nodded. "Sure thing, Captain."

Chapter 81

Gabriella trembled and squealed, "Oooh," and dug her nails into Ricky's bare back as they tumbled off the cot and onto the floor of their tent, their lips locked together, and their bodies intertwined, dripping with sweat and quaking. Ricky ran his fingers through her hair and the rhythm of their coupling increased as they rolled across the floor.

"Captain," they heard someone call out loudly.

Ricky glanced reflexively at his watch. 5:00 AM.

"Captain!"

"Just a minute," Ricky barked as he wrapped a blanket around Gabriella. He shrugged into his trousers and slapped the door flap back. "This better be important, Private," he said to the baby-faced soldier standing outside the tent, saluting. "At ease."

"Sir, your cell phone," the soldier stammered, "you left it at the gate yesterday. The guard on duty says it's been going off all night and twice already this morning."

Ricky snatched the phone from the private's hand. "Oh crap."

The private said, "Sir?"

"I just realized I also forgot to retrieve my dog." Ricky chuckled. "Dismissed, Private."

Ricky jerked the canvas flaps shut and knelt back down in front of Gabriella, gazing into her eyes, and gently caressed her shoulders. "Where were we?"

She giggled and said, "Knock knock."

Ricky played along. "Who's there?"

331

Gabriella giggled again, her face flushed, and she parted the blanket and licked her lips seductively. "Mrs. Ricky Santana. Want to come in?"

"More than anything," Ricky said, and his heartrate kicked back into high gear as he snuggled into her soft flesh. Gabriella drew the blanket around him, and their lips met in a tender kiss that grew more passionate by the second. She rested her cheek on his shoulder and nibbled at his earlobe, her warm breath sending goosebumps up and down his body. She tugged at his zipper.

Ricky's cell phone rang.

"Grrr." He glanced down at the caller ID and saw that the call was coming from the medical center. Dawn probably, wondering why he hadn't come for Bernice last night.

Gabriella pounded on Ricky's chest. "Leave it."

"Right," he said, and powered off the phone and tossed it aside. He took her face in his hands and kissed her again, twirling her curls around his fingers as he did.

Gabriella traced the sides of his ribs down to his hips, then laid back, pulling him down with her, and they made love again, then fell back to sleep until long after sunrise.

Ricky lifted Gabriella's head off his chest and eased it gently onto a pillow, careful not to wake her, then quickly dressed and slipped away into town and picked up a gift he'd looked forward for years to giving her.

"Honey, I'm home," Ricky called out in his best *Ricky Ricardo* impression when he returned a couple of hours later with the gift-wrapped box concealed behind his back.

Gabriella looked up at him from the cot where she was stretched out in a pair of his boxers and a sleeveless undershirt with legs crossed, fiddling with her laptop. She smiled. "I was beginning to think you got a case of buyer's remorse and ran off again."

"That will never ever happen," Ricky said. "What you doing there?"

"Loading some pictures I took on the Island. They aren't great, but they aren't bad either, considering they were taken with a phone." She pointed at him. "Hey, are you hiding something from me?"

"It's a surprise. Close your eyes."

"No," Gabriella giggled, "I'm never closing my eyes ever again."

Ricky should have anticipated a response like that. He held the box out.

"What's this?" Gabriella set her laptop aside and took the gift from him.

"Oh, just a little something I picked up for you in town."

She untied the ribbon and peeled the wrapping paper off. "Oh, Ricky." She gleamed. "A new Nikon camera. I guess you realize it's going to take me a little while to figure out how to use this modern technology." She sprung up from the cot and snuggled into Ricky's arms.

Dawn stormed into the tent without announcing herself, and Chick scurried in behind her. "Ricky," she said frantically. "Why aren't you answering your cell phone?"

Gabriella wrapped herself in a blanket.

"Dawn, I'm in the middle of something right now." Ricky sighed.

Dawn held a fisted hand out and opened it, revealing a tiny metallic device in her palm. "Do you recognize this?"

Ricky's eyes widened. He glanced over at Chick who was rubbing a bandage covering his right temple area, and said, "Are you telling me –?"

Dawn nodded. "Yes. That was implanted in Chick's head. And before you ask, I confirmed his eyes are biological. But listen, there's more." She opened her other hand and showed Ricky two small transparent objects. "I found these stitched into Chick's eyes, and just so you know, they are not contact lenses. At least not in the conventional sense. I examined them under the microscope and they're…well, Chick, you speak computer better than I do. Tell Ricky what you told me."

"They're like the contact lens version of google glasses, more or less," Chick said, "little bitty monitors that fit over the eyes." He tugged Bernice's goggles away from Dawn and dangled them out to Ricky. "These got the same thing in them, plus a GPS tracker and a transmitter that sends video somewhere from a pin-sized webcam. I know that stuff ain't got nothing to do with that retina correction thing you rigged up for the dog."

"Darn straight it doesn't," said Ricky. He peered into the googles. "Mm-huh." He closed his eyes, contemplating. His mind shifted to the tour Levi had given him of the lower level of the Leviathan building a few months back, and more specifically, Levi's demonstration of the harmonizer 3.0's satellite fed sight system with the overlay feature that allowed someone somewhere to manipulate the appearance of targets, to make something as benign as an innocent little girl appear to be as threatening as a rabid beast. Ricky pressed a hand against his forehead. "Oh my God," he whispered.

"What, Ricky?" Gabriella and Dawn said simultaneously.

Chick said, "Them little bitty computers got something to do with the harmonization vaccine, don't they?"

Ricky cringed. "Sure seems like it."

If Ricky's suspicions were right, the microcomputers were not simply related to the harmonization vaccine, they were critical to it. And the purpose of that vaccine was quite the opposite of what it was billed to be. He thought about Boston, how the millions of citizens gathered in solidarity had instantly turned violently and viciously against one another. He remembered Chick describing President Grant's transformation into a monster onboard the Cole Brothers ship…Google glasses in the form of contact lenses powered by the tiny client computers. If that combination did comprise the so-called harmonization vaccine, everyone who received it must be connected to the harmonizer sight-system or some version of it, and everything they see can be manipulated. Ricky shuddered at the thought.

"What does it mean?" Gabriella said.

"It means the U.S. political establishment is manipulating everything the citizens see, at least everything citizens that have had that vaccine see," Ricky said. He went on to explain how the overlays were used to superimpose frightening images over reality in the line of sight of the harmonizer pilots, or in this case, the line of sight of harmonization vaccine recipients. "They're using the most powerful motivator of bad decisions known to mankind to divide the people and overcome their common sense – fear."

It pained Ricky to ask what he asked next, but he had to. "Gabby, have you seen anything, ah, unusual, since we got your eyes working properly?"

Gabriella chuckled nervously, trying to make light of the question, though she did grasp the implications of it for her. "Ricky, the world has changed a lot over the last thirty-some years. Practically everything I see is unusual to me. But no little girls turning into fanged aliens from outer space or anything like that."

Ricky hoped his concern would prove to be unfounded, and so far it seemed it was. "Say, where's Bernice?" he said to Dawn.

Chick said, "She's in our tent resting. You want me to go fetch her?"

"Actually, would y'all mind looking after her for a couple more days?"

Chick smiled. "Whatever you want, Captain."

Late that evening after another round of lovemaking, Ricky and Gabriella lay with bodies and faces scrunched together like sardines in a can on the single canvas cot that had been their marriage bed since they returned from the honeymoon.

"Ricky," Gabriella whispered, "are you awake?"

"Mm-huh," Ricky said with eyes closed.

Gabriella said, "It's hard to sleep like this, isn't it?"

Ricky nodded, eyes still closed. "Mm-huh."

"Ricky?"

"Yeah, babe?"

"Living in this tent is getting old. If you could live anywhere in the world, where would that be?"

Ricky propped himself up on an elbow and looked at Gabriella. "Anywhere's alright with me as long as I'm with you...Even a tent."

She smiled, and ran a fingertip down the hollow between his pecs. "That's not really an answer."

"Well, where do you want to live?" said Ricky.

"I don't know," Gabriella said. "After the first day at the ranch...before I thought you...What I mean is before I knew you weren't...Okay this isn't coming out right. What I'm trying to say is, of all the places I've been over the past several years the ranch was the most beautiful of them all. But I measured that beauty in smells, the sweet smell of the bluebonnets, and tastes, and touch, the feeling of the horse beneath me, the cool river water on my toes, that kind of thing; and sounds and...I don't know, words, I guess, your words, and people, all the others, your folks, Juan, all of them. It just felt like home. Do you understand what I mean?"

Ricky gently stroked the side of her face with the backside of his hand. "I know exactly what you mean. Would you like to see it?"

Gabriella peered into his eyes. "More than anything. But it's too dangerous. Isn't it?"

Ricky took a deep breath and closed his eyes, trying to block the images of carnage from the last time he saw the ranch. He felt his pent up rage boiling to the surface along with disappointment in himself and the Republic of Texas for letting months go by without retaliating against the U.S., much less taking the Red River land back.

A shrill of sirens pierced the night. Gabriella pressed her hands over the sides of her head to keep her eardrums from bursting. "What's going on?" she yelled.

A text appeared on Ricky's cell phone – DEFCON 3. He tumbled off the cot, quickly attached his prosthetics, then tugged Gabriella up. "Get dressed now!" he shouted as he shucked his pants on. A voice call came in.

"Captain Santana here," Ricky yelled into the phone.

The sirens continued to blare.

Ricky hollered to Gabriella, "DHS harmonizers breached the south Dodge City wall. All civilians are to report to the bomb shelter and all pilots to proceed as planned for this contingency."

"What does that mean?" Gabriella screamed over the sirens.

"It means we've got to get our attack aircraft up to Dodge City. Now."

Dawn rushed over from her and Chick's place a couple of tent's down and jerked the door flap open and reached in and took Gabriella by the hand. "Come on girlfriend, we've got to get underground."

"Wait," Gabriella said. "Let me grab my laptop bag."

Ricky kissed them both on the cheek and ran to the apache gunship he'd been assigned to. He saw Chick on the ramp rushing from aircraft to aircraft with other ground support troops stripping tie-downs off choppers and airplanes.

By the time air support from Sheppard reached south Dodge City, the Texas troops there were in full retreat. Ricky peered through night vision goggles at the chaos below. From two thousand feet altitude, the harmonizers' human façade made it hard to distinguish them from the Texans. He clicked his mic and said to the others in his chopper squadron, "Blackbird flock, this is Bad-bird, looks like a hot mess down there. Descend to five-hundred feet and engage. And make damn sure you're shooting at the enemy."

Chapter 82

"How long do we have to stay down here?" Gabriella said to Dawn as they huddled in the crowded bomb shelter they'd shared for the last few hours with hundreds of frightened civilians. Isabella dozed on the bench next to them after worrying herself to sleep over Ricardo who had ridden off into the night on the Palo Pinto tugging the mustang along with him.

"I have no idea," Dawn said.

Gabriella sighed, and nudged Bernice's head off her computer bag so she could get at her laptop and Josh's DNA profile that she had found lying on the floor in the tent. Then she pulled up the electronic copies of the DNA profiles from the rape victim samples. "Can you help me with this?" she said.

Dawn looked at the files displayed on the laptop screen. "What're you trying to do?"

"Just killing time. Can you tell if either of these matches Josh's here?" Gabriella pointed at the electronic files and tapped the hardcopy file with her other hand.

"Let me have a look." Dawn took the laptop from her and alternately scrutinized the DNA markers there and those on the hardcopy file. She scratched her head after a few minutes, then said, "One of them is a perfect match for this one," she pointed to the hardcopy, "and the other appears to have come from a close relative."

Gabriella felt the blood drain from her face. She told Dawn about the rapes then, ending with, "I can't believe Josh is the one. But he does smoke cigars, and he has been to Max's place, so that explains the sample Ricky gave me. And I never really thought it was Max. This makes a lot more sense than Levi being the other perp." She paused. "Hmm. Do you suppose Josh has a brother or something he never told us about?"

"Must have," said Dawn. "Wow. I can't believe –"

Gabriella grasped Dawn's hand. "Listen, I don't think we should bother Ricky with this. He and Chick have enough on their plates with the war or whatever this is and…" The two women hugged and cried together.

After a minute, Dawn said, "Where did Isabella say Ricardo went?"

She didn't say exactly," Gabriella shook her head, "just that he told her he had to get the horses someplace safe."

The door clapped open and the roars and rumbles and screeching tires of landing aircraft flooded the bomb shelter. "Alright people, listen up," Colonel White barked. "I've been ordered to evacuate all civilians to San Antonio." He glanced over at Dawn. "And you as well, Doctor. The buses are on the way, so get your things together."

"Colonel," Gabriella yelled, "is that our pilots I hear landing?"

Chapter 83

Josh and Farnsworth gathered around a computer screen in the not-so-oval office watching the live feed from a drone monitoring the U.S. offensive. By 4:00 AM, harmonizers had pushed the Texans out of Kansas and all the way across the thirty-four mile wide Oklahoma panhandle back into Texas proper. "How do you like me now, Grant?" Farnsworth chuckled.

Helen stood at the window glaring out at the lack of progress on the Dodge City VP residence. "When I signed on with the unity presidency, I hadn't intended to spend the next four years at a slumber party in this...this shack...with you gentlemen," she complained. "What on Earth is taking so long to get my mansion built? They've been at it for over three years now, haven't they?"

"Same thing that's delayed completion of the new Whitehouse," Farnsworth said, "regulations, licensing, permitting, inspections, environmental impact studies, all of that business. And by the way, Vizion hasn't even taken the oath of office yet, nor have you. Feel free to reside elsewhere."

Helen fiddled with the draperies. "Joshua darling, why don't you issue an executive order or something to move things along on my mansion first thing once Vizion's inaugurated, and if you can't do that, at least order someone to change these atrocious window treatments."

"I can't think of anything I'd like better than not having you for a roommate, *mother,*" Josh smirked, "but right now I'm far more concerned with bringing Texas to its knees. I intend to show Ricky and those... those, whatever they are, in the incoming House of Representatives where the real power lies in this country."

Farnsworth snickered. "Still hung up on that woman, are you?"

"Screw you." Josh took a seat behind the presidential desk, picked up the phone and dialed the GTP enforcement director. "How much longer before your assets are in the Gulf? ...Excellent." Josh cupped a hand over the mouthpiece. "Farnsworth, they want to know if our DHS harmonizers along the Red River can be ready to strike at sunup."

Farnsworth's eyes flickered. "They're ready now."

Josh uncovered the mouthpiece and said, "They'll be ready." He smiled. "See you in Austin."

Chapter 84

Colonel White met Ricky's Apache on the ramp as soon as it landed. Chick ran out and started to chain it down. "Leave it," the Colonel yelled over the whapping of rotor blades and screaming of aircraft engines. Our birds are going back up as soon as they're refueled." He waved at Ricky.

"Listen, I know you and your airmen are exhausted but we've got more trouble on the way," the colonel told Ricky. "Big trouble. We intercepted a communication between the DHS commander across the Red River and the enforcement director at the GTP. They're planning an all-out assault at sunup – DHS harmonizers from the north and west and fighter jets off the GTP carrier in the Gulf. And an additional GTP battle group is being dispatched from Dubai. We've got to get all the aircraft out of here."

"You mean retreat?"

"We've already evacuated most of the civilians." He paused. "Look, Captain, we don't have a navy. We're going to need all the aircraft we can muster to take out those GTP ships and planes. And we've got to protect our people and our capitol. Those are our priorities. We'll have to stop the harmonizers with ground forces."

"Ground forces, huh?" Ricky baulked. "In case you haven't noticed, small arms aren't particularly effective against those things."

"I've noticed, Captain. Additional assets, including artillery and shoulder mount tank-killers are on the way from Fort Hood as we speak. I asked for an armored column from Fort Bliss too, but they've got their hands full trying to hold back the harmonizers in the panhandle and evacuate the wounded brought down from south Dodge City."

The colonel went on to explain that the orders were to redeploy most of the aircraft from Texas's northern airbases to the naval air station at Corpus Christi and Ellington field in Houston to protect the tidal power system against the GTP fleet in the gulf. The residual aircraft would be shared between Camp Mabry in Austin to defend the capitol and Lackland air base in San Antonio to protect the local civilian population.

"You sure you wouldn't rather send me and my flyboys up to bomb Dodge City into the stone age, Colonel?"

"I can't think of a thing I'd rather do than rid this Earth of that bunch of establishment crooks," Colonel White said, "but we can't risk the civilian casualties. Those civilians are our brothers and sisters."

Ricky nodded. "Right. Colonel?"

"Yes, Captain."

"I understand how grave the situation is and I'd like to see my ranch one last time in case… and I'd like to take my wife with me."

Colonel White glanced at his watch. "You've got an hour. Be careful."

Chapter 85

Gabriella stood next to Ricky, holding a half-frozen bluebonnet on the southern bank where the Santana Ranch met the Red River. The glow of the predawn sun nudged at the horizon just enough that she could see her breath and his in the crisp November air. "It's beautiful, even in the dark," she said. "And the smells…mmm, it's just like I remember. When this is all over, I hope we can come back here to live forever."

Ricky wrapped his arms around her. "I hope so too."

Gabriella pulled back and peered into his eyes. "It's just wishful thinking, isn't it?"

"I don't know," Ricky whispered.

The ground beneath them began to rumble, and they heard mechanical feet sloshing into the water. Gabriella gazed in horror at the eye-lights of thousands upon thousands of harmonizers crossing the river from the north. Ricky grasped her hand and said, "Time to go."

Chapter 86

Several hours later, Josh stepped into the Situation Room. He shook the hands of the DHS Secretary and Farnsworth and asked where Helen was.

"Shopping, where else?" Farnsworth said. "It's a ritual with her, you know. Start off each week bright and early with a shopping spree." He sat down in front of a widescreen monitor and continued amusing himself with the drone feed of the dog fights playing out over the Gulf.

The DHS Secretary said, "the Red River harmonizers have advanced into Dallas, and so far we've only lost eight thousand units. Most of those to airstrikes."

"And Sheppard air base?" said Josh. "Was Ricky Santana there? Did they kill him?"

The DHS secretary shook his head. "No. They found the base abandoned. Troops, aircraft, everything, gone. Different story out west. We lost over twenty thousand harmonizers between Amarillo and El Paso. But they've got Fort Bliss surrounded now. I expect it will fall within the hour."

Farnsworth squinted as he watched the bow of the GTP carrier off the coast of Galveston Island rise into the smoke-filled air. He shouted, "The Texans have sunk the carrier."

Josh and the DHS Secretary turned in shock toward the screen.

The phone rang, and Farnsworth snatched it up. "President Farnsworth here....Yes, I saw it...How long before that GTP battle group gets there? ...You have got to be kidding." He slammed the phone down.

The DHS secretary stood wide-eyed and silent.

"What?" Josh said.

Farnsworth shook his head and clicked through channel after channel of video of massive protests in capitols throughout the world, many of the protesters waving Texas flags. "Look for yourself. It's a global uprising."

Josh sat down next to him. "Why don't they just shoot those thugs?"

The DHS Secretary paced.

"Because national governments don't have militaries anymore," Farnsworth growled. "Remember?"

Josh sighed. "I know. But what about their domestic forces? Can't they handle civil unrest?"

"Of course they can," Farnsworth jabbed his finger at the monitor, pointing out tens of thousands of uniformed officers mixed in with the crowds, "but, as you can see, their domestic forces have joined the protesters instead. And before you ask, the GTP trade enforcement wing is too busy dodging terrorists' torpedoes right now to deal with it."

The DHS secretary picked up the clicker and brought up a video feed of billowing black smoke and the wreckage that had been the GTP's fleet at Dubai's Jebel Ali Harbour. "The Kurds and the Jews have been busy," he said. "Apparently they maintained national militaries and equipment, including subs and bombers, in violation of the trade agreement."

"Where in the hell did the Kurds get subs?" Josh said.

"From the Jews, where else," said Farnsworth.

Josh turned to the DHS Secretary and said, "If domestic forces won't stop those protests, why doesn't the GTP send ground forces into the capitols to do it?"

The DHS Secretary pointed at the smoldering wreckage of the fleet onscreen again. "No ships to transport them." He clicked over to a feed of cratered runways and mangled steel remains of aircraft at the GTP's only significant airbase. "Nor airplanes."

Josh stood and sighed. "So, where does that leave us?"

Farnsworth clicked back to drone footage of a section of the I-35W corridor midway between Dallas and Waco. He smiled when he saw Texas' Fort Hood forces in full retreat, leaving behind a convoy of obliterated trucks and artillery pieces. Then he clicked over to the rubble that had been Fort Bliss a short while earlier. "Looks like we're doing just fine without the GTP's help. At this rate, the Red River harmonizers should be in Austin by tomorrow morning."

Chapter 87

The celebration at Houston's Ellington Field ended abruptly when Colonel White stepped into the mess hall where the airmen had gathered. "Men, listen up," he said. "You're all to be commended for your fine work in taking out that GTP menace in the Gulf. And we owe a debt of gratitude to our Kurdish and Israeli friends for neutralizing the remainder of the GTP forces.

The airmen hooted and whistled.

"By the way," the colonel continued, "in case you weren't aware of it, the whole world is rooting for us. At least the people of the world are – with the apparent exception of our harmonized brethren in the U.S. But this is a long way from finished. We've taken heavy casualties up north and out west. Fort Bliss has fallen. Our Fort Hood interdiction forces have been destroyed. And the Red River harmonizers are damn near to Waco."

Colonel White caught Ricky's eye. He did not have the heart to tell him that Juan had been killed at south Dodge City. He needed Ricky in the fight with a clear head. The colonel clapped his hands together. "So, now that the threat from the Gulf has been neutralized, we're moving our coastal air assets inland to supplement those at Camp Mabry in destroying the harmonizers. At the rate those machines are advancing, they'll be in Austin by tomorrow morning. It's up to you boys to stop them. We'll be flying sorties round the clock."

Ricky raised a hand. "Colonel?"

"Speak, Captain."

"What about the civilians?"

"They're already being transferred from Austin to San Antonio to be on the safe side," the colonel said. "And we'll be joining them if Austin falls."

"What about ammunition?" said Ricky. "We're dangerously low."

Colonel White nodded. "You've got to make every missile count. Now, one last thing before we get to it." He dialed a number on his cell phone. "Mr. President, it's Colonel White," he said when Grant answered. "I have you on speaker." The colonel held the phone up, and the airmen gathered around to listen.

"Men, this is President Grant. Congratulations on knocking out that GTP carrier. I have my friend, Prime Minister Ajar of Kurdistan here with me. He has some news to share. Mr. Prime Minister."

"Hello, fellow Americans," said Ajar with a distinctly Arabic accent. "I too wish to congratulate you on your victory in the Gulf."

Ricky turned to the airman beside him. "Did he say *fellow* Americans?"

"You caught that too?" said the airman.

Ajar went on, "I am also proud to announce that President Grant and the Texas legislature have recognized the independent nation of Kurdistan and offered to us to become the second state, alongside Israel, in the United States of Texas. We graciously accept."

Chapter 88

343

By dusk the next day, Texas air forces had destroyed almost half of the Red River harmonizers, but that did not stop the other half from advancing into Austin; nor did it stop the western harmonizers from marching down I-10 all the way to the outskirts of Sonora, less than two-hundred miles from San Antonio where a river of civilians flowed into the courtyard of the Alamo. "Corporal, get these people into the shelters," Colonel White ordered Chick. "We're about out of daylight."

"Yes, sir," Chick said, and switched on the courtyard floodlights.

Dawn rushed about, directing nurses and medics to treat the refugees for blistered feet, fatigue, and various other maladies suffered during the evacuation from Austin.

Ricky scanned the crowd and saw Ricardo and Isabella straggle in tugging the horses along, and Gabriella right behind them with Bernice. "Gabriella!" he hollered, and ran to her.

"Baby," Gabriella breathed and wrapped her arms around him. Ricky held her tightly for a minute, then he heard Grant call out from the makeshift presidential office, "Captain Santana, Colonel White."

Ricky kissed Gabriella.

"Ricky," she said through trembling lips, "I love you."

"I love you too." He brushed her cheek with the backside of his hand. "I gotta go. You best get to the shelter."

Colonel White and Ricky joined Grant around the map on the war table in his office. Grant tapped a finger on it. "The western harmonizers are here. The Red River harmonizers are here." She folded her arms across her chest. "Give it to me straight, gentlemen. Is there any way we can win this thing? If we don't hold San Antonio, there's going to be a civilian bloodbath, a massacre."

Ricky said, "Without more ammunition, we're screwed, Madam President."

Colonel White held up a finger. "Unless."

"Unless what?" Grant said impatiently.

"Unless we could disable them."

"What do you have in mind?"

"An ASM –"

"As in anti-satellite missile?" Grant said.

"Yes, ma'am, Madam President." said Colonel White. He glanced at Ricky. "The harmonizers' sight system relies on a dedicated satellite to distribute the video to the operators, right?" The colonel's eyes shifted back to Grant. "With an ASM, we could knock it out of the sky, effectively blinding every last one of those damn machines. They'd be easy pickins after that."

Grant glanced at Ricky. "Do you concur, Captain?"

Ricky choked. "Uh...ah..."

"Well?" Grant said, "Do you agree with Colonel White or not?"

Ricky nodded. "Yes, but," he stammered, "we don't have any ASMs... Do we?"

"I'm afraid not," said the colonel.

Grant thought for a few seconds. "Say, any reason we couldn't have TASA repurpose a satellite launch vehicle to mail a bomb up to that sight system satellite's address?" Grant didn't wait for an answer before calling Texas Aeronautics and Space Administration.

"Houston, we have a problem," Grant told the lady at TASA. Then she explained to her what she needed. "Only one, huh?" She turned to the colonel. "Will one do it?"

Colonel White nodded. "As long as we don't miss."

Grant glanced at Ricky who reluctantly nodded agreement with the colonel.

"One'll do," Grant told the lady at TASA. "Hold on a moment." She handed the phone to Ricky. "Here. Tell her what she needs to know to identify that satellite."

Ricky clicked the phone back into its cradle, and Gabriella approached the door to the presidential office just in time to hear him say to Grant, "I can't. The sight system for Gabby's eyes operates off the same satellite. Blinding the harmonizers will blind her too."

Gabriella covered her mouth and gasped, "Oh my God." She left Bernice and fled to the other side of a convoy just arriving outside the Alamo."

Grant shook her head and sighed. "Captain, if there was any other way...Listen, I'm sorry, but we don't have any choice. I'm ordering you, as the Commander in Chief of the Republic of Texas to call TASA back right this instance and tell them what they need to know."

"Madam President, I don't have the information with me," Ricky said.

Grant grabbed Ricky by the arm. "What do you mean you don't have it with you? Where is it?"

Colonel White rested his hand on his sidearm, then the sound of semi-truck horns blasting and a bugler trumpeting the cavalry call shook the windows. Grant jerked the door open and peered out. "Well, I'll be a son of a gun. It's Ben Black and…who's that, somebody's grandparents on that wagon with him."

Ricky saw Miss Sally and her bearded cousins and Trucker JB and a mess of TEA- partiers wielding rifles on horseback, and several horse-drawn covered wagons interspersed within a mile-long convoy of big-rigs with small flags from Texas and each of the forty-nine American states fluttering from their hoods.

Ben Black hopped off the seat of a wagon, and Ricky rushed out to meet him.

"Captain Santana," Ben Black said as he gripped Ricky's hand in a firm shake. He waved his other arm toward the elderly couple in the wagon seat. "Meet Mr. and Mrs. Swanson, formerly of Dodge City, Kansas."

Ricky's mouth fell open. The *Swansons*. "Pleasure to finally make your acquaintance," he said, and turned back to Ben Black, noting the pair of AR-15s slung over each of his shoulders, the bullet belts crisscrossing his chest, and the pistols tucked into his dual hip-holsters. "I see you came prepared."

"That I did," said Ben Black. "Times like these are what the 2nd Amendment's all about. It never had anything to do with hunting." He angled his thumb at the wagon as he reached into his pocket and pulled out a stick of dynamite. "Between the wagons and the trucks, we've got five-hundred tons of boom-boom, give or take. Compliments of West Virginia's former coal mining industry.

Gabriella, who was crouched behind the wagon, reached into it and fished out a couple of sticks of dynamite and shoved them in her jacket pocket, then crept away quietly into the night to East Houston Street. She took out her cell phone and texted Josh.

Grant approached the wagon with Colonel White at her side and shook Ben Black's hand, said, "Good to see you, Ben," then said to Ricky, "I asked you a question."

Ricky stubbed the toe of his boot at the ground. "The satellite information's on my laptop," he said.

"Fine," said Grant. "Go and get it. Quickly. We're running out of time."

Ricky went back into the Alamo and seconds later a burst of M-4 machinegun fire echoed out from the barracks there.

346

Colonel White drew his sidearm and rushed in and found Ricky standing over smoking bits of metal, plastic, and electronic components – all that was left of his laptop.

"Sorry," Ricky said, and surrendered his rifle to the colonel.

Grant stepped in. "What's happened here?"

"He destroyed the laptop," Colonel White said.

Grant grimaced. "I know good and well that laptop wasn't the only place that information was stored, " she said. "Colonel, take the captain to an interrogation room and do whatever you have to. We've got less than ten hours before those harmonizers get here.

Chapter 89

Josh's jaw dropped when he saw Gabriella's text message on his cell phone – *I will divorce Ricky and marry you if you stop the invasion.* He dialed the not-so-oval office. "Farnsworth, it's Josh. I need a stealth chopper and a pilot immediately."

Farnsworth chuckled. "Oh? Where're you headed?"

"San Antonio," said Josh.

Four hours later, Gabriella slipped the engagement ring that Josh had given her back onto her finger. She held a forearm up to shield her eyes from the dust whipped up by the chopper hovering down for her.

Josh shoved the door open and reached out for her hand and pulled her into the rear seat.

Gabriella winced when she looked at him. His beady little eyes bearing down on her through those round-lensed glasses made her skin crawl.

Josh smiled. "How have you been, Gabby?"

"It's hot in here," she said, then turned away and stared at the back of the seat in front of her for a minute before saying, "I know who you are."

Josh draped an arm around Gabriella and she cringed. "Of course you know who I am, honey. Oh, you mean you can see me now. Yes, I heard about that. All the better now that we're back together. I've done a little research and you'll be pleased to know that you've got a sufficient basis for annulling that mistake you made with Ricky so you won't have to get a divorce."

Gabriella jerked her head around and glared at him. "I mean I know you were the driver in the accident." She paused. "And I know you're one of the rapists. You want to tell me who the other is or do I have to keep digging on my own? Because I will find out. Trust me."

Josh's eyes widened. "Where did you get an idea like that? From Ricky? He'd say anything to get his way with you. Anyway, now is not the time."

"Tell me about your sibling," Gabriella pressed. "Or is it multiple siblings?"

Josh gulped. Did she somehow know he was Levi's son? "I said, now is not the time."

Neither of them spoke another word until the chopper touched down on the lawn of the temporary presidential mansion where an army of secret service agents swarmed to escort them inside.

Josh led Gabriella down the hall to their sleeping quarters and peeled out of his suit jacket and tossed it in a chair. Then he stripped his tie off and started unbuttoning his shirt.

Gabriella folded her arms across her chest and said, "Um. What are you doing?"

"Getting ready for bed. It's almost four AM." Josh pointed to the dresser. "I bought you some lingerie. Top drawer."

Gabriella rolled her eyes. "Are you going to tell me the truth about that night at the Green Dragon? And about the rapes?" She clenched her hands in fists and silently scolded herself for putting her own issues above stopping the impending massacre in Texas. What was she thinking?

Josh plunked down on the edge of the bed. "I'm not so sure you're in a negotiating position," he said, then he noticed the irritated wrinkle above the bridge of Gabriella's nose and her jaw muscles flexing as she ground her teeth. "Okay." He washed his hands across his face. "Look, it's true that I was the driver. And for that I am truly sorry. It was an accident. But I never raped anyone."

The irritated wrinkle above Gabriella's nose became more pronounced.

"Alright, alright," Josh said. "What happened at the Green Dragon: While you and Ricky were in the restrooms, Max dropped a ruffie in your drink. Max didn't know I saw him do it. Anyway, Ricky got back from the restroom first, and he drank your drink instead of his own."

Gabriella had to respond to that. "Wait. What? Max tried to drug me?"

"You asked me what happened and I'm trying to tell you," said Josh.

Gabriella took a deep breath. "Go on."

Josh continued, "So the three of us left in your car right after that because Ricky was passing out. The headlights from the other car blinded me... And after the crash, I dragged Ricky from the backseat into the driver seat. I was afraid I'd go to jail. No way I could have passed a breathalyzer."

"But you were okay with Ricky going to jail?" Gabriella shrieked. "Your friend. For something you did?"

"No," Josh said. "Not exactly, I mean. Yes. He would go to jail. But he had a defense. I knew there would be a blood test, and that the test would reveal the drug in his system. But he'd have a star witness, me, to testify that he had not purposely ingested it, that he'd been drugged by someone else. But then Max appeared. He'd been behind us in his car. He witnessed the accident, the whole thing, and he threatened to tell the cops I was the driver. So, we came to an agreement. If I kept Max's secret about the ruffies, he'd keep mine, and he'd use the connections he'd established through his work with the police officers' union to make sure the charges against Ricky were never forwarded to the prosecutor's office. Everybody won."

"Except me," Gabriella said, and slapped him across the face.

Josh grabbed her by the wrists and shook her. "Gabriella, my going to jail and ruining my future wouldn't have changed what happened to you?"

Gabriella broke away from him. "Finish your sordid tale, rapist."

"I told you, I never raped anyone. Must be some kind of mistake in the DNA samples."

"So you keep saying, Josh." That was all Gabriella could take. She could not marry him, not even to save Texas. There must be some way. She shoved her hands into her jacket pockets and felt the dynamite sticks there. Yes. She flung the door open and stormed out.

Josh buttoned his shirt up, slung his jacket over his shoulder, and ran after her. "Where are you going?" he hollered.

"Vizion," Gabriella hissed. She stopped abruptly and turned to face him, hands in her pockets still, firmly gripping the dynamite. "I'd like to see that amazing computer system that's made it possible for me to

349

look upon this historic town, this beautiful world, and Texas again, before those awful killing machines run by you and your corporate Frankenstein president destroy it all."

"Fine," said Josh, "I'll take you there. But it's Grant and your beloved Ricky that caused all this, not me." He slipped a cigar into his mouth and clenched it between his teeth. Gabriella smiled at the flame flickering from his lighter as he lit it.

Chapter 90

Grant stood with Colonel White atop a lookout tower as dawn rapidly approached.

"We've tried everything short of jerking Ricky's fingernails out, and he won't talk," the colonel said.

Grant rubbed her forehead. "Damn. Any other ideas?"

"You mean besides jerking his fingernails out?" Colonel White said.

"No no. I mean –"

The colonel broke in. "I know what you mean. I've been thinking about it all night."

"And?"

"And we may not have a fix on that satellite but we might know where the computer that controls it is."

Grant's eyes beamed. "Vizion, right?"

Colonel White nodded. "Right. We could send a bomber up there and–"

Grant peered out through a field telescope and saw a tidal wave of harmonizers crashing through San Antonio. "Holy mother of God." She grabbed Colonel White by the arm. "It's too late. They're here."

Sirens shrieked.

Texas aircraft crisscrossed the skies.

Troops and militiamen flooded the courtyard as officers barked out orders. "Snipers to the towers. Man the cannons."

Exploding artillery shells whistled and banged.

Grant scanned the tanks and artillery pieces surrounding the outside perimeter and saw the avalanche of harmonizers rumbling toward them. "Fiiiire!" she hollered. "Madam President," she heard someone yell. She turned to see Ricky leaping up the steps with a pair of RPG launchers slinging from his shoulders and several sticks of dynamite tucked into his waistband.

Colonel White drew his sidearm.

Grant said, "Hold your fire, Colonel."

"How did you get out?" the colonel said to Ricky.

Ricky rapped his knuckles against his shin. "I kicked the door down," he said through labored breath. "Titanium legs have their advantages." He leveled one of the RPG launchers at a harmonizer and fired. Swish. Boom! He grinned. "One down, ninety-thousand to go." He lit a stick of dynamite and hurled it, taking out another one.

A mortar round crashed into the wall and Grant and the two men tumbled to the ground as the floor of the tower collapsed beneath them. "You alright?" Ricky said to Colonel White who was laying on top of him now.

"Yeah. You?" the colonel said.

"I'm okay." Ricky glanced at the harmonizers approaching the gaping hole in the wall.

They heard Grant murmur.

"We've got to get the president to safety," Colonel White said. He and Ricky dug through the rubble.

"Madam President," Ricky said.

Grant groaned. "My leg's broken."

Ricky stood in the gap and fired another RPG while Colonel White hoisted Grant up over his shoulders. The harmonizers were obliterating the ring of tanks and artillery.

"You stay here and help hold them off," the colonel said.

Ricky nodded. "I'll do my best." He pulled out another stick of dynamite and lit it, and the colonel rushed off with Grant.

Patriots plunged from the tops of what was left of the Alamo walls as harmonizers strafed them with machinegun fire. Ricky winced when he heard the thud of a body striking the ground and saw that it was Chick. Tears welled up in his eyes, blurring his vision as he hurled another stick of dynamite.

Bullets ricocheted off the rubble in the gap.

Ricky hurled another stick of dynamite, and then another, and another, until the last one. The harmonizers kept coming. He picked up the RPG launcher. Two grenades left. He planted himself on one knee in the middle of the gap and aimed the launcher.

Another mortar round exploded nearby.

Ricky fired the RPG. Another harmonizer disintegrated.

One grenade left.

Ricky heard horses whinny and he glanced over his shoulder.

Ben Black rolled up and leapt from his wagon, stripping the cover off of it for easy access to the cases of dynamite. Miss Sally and her cousins and trucker JB rushed up right behind him. "You look like you could use a little help," Ben Black said.

Ricky nodded and fired off the last RPG. Then he reached into the wagon for a handful of dynamite and he felt another hand reaching in. He looked up.

"You didn't seriously think I wouldn't be here for the fight, did you?" said the man attached to that other hand.

Ricky's eyes widened. "Ted Cruz?"

"One and the same," Cruz said, grinning from ear to ear. He lit a stick of dynamite and through it into the crush of harmonizers.

The others followed his lead, hurling stick after stick of dynamite.

The harmonizers continued to close in. There were just too many of them.

Jet engines roared overhead and the ground shook from the massive explosion of ordinance dropped from the aircraft. Ricky looked up.

All went quiet for a moment.

"Was that what I thought it was?" Ricky said.

Ben Black grinned. "Looked to me like corporate jets," he said. "Cole Brothers and Attorney Miller's jets, as a matter of fact."

"Well I'll be damned," said Ricky, then he felt a tap on his shoulder. He lurched back when he saw the long green fingernails. "Sis?" From the Dodge City impound lot?"

She smiled. "You didn't seriously think I'd let you have all the fun, did you?"

The smoke from the explosions drifted away, revealing another massive wall of harmonizers. "Looks like this is it." Ricky said. They embraced in a group hug and Ben Black said a quick prayer, then they set the horses loose and pushed the wagon full of dynamite into the gap and backed away from it and huddled close to the ground.

The wall of harmonizers closed in, tighter and tighter around the Alamo. When the first of this wave of them approached the gap, Ricky pulled out his sidearm and fired several rounds into the wagon. Boom!

A river of harmonizers poured into the courtyard through the cloud of flying debris.

Bernice charged out from somewhere, growling, and bit into the ankle of one of the harmonizers. It aimed its weapon down at her in what seemed to Ricky like slow motion time-lapse.

Ricky screamed, "Nooooo." He raised his sidearm.

The harmonizer froze. Several other harmonizers' movements became suddenly awkward. Some stopped. Others stumbled clumsily in different directions. Still others bumped into one another.

"What's happening?" Miss Sally said.

Ricky crept up to the one Bernice was tearing at with her teeth and waved a hand in front of its eyes. "They're blind," he said. He reached around behind it and disconnected its battery, then lightly shoved it and it tumbled to the ground. "Hey," he said to the dog, "you can let go now."

Ben Black scrambled up into a tower and called out over a bullhorn. "The harmonizers are blind!" The courtyard filled with cheers, and the Alamo defenders poured down from the walls and rushed from harmonizer to harmonizer disconnecting batteries for the next several hours until every last one was disabled.

Ricky stood amidst the crowd in the courtyard, dejected after searching the now empty shelters for Gabriella. Colonel White rolled President Grant out in a wheelchair. A hush swept over the crowd of patriots.

A recon report Grant had received that Gabriella had paid a very high price for this victory caused her to avoid eye contact with Ricky. "Fellow Texans," Grant said solemnly, "I'm pleased to inform you that I have accepted an offer of a temporary ceasefire by President Farnsworth and I'll be meeting with him at the Dodge City presidential office to discuss terms of a permanent settlement this evening." She nodded at Ricky then. "Captain Santana, get your gear together. I'd like you to fly me up there."

After a several hour aerial survey of the swath of devastation the harmonizers had wrought across Texas, Ricky navigated Grant's helicopter toward Dodge City. "What a mess," Grant said, and sighed. "It'll cost a fortune to rebuild."

Ricky nodded silently.

Grant spoke again. "I'm going to push Farnsworth for reunification."

Ricky said, "And what would we call this happy new union, Texas and her forty-nine bitches? Or is that fifty-one bitches counting Israel and Kurdistan?"

Grant chuckled at that, then said, "I doubt the Kurds and Israelis would appreciate that, much less the others. Not that it's an issue. Kurdistan and Israel both requested to withdraw as soon as they got word of our victory at the Alamo. I'm confident our legislature won't argue."

"So," said Ricky, trying to maintain interest, despite his thoughts continually drifting to his worry over Gabriella, "you really think reunification is a good idea? I was just starting to get use to the idea of the new Republic of Texas."

"A lot would have to change," Grant said. "We could never go back to the way things were. What I'm thinking is that we call for an article five convention of the states where Texas and likeminded states can propose amendments to the Constitution as part of the settlement."

"You mean like term limits for Congress and that kind of thing?" said Ricky, still feigning interest.

Grant nodded. "Yes, and a few more. You ever read Mark Levin's book, *The Liberty Amendments*? She didn't wait for Ricky to answer before going on, "In addition to term limits for the House and Senate, Levin recommends at least nine other amendments, including: Repealing the seventeenth amendment, Restoring the judiciary to its proper role, Limiting taxation and spending, Limiting bureaucracy, Defining the Commerce Clause, Limiting federal power to take private property, Allowing state legislatures to amend the Constitution, Giving states the authority to override Congress, and protecting the vote by a voter ID requirement and limits on early voting. Levin details how all this would work in his book." Grant noticed Ricky gazing down as they entered the airspace over south Dodge City. "Ricky are you listening to me?"

Ricky glanced back at Grant. "Yes, ma'am, Madam President. Amendments. Lots of them."

Grant sighed. "Listen, Ricky, I'm granting you a full pardon for what you did…And there's something else I need to tell you before we get to the presidential mansion."

"Thanks," said Ricky, and his gaze returned to the landscape below.

"It's about what stopped those harmonizers…no…it's about *who* stopped them." Grant hesitated before going on. "Look, there's no easy way to tell you this, so I here it is. Your wife, she –"

Ricky gasped when Josh's limo came into view below, parked next to a burned out pile of rubble that just this morning had been Vizion Inc.'s headquarters. "What happened?"

"That's what I'm trying to tell you," said Grant. "Someone saved our bacon by blowing up the sight-system computers, and…we have reason to believe it was Gabriella. The thing is neither she nor Joshua Horowitz have been seen since."

"She..she…no." Ricky's hands began to tremble. "May I?" he said, and pulled back on the throttle.

Grant nodded. "Go ahead."

"Thanks," Ricky said.

He brought the chopper down for a landing in Vizion's parking lot.

Grant waited while Ricky wandered through the scattered ash and debris. Ricky saw something, a tiny flicker. He approached slowly, his gut twisting into agonizing knots. Tears flooded his eyes as he reached down for the simple silver necklace. He dropped to his knees, cradling that strand of silver against his heart, and wept. "Gabby."

Chapter 91

Several weeks after reunification of the nation, the Convention of the States was still in session. So far the delegates had agreed on only two amendments. One, clarifying that the Commerce Clause does not grant Congress the power to do anything besides preventing states from imposing import tariffs or similar measures on one another that impede interstate commerce. The second, prohibiting corporations and robots from holding electoral office; a proposal made easier by Ricky's transfer of a single share of Vizion Inc. stock to Ricardo – not a *natural born* citizen – which effectively destroyed Vizion's qualifications and terminated its presidency.

The breakfast bell clanged and Ricky sauntered into the freshly constructed new main-house at the ranch and took a seat at the dining room table where Ricardo sat reading a Bible.

"What's with that?" Ricky said. "You always read your newspaper in the morning."

Ricardo grunted, "Your mama says – "

355

Isabella stepped in with a coffee pot in hand. "Your Papa was wondering what God wished us to do now that the war is over," she said as she filled his cup, "so I told him to stop wondering and read the answers. I cannot understand why people are always wondering when all of the answers are right there in the Bible for anyone to see if only they will open their eyes and look."

Ricardo set the Bible aside and picked up the newspaper.

Dawn came in and helped Isabella serve the food.

Ricardo chuckled at the headlines. "President Helen is threatening to sue the new congress for defunding her executive agencies. Esa senora esta´ loca."

Ricky laughed. "Crazy or not, I don't expect she can cause much trouble now that we have a congress with the spine to use the power of the purse."

"And look at this." Ricardo slapped at another headline. "Our new governor is trying to strike a deal with the Federal Reserve for a big infrastructure loan to rebuild Texas."

"No kidding?" said Ricky, remembering the conversation with Ben Black onboard the Cole Brothers tanker about the evils of central banks. "I wonder what Grant would do if she was still president...or governor now, I should say."

Dawn filled Ricardo's coffee cup and scrutinized the headline. She shook her head and said, "Do you think Texas would be better off if Grant hadn't been appointed Speaker of the House? And is it even legal for her to be Speaker of the House when she wasn't elected to Congress? Nothing makes sense anymore."

"Of course it is legal," Ricardo grumbled. "The speaker does not have to be a member of Congress. Congress may appoint whoever it wishes as speaker. This is why we have so much trouble in this country. Even our best and brightest cannot be bothered with learning the basics of how the government works."

Dawn ignored the slight.

Ricardo laid the newspaper aside.

Ricky picked it up and peeled it back to the next page. His eyes widened frightfully.

Dawn clutched his hands. "Ricky, what is it?"

He slid the paper across the table to her, speechless.

"Oh My God," she gasped as she looked at the photograph of Levi smiling confidently from his Palm Island, Dubai retreat, with his arms wrapped around four very pregnant young women at his sides. Dawn read, "The births of corporate magnate Levi' Baxter's children are expected to coincide with the signing of a global stimulus loan from the GTP international bank. The three-hundred trillion dollar investment will fund the first ever global infrastructure project as well as the rebuilding of the GTP free-trade enforcement forces."

Ricky changed the subject to avoid dwelling again on Ben Black's warnings about central banking. "So," he said to Dawn, "you going out to the Lawton harmonization center today."

"No." Dawn smiled. "Thank goodness, my work is finally all done there. I'd have never believed it when I started medical school if anyone had told me I'd be using that knowledge to work with an army of other surgeons extracting tiny lenses and microcomputers from the eyes and heads of half the population of the United States."

"I reckon that's my fault," Ricky said.

Dawn squeezed his hand firmly. "Ricky, bad people will always find ways to do harm with the technological advances good people make. That is not your fault."

"Maybe you're right," said Ricky. "Say, since you're off today, how about a horseback ride?"

Dawn smiled again. "I'd like that."

"All technology is evil," Ricardo mumbled. "Except for the radio."

Isabella set Ricardo's pill organizer on the table and said, "It is time to take your medicine, Papa."

Ricky gobbled down his bacon and eggs and grabbed the Bible off the table.

Dawn eyed him curiously. "Thinking of taking your mom's advice?"

"Actually I was thinking of stopping by the oak tree to say a few words for Gabby and Chick and Juan, but I've never been much good with words." He held up the Bible. "Must be something applicable in here."

Chapter 92

"Hey," Dawn yelled from her perch on the mustang, waving at Francisco and his boys who were out working the cattle.

The boys waved back.

Dawn and Ricky rode on to the old oak tree.

"It was thoughtful of you to do this for him," Dawn said, gazing at the monument Ricky had fashioned from Chick's ice cream cart.

The horses meandered a few feet away, nibbling at grass.

"He might have gotten off to a rocky start, but he turned out to be a heck of a man," Ricky said. "Died a hero." He glanced at the life-sized bronze vaquero on horseback to the right of the ice cream cart. "As did Juan. If only I were half the man those two were."

Dawn ran her fingers gently across the face of a granite angel towering above Juan and Chick's monuments. Ricky's brother's simple headstone stood just to the left of it. *Gabriella Santana* was etched into the base of the angel. "It's beautiful," Dawn said. She dabbed at a tear. "Just like she was."

Ricky felt something not quite solace in the knowledge that the grave beneath that angel was empty. He could choose to believe whatever he wanted about that. And that was something. He opened the Bible and thumbed through the pages until his finger landed on a verse, John 9:39: *For judgment I have come into this world, so that the blind will see and those who see will become blind.*

"Not the verse I would have chosen," Dawn said, but it does seem oddly appropriate.

Ricky stroked her back and said, "So, what's next for you?"

"Oh, I don't know," she said. "I guess it depends on whether the Cole Brothers want to rebuild the artificial sight system after all that's happened. If not, I might go back east. I hear Boston is open for business again. I mean, it is still in shambles, but... well, regular flights have resumed. And lots of people are moving back – so they say on the news. I reckon some of those folks could use a good neurosurgeon. What's next for you?"

Ricky laughed out loud. "Did you just say *reckon*?"

Dawn laughed too, and God, it was good to hear her laugh. "I reckon I did say reckon, partner," she said, and flicked at the brim of an imaginary cowboy hat on her head.

Ricky fiddled with the simple silver necklace that he'd carried in his pocket every day since he retrieved it from the ashes of Vizion. "Dawn?"

"Yes?"

"I was just wondering, do you think a silver necklace would have went well with that beautiful evening gown you wore to that fundraiser at the Dodge House?"

Dawn searched his eyes and in the process she noticed the stubble on his face. She couldn't decide whether it made him look rugged sexy or just unkempt, but after all those weeks spent with that aloof stranger with the shaggy beard he had been she didn't even want to think about it. "I don't know," she said. She clutched Ricky's hand, lacing her fingers together with his.

About the Author

Hollis Joslin studied creative writing at the University of Arizona and graduated with a degree in Political Science. He completed his aircraft pilot training at Fulton Aviation, and earned his Juris Doctor degree at the University of Massachusetts at Dartmouth School of Law. He currently lives in Phoenix, Arizona where he writes and practices law. You can reach Hollis by email at Hollis@HollisJoslin.com. Hollis values the opinions of all of his readers, so whether you loved this book or hated it, please leave a review on Amazon, on his website, HollisJoslin.com, and on his facebook page, Hollis Joslin, Author.

CPSIA information can be obtained
at www.ICGtesting.com
Printed in the USA
LVHW031044150423
744456LV00014B/180

9 781792 884955